I0590452

ZONE PROTECTION

ZONE PROTECTION

WALKER UNIVERSITY STALLIONS
BOOK 2

AVA SUTTON

COMPASS PRESS

Copyright © 2025 by Ava Sutton
Published by Compass Press
All rights reserved.

Visit my website at avasuttonbooks.com
Cover Designer, Enchanting Romance Designs
Developmental Editor: Jeannine Colette, www.jeanninecolette.com
Editor: Jovana Shirley, Unforeseen Editing, www.unforeseenediting.com
Proofreading, Tina Otero

No part of this book may be reproduced or transmitted in any form or by any means, electronic or mechanical, including photocopying, recording, or by any information storage and retrieval system without the written permission of the author, except for the use of brief quotations in a book review.

This book is a work of fiction. Names, characters, places, and incidents either are products of the author's imagination or are used fictitiously. Any resemblance to actual persons, living or dead, events, or locales is entirely coincidental.

ISBN-13: 979-8-9929966-3-0

Playlist

Speechless - Dan + Shay

I'm Gonna Love You - Cody Johnson & Carrie Underwood

Tennessee Orange - Megan Moroney

Hands to Myself - Selena Gomez

If You Think I'm Pretty - Artemas

Sports Car - Tate McRae

Cowgirls - Morgan Wallen

Am I Okay - Megan Moroney

Beautiful Crazy - Luke Combs

The Good Ones - Gabby Barrett

Body Like a Back Road - Sam Hunt

Play It Again - Luke Bryan

What If's - Kane Brown, Lauren Alaina

Wagon Wheel - Darius Rucker

One Man Band - Old Dominion

Do I Make You Wanna - Billy Currington

Head Over Boots - Jon Pardi

Spin You Around - Morgan Wallen

Oklahoma Smokeshow - Zach Bryan

Father Figure - George Michael

Feelin' Love - Paula Cole

Pony - Ginuwine

You Make It Easy - Jason Aldean

This one's for the girlies who melt for a man who doesn't hesitate, doesn't run, and doesn't hold back.

PROLOGUE

EMMA—THEN

MY LITTLE SISTER, Sunny, had surgery a few days ago. She had something wrong with her heart that I didn't understand, and they went in to sew it up. After poking at her today with needles, they ran some tests. From what the doctor said yesterday, she should be starting to feel better.

The doctor comes into her room, and he has the kind of look on his face that my dad gets when he gets home from a hard day at work. Tired.

Dr. Norton walks over to the side of Sunny's bed and places both hands on the bedrail. His mouth is turned down. Doc doesn't usually have a frown. He's a smiley kinda doctor who gives out lollipops.

"Mr. and Mrs. Tucker, there is no easy way to say this, especially after a successful surgery, but Sunny has developed a bacterial infection, and it has spread into her lungs. We already have her on antibiotics, but we're going to have to try something stronger to see if we can knock it out before it worsens and turns septic."

My parents don't say anything at first. I'm confused because

I've been sick before and I took antibiotics. It's the pink drink that Mom keeps in the fridge that tastes like a foot.

Dad's brows narrow as he moves from the chair he was sitting in and walks over to Mom, who's sitting next to where Sunny is sleeping. He stands behind her and puts his hands on her shoulders. "I'm sorry. I don't understand. What do you mean, she has an infection? We went through this surgery after she was born, and there were no complications."

Mom's hand moves from her lap, and she takes my sister's hand in hers—the three of them clinging to each other. I'm not sure what to do, so I just sit in the recliner and don't make a sound. By the worry in the doctor's voice and my dad's, I know to stay quiet and listen.

"Your tone makes this sound rather grave, so I just want to make sure I understand it properly." My mom clears her throat. "So, at some point in the last few days, she has developed an infection, and you're giving her different antibiotics to see if you can kill the infection before it spreads?"

"That's correct. As you know, pulmonary atresia prevents blood from flowing from the heart into the lungs. While this is her second surgery and the correct-sized valve has replaced the one from her first surgery, her lungs and heart are working over-time to function, which also compromises the immune system. However, I believe there is a chance we caught it in time and can start this new round of antibiotics, and she should be progressing in the next few days." He moves his hands to his waist and glances over at me.

I don't understand what he's saying, but my parents' silence starts to make me feel scared. I place the book I was reading on the footstool next to my chair and stand up to walk over to my dad. I wrap my hands around one of his arms, and I can feel the muscles in his arm tense.

My dad mumbles something I can't hear, then says, "Doctor, my baby has been lying in this bed, fighting an infection, and no one noticed it until now? You've been checking on her regularly for the last few days. I don't understand how this is possible. Are you sure you can treat it in time?"

"We have every reason to believe we caught it early, and she should continue with a normal recovery."

He removes his stethoscope from his neck, places the earpieces in his ears, and leans down toward my sister. Placing the cold round part that I never like on her heart, he listens.

I hear my mom sniffle—something I've heard a lot lately—so I let go of my dad and step to the side of my mom's chair. She looks up at me and squeezes my hand lightly with her free hand.

"She'll be okay, sweetie. They just need to give Sunny some more medicine to help her get better faster."

Not really sure what to say, I nod.

After the doctor leaves the room, we sit quietly until my sister begins to stir. My parents jump and lean over the side of the bed.

My mom takes her hand in hers. "Hi, pumpkin. Did you have a good sleep?"

Sunny gives Mom a soft smile. She's always happy, always smiling. Even when she's sick, she's smiling. "Yes, I had a dream, and Emma was in it with me. We were playing in the sunflowers by Grandma's house."

The last time we were there, Sunny grabbed my hand and begged me to take her into the flowers. We walked a little ways in, hand in hand. After finding the perfect spot, we lay down on the ground and looked up at the sunflowers. She said she loved lying in the garden and that it felt like we were in a tent in a magical wonderland. The sun filtered in through the stems, and when I looked over at her, she was looking up. Between the sun's rays and the big flowers' shadows, it looked like she was wearing a halo. She asked me if we could stay there forever that day.

A few days later, we found out she needed another surgery.

"You have always loved the sunflowers, even as a baby. I

think it's because we named you Sunny. What do you think?" Mom smiles and holds her hand lightly.

Sunny giggles softly. "I do love them. They get so big, and they're so happy."

She pulls her hand out of my mom's and waves me over to her. "Emma Bean, did you know you're my bestest friend?" Her voice is so low that I have to lean in to hear her.

I rest my forearms on the bedrail. "I do know that because you're my bestie too."

Weakly, she lifts her other hand and puts it on my arm. "Emma Bean ..."

I look from her hand to her face and see her smile.

"I'll be waiting for you in the sunflowers." As she finishes talking, her eyes close again. So sleepy.

Seconds later, alarms begin beeping, and nurses rush into the room. My dad grabs my shoulders and pulls me away from the bed and into the corner of the room while Mom cries out for a nurse. The nurses move to Sunny's bed as Dad pulls Mom by the waist and out of the way.

Then the doctor comes in. "Someone, get the family out of the room."

One of the nurses walks over to us. "Mr. and Mrs. Tucker, we're going to take you to the waiting room just a few doors down. Let us see what's going on, and we'll come get you as soon as we can."

My mom's hands are covering her mouth, and tears are starting to fall down her face. "I'm not leaving my baby." Her hands drop from her face, and she yells, "I won't get in the way, I promise! But I'm not leaving my baby!"

Another nurse enters from the hall and comes over to me. "Hey, sugar. Let's go into the other room for a bit. I'll stay with you in there until your mom and dad come in, okay?"

She doesn't wait for me to answer. She takes my hand and leads me out. As I leave the room, I look back to see my dad wrapping his arms around my mom. They watch with wide eyes and open mouths as the doctor and nurses fuss over Sunny.

The nurse keeps calling me sugar and tries to be nice by giving me soda and snacks from the vending machine, but I just want my mom and dad. I want my sister.

My parents never come into the room I'm in with the other nurse.

Everything seems to happen so fast, but the wait is forever ...

Death isn't something you really understand when you're nine years old. And I can't believe my sister is gone. My mom can hardly speak because she's crying so hard. My dad, he is crying and holding me tighter than he ever has.

I'm not sure how we ended up at the little church at the hospital, but we've sat there all night, wrapped in each other's arms. My shirt is wet from our tears, and all I keep thinking about is how much this hurts and how much I never want to feel like this again.

CHAPTER
ONE

EMMA—NOW

THE LAST PLACE I want to be tonight is at a party at some football player's house. My next paper for my Organic Chemistry class is due on Tuesday and isn't going to write itself. But my roommates—who are also my teammates on Walker University women's golf team—have dragged me out, thinking I need to let off some steam and have a little fun.

Our first tournament in California wasn't my finest performance, and the pressure I feel from my course load this semester is enough to drive an average person crazy. I'll compartmentalize it, as I usually do, and keep moving, but my friends might be right. I'm a perfectionist to a fault, and admittedly, I take on more than I should from time to time.

Okay, all the time, but I can't help it. So, maybe I should just let myself have some fun tonight.

Problem is, this house is filled with ego-driven fuckboys. Don't get me wrong; I've played around with my fair share, but I'm just not in the mood tonight. The music is too loud, most of the girls here are decked out in their short skirts while I'm in jeans and a cropped T-shirt, and it smells like a distillery in here.

I feel like one drop of a match, and this place would go up in flames just because of the amount of alcohol in here alone.

Which surprises me a little bit, to be honest. The football team won today, so they deserve to celebrate, but most athletes don't drink too heavily during the season. Or at least the ones who plan to take their career past college.

I don't plan on playing golf beyond my college years. My track has been clear to me since my sister died when I was only nine years old. I need to finish my four years here at Walker near the top of my class in order to get into the best med schools. Right now, my top choices are NYU, Case Western Reserve, and Duke. They have the best pediatric cardiology programs, which is what my specialty will be.

"Emma, did you hear me?" my friend Olivia Lewis—aka Livi —asks.

"I can barely hear anything in here. What did you say?" I lean in closer to her to hear her more clearly.

"You need to get out of your head. Your paper will still be there tomorrow. This place is swimming with endless possibilities. I feel like you need to get laid. Like not only let loose and have a few drinks, but you need to get some D, my friend." She wraps her arm around my shoulders and laughs.

"Why is sex the only avenue to letting loose?"

"Because if sitting in your room and studying released tension, you wouldn't have gotten a double bogey on a par three."

"I blame the wind."

"I blame your inability to get out of your head, and the way you're gonna do that is by using your body with the next fuckboy who walks into this room."

Just as she says it, a loud boom of a voice comes from the doorway. Now, I'm standing next to the speaker, but I can still hear Archie Griffith's voice over the sound.

"Ladies and dicks, the party can begin. I have arrived! Let's get fucked up, motherfuckers! Cowboy up!" he yells, then gallops. Yes, he gallops into the room and straight for my other two friends, Peyton Adams and Mia Wallace, who are dancing on the makeshift dance floor in what is probably the dining room.

"Holy shit, that man is a snack!" Livi laughs.

I mean, she's not wrong. He's tall with blond hair that's long enough that he can pull it back and covered in tattoos. Not at all my usual type. But he's fucking fine. I can only imagine what he looks like under that T-shirt and jeans that fit like a glove. He's gotta have one of those Adonis belts—the holy grail for thirsty women everywhere.

"I'm going over there. You should definitely come too! Come on, Em."

She tugs on my arm, but I pull it back.

"A shot is calling my name. I'll be right back."

She nods and heads out to the dance floor.

I walk into the kitchen, which is the room next to where I've been standing. There's a bar set up on the island in the center of the kitchen. *Bar* is a loose term. Really, it's just a bunch of liquor bottles, although they are lined up neatly.

"Can I get you something?" a cute guy asks. He has brown hair and an interesting T-shirt that says *Two-Seater* with one arrow pointing up to his face and another pointing down to his junk. "I'm the rookie on bar duty tonight. Whatcha thinkin'? Wait, don't I know you from somewhere? Emma, right? Golf?" He holds out his hand for me to shake. "Leo Morris. I'm the new kicker for the football team. I saw you at the Fellowship of Athletes meeting a few weeks ago."

I take his hand and shake it. "Oh, cool. Nice to meet you, Leo. Congrats on the win today."

"Thank you. It was—"

He's cut off by Dan Smith, who I've known for a few years now. I actually hooked up with him once.

"Sup, Emma? Looking good. Want to come out back and get a beer?" He loops his arm around Leo's shoulders and basically puts him in a headlock. "It's time for this guy to pay his dues."

"I thought I was paying my dues by manning the bar!" He coughs out a laugh.

"I'm gonna pass, but you guys have fun. Nice to meet you, Leo." I wave.

Dan gives me a wink and turns with Leo still in his hold toward the back porch. I'll admit, Dan is hot and a possible contender for the D, but I don't really do repeats. That gets messy, and I don't have time for messy. Or feelings. Easy hookups are all I can manage right now, so one-night stands work for me.

I peruse the options on the bar and settle on a shot of Fireball. I have no intention of getting fucked up tonight, but maybe a shot will make being here less … annoying. So, I grab one of the red plastic shot glasses and fill it to the top. At least my breath won't smell as horrible with the cinnamon aftertaste.

Wasting no time—because I don't want to stand around with a shot in my hand like a weirdo as people wander in and out of the kitchen—I knock it back in one go. It burns like a mother-fucker, and I wince, while also trying to seem unaffected.

I grab a bottle of water from the fridge on my way back to the dance floor. One shot was enough for me tonight, though I've never been a big drinker anyway.

Finding my spot by the speaker again, I see my friends still dancing with Archie. Well, *dancing* isn't really the term I would use. They're grinding up against each other. Peyton is in the front, and Mia is behind him. Livi is dancing near them, but with some guy I don't recognize.

Honestly, there isn't a guy in here who isn't hot, but there is something about Archie Griffith that draws you in. I don't know him personally, but watching him on the field and in interviews, I see he's got that Southern boy charm that apparently makes guys envious and girls lose their panties. Literally.

His arms are draped over Peyton's shoulders, but he's not

touching her with his hands. He leans in to hear something she's saying, and when he looks up, our eyes meet.

I'm not sure if it's the Fireball making its way through my body or if it's him, but heat rises from my toes to my cheeks. With a little extra heat making a pit stop at my lady business. I can't say a guy has ever had this effect on me before.

I break my gaze first so I don't look like some stalker. But I can't help but look back, and when I do, he's still looking at me, and now he has the sexiest little smirk on his face.

He says something to Peyton and moves his hands to Mia's wrists, which are wrapped around his waist, and removes them from his body. His eyes never leaving mine.

Jesus, this man is sex on a stick and is now walking toward me.

Wait! He's walking toward me. Do not act like a nerd, Emma.

"Hey. You having fun tonight?" he asks me, crossing his arms across his chest, making his biceps look enormous.

With him standing this close to me, I can see just how big he is. And I'm not short by any means. I'm five-eight, and he still towers over me.

"Huh? I can't hear you over the bass. What did you say?" *Way to play it cool, Em.*

He takes hold of my elbow and drifts us a little farther away from the speaker.

"I asked if you were having fun." He gives me a sexy smile.

Leaning in a little closer to him, I say, "Yeah, I guess so. These parties aren't really my thing, but it's been a stressful week, so my friends insisted on getting me out tonight. How about you? Are you having fun?"

"Sweetness, I'm always having fun. Even better now that I'm talking with you," he says a little too smoothly.

"Ha! Look, I know who you are. Everyone on campus knows who you are. If you're looking for a hookup, you don't need to use fancy lines. Just come out and say it." I turn my head toward where my friends are dancing.

What am I doing? I'm not one to flirt or play games with any guy. When I want a hookup, I'm pretty clear about it, so I don't know why I'm acting flustered and kind of bitchy. I don't mean to be. And I'm also a big fat liar. I absolutely wouldn't mind hooking up with him.

Lifting his hand up, he reaches for my face and cups my cheek while his other hand takes hold of my waist. "Hey, darlin'."

He guides my face to look at him, then drags his fingers to my chin and tilts it up. When I finally look at him, that heat, it's back.

His smirk falls, and he sucks in a breath. "Goddamn. You are fucking beautiful."

I huff out a laugh. "Yeah, okay, player." But I don't move away.

He brings his hand back up to my cheek. "I'm dead serious. I don't think I've ever seen anyone so pretty."

We're locked in a staredown when a slower song comes on.

"Dance with me."

He strokes his hand from my face to my waist and pulls me into him. Instead of moving away, I wrap my arms around his shoulders.

We're dancing together, and neither one of us has taken our eyes off each other. I'm not sure what it is about him, but I like the way it feels to be in his arms.

I can't help but drift my hands over his shoulder muscles and to his back, winding my arms around his neck. My breasts are brushing against his chest, and I can feel his warmth through his shirt and mine.

He moves his hands from my waist to my lower back, drifting a little lower. I'm not gonna stop him, so he keeps sliding his hands down until they're cupping my ass.

He pulls me in a little closer, and our noses practically touch. "You wanna have some fun with me, darlin'?"

My tongue peeks out and touches my top lip, and then I look

over at my friends. Mia gives me a nod and a wide smile while Peyton gives me two thumbs-up and smiles. Livi … she's sucking face with the guy she was dancing with. I roll my eyes at them, but smile and rest my forehead on Archie's chest.

"So, you know who I am, but I don't know your name. Are you gonna tell me?" he asks, tipping my chin up with his finger.

When I meet his eyes again, butterflies flutter around my belly like they're having a party that only Archie is invited to. He smiles at me, like a real smile, not a *let me get in your panties* smile, and I'm done. I surrender all the panties to this man.

"Emma. My name is Emma." My hands slide from his neck to the sides of his face. "So, Archie Griffith, are you gonna keep giving me lines, or are we gonna have some fun?"

He leans in a little closer to my face, close enough to kiss me. "That's up to you. I'm more than ready to have some fun with you, *Emma*."

No guy has ever made me feel like this. Regardless, this can only be one night.

I level with him. "Here's the deal. My friends dragged me out because, like I said, it's been a shit week. But what the hell? Maybe my friends are right, and I just need a good lay. Do you think you're up for that, Archie?"

I'm so close to him now; I can feel his breath on my lips.

"Oh, I'm up for it. You gonna let me kiss you? I really want to taste those lips."

Instead of answering him, I lean in and kiss him. If I thought his eyes and smile did me in, nothing could have prepared me for this kiss. Our tongues tangle almost immediately, and there's no way in hell he doesn't feel this too.

It's electric.

His hands grab on to my ass, and he pulls me in even closer. I can feel his hard-on through his jeans, and I think … he might not be wearing boxers. Just that thought alone makes me moan into his mouth, feeling a bit feral. I'm completely lost in him and practically forget where we are when he pulls back.

His blue eyes are dancing with mischief and sexual energy.

"Do you want to go upstairs?" I ask him.

He tilts his head and smirks. "Yeah, darlin', I do. But you know, I live right down the street. We could have a little more privacy and more time for me to do everything I want to do with you. This ain't gonna be a fast fuck. I wanna take my time."

"If we leave to go to your house, there's a chance I might change my mind. So, while the thought of having sex in this house makes me question my sanity, it's now or never, Archie."

He nods and slides his hands from my butt to my waist. Leaning in, he kisses me. "Come with me. I know where we can go." He lets go of my waist and grabs my hands.

I nod and release one of his hands. "Show me the way."

When we get upstairs, he knocks on a door, and when no one answers, he opens it.

As soon as I get in the door, he spins to face me and closes it behind me with one hand and turns the lock.

Neither of us says anything, but I can see the heat in his eyes.

"Are you sure about this, darlin'?" he asks.

I appreciate that he's asking for my consent, but I really just need him to take my clothes off. Like now.

"Oh, yeah. I'm sure." I reach up and wrap my hands around the back of his neck and lean in and kiss him, slipping my tongue inside of his mouth.

The kiss goes to an inferno level immediately.

I slide my hands from his neck down to the hem of his shirt and lift it up as he raises his arms. Wrapping his now-bare arms around my waist, he lifts me and carries me over to the bed and sets me down at the edge.

He kisses me again, then pulls back and kneels in front of me, dragging his hands down my chest and pulling the neck of my shirt down a little. I lean back on my elbows and watch him. When he gets to my waist, he pops open the button of my jeans and pulls the zipper down. He doesn't say anything but looks up at me as I lift my hips as he pulls my jeans from my legs.

Moving his hands from my calves to my hips, he dips his head and starts kissing up my thigh and to my center. "You smell so good, darlin'. I can't wait to taste you."

Annnd why does that sound so fucking hot? But also, I'm glad I didn't wear my comfy panties tonight. Archie Griffith should not see my comfy panties.

He pushes my thighs apart and swipes his tongue over the lace from my opening to my clit. Then, sliding his hands under the waistband in the front, he grabs my underwear and pulls them off and continues to lick me.

"Archie, you really don't have to do that. I mean, it feels so good, but I don't usually get off from oral." I'm almost embarrassed to admit it while his face is literally in my vagina, but I'm kinda anxious to get to the good part.

Instead of replying, he presses his hand on my stomach gently to get me to lie down. He continues to flick my clit with his tongue, and I buck slightly. The feeling is a zing that radiates down my thighs and makes my nipples tighten at the same time. He flicks again, and I let out a gasp.

He smiles against my core as he does it again—and I nearly lose my mind.

When I say I don't get off from oral, I should admit I've never had oral like this before.

He slips his index finger inside me, and I gasp. It feels so good; I start to rock my hips to move his mouth back and forth.

"I'm gonna make you come, Emma. You're gonna be a good girl and come all over my tongue. Then I'm gonna fuck you so hard, you'll feel me all week." He dips his head back between my legs. "You taste so fucking good, and I love hearing those soft moans coming from your pretty little lips. I could do this all night."

Yes, please. Sign me up for the all-nighter!

His arm is wrapped around my thigh, and he's using his hand to keep me open as he licks and sucks my clit while his other hand continues to pump in and out of me.

The sensations are overwhelming. I'm on the verge of coming. I move my hands from my sides, which are gripping the comforter, and put them on his head, sliding my fingers through his hair. I hear him moan when I pull on his hair slightly, which only turns me on more.

My head falls back onto the bed, and I'm gripping his hair so tightly as I start to come. "Oh my God, Archie, don't stop. I'm so close."

I move my hips in sync with his mouth moving back and forth over my clit. I'm just about to explode when he adds another finger and presses on my G-spot. I swear I black out for a minute until I feel him kissing his way up my stomach.

"Holy shit," I pant. "I've literally never come like that before."

I'm not even worried about this going to his head because the man deserves a round of applause for that performance.

"I'm just getting started, darlin'."

Then he leans in and kisses me. I can taste myself on his tongue, and I don't hate it like I thought I would.

"Do you have a condom?" I ask him.

He lifts his head and nods, looking into my eyes. "I do."

Then he stands and pulls his wallet from his pocket and grabs a condom. He tosses the wallet on the table beside the bed.

I scoot back toward the headboard and watch him unbutton his jeans. Just like I thought, he's not wearing any boxers. And what's hanging between those gorgeous thighs is impressive. In fact, I'm slightly nervous about it.

"Umm … do you think we need lube or something?"

Archie smirks but shakes his head. "Don't you worry, darlin'. I'll make it fit."

And now I definitely don't need lube with those words.

He tears open the wrapper and starts to roll it onto his cock. My eyes devour his body. This man is a work of art. Muscles for days, and the tattoos, he's got quite a few. Including what looks like a deck of cards, all aces and one joker, resting on his heart.

"You a poker player?" I nod to his chest.

With both hands, he pulls my legs apart again and crawls up the bed. Crawls. To. Me. Could this man get any sexier?

"Texas Hold'em is my specialty." He laughs. "But let's talk about my tattoos later, yeah?"

Leaning over me now, he dips his head for a kiss. His body is pressed against mine, and I can feel his covered cock at my entrance. As we kiss, our bodies begin to rock in sync. Archie deepens the kiss as he pushes into me.

I gasp with the sensation as he continues kissing me. He's moving slowly, letting me adjust to his size.

He stops for a second and asks, "You okay?"

"More than okay. You feel so good, Archie." I take hold of the back of his neck and bring his lips back to mine. I slip my tongue inside his mouth and twirl it around his.

His hips start to roll into mine, and his pelvis hits my clit in just the right spot. I'm not sure I've ever felt so in tune with someone during sex. It's like our bodies instinctively know how to move together.

"You gonna come again for me, beautiful? I want to feel you choke my cock." His breathing is getting heavier, and his thrusts are getting faster.

I nod because I don't think I can speak right now.

When he leans in to kiss me again, I pull in his bottom lip with my teeth and suck, making him moan.

The moan triggers me, and my orgasm hits me hard, and my whole body feels like it's shaking.

"Fuck!" he yells as he comes.

Our bodies still connected, he gives me a soft kiss, once, twice, then pulls his head back. "I think it's safe to say you rocked my fuckin' world, darlin'. Give me a minute, and we can go again. I need more of that."

I start to laugh, and he groans.

"Sorry, did I hurt you?"

"No, but your pussy just squeezed my cock when you laughed, and I might just be ready to go again. I think you have a unicorn pussy, Emma." He's smiling, but his hips are already moving in and out.

It feels so good that I almost forget to remind him to get another condom. "Archie, wait. You need a new condom."

"Give me one more minute." He pushes in to the hilt and pauses. "I want you to ride me this time."

He doesn't need to ask me twice.

"Yes, let's do the riding." I nod, and he laughs.

Reaching between us, he grabs the base of the condom and pulls out, then gets off the bed. He takes off the condom and ties it, then wraps it in tissue sitting on the bedside table and tosses it in the garbage.

"Do you have another one?" I ask as he looks through his wallet.

"Fuck. I don't. Let me see if Schuster has some in this drawer." He pulls the drawer open and rustles through it. "Got it!"

I sit up and scoot over to give him room on the bed. He lies next to me and pulls me to him, setting the unopened condom on his stomach. "Come here."

Everything that comes out of this man's mouth sounds sexy. He's got this husky, deep voice with a Southern accent. No wonder girls fall at his feet all around campus.

My head is resting on his chest, and I listen to his heart, strong and steady. This man just commanded and owned my body. But his fingers, now strumming along my back, are soft. Almost too tender. A girl could get ideas from a move like that.

I tilt my head up and kiss his jaw first before propping myself onto my elbow to lean over him. "What do you say, cowboy? You up"—I pause and look down at his dick—"for a ride?"

He barks out a laugh and pulls me in for a kiss. "Giddyup, darlin'."

CHAPTER
TWO

ARCHIE

NOTHING IS BETTER THAN A WIN. Well, nah, wait. Pussy is better than a win. But tonight … I got the win, *and* I'm going to get the pussy. Or I hope to anyway. Ever since that night after our first game, I haven't been able to find Emma. I should have asked for her last name, but I'm a certifiable idiot.

When she left that night, I didn't think I'd be feeling her the way I was the next morning and the morning after that. It's been almost four weeks, and I still wouldn't mind seeing her again.

There's another party at Chris Schuster and Dan Smith's house, the same house we met at, so I'm really hoping to see her there. That girl done rocked my world.

I drop the towel from my waist and get my jeans from the dresser drawer, pulling them on. Am I going to put boxers on? Nope. I like to let my balls roam free after a game. Besides, I don't plan to have the jeans on for long if Emma is there.

I grab a pair of socks from another drawer, then move to my closet and take a T-shirt from a hanger. I put the shirt on, then walk over to my bed and sit down to put my socks on. My boots are sitting next to the bed, so I reach over to grab them and slide them on.

I'm a Texas boy through and through. I love football and my family—especially my mom. Not saying I'm a mama's boy though. I just love the shit out of that woman. She's put up with six rowdy athletic boys while my dad worked our family ranch.

With one last look in the mirror, I run my hand through my wavy blond hair, spray one puff of my Nautica Voyage on my neck, and walk out my bedroom door and down the hall.

"Pitzy," I yell.

Liam Pitz is one of my roommates and the starting quarterback. We've been living together since our freshman year. I have a feeling this year is going to be tough on him though. Our rookie QB is gunning to start, and honestly, he's damn good.

We have two other roommates.

Beckham Linson, who's also become a good friend. I took him under my wing, so to speak, when he came to Walker last year. Kid's wicked talented, and he will definitely make it pro.

Casey King is the other, and he and Beckham grew up together. He's a chill guy and easy to hang with.

Oh, and plot twist … his twin sister, Charlie, moved in with us because her housing fell apart. Not only is she King's sister, but she's also Linson's ex-girlfriend. He still has a thing for her though, so I love fucking with him. I flirt with her just to get under his skin. It's fuckin' funny.

I find Pitz in the kitchen, eating something over the sink. "Dude, just get a plate. That's gross."

"Nah, I'm good," he says while shoving another bite of pizza in his mouth.

"You comin' out with me tonight?" I ask with a nod of my head toward the door. "I think I'll head over to Schuster and Smith's again."

Pitz looks over at me and grins.

"What, asshole?"

"Dude, I see you. You're going to look for that girl again, aren't you?" He laughs.

I scoff. "No, I mean, I wouldn't be mad if she was there. But I'm not going for her." Lies.

"Okay, buddy. Keep telling yourself that. You know, it's okay to like someone as more than just a fuck."

Shaking my head, I turn to walk into the living room and toward the front door. My favorite cowboy hat sits on a hook in the entryway, so I head over to grab it. I brush the hair back from my face and put the hat on. It's a hat night.

"Arch, you know I'm just fucking with you," he yells from the kitchen.

I sigh and walk back into the kitchen. Pitz looks at me.

"Look, if you're coming with me, let's roll."

"Okay, give me five. I just need to change my shirt. A pepperoni fell off my slice and the grease stained it." He pulls his shirt off as he walks out of the kitchen toward his room down the hall.

While I wait, I check my phone and see a few texts from my brother Aiden. He plays hockey in a major junior league in New England, but it looks like he'll be getting drafted this year too. He's not even eighteen yet, but he will be by spring and won't be playing college hockey.

Aiden: Sup, brotha?

Archie: Yo. Where are you? You're on the road this week, yeah?

Aiden: Yep, we're in sunny Wisconsin. We have a two-game series here, and then we'll head back to NE. I didn't catch your game, but saw the score. Congrats.

Archie: Yep. Thanks, bro. I have a feeling it's going to be a good season.

Aiden: You heading out to celebrate?

Archie: Yeah, we're just leaving now. I'll text you tomorrow night.

Aiden: Later. Be careful. Gotta keep everything on the straight and narrow.

Archie: Where's the fun in that?

I pocket my phone when Liam walks back into the kitchen.

"Let's go, Griff. I've been waiting on you for hours."

I shake my head and laugh. "Let's do it."

"What, no pre-party speech tonight?" he asks.

"Nah, I probably won't stay long. Maybe just a few beers." In truth, if Emma isn't there, I'll stay for a beer and check in with my teammates, but I won't hang around.

I walk out first, and Liam shuts and locks the door. We don't have far to go. Our friends live pretty much around the corner.

"How you feeling about the last few games?" I ask Pitz.

Our coach has been playing our rookie more and more in games, but Pitz got the win tonight.

He shifts his head from side to side. "I don't know, man. I'm psyched that I got the win today, but it's pretty clear that Coach is going to be using Callaway more. And I get it; I want to go all the way this season too. Just sucks for me if I don't get the playing time, you know?"

I nod.

"I need to do some serious thinking about it though. I can't sit on the bench this season if I want to enter the draft next year." He looks over at me. "No joke though, it'll kill me to leave Walker if that's what I need to do."

"Listen, try to stay focused on one game at a time. Keep working hard and prove to Coach you are a killer QB. Because you are. I hope you aren't doubting yourself. Callaway is good—I can't deny it—but you are too. Coach will do what he thinks is best for the team, but whatever he decides, try not to let it get in your head. Whether you stay or go, you need to show the coaches you'll do whatever it takes. You feel me?" I put my arm around his neck and pull him in. I rub my knuckles across his short brown hair.

"Fucker! Don't noogie me."

We both laugh.

When we round the corner, the house comes into view. Music is thumping, though not as loud as it usually is. A neighbor might have finally complained, or it's not as wild. Yet.

"Okay, let's do this. Not gonna lie—I'm hoping that girl I hooked up with last weekend isn't here tonight," he says. "She was blowing up my phone all week. I probably shouldn't have answered the first text. So, if I see her here, I'm bolting, just so you know." He looks over at me, eyes wide.

"All good. Let's see what's up. If it sucks, we can go home and get some food or something." I have to admit, this is a big shift for me, but Emma blew my mind, and I can't stop thinking about her.

The porch is empty for once as we walk up to the front door.

I open it, and because I am who I am, I yell out, "Ladies and gentlemen, I have arrived! Let the party begin!"

Pitz laughs as he walks by me toward the kitchen. A few girls try to catch my attention as I follow Pitz.

I don't stop walking but look over at them. "Hello, ladies. How you doin' tonight?"

"Hey, Archie! Come dance with us later," one of the girls says.

She looks familiar, as in she's always at our parties, but I don't have a clue what her name is. I probably hooked up with her at some point.

"We'll see. May just do that." I wink, but I'm not feeling it.

Liam looks back at me with a smirk. "Not entertaining the ladies tonight?"

I flip him off.

We get into the kitchen and find Schuster and Smith standing around the island with beers in their hands. Where there is typically a bunch of liquor on the countertop, it's empty tonight.

"Sup, fellas?" I fist-bump them both. "Quiet night tonight, yeah?" I walk over to the fridge and grab myself and Pitz a beer.

"Bro, I got trucked today. I'm so sore; I can hardly move. There's no way I'd be able to do cleanup and shit tomorrow. I could use a good rubdown from that blonde out there," Smith says, pointing his finger at one of the girls we just walked by. "But I'm ready to kick all these people out and just play some video games and crash."

"I feel that. I'm not planning to stay late myself." I look around to see who else is here.

Am I looking for Emma? You bet.

"Arch, you're pathetic, man." Liam laughs and looks at our friends. "He's looking for a chick he hooked up with, like, over a month ago. Got her first name, and that's it. Hasn't seen her since. Dude's down bad for her."

I glare at him. "Fuck you. I am not down bad for her. I just had a good time, is all."

I know I'm downplaying it, but the last two years at Walker, I've never tied myself to a girl, let alone had more than one night with one. I've never misled any chick into thinking it would be anything more either. Like I said, I love women, and my mom would kick my ass if I ever disrespected one.

"Who was it?" Schuster asks.

"Her name was Emma," Pitz answers for me.

Schuster punches him in the chest. "There've probably been at least a dozen Emmas who came through here in the past month alone."

"What did she look like?" Smith asks.

I take a drink of my beer before I answer. "Long blonde hair. Green eyes. Complete baddie."

I could say more, but like I said, I respect women, and they don't need to know anything else. Like how she tasted like the sweetest honey. How she rode me like a rodeo queen. How tight her body was …

Fuck. I'm gonna get hard if I keep thinking about her.

"That narrows it down. Blonde, green eyes, Emma. Yep," Schuster says sarcastically and nods.

"Fuck you, Travis," I say with a laugh.

He has a point though. But this girl isn't like any of the other Emmas who have come through here.

"Go walk around and see if she's here tonight." Pitz nods to the other room, where we saw the girls walking in. There are also some girls dancing in the dining room. "I'll come with you."

"Good luck!" Smith laughs as we walk out.

We walk into the dining room first. I look around, but don't see anyone who looks like her.

A brunette latches on to Liam, wrapping her arms around him. "Hey, Pitzy! I'm so glad you came tonight. You had an awesome game today." She looks up at him with a very clear *fuck me* look.

"Thank you, babe. Come dance with me to celebrate." He hands me his beer, then unwinds her arms from around his waist and takes her by the hand. She's good-looking for sure—brown hair with some blue streaks running through, tight body.

One of the girls she was standing with comes over to me. "Hey, Archie. Wanna dance?"

I put both beer bottles into one hand and take off my hat with my other hand and put it over my heart. "I appreciate it, doll, but I'm not gonna stay long tonight. But next time." I wink at her.

Placing my hat back on my head, I look at Pitz dancing with his girl. "Yo, Pitz. I think I'm gonna head out."

He lifts his chin and smirks. "Later, lover boy."

Fucker.

Walking back through the kitchen, I set his bottle on the counter, down my beer, and toss it into the garbage on the side of the island.

As I walk back toward the front door, I see more of my friends hanging out, talking to some of the girls who were at the front of the house when we arrived. I take off my hat again and lift it in the air.

"Boys, I'm out. Good game today, fellas. Ladies … have a good night."

Goodbyes are said as I walk out, but I don't look back.

I make it back home in less than five minutes.

When I walk in the door, I set my hat on the hook and kick my boots off. Our family room is off the entryway, so I make my way over to the couch and turn on *SportsCenter*.

The highlights are on from today's games, and I catch some footage of one of the tackles I made—and not trying to hype myself up, but I'm one of the best tackles in NCAA football— even though the commentators are talking about Liam.

Once they move on to other news in the sports world, I pull out my phone from my pocket and scroll through Instagram. I might have looked for Emma on social media a time or two without success. But it's not gonna stop me from trying again.

CHAPTER
THREE

EMMA

IT'S BEEN A ROUGH DAY. We're playing our third tournament of the season in Tulsa, and I'm not having my best outing, partially because I've been nauseous all day. Over the last week or so, I've felt like I had some kind of stomach bug. I brushed it aside and kept powering on through classes and practices. But today, being in the heat is getting to me.

Coach walks over to me as I set up my tee. "Emma, you need to try to aim for that straight to get as close as you can to the green on the other side of the hill. Use your 4-iron to get the drive you need to try to make up some ground in the standings. We really need your score to move up in order to win the tournament."

"Yes, Coach."

I know what I need to do, and I also know my team is counting on me, but I'm feeling worse and worse as the day goes by. I've chugged some Gatorade, but that almost made me puke too, so I don't think I'm dehydrated. I just need to get through the next four holes, and then we'll be done. I'm going to crash for the rest of the weekend.

I walk back over to my bag and pull out my 4-iron, then walk back over to the tee. I gaze out over the green to try to gauge how much power I need to put into my swing. Then I line myself up with the tee, move my hips back and forth, and curve my back just right to get the power I need in this hit.

I pull my club back and swing. It sails a little farther to the right than I needed to or planned to. *Shit.* I look over at my coach, and she's marking her clipboard. As I turn back to go to my bag, Mia walks up to me.

"Em, are you okay? You usually rock this course." She takes my hand in hers.

Just moving my head back and forth is making me queasy so I look down and close my eyes. "I'm not really sure what's going on, but I've been feeling bad all week. I think I must have caught some kind of bug or something. You know me; I never get sick."

And that's true. I've always been a healthy person, even as a kid.

"Okay, well if you want me to get you some water or anything, just let me know." She squeezes my hand and lets go to take her turn.

We don't use golf carts for our tournaments, so I have no place to sit and get out of the sun for a few minutes. I do grab a water from my bag and then lean against it, which is bent on its stand. The last thing I see is Mia taking her swing.

When I come to, my coach and Mia are on the ground next to me.

"What happened?"

"Em, OMG, I took my swing, and then I heard a thump behind me. For a minute, I thought I'd hit something, which made no sense because there was nothing behind me, but anyway ... I turned around, and you were on the ground!" Her eyes are wild, and she's moving her hands around while she speaks.

My coach gets on her walkie-talkie.

"Miranda, can you please meet us at the sixth hole? Emma

Tucker just passed out." She releases the walkie-talkie and leans over me. "Are you okay, Emma? Did you bump your head or anything when you fell?"

There's no pain, so I shake my head.

"Good, good. Okay, let's get you some ice packs and see if we can get you cooled down. You probably just passed out from the heat. It's a hot one out here today." She looks back at the official at this hole. "I'm going to go tell him what's going on. Mia, pack up your bag and make your way to the seventh hole."

"Yes, Coach." Mia nods, then looks back down at me. "Are you sure you're okay? I don't like leaving you here."

"I'll be fine. I'm sure Coach is right, and it's just the heat." As I say it, my stomach rolls. I sit up quickly and lean to the side just in time for vomit to come flying out of my mouth. Like, seriously, projectile type of vomiting.

"HOLY SHIT! Coach! She's throwing up now!" Mia yells over to the coach.

I'm still leaning over because I don't think I'm done puking yet. Then my ponytail falls over my shoulder just as I start to heave again. Mia takes it in her hand and holds it back from falling.

"Oh God, Em. I think I'm gonna puke. Girl, that stinks, and you know I'm a sympathetic puker!" Mia says with a gag.

I see Coach rush back over to me—well, I see her shoes. "Okay, I think we need to call it a day for you, Emma. I'm going to get Miranda to call for a cart to come get you. We'll have you monitored in the clubhouse while we finish playing. I want you to stay off your feet and drink some electrolytes. If you think you can eat some crackers or something, try that too."

Not able to speak, I nod.

Mia releases my ponytail when I sit back up. "Babe, I'm sorry, but I have to go. Are you going to be okay?" She brushes some loose hair from my face.

"Yeah, I'll be fine. Go. I'll see you at the clubhouse. Don't forget about the sharp dip in that hill on the eighth hole; you can't see it from the green."

"I'm on it! See you in a bit. Huggies!" She blows me a kiss as she grabs her bag and starts walking.

Miranda, our team trainer, comes driving up in a golf cart right next to me. "Emma, how are you feeling?" She exits the cart and walks over to me. "Yuck," she whispers.

"Yeah, sorry about that. Couldn't get to a garbage can," I say sarcastically.

She just laughs. "Okay, let's get you up and back down the hill."

From my position on the ground, I turn to my side and push off the ground with my hands. When I stand, a wave of nausea and dizziness hits me again, and Miranda must see it on my face because she grabs my arm to steady me.

"Whoa, you okay? Do you think you can walk a few feet to the cart?"

I nod and try to stand still for a minute. I'm racking my brain, trying to figure out who has been sick lately. None of my roommates have had any viruses, and all of my classes have been full, so I don't think anything is going around.

Miranda helps me get to the seat, and once I'm sitting, she rounds the cart and walks over to my golf bag and sets it in the back of the cart.

"Do you need some water to rinse out your mouth?"

"That would be great. I think my water must have fallen when I fell. Do you see it on the ground anywhere?"

She looks around the grass and shakes her head. Leaning down, she looks under the cart and says, "Found it."

When she stands, she hands me the water, then takes her seat behind the wheel.

I open the bottle and swish some of the water around in my mouth. Before she starts driving, I spit it out the side of the cart. "Sorry, I know that's gross."

"Doesn't bother me. I see all kinds of things with the teams I work with." She laughs.

Our speed on the way to the clubhouse is a little fast, but she probably doesn't want me to puke in the cart while she's driving. Can't say I blame her.

We reach the clubhouse, and she parks near the back entrance. "Do you need to use the restroom before we get you settled?"

"No, I'm good. I just want to sit down in the air-conditioning for a bit. I'm hoping that will help me feel a little better." I move my legs from the cart and stand slowly. I don't feel dizzy anymore, so I'll take that as a win.

Miranda takes my arm and leads me into the building. We make our way to a room that has a small couch, two oversized chairs, and a coffee table in the center. There's also a fireplace in here, but thankfully, it's not running.

I can see the course through the floor-to-ceiling windows and watch as people move around outside. Some of the teams are likely finishing up by now. Livi and Peyton were a few holes behind me and Mia, so they probably won't be back for a while.

Miranda leads me to one of the chairs. "I'll be right back. I'm going to go grab you some ice packs and some Gatorade."

"Thanks, Miranda. Should I put my feet up or anything?" I ask.

"Try just sitting for a few minutes, but if you feel like you need to lie down, absolutely do it," she tells me, hurrying out of the room.

Underneath my golf skirt are shorts, which have a pocket I keep my phone in. I pull it out and start googling to see if there is anything going around right now. As I'm looking, Miranda comes back into the room with a cold cloth, some ice packs, and some Gatorade.

"I got you the orange flavor; I hope that's okay. Our choices were limited." She hands me the drink.

I open the bottle and carefully sip it. It's not turning my

stomach, so I take that as a good sign and try to drink some more. When I put the cap back on, I set it on the coffee table in front of me. Miranda hands me the ice packs and cold cloth.

"Try putting the cloth on the back of your neck first. If that doesn't seem to help, go ahead and add in the ice packs for a bit."

"Okay, thanks, Miranda. You don't have to sit in here with me. I'll be fine. Just tell me where the bathroom is, in case I feel like I'm going to be sick again."

She tells me where to go, then leaves the room.

I place the cold cloth on the back of my neck and lean back on the chair. I must drift off because the next thing I know, Livi is standing next to me, telling me it's time to get on the bus to go back to Walker.

Our drive back to campus takes a few hours, and I'm not feeling as bad as I was, so the girls fill me in on what I missed from the tournament once the coach has given us her speech.

As soon as we get home, I hop in the shower and practically dive into bed, even though it's early for a Saturday night. My friends are planning to go out, but there's just no way.

They all stop in before they leave to check on me. As soon as I hear the door to the apartment close and lock, I shut my eyes and sleep.

The sun is shining right through my blinds in my room. It must be pretty early still, but once I'm up, I can't fall back to sleep.

I don't remember hearing my roommates come home last night. I was so dead to the world. But I can hear music coming from the kitchen, which is next to my room, so someone must be up already. We don't have practice today, so I'm surprised one of them is up before me. I'm usually the earliest riser in the apartment.

I'm not feeling as dizzy this morning or sick to my stomach, so I sit up and pause for a minute to test if I'll get sick. Nothing, which is a good sign. Maybe I just needed a good night's sleep. I've been moving on all cylinders lately between classes and golf.

I move my legs to the side of the bed and stand. Again, I wait for a minute to make sure I don't get dizzy. The coast is clear, so I make my way to my door, unwrapping my ponytail and retying it.

When I open the door, I see Livi standing in front of the coffee maker in the kitchen, her back to me.

"Morning, Liv."

She turns and looks at me with a smile. "Hey there, sleepy-head. Are you feeling better today?"

"Yeah, so far, so good. I think I'm just tired from everything I've had going on lately. The heat didn't help yesterday either. And why is it so hot in October? Freakin' wild Oklahoma weather."

"Girl, I know. It was brutal yesterday. I'm ready for the temperature to drop. My hair was a frizz ball from the heat." She reaches up to grab a coffee mug from the cabinet. "You want some?"

"Yes, please. I need a pick-me-up so I can start working on some homework." I walk over to the refrigerator to grab my almond milk creamer, which no one likes but me.

I move over to stand next to her, and she sets the coffee in front of me on the counter. I grab a stevia from the jar next to the coffee maker and rip it open and drop it in my mug, followed by my creamer.

"Em, that stuff is so gross. How can you drink that? It's not even sweet." She scrunches her nose.

"You know I'm lactose intolerant, and the artificial sweeteners in some of the creamers are so bad for you." I bump her hip with mine.

"I will gladly take my artificial sweeteners over that. Yuck."

She takes her coffee mug, I raise mine, and we clink mugs.

"What do you have going on today?" I ask her.

She takes a sip then sets down her mug. "I'm gonna drink my coffee, and then I'm going to go to the gym for a bit. You know I'm trying to work on my swing, and Coach told me to do some strength training with the medicine ball. After that, I'll probably come home and get ready for the week. Do you want to come to the gym with me?"

"No, I think I should probably sit out today and get some more rest. I can't miss class this week, so I'll stick around here and get ahead of some of my homework. I am hungry though. Should we go grab something or make something here?" My stomach is rumbling, which is a good sign since I haven't been able to eat much this week.

"I'm just going to have some yogurt and granola before I head out. Plus, I'm broke until my parents add more money to my account next week." She laughs.

I set my mug down and walk back over to the refrigerator. I put the creamer back and grab the yogurt for Livi. When I set it on the counter and open it, my stomach rolls. "Urgh. I was going to have some with you, but I think it's spoiled. Does it smell weird to you?"

She pulls it over to her and leans down to smell it. "Nope, smells fine to me. Do you think it's still that bug you caught?"

"I don't know. Might have to go to the clinic if it doesn't feel better by tomorrow." I put my hand on my stomach and rub in a circle.

"Yeah, it's not like you to be sick like this." She walks over to the pantry and grabs the granola, comes back out, then pulls a bowl from the cabinet. "Maybe you should just try eating some of the granola without the yogurt, just to get something in your stomach. Do you want a bowl?"

Nodding, I say, "Let me try that and see if it helps."

She hands me my bowl first, then finishes hers by adding the yogurt. As she does that, I walk around the counter, coffee in hand, and sit at the four-top table we have in our little kitchen nook.

I'm picking at the granola, and the smell doesn't seem to bother me, so I take a bite. But when Livi comes to sit next to me, I smell the yogurt again, and I jump up, barely making it to the sink to puke.

There's nothing in my stomach to bring up, so I'm really just heaving. I feel Livi's hand on my back, rubbing it in circles.

"Babe, I'm starting to get worried about you. Are you running a fever or anything, or is it just the stomach and dizziness?" She reaches over and turns on the sink to rinse out the bile I threw up.

I shake my head in reply. After a few deep breaths, I lean into the water and pull some into my mouth. I gargle and spit it out in the sink.

"So, um, question then. When was your last period? Because I just had mine and I feel like we all usually sync up, but I don't remember you saying anything about it." She drops her hand from my back.

I close my eyes and think about when my last cycle was. I had to go off the pill last spring because I kept getting migraines, no matter which one they switched me to. I tried keeping track using one of those apps on my phone, but my cycle was irregular for a while, so it was difficult to keep the timing accurate.

Livi gets up from the table and walks over toward the coffee machine, where she left her phone. She walks back over and lays it in front of me with the Calendar app open. "I think you should try to figure it out."

There's no way I've missed my period. I take her phone in my hand and start scrolling through the calendar, thinking back to when I last remember having it. Between school and golf, it's honestly slipped my mind. It's one of those things that I don't really think about until I actually get it.

It's late October now, so I scroll back to September, and … nope. Go back to August. I do remember having a period in August, right before we went to California for our first tournament of the fall season. So, I'm only … shit. I'm nearly eight weeks late.

"Em, how late?" Livi puts her hand on top of my hand that's now resting on the table.

"Umm …" I swallow hard.

My stomach rumbles again, and I drop her phone on the table and rush to the sink. I heave once, twice. This can't be possible. I haven't even been to any parties or even around any guys since—fuck. The end of August was when I hooked up with Archie freaking Griffith.

I turn on the water and cup my hand, filling it with the cool water coming out of the faucet. I take a drink and rinse out my mouth again. I put my hands back under the faucet and splash my face with water. I can't even bring myself to say in my mind what I suspect has happened.

Livi comes over to me at the sink and puts her hand on my back again. "Babe, I think we should go to the store."

Tears start pooling in my eyes. There's no way this could be happening. I'll lose my scholarship. Not to mention med school. And my parents. They will … I don't even know what they'll say.

"Okay, so before you start spiraling, let's go. Or I'll go and you go take a shower. Maybe you'll feel better if you do that. And then you won't be sitting here, freaking out." Livi takes my arm and guides me over to the couch. She sits first and gently pulls me down to sit next to her.

"Where are Mia and Peyton?" The thought pops into my head when I think about how I'm going to deal with this.

"Neither one of them came home with me last night. They were both hooking up with some basketball players, and I think they ended up going back to their place. They texted us in the group chat at, like, two a.m." She puts her hand on my knee.

I nod.

"Em, look at me. Let's get some answers and then figure out what to do. If you're not preg—"

The P-word snaps me out of my haze, and I whip my head to her. "Shh. Don't say it out loud. We don't know anything yet. This could all just be stress-related or something."

"Okay, yeah. You're totally right. I'm gonna go put a sports bra and a sweatshirt on and run to the store. Go get in the shower. I'll be back in a few." She stands and puts her hands out to me.

"Just take my debit card. It's in my wallet. I don't want you to have to pay for this."

I reach for her hands, and she pulls me up to stand. She

squeezes my hands, then releases them and turns to walk toward her room. Me? I'm frozen in place.

My mind feels muddled as I try to run through how this could have happened. And…what the fuck am I going to do if I'm pregnant. This certainly doesn't fall into any plan I've made for myself, my schooling, my career. I'm feeling panicked by the thought of trying to go through medical school with a baby. Is that even possible?

And what the hell will I tell my parents? *Oh, hey, Mom and Dad, I needed to get laid, and oopsie, now I'm pregnant.* I've tried so hard to be the perfect daughter since my sister's death. I have no idea how they'll react if I am pregnant.

Slumping back into the chair, I take some deep breaths to try to ground myself. I'm a logical, fact-based person, and I know I can't create a plan of action until I know the results.

Forty minutes later, I've showered and had a bottle of water, and now Livi and I are sitting in the bathroom, staring at three sticks lined up on the countertop. My back is turned to them— because if I can't see them, I can live in denial for just a little longer.

Livi keeps trying to say things to make me feel better, but really, nothing is helping.

"Hey, Liv. You can't say anything to anyone yet. Like, when the girls come home, you can't tell them. If I am ... you know. I need to figure out what to do about golf and everything."

"Absolutely. Not a word to anyone. But, Em, I'm totally here for you. If you are, we'll *all* be here with you the whole time. And besides, I'll be an amazing auntie."

"Livi, really? I'm trying not to have a complete breakdown here. How many more minutes?"

She giggles, and I turn my head and glare at her.

"Sorry. Sorry. Not funny at all. Not in any way, shape, or form. We have two more minutes left, but do you want me to look and tell you now?"

"You already looked, didn't you?" I reach for her hand.

With a sympathetic smile, she nods.

A sob breaks free, and I can't hold back my tears any longer. This can't be happening.

Livi wraps me in her arms. "Em, it's going to be okay. I promise. We'll be right here with you. But I gotta ask, are you going to tell Archie?"

I pull back and wipe the tears from my eyes with both hands. "I mean, how can I not? I'm not going to hide it; I wouldn't even be able to. My biggest concerns are school and golf. What am I going to do? And I'll have to talk to Archie. I saw something on *SportsCenter* about him entering the draft this year. I mean, this couldn't be more complicated."

What I don't say is that I'm also terrified. My little sister died of a genetic heart condition. I was fortunate not to have any issues, but that doesn't mean my kids won't. So I never really even thought about having kids. I've been so focused on getting through my four years here at Walker and then working toward applying to med school.

I clear my throat. "So, I think the best thing for me to do is find a doctor off campus for now. I'm afraid that if I go to the clinic, they will report it to the athletic department before I can figure out a plan. I really can't have that on my plate right now."

"I totally agree. I think that's probably for the best. But you should talk to Archie first. Have you seen him since that night?"

I sigh. "I know." I close my eyes and tilt my head back. "No, I haven't seen him, but haven't exactly been looking either. Of course I would have to get knocked up by the campus playboy."

"Yeah, but at least he's hot."

"Really, Liv?" I look at her incredulously.

She laughs. "Sorry, I guess it's too soon."

"You think? I need to try to get his number. I bet I could get it from Dan Smith, but then he'll ask questions."

"Smith is a nosy fucker; he would definitely ask questions. Most of those guys are bigger gossips than any girls I know. But I think I might know someone who knows where he lives."

"You just want me to go in guns blazing and see him instead of texting him like a normal person?" I look at her, eyes wide.

She pulls me into her arms again. "Yeah, babe. You need to go see him."

I tilt my head on her shoulder and see myself in the mirror, then look down at the counter at the three positive pregnancy tests. Yep, I guess it's as real as it gets.

CHAPTER
FOUR

ARCHIE

I JUST GOT HOME from my last class of the day, and I'm in the kitchen, making a protein shake before I have to leave for practice. I think the other guys already left without me, and I know Charlie has her long day of classes today. So, I might just take my time and have my shake here instead of bringing it with me.

My cell rings over the noise of the blender. The ringtone is the Walker U fight song, and it's loud as shit. It startles even me sometimes. I know it drives my roommates crazy.

I turn off the blender and walk over to the kitchen table, where I left my phone. *Mama Bear* shows on the screen. I swipe the Answer button and tap Speaker.

"Hey, Mama."

"Hi, honey. How was class today? Did you find out what you got on that last test in your History class?"

My mom is the best. Seriously, the best. Three of my brothers are still at home, but she makes it a point to call me and Aiden every day to check in.

"Yeah, I got an eighty-four on it. Not too bad. I'm happy with it. Keeps me eligible." I laugh.

"Okay, well, that's good! It's hard to believe this is pretty much your last semester, isn't it? I know you plan to keep the house as your home base until the draft, but this is it, huh?"

I nod, even though she can't see me. "Yep. I can't believe it either. But I promised you and Dad that I would still get my degree, so don't worry. I'll either take classes online or finish when I'm not in training or in season. Might take me a while, but I do want a backup plan. You never know what can happen."

"Archie, please don't even say things like that. I know injuries can happen, but I'm practically in need of anti-anxiety meds as it is between you and your brothers. I swear you all think you're indestructible." She huffs.

"Mama, if you really think about it, it's your fault. You raised us this way. Fearless, just like you." I belt out a laugh. Not laughing because it's not true. My mom is the most fearless woman I know.

"Ha-ha. So, there is actually a reason for my call. I, of course, wanted to do our daily check-in, but I wanted to let you know I can't make it up for the game this weekend. I'm so sorry. Ace and Aston have a game on Friday night, and then Austin and Jesse have games on Saturday morning and afternoon. So, Dad is going to come up by himself, and I'll cart the boys around here."

I walk back over to the blender and pour my shake into a cup.

"Not a problem, Mama. It's the busiest time of year for the Griffs. I get it. This game is gonna be a good one though."

She sighs. "I know, and I really am sorry to miss it. I also need to be here for the ranch hands in case they have any problems while Dad is up there. We have a few horses that are due any day now."

The doorbell rings before I can reply. "Hang on, Ma. Someone is at the door."

I walk over to the door and pull it open to see Emma standing on the other side. The girl I've been thinking about for two months is on my freaking doorstep, wearing leggings, an oversize sweatshirt, and one of those messy buns girls like to wear. She doesn't have on a stitch of makeup and is still the prettiest girl on campus.

I have to clear my throat and lift my chin to make sure I'm not looking like a total puppy dog in heat at the sight of her.

"Holy shit. Emma! What are you doing here?"

"Hey, Archie. Sorry to stop by like this, but I really need to talk to you. Is this a bad time?"

I shake my head, probably a little too much. "No, it's great. Come on in."

"Archie, who is Emma?" my mom asks.

"Oh shit. Sorry, Ma. My friend Emma is here, I gotta go. I'll call you later. Love you, Mama."

"To the moon, baby. Call me later. I want to know wh—"

I end the call before she can say anything else.

Emma smiles. "Mama's boy?"

I shrug. "I mean ... no? I'm the oldest of six and the favorite though, so you know how it is," I say, laughing.

Her smile falls. "Right. So, wow ... you have a big family then?"

"Yeah, all boys too."

"Are they all, like, your size?" She has her backpack over her shoulder, and she shifts it to the other one.

"Uh, yeah, pretty much. Aiden is close to my size. And the four youngest brothers are getting close." I stop talking and smile at her. "But I don't think you came here to ask about my family, did you?"

"Oh, right. Yeah, no, I didn't. So, um, how are you?" She's gripping the strap of her bag so tight that her knuckles are turning white.

"Hey, let me take your bag for you. You want to come in? I just made a protein shake. I can make you one, if you want." I reach my hand out, and she hands me her backpack.

"No, thanks. I'm sorry to drop by like this, but there's something I need to tell you." Her face is turning a little pink.

I'm not sure what it is she needs to tell me, but I'm pretty fucking happy she's here.

"Oh yeah. Shoot. Follow me to the kitchen. Water? Gatorade? We don't drink soda during the season, but I think my roommate has some of those sparkling waters if you want one of those."

"I'm good. Are your roommates here right now?" she asks.

I pull out one of the chairs at the kitchen table and drop her bag on it. "No, it's almost time for practice, so I think they left for the field house already. And Charlie, our other roommate, is in class or her sorority house."

"Oh! I didn't realize a girl lived here."

I nod. "Yep. She is Casey King's twin and Beckham Linson's girl."

She releases a breath. "Oh good. That's good. Sounds fun."

I can tell she's nervous, but I'm not sure why. Is she embarrassed by the night we spent together? She did take off at some point during the night. When I woke up, she was gone, as was my Texas Forever shirt.

"So, Emma with no last name, I've been looking for you."

Her eyes widen. "You've been looking for me? Why?"

I bark out a laugh. "Well, you pretty much blew my mind that night we spent together, and I haven't been able to stop thinking about you."

She stands there, looking at me with a shocked expression on her face.

"Does that surprise you?" I mean, it is out of the norm for me, but she doesn't need me to tell her that.

"Sorry." She shakes her head. "I'm just trying to figure out why you would be looking for me. I know your reputation—which is totally fine, by the way! I get it. College fun and all that. But, um, yeah. I think I'll just come out and say it. I find it's easier if I just blurt things out when I'm nervous."

I reach out to take her arm, and she lets me.

"Hey, are you okay? You don't need to be nervous with me. I'm stoked to see you. I'm not lying when I said I've been looking for you. I've been to Schuster and Smith's house more times than I'd like to admit. I even scoped out a few other parties to see if you were there."

She tries not to smile and rolls her lips in. "Good to know."

"Do you want to sit down?"

Nodding, she sits when I pull the chair out for her. "Archie ..." She looks up at me.

"Yes, darlin'?" I want her to relax a little. And honestly, I'm just happy she's here.

"So, I'm pregnant." She looks up and meets my eyes.

I'm not completely sure if this is a prank or if she said what I think she just said.

"Come again? Did you say you're pregnant?" I tilt my head and watch her face for any sign that this could be a joke.

"Yes, I did. And, Archie, just so you know, I obviously didn't intend for this to happen. I'm completely freaking out right now, but I'm trying to stay calm so I can get through telling you all of this. But I had to tell you. I have no idea how I'm going to do this, but I wanted to give you the choice to be a part of the baby's life. If you want to, that is. I'm sorry I'm rambling. This didn't fit into my plan, so I have no clue what I'm doing or how this will all work." She moves her hands from under mine and covers her face.

On instinct, I move toward her.

"Hey, hey. Okay, so you're pregnant. And I'm sorry to ask, but you're sure it's mine?" I reach for her hands and pull them away from her face. I need to see her when she tells me her answer.

Tears are running down her face, and I release one of her hands and wipe one off.

"Talk to me."

She inhales deeply. "I totally understand why you're asking, but I want you to know I don't sleep around. Regular hookups aren't really my thing, like they are yours."

"Ouch. Okay, good to know." I nod a few times. "But just so you know, I haven't been with anyone since you. I haven't wanted to. I haven't been able to look at any other girl without seeing your face in my mind."

"Really?" she whispers.

"Really." I try to keep my tone earnest. The gorgeous girl who I had the best sex of my life with has turned up on my doorstep to say she's having my kid. I've gone from elated, to confused, to—I'll admit—shitting a brick, to wanting to make this girl feel safe, to full-on excited in a matter of moments.

She's staring at me as if trying to decipher if I'm full of shit.

I lower my gaze to hers and try to get her attention to me and away from whatever thoughts that are going on in her head.

"So, tell me how you know you're pregnant. Did you see a doctor yet? How does that all work? I'm gonna be with you through all of this, by the way. You will never have to worry about that. I could probably get you in to see one of the team doctors or something. A guy I played with a few years ago had a baby, and I'm pretty sure they used the university doctors during her pregnancy, but I can find out for sure."

She starts shaking her head while I'm talking. "No, we can't do that. I'm also an athlete."

"Wait, what? What sport?" I'm going through every athlete event we've been required to attend over the last few years, and there's no way I wouldn't remember her face.

"I'm a golfer. I've been playing for Walker since my freshman year. So, yeah, I can't use the university doctors until I figure out what to do. I can't lose my scholarship. If the pregnancy is confirmed, I'm going to have to try to play out the rest of the fall season at the very least. The other issue is that I'm premed. And I've heard you have your own plans, so honestly, Archie, I'm completely overwhelmed, trying to think about how this will all work. And I wasn't really sure what you were going to say. It would almost be easier if you didn't want to be invol—"

"I'm gonna stop you right there, Emma. Don't think for a second that I'm going to let you do this alone. And if you're pregnant, that is my baby you're carrying. I will never abandon my child or you. We'll figure it out, but let's take this one step at a time. What do you want to do about a doctor then? Since you're premed, can you get some referrals or something?" I release her hand and scoot my chair closer to her.

She looks down at the table. "I could probably find someone, but worst case, we go to an OB-GYN in town through the hospital here just to get it confirmed, then decide what works from there. What do you think?" Her gaze meets mine again. She looks scared, uncertain.

I'm going to do everything I can to make sure she doesn't feel alone in this. And okay, fine, there's a little bit of caveman trying to break through. I can't believe I'm gonna be a dad. My little swimmers are pretty fucking strong to break through latex.

"Whatever you want to do, I'll do. You need me to look for doctors, I can. I want to be at every appointment I can be. The timing is not particularly great, but we'll figure it out together. Come here." I lean forward and wrap my arms around her.

"What are you doing?" she mumbles into my shoulder.

I lean back and tilt her face to look at me. "Emma, everything will be okay."

My ringtone goes off and startles us both.

"Holy shit, Archie. What is that?"

I laugh, letting go of her, and reach for my phone in my back pocket. "It's my ringtone for my phone. It's the Walker fight song."

When I look at the screen, I see a text from Beck, asking where I am, and then I look at the clock to see I have ten minutes to get to practice.

"You need to go, don't you?" she asks.

"I'm sorry, but I do. You aren't leaving without giving me

your number this time. Oh, and by the way, do you have my T-shirt from that night?"

She smirks. "I have no idea what you're talking about."

"Darlin' ... I think you do." I laugh. Glad to be able to laugh too. "Can I drop you at yours on my way, or do you have a ride?"

"Oh, no, I'm good. I parked on campus for class, so I'll just go grab my car before I also have to get to practice." She stands from my lap.

"I really don't want you to go. I feel like we should talk some more. Plug your number into my phone, and I'll call you later? Maybe we can grab dinner or something and talk some more?" I hand her my phone.

"Sure, we can probably do that. And, Archie, can I ask you not to say anything to anyone? Only one of my roommates— who is also my best friend and a teammate—knows, but my other two roommates don't know yet. I just want to figure out how to deal with my scholarship before I tell anyone. And because I don't know your friends, can I ask that you keep it between us for now too?"

She's looking up at me, and I see vulnerability in her eyes.

"You got it, darlin'. I'll call you later, and we'll figure out a plan." I take her hand and lead her to the door.

"Thanks, Archie. I wasn't sure what to expect, but I'm feeling a little less scared now."

We stop at the door, and she glances up at me.

I open the door for her; she walks out, and then I follow. I don't want her to leave. I want to keep talking to her, spending time with her.

"I'm glad you feel better. I think it'll take a minute for it to settle in, but I know everything will be okay. Besides, whether it's a boy or a girl, this is gonna be one good-lookin' kid. Am I right?" I wink at her, trying to lighten the mood again.

She laughs and steps off the porch stoop and down the walkway.

When she reaches the sidewalk, I call out to her, "Oh, wait, Emma! What's your last name?"

She stops and turns toward me. "Tucker." She smiles and starts walking away.

"I'll call you later, Emma Tucker, and you'd better answer!" I know I'm shouting now, but I don't really give a shit.

She waves a hand over her head and turns the corner. Once she's out of my sight, I rush back into the house to grab my shake and my bag.

As I'm running toward my room, Liam calls my name.

Fuck.

"Duuude, Arch. What in the actual fuck? You're gonna be a dad?"

"Pitzy, why aren't you at practice right now? I thought I was here alone." I go into my room and grab my bag, then turn and walk back out.

"Bro, are you not gonna answer me? I was taking a little siesta, and my alarm clock didn't go off—which thank fuck I heard you out here, or I would have missed practice. Then I opened the door, just as I heard, 'I'm pregnant.'"

Pitz reaches down and grabs his bag while I pass.

I stop in front of him and try not to smile. "Look, she doesn't want anyone to know. Like, at all. So, you have to promise me you won't say a word to anyone. We still don't know for sure anyway. Give me your word you won't say anything. This is bigger than gossip. Her scholarship is at risk with this."

"Damn. No, of course you have my word. I'm just ... speechless. And why aren't you freaking out? I would be toast if a chick came in, telling me she was pregnant!"

I shrug. "Because I'm not freaked out. If she's pregnant, I'm gonna be a daddy. If she's not, I got her number." I wink and walk away.

"Arch, I gotta say, I'm a little nervous about how you're acting here," he says from behind me.

I pull open the front door, and we walk out to my truck that is sitting in the front of the house on the street.

"I mean, it's not ideal timing for either one of us. But I gotta tell you, there's something about this girl. It wasn't just good sex. For the first time in my life, I felt a connection. I haven't stopped thinking about her since that night. You know I've been looking for her. And regardless of how this turns out, I'm not letting her out of my sight again."

I round the front of the truck to get in on the driver's side, and Pitz opens the passenger side and hops in. When I get in the truck, Pitz looks at me.

"You really do like her then." He barks out a laugh. "You know, just because she's carrying your kid, doesn't mean she's gonna fall in love with you."

"Who said anything about love?"

"The way you're swooning all over the damn living room says a lot. This could be the first girl who breaks your heart."

"I just found out I'm gonna be a dad, and you're already trying to spoil the good news."

"Just looking out for my boy. This is a lot to take in. Never thought I'd see the day, man. I mean, maybe when we're in our thirties, but not now, for sure."

"You know how much my family means to me. I had the best role models for parents. Marriage, kids—I've always wanted that. I was just having a good time while I was here. But this changes things." I turn on the truck and pull out onto the road.

"Daddy Archie. Who woulda thought?" He laughs.

And me? A deep sense of pride fills me. I'm gonna rock the shit out of being a dad, but also, I'm gonna show Emma that I'm all in. For her and the baby.

CHAPTER
FIVE

EMMA

AFTER I LEFT ARCHIE'S, I got my car from one of the lots on campus and made my way to practice.

We ran some swing drills, but then the sky opened up and started pouring rain, so we had to call it early. Coach asked me how I was feeling today, and while I didn't feel my best, I needed to suck it up while I was golfing, or my teammates will figure it out fast.

I'm on my way back to my apartment now, and my cell starts ringing. I see a 940 area code, and it says Denton, Texas. In a college in Oklahoma, it's not uncommon to see a Texas area code. But I'm guessing this is Archie.

I tap Accept on the screen in my car that connects to my phone. "Hello?"

"Emmaaaa," Archie's deep grumble rolls out.

I can't help but smile. "Hey, Archie. You called, and I answered."

Despite the stress of the situation, I don't think going through this with him will suck. I wasn't sure what to expect when I went over to his house today, but the fact that he actually made me feel … okayish about this pregnancy helped defuse the anxiety a little. Gives me hope that we'll be able to co-parent together. We still have so much to talk about and figure out, but at least he's sweet. And nice to look at. And those butterflies, yep, they're there, but I'll just squash those down for now.

"I'm a man of my word, Emma. So, what are you up to? Y'all get rained out?" It sounds like he might be in his car too.

"Yeah, we called practice early, so I'm on my way home. Did you finish early too?"

"Yep, I'm on my way home now, but I wanted to see if you might be up for getting some food with me. I figure we should probably spend some time together and make some tentative plans, yeah?"

At the mention of food, my stomach rolls. I know I need to try to eat though, so maybe I could try some soup or something. "I can meet you now, if you want. I was just on my way home, too, but I can detour. My appetite is a little picky right now, so can we try something simple?"

"Oh, right. I didn't think about that." He clears his throat. "Are you, like, sick to your stomach?"

"It's really only been a week or so, but it's been a rough one. I passed out at my tournament on Saturday." I huff a laugh, trying to play it down.

"You did what now? You passed out on, like, the course?" His voice inches up a notch.

"Yeah, I did. It wasn't fun. And I threw up on the course after my rotation. I was mortified. But I thought it was just a bug or something, but then yesterday, my roommate was eating some yogurt, and the smell did me in. That's when we figured that I had better take a test. It's been a wild weekend, for sure." I wince.

"That sucks. I'm sorry you had to go through that. Well, let's try something easy. You aren't worried about being seen with me, right?"

I shake my head even though he can't see me. "No. I mean, at some point, everyone will know, and I'd rather it not be as big of a surprise as it will be anyway. Unless you have a problem being seen with me."

"Fuck no, darlin'. I can't wait to hang out with you. How about we meet at Scratch and get a burger or something?"

"Not sure about the burger, but I'm sure I can find something there. I can be there in five. How far are you?"

"I'm just a few blocks from there, so I'll grab a table."

"Okay, see you soon." I lift my hand to press End, but Archie speaks before I do.

"I can't wait to see you, Emma."

My stomach flutters. "Bye, Archie."

I pull up to the restaurant a few minutes later and park next to a big black truck, similar to the one I saw parked outside Archie's house earlier today. And by the big decal—a 69 inside a football—in the corner of the rear window, I'm gonna guess it's his.

There aren't many people in the restaurant, but even if there were, I would see Archie over everyone. He stands when he sees me and walks over to me, wearing a smile.

He reaches for my hand. "Hey. I ordered you a club soda in case your stomach was bothering you. I searched it, and Google said that would settle an upset stomach, so if it lied, don't be mad at me." He laughs and gently squeezes my hand.

We reach the table, and he pulls out my chair for me.

"Thank you," I say as I take my seat.

He rounds the table and sits across from me. The smile ... it's still there. "So, Emma, where should we start?"

His hair is damp, and he's wearing a red Walker University football shirt with a number sixty-nine right over his heart and black gym shorts. He looks hotter than he should just after practice.

Me? I had to change into my practice uniform, so I'm in my skort and oxford shirt, with *Walker Golf* on the chest. Hair pulled back in a ponytail. I have zero makeup on today because I could barely get out of bed this morning.

So, he looks like a snack, and I look … like I just got caught in a rainstorm in my golf gear.

I look around and see the place is pretty much empty, but I still lower my voice and take a deep breath in. "Well, I will call and see if I can get an appointment with one of the doctors through the hospital website, but based on what I saw online, they probably won't take me until it's been ten weeks from my last period, which is, by my best guess, in two weeks."

He nods and moves his hands from his lap and folds them on top of the table. "Okay, sounds good. If you're open to it, I would like to go to your appointment with you. I don't want you to do any of this without me, if that's okay."

I really don't know what I was expecting from him, but it wasn't this. Not that I thought he would be a jerk, but I didn't think he would want to be so involved.

"Of course. I have no problem with that, but I don't want you to feel obligated to be at every one. I know you have a full schedule with football right now." I take a sip of the club soda in front of me, and it's not bad.

The waiter comes over to us before he can reply. Archie orders a burger, and I order soup. I'm just not sure I can handle much more than that right now, and the very last thing I want to do is throw up in front of Archie. In the middle of the restaurant.

After he walks away, Archie reaches for my hands, and I let him take them. He seems to be a touchy guy. "Here's what I would like to happen. I would like to be a part of this whole thing, Emma. I don't want to miss anything unless I absolutely have to, meaning if I'm out of town for a game. But, if possible, I'd like to schedule anything you need to do around my commitments and yours."

"Okay, I think we can make that work." I smile at him.

He starts rubbing his thumb across my knuckles. It seems like a simple gesture, but it's making me feel a little flushed. I have never in my life had a reaction to a man like I have to Archie.

"Glad we have that settled." He smirks. "I don't know what your reasons were for not seeking me out, but I'm pretty sure they had something to do with my player reputation. Whatever it was, the reality is that you and I are now connected. I know we only know each other from that one night, but I would really like to hang out with you and get to know you—and not just because you're pregnant. Although that seems like the biggest reason to. Even if you hadn't knocked on my door and told me you were pregnant, I was gonna find you, and I was going to ask you out. I don't think that has to change. In fact, I think it's even more of a reason why I should."

I know I'm full-blown blushing now. I can feel a rush of heat go to my face. I've had guys hit on me, dated a guy in high school, but no one has ever come right out and asked me to spend time with him like this.

And I can't deny it and say I didn't feel a connection that night. I absolutely did, which was why I bolted before he woke up. And I had to keep my head on straight and stay focused on school and golf. He was a hookup, plain and simple, which was what I told myself—repeatedly. Guys like Archie can break your heart if you let them.

"So, are you saying you want to date me?" I smirk.

"I'm gonna date the shit out of you," he says with a laugh, leaning forward. "And I'm not gonna lie—I wouldn't mind getting into that cute little skirt you have on."

My eyes widen, and I bark out a laugh. People turn to look at us then. "Oops, guess that was a little loud."

"I like it when you're loud." He smiles and pulls his hands away from mine. He takes a drink of what looks like water, eyes not leaving mine.

"No, wait. This could get messy, Archie. If it goes wrong, we could really mess up our relationship."

"It could. Or it could lead to something pretty special. We

have to get to know each other, and I'm pretty sure it would be nice to tell our child that he or she was conceived while we were dating in college and not because Mom and Dad were horny at a college party and Mom snuck out in the middle of the night, wearing Dad's T-shirt."

"Yeah, that would make a better story. And I do want to get to know you. The real you and not just the stories that float around this campus."

"I mean, the stories are pretty epic, I'm sure," he drawls, completely unashamed of his life.

People would kill for his self-confidence. As for me, I'm drawn to it.

I bite my lower lip and contemplate what kind of mess this could be.

Archie Griffith, one of the biggest fuckboys of Walker, who only found out hours ago that he's gonna be a father—and has yet to freak out, by the way—wants to show me what kind of man he is by dating me. A guy who could have questioned my motives, asked for a paternity test, and ignored me for eight months while we awaited results is being the most chivalrous man by not only supporting me, but doubling down on this notion that he wants to—and I quote—"date the shit" out of me. It's crazy and absurd. And yet it's so damn sweet that I'd be a fool to not give this man a try.

My stomach flutters, and yet I try to maintain an almost businesslike approach, keeping my emotions in check.

"All right, if we're gonna try the dating thing, tell me more about your family. You have brothers? Five? You're from Texas, right?" I ask, sitting back in my seat.

He nods. "I do. I have five brothers, and I am from Texas. My dad is a cattle rancher. We live on the same ranch where my dad was raised. He took over before I was born, but my grandparents still live on the land. They live in a smaller house about two miles from the main house. Gramps still tries to help out, but my dad won't let him do too much. He has ranch hands to help him with most of it."

"You and your brothers ever work the ranch too?" I take another drink of my club soda, then put it down. Crossing my arms, I rest on my forearms and lean in.

"Yeah, growing up, we all had chores. Four of my younger brothers still live at home, so they help out a lot when they aren't playing sports. My brother Aiden is away, playing hockey right now. He lives up in New England and plays for a league there. But he's entering the draft in the spring after he turns eighteen." He mirrors me and also leans in.

"Oh, wow, that's cool. He doesn't want to play in college then?" I ask, not familiar with how the hockey draft process works.

Archie shakes his head. "No, he's in the major junior league, so he does have the choice to play in college, but he's good enough to get drafted and go straight to the pros. It's a different process from football—that's for sure."

The waiter brings our food out, so we sit in silence for a few minutes and start eating. My stomach isn't rolling right now, so I'm taking advantage of that and trying to get some of the soup in. I just hope I don't throw it up later.

Thankfully, he chews with his mouth closed. I couldn't deal with it otherwise. I think if I had to hear him chew, it might make me gag. Pregnant or not.

"Tell me about you, Emma. Are you from here?" he asks.

I grab a pack of crackers from the bowl they gave me with my soup, scrunch it up, then open it, and scatter it in the bowl.

"Well, let's see. I'm from this area. I grew up in Midwest City. I started playing golf when I was twelve, and I really liked it. I was good enough to get a scholarship here. I'm close to my parents, and they come to my tournaments that they can drive to. My dad is in insurance, and my mom is a freelance writer. And that's about it. Fairly normal."

I am not ready to talk about my sister with him yet, so I leave her out. Even all these years later, it still hurts to think about what happened, and I know it's not particularly good that I don't talk about her, but it's my way of coping with it.

Well, and becoming a doctor. I hope I can someday help kids who have the same defect my sister did. Although technology has come a long way in the last thirteen years, there's still a lot of research to be done.

My sister's death rocked my family for a long time. I felt like I tried my hardest to fill that void. I've been a good student, and I've stayed focused, never getting in trouble for anything. Doesn't mean we don't talk about her at all, just not a lot. Which makes me sad. She was such a bright light in our family in the short time she was with us.

"How do you think your parents will feel about your pregnancy? Will they freak out?" he asks.

I nod. "Pretty much. I think they'll be shocked. I've been on the doctor path for so long, and they know how important it is for me, so they'll worry for sure."

"What kind of doctor do you want to be?" He takes another bite of his burger, nearly done with his meal, while I've only taken a few of mine.

"I'll get my degree in chemistry and biology, and then I'll need to apply to med schools, where my specialty will be pediatric cardiology." I take a sip of the broth in my soup, still testing my stomach strength.

"Wow, that's amazing. You must be smart then, huh?" He smirks.

"I mean, yeah." I laugh. "My grades are good, and my mock exam scores for the MCAT have been high, so I should be able to get into my pick of med schools."

Archie wipes his hands on his napkin. "Well, I'm guessing the baby will change a lot of that, right?"

I look down and swallow. "For sure. I think we just need to see what the doctor says. I feel like there is a lot we still need to know and talk about. I mean, you're going into the draft this year, right?"

"Emma"—he smiles widely—"have you looked me up?"

Listen, I'm not shy, and I'm a confident gal, so I have no problem admitting I have, in fact, looked him up. But also, his face is everywhere on this campus. And I've seen him on *Sports-Center* more than once.

"Yeah, I have. But don't act like you aren't basically a celebrity on campus." I roll my eyes, smiling.

"You looked me up." His grin is so wide that I can't help but laugh.

The waiter comes back over and places the check on the table, then takes Archie's plate. Archie reaches for it and pulls out his wallet.

"I can pay for my half," I offer.

"Darlin', don't insult me. I would never in a million years let you pay. Call me old-fashioned, but not happening." He hands the waiter his card and nods to him.

"You can take your time eating. I'm in no rush." He nods to my bowl.

"No, I'm good. I wasn't really hungry, but while I wasn't nauseous, I wanted to try to eat something." I wipe my mouth with my napkin and set it back in my lap.

"Is that all you wanted to know about me? About my family?"

I cross my arms and look at him with an arched brow. There are so many things I want to know about him, yet there are only so many hours in the day. "Okay, Archie. I need to ask you three very important questions that could make or break this relationship."

He leans forward, as if ready for the challenge. "Fire away."

"One, when you travel, do you need a packed itinerary for max efficiency, or are you a *go where the wind takes you* kinda guy?"

He purses his mouth in contemplation. "I like a loose itinerary. The main hits of the trip are planned, like dinner or a tour, with some wiggle room on what we do in between."

I nod in appreciation. I am a consummate planner who even schedules my time to relax, which is probably not the best.

Liking his answer, I continue, "Two, what is a movie you've seen a million times and would watch again if it came on TV?"

"*The Parent Trap*," he answers easily. "The Lindsay Lohan version. Don't look at me like that. It's a great movie, and when I'm home, it always happens to be playing on cable. My mom loves those sappy channels. No lie—I've seen that movie so many times, and I'd totally watch it again if it were on right now. That, and *Crazy, Stupid, Love*. So cool how all the stories just wind into each other. You've seen that?"

I grin. "I have. Why did I expect you to say a football movie or a Marvel film?"

"Because that's what all guys like, but I'm not your typical guy."

"That you're not."

"Okay, what's your last question?"

I smash my lips together for a moment before asking, "What is the one thing you're most passionate about?"

His eyes zero in on mine and widen slightly. The dark orbs hold my gaze and pierce me with a searing heat that warms me more than the soup. It feels like I'm the one thing he is most passionate about, which is ridiculous because we've known each other for a combination of hours—yet it already feels like one of the most important relationships I've ever had in my life.

I suppose it is.

I sit back and wait for him to answer. When he does, it's with sheer conviction.

"Being a man."

I blink at him and then scowl slightly, wondering where he's going with that comment.

"Faith, family, and hard work. That's what it takes to be a man, and I work damn hard every day to be a good one."

Well, color me taken aback, but that was perhaps the best answer to a question I've ever heard.

I like this man. I like him so much. My chest feels like it's tightening, which could be good or bad. I'm either smitten or having a heart attack. Verdict's currently out.

He has a smug smile. "Are these the questions you ask all your dates?"

I lift a shoulder. "No. I just made them up."

He laughs out loud. "So, they were just special for me?"

"I wanted to learn more about you, and those are what came to mind."

"You're an interesting one. I have to keep my eye on you."

When Archie gets his card back from the waiter, he puts it back into his wallet. "You ready to go then?"

I nod and place my napkin on the table next to the bowl. I start to get up, but Archie comes around the table before I do and holds out his hand to help me up. Not that I need help, but it's kinda cute.

He keeps my hand in his as we walk out. I look around the restaurant and notice people watching us leave. This must happen to him a lot.

When we walk out of the restaurant, I move next to him, and we walk toward my car. "This is me."

I turn to face him and rest my back against the driver's door. We're still holding hands, and I haven't let go yet.

He comes in closer and brings his other arm to rest against the top of the car over my shoulder. Our faces are a breath apart.

"Emma, I gotta tell you. That little skirt thing you're wearing is fucking hot." The heat in his eyes makes me believe him.

"Oh, yeah?" I say breathily.

There's something so sexy about the way Archie says exactly what he's thinking, when he's thinking it.

No games.

Just pure honesty.

He leans in closer. "Definitely. Are you gonna let me give you a kiss good night? You know, since this was our first date and all."

I pull my head back and look at him. "Is that what this was? Our first date? Hmm … not sure I'd count this as a date, but I'll let you kiss me."

With no hesitation, he releases my hand and cups my face with both of his hands. When his lips cover mine, I can't keep my moan from slipping out. He was the last person I kissed, and I gotta say, my memory was accurate.

The kiss starts slow. He's teasing the seam of my lips with his tongue, and I gladly open for him. I meet his tongue stroke for stroke. My hands move to his waist, and I grab on to the bottom of his shirt. When our mouths open just a bit more, he deepens the kiss. This time, he groans.

Needing to feel his body, I pull him in closer to me. I let my hands drift up his chest, then around his neck, and slide my hands into his hair. With his body against mine, I can feel his erection poking into my belly. The burst of heat that rips through me makes me hold him tighter.

He pulls back, breathing heavy. "Darlin', I'm about two seconds away from picking you up and fucking you against this car. Not that I don't want that—because believe me, I do—but we're in a parking lot at a restaurant. I want to ask you to come home with me, but I really don't think that's what you need right now. You should probably get home and get some rest. Do you want me to follow you home?"

I close my eyes and take a few deep breaths. "Yeah, I should probably get home. I need to do some reading and get to bed early. I have an eight thirty a.m. class."

"Why on earth would you pick a class that early in the mornin'?" He chuckles.

I look up at him and shrug. "I'm an early riser, and it just fit with my course schedule and golf."

His hands are still holding my face, and his thumb swipes my cheek softly. "You're so pretty. I can't wait to spend more time with you, Emma Tucker." He leans in and kisses me gently on the lips.

When he pulls back, he releases me and steps back. He reaches down and adjusts his erection. "Hate wearing boxers. So restrictive."

I shake my head and smile. "Night, Archie. Thanks for dinner."

I turn and open my door. He grabs of the top of the door, holding it open while I get in.

Once I'm buckled, he bends down slightly. "Text me when you get home?"

"Will do." I nod.

He stands and closes the door, taps the hood twice, then backs up.

I pull out of the spot and start driving. I can't help but look in my rearview mirror and see him standing there with his hands in his pockets, watching me drive away.

CHAPTER
SIX

ARCHIE

IT'S BEEN two weeks since Emma told me she was pregnant. We've talked every day, and we've seen each other just about every day too. Our schedules are busy, but we've been able to meet for lunch on campus, and we've spent some time together at her apartment, getting food, and running errands together. Coupley type of shit. And I love it.

Emma seems to have gotten over the complete freak-out about being pregnant. I like to think I have something to do with that. I try to make her feel good every time I see her or talk to her. We talk about the baby some, but I really want to get to know her too. It turns out, she's not just a smokeshow, but she's really cool too.

Like how in the summer months, she mentors young golf players who are pediatric oncology patients from the nearby hospital. She's also crazy smart, and she's taking the most advanced science classes the college offers. There are words on the page that I can't even pronounce. She takes school seriously and studies a ton.

She loves comedians. Her reels are full of clips of stand-ups that make her giggle. Don't ask her to recite one though because she's terrible at delivering a punch line.

She's also mad competitive. We've played a few board games she keeps in her closet. The old-school kind, like Monopoly. The girl can't handle losing her cash to my epic hotel empire. Not gonna lie—I'm equally competitive so I refuse to let her win just because she's a girl.

I did, however, take my shirt off to distract her as I put her homes in foreclosure. I caught her ogling my chest and might have kept my shirt off the rest of the night just to keep her hot and bothered.

My favorite thing is how when she scratches her nose, she uses two hands, which makes her look like a rabbit, and it's really fucking cute.

And we've done a whole lot of kissing, but nothing much more than that, even though I'm dying to, but up until a few days ago, she hasn't been feeling all that great, so I'm letting her take the lead.

Today is our first appointment with the obstetrician. My last class ended just before it was time to leave to get there, so I'm meeting her at the office.

I'm taking the stairs two at a time so I don't miss anything. Plus, she told me she'll have to fill out some paperwork and might need some of my medical history. I've never had anything happen to me minus minor injuries from football, and other than my gramps's heart attack, my family is pretty healthy.

I find the doctor's office and open the door. As soon as I walk in, every lady in there turns to look my way. There are a few other men in the waiting room, too, and they nod at me.

Emma is sitting in the corner, filling something out on a clipboard. I walk over and sit in the seat next to hers. "Hey, darlin'. How's it going?"

She looks up at me and smiles. "Hey. It's going … I'm almost done with the paperwork. I just need you to answer these four questions, and then I can go turn it in. I've used my insurance card from my parents, so I'm gonna have to tell them before they get the explanation of benefits." She winces. "Maybe we should coordinate our timing for telling our families?"

"Yeah, baby, we can do that." I look at the form. "The answers are no, no, no, no. BOOM. Done." I clap my hands together.

"Archie, shh! There are other people in here with us." But she says it with a laugh.

Her laugh makes me smile, and I want to kiss her.

"Come here." I crook my finger at her.

She turns her head toward mine. "What?"

"I want those lips." I take her chin between my thumb and forefinger and lead her closer.

Her lips pucker, and she leans in to kiss me.

I hum against her lips. I'm getting addicted to kissing her, and—I can't lie—I'm dying to get into her pants again. The number of nights I've come home and jerked off … I feel like a teenager. I've never really *dated* anyone, and considering we've only just started spending time together, I'm trying to be patient. It's not easy. I like sex, and I liked sex with Emma a lot. Big fan. Can't wait to do it again. When she's ready, of course.

A door opens, and a lady in scrubs props the door. "Emma Tucker."

Emma stands and grabs her purse from the floor and slides it over her shoulder, then moves the clipboard to one hand and reaches for my hand with the other.

Despite the fact that we're really still getting to know each other, I love that Emma feels comfortable with me. She's not timid, so her affection with me is natural.

We walk through the doorway and pause, waiting for the nurse to tell us where we need to go.

She starts walking, then stops at a door next to a small counter space that has a computer, a tablet, and some urine cups. She picks up one of the cups and wraps a label around it, then hands it to Emma.

"I need you to give us a urine sample to confirm the pregnancy. Use the sanitizing wipes first, then fill to this line." She points to a line on the cup and then hands it over to Emma.

Emma looks at me, hands me her backpack and the clipboard, then goes into the restroom.

"Oh, here, I can take that for you."

The nurse reaches for the clipboard. I gladly hand it over. She walks away with it, then comes back just as Emma is coming out of the restroom, urine in hand.

The nurse takes it from her and sets it on the counter. She steps around us, and we follow her down the hallway to a scale. She instructs Emma to step on.

Emma looks over at me. "Turn around. You don't need to see how much I weigh."

I bark out a laugh. "Darlin', you can't be serious?"

With her finger, she twirls it in a circular motion. I sigh but turn around.

I hear something sliding, then hear the nurse say, "Sixty-nine inches."

I can't help myself. I turn my head and meet Emma's eyes with a big-ass smile on my face.

She rolls her eyes and steps off the scale.

We follow the nurse farther down the hall to an open doorway. "Go ahead and have a seat. I'm just going to take your blood pressure and vitals."

Emma sits in the chair next to the countertop that has a jar of cotton balls, long Q-tip-looking things, and a box of gloves.

The nurse takes Emma's arm and wraps the cuff around it. While that expands, she drags a thermometer across Emma's forehead, then places a heartbeat-button thing on her finger. She writes something on a paper on the desk, then looks at a box, checking her blood pressure.

"One eighteen over seventy. Good. Are you taking any medications right now? Even over-the-counter ones count."

"No prescription meds, but I do take a multivitamin and a probiotic," Emma answers.

"Okay, that's fine. And when was the first day of your last period? Doesn't have to be exact, but as close as you can estimate," she says.

"I can't remember the exact date, but it was mid-August."

The nurse nods and writes something on the paper, then stands. "Dr. Landy will be in soon. Go ahead and undress completely and put the gown on." She points to the exam table, then opens the door and leaves the room.

Emma and I look at each other. I smile, but she looks a little shy.

"Do you want me to leave the room, darlin'?" I ask her. I never want her to feel uncomfortable with me.

She shakes her head. "No, it's fine. Not like you haven't seen it, but I'm just feeling a little bloated now."

"Emma, you are the most gorgeous girl I've ever seen." I smirk.

She laughs. "You are ridiculous." But she starts to remove her clothes.

Do I watch? You bet I do. I'm not missing a minute of seeing her body again. It's been months, and I still see it in my mind. Seeing the real thing? Yeah, nothing could pull me away.

Her back is to me, but when she bends down to remove her pants, I see a tiny tattoo on the small of her back that I make a note of to ask about later and the swell of her breast from the side.

"Hey, Em, are your boobs starting to hurt yet?"

She whips her head back to me. "Archie, seriously?"

"What? I'm just curious. I read that they might start to get sore early in the pregnancy, all the way to the end. So, I was just curious."

My eyes are still glued to her as she wraps the gown around her. Once it's tied, she reaches under it and pulls her panties off. They're pink.

She hands me her clothes and settles herself on the exam table. I set her bag down and fold her clothes before placing them on the counter next to me.

"Are you good? Do you need anything?" I ask.

"I'm good." She holds out her hand to me so I lean forward and take it in mine. "Are you nervous at all? You seem so calm. I'm kinda freaking out a little. Like, Archie, this appointment is going to make this very real."

Before I can reply, there's a knock on the door, and then it opens. The doctor walks in, followed by the nurse, and the door closes.

"Hi, Emma. I'm Dr. Landy. So, I can confirm that you are pregnant. Congratulations. I'm going to do a short exam here, but then I'm going to bring in the technician for an ultrasound. She'll do a transvaginal ultrasound to help me confirm your due date and just make sure we don't have any additional challenges. But you're young and healthy, so I don't anticipate any issues. We also need to discuss your family history based on your intake form."

She looks over at me. "Are you the father?"

"I am." I beam.

"Congratulations to you both then. Go ahead and lie back, Emma." The doctor pulls a pair of gloves on and sits on a rolling stool and rolls her way right up into Emma's honeypot. I mean, right on in there.

I'm still holding Emma's hand, but locked in on what's happening at the end of the exam table when I feel Emma squeeze my hand. I look at her, and she's watching me.

"Look at me, please." Her eyebrows rise.

"You got it, darlin'." I wink at her.

"Okay, Emma. You can sit up. Everything feels okay, so let's get the tech in here and get the ultrasound done. I'll see you in four weeks, unless you have any concerns." She takes off her gloves, tosses them in a bin, and smiles at us both.

Emma clears her throat. "So, about that family history. I do need to know what to be prepared for since my sister died from complications of pulmonary atresia."

"I did see that on your form, and I understand your concerns. We will be monitoring your pregnancy closely, and if we see anything that we need to look at further, I promise you, we will do so immediately. But there have been so many advances in pediatric cardiology in the last ten years, so I'm confident that if there are any issues, we can keep you and the baby safe. Okay?" She smiles gently. "Now let's get that ultrasound so we can get some measurements and the baby's heart rate."

I turn my gaze to Emma, a little shocked by the fact that she hasn't told me she lost a sibling. I can't imagine losing any of my brothers, so that must have been horrible for her and her family.

Emma nods. "Thank you, Doctor."

Dr. Landy smiles and leaves the room with the nurse.

"So, Emma, can you tell me about your sister?" I ask quietly.

She sighs. "I will. It's just not something that's easy for me to talk about. I remember the day she died. I was nine, so while I didn't understand a lot of the medical jargon then, I knew something was wrong. It happened so fast, and then she was gone. She's why I want to be a doctor."

"I'm so sorry, darlin'. I can't imagine. But, Em, look at me."

She looks at me, and our eyes meet.

"Our baby is going to be healthy, happy, and smothered in love."

She smiles and nods. "You're right. This is a lucky baby, huh?"

"The luckiest." I lean forward and kiss her.

Another knock on the door interrupts our kiss.

"Emma, I'm here to do your ultrasound." A woman in scrubs comes into the room, pushing a cart with a screen and ... a dildo?

My eyes shoot to Emma's. I'm trying to keep my mouth shut, but I can't help the smile that breaks across my face. I pull in a deep breath through my nose to keep from laughing.

Emma closes her eyes and shakes her head. "You are a child, Archie."

That just makes me grin wider. "Now, darlin', you know that's not true."

"Okay, Emma, I'm going to have you lie back. I'm going to insert the wand into your vagina, and we'll be able to get some pictures of your baby. You might feel some pressure, but don't worry; it won't hurt the baby," she says as she rolls a condom over the wand, then squirts some lube over it.

I can't stop the words before they fly out of my mouth. "Um, ma'am, is that a condom and lube?"

"Archie!" Emma screeches. "I'm sorry about him. Just carry on and ignore anything he says." She turns to me and shakes her head once.

"It's all good. I've heard it and seen it all," the technician says with a laugh. "First baby?"

Emma and I look at each other.

"Yes, ma'am, it is," I answer for us.

She stands between Emma's legs and pulls her cart closer. After she taps some buttons on the computer keyboard, the screen lights up on the monitor. "Okay, let's get started. Again, Emma, you'll feel a little bit of pressure."

I can't watch her put the wand into Emma, even though I can't see anything under the gown she's wearing. So, I squeeze her hand, and she looks over at me. I smile and pull her hand up and kiss it.

"Okay, here we go."

We hear a swooshing sound come over the speaker.

"Do you see this dot right here?" she asks.

We both nod.

"That's your baby. I'm just going to take some measurements of the embryo and the uterus. That should confirm your due date." She holds the wand in place, then takes the mouse and drags it across different points on the screen. Kind of looks like geometry.

Emma's eyes are glued on the screen. A faint smile on her lips. "Is the swooshing noise the heartbeat?" she asks.

I didn't even realize that's what it could be, so my head turns to the technician to hear her reply.

She smiles. "It sure is. Nice and steady, too, at one hundred fifty-three beats per minute. I'll get some pictures for you to take home too."

The reality of this whole experience hits me like a truck. *I'm going to be a dad. Emma is carrying my baby.*

The sense of pride and this need to protect her rush over me. I never in a million years expected I would be sitting in a room with this hot-as-fuck girl I was lucky enough to hook up with, hearing and seeing our baby. It's wild, to say the least.

I lean in and kiss the side of her head. "You doing okay?"

She turns to look at me, and tears pool in her eyes. "I'm good. This is pretty amazing, isn't it?" She smiles, then wipes a tear that ran down her cheek.

I return her smile, feeling my own eyes getting glassy. "Yeah, darlin', it's fucking incredible."

Emma puckers her lips for a kiss, and I oblige.

The technician taps a few more buttons on the keyboard, then pulls the wand out. She pulls off the condom and wipes down the wand with a towel, then hands Emma a clean one for herself.

"Okay, Emma, you're all set. I'm just going to submit the results to the doctor to review, and then we'll call you with the report. Once you get dressed, go ahead to the checkout counter, and don't forget to schedule your next appointment." She looks at the paperwork in front of her. "Looks like she wants to see you again in four weeks. If you have any questions or concerns in the meantime, don't hesitate to call."

"Thank you so much." Emma places the towel between her legs.

Once the technician leaves the room, Emma sits up. "Turn around, Archie."

"What, why?" I sit up straighter.

"Because I need to wipe down the lady business and I don't want you to watch me do it." She looks at me incredulously.

I bark out a laugh. "Okay, fair." I stand and move to the other side of the small room and turn my back to her.

She must be done when I hear the paper crunch on the table. I take a look over my shoulder and see her drop the gown from her body. She hasn't looked back at me, so I keep looking. Her perfect ass is right there, begging for me to grab on. And I'm just about to do it when she pulls up her panties and grabs her bra off the counter I set it on. She finishes dressing, then turns around to face me.

"Archie, you totally watched me get dressed, didn't you?" she asks, but she's smiling.

"Darlin', I couldn't help it. I was about two seconds away from taking hold of that juicy ass and bending you over the table." I wink and smirk at her.

Her smile hits me right in the gut. This girl is doing something to me that I might not be ready for, but I want it all at the same time.

She walks over to me and lifts up on her toes and kisses me. "Come on, Daddy. Let's go."

"Oh ho ho, baby. I like the sound of that. You can call me Daddy anytime." I laugh.

"Archie, don't be gross," she says, laughing.

I take her hand and start to lead her out of the room.

"Oh, wait! Let me grab the pictures." She walks over to the countertop, where the technician left the ultrasound photos.

When she reaches me again, I open the door and place my hand on her lower back. We walk to the checkout and make her next appointment, which falls just before our Thanksgiving break.

After we leave the office, I walk her to her car.

"So, do you want to come over and hang out for a bit?" she asks with a smile.

I nod. "Yeah, for sure. Do you want me to pick up some food on my way?"

"That would be good. I seem to be tolerating pasta pretty well. Do you want to stop at that pizza place on Campus Corner and pick some up there? I can call in the order." She pulls out her cell from her bag.

"Whatever sounds good to you is fine with me. I'll take a pizza. Cheese is good."

"What size pizza?"

"The biggest one they have, I guess. I'm pretty hungry."

I rub my stomach, and it pulls my shirt up a little. She looks at my hand. Biting her lip, she keeps watching until I stop. I can't help but smile. I think I might just be getting to her like she's getting to me. Although I don't think either of us would deny our chemistry. It's just a matter of time before we cave in to each other.

I reach out and cup her face. "Em, do you need help ordering?"

"Huh? What? No, of course not," she stammers, looking back down at her phone. "Okay, done. I'll meet you at my place?"

"Sounds good."

I lean in and kiss her. When she pulls away, I reach down and open her door. She turns and bends down to get into the car. Once she's buckled, she looks up at me.

"See you in a few."

She starts the car, and I close the door. Once she's gone, I walk to my car.

I pull my phone out while I walk and see a missed call from Pitz. I hit Call, and after a few rings, he answers.

"Yo. Have you eaten yet?" he asks.

"I'm about to go grab something with a friend. Not sure when I'll be back." I reach my car and push the key fob to unlock it.

"Friend, as in Emma?" he asks.

"Maybe. Why do you want to know, you nosy fucker?" I chuckle.

"All good, man. You've been gone a lot since the *surprise*. I was just curious. You know, the guys are gonna start to notice you aren't here."

"Yeah, I know. I'll be home tomorrow night for family dinner." I step up into the driver's seat, then close the door and start the ignition.

Charlie created a schedule for meals in the house. It's been fun, having a day each of us has to cook dinner for the house. My turn was last week, so all I have to do is show up this week. It's a good way for us to catch up and bond and shit. I love it.

"All right, man. Later." He hangs up the call before I can reply.

Today was a big day. Not that I hadn't believed her when she told me she was pregnant, but seeing my baby on that little screen made this for real. We're going to be parents. Emma and I will be tied together forever. Or at least until our baby becomes an adult. It's so wild to think about now with the baby the size of, like, a peach pit or something.

Not telling my friends and family is going to be hard. I'm so close with my family, and I've never *not* told them anything. But I'll honor Emma's wishes and wait to tell them until she's ready.

In the meantime, I'm going to keep working on getting to know her and showing her that she can trust me to be there for her.

CHAPTER
SEVEN

EMMA

AFTER WALKING around campus all day, an early practice, then the doctor, I felt sweaty and a little stinky. When I got home, I jumped into the shower.

Just as I'm walking out of the bathroom in shorts and a T-shirt, there's a knock on the door. I unwrap the towel from my head as I walk to the door. Seeing it's Archie in the peephole, I unlock it and open it.

"Hey. Did you get everything okay?"

"Yep. I got my pizza and your pasta. I almost ate a few slices on the way here. I am so hungry," he says as he walks over to the kitchen table, setting the bag with the food on it.

I walk into the kitchen and grab some plates from the cabinet, then some napkins. "Do you want something to drink?" I ask after setting everything on the table.

"Water is good for me. Thank you," he says with a smile.

I grab him a bottle of water, a can of 7UP and a blue Power-ade, and my Stanley, then walk back over to the table. Archie is standing, holding my chair out for me. Once I sit down and scoot myself in, he walks to his seat and sits.

"So, that was wild, right?" he asks.

My roommates aren't home right now, so I don't mind talking about it openly.

"For sure. Obviously, I knew it was real because of how I've been feeling and, of course, the tests, but seeing it on the screen and hearing the heartbeat made it so very real, you know. Like, Archie, we're going to be parents." I shake my head.

"Yeah, I agree. It made it all so real. And like you said in the room, we have to make some decisions. I know we're hanging out, and I'd really like to continue to do that, but I also don't want to be a part-time dad, you know?" He looks at me with a soft smile.

"I get it, and I wouldn't ask you to be. If you want to be a part of the baby's life, you can absolutely be there." I run my teeth against my lower lip and tilt my head at him. "Archie, I need you to understand that I'd never keep you from your child. You don't have to ..." With my hands, I motion between the two of us. "You don't have to do this."

"By *this*, you mean?"

"The hanging-out thing. The kisses and attentiveness. The pizza. All of it."

His eyes narrow a touch as he looks down and comprehends what I'm saying. With a nod, he looks up and gives a crooked smile.

"Okay, but here's the thing." He scoots closer. "I really want to keep hanging out with you and getting to know you too. I think you know I'm attracted to you, but I also just like you. I feel good when I'm around you—you know what I mean? I look forward to seeing you every day between classes or talking to you on the phone, texting. I want to keep this going not because of the baby, but because of that. Do you think you want to give me a chance?" He reaches over and places his hand on mine that's resting on the table.

"Archie, I'm going to be completely honest here. I didn't intend on getting involved with anyone in college because my plan was to move on and go to medical school. Having time for relationships when you're going through that is hard. Or I imagine it would be."

He raises a brow. "Is that why you ran off the night we were together without giving me your name and number?"

"Kind of. I mean, it's not that I wasn't incredibly into you. I have my boundaries, and getting involved with someone wasn't in the cards. Going to medical school is all I've ever wanted."

"You're driven. And guarded. So, you bolted. That makes sense."

There's a piece of lint on his shirt. I zero in on it because it's easier than looking at his intense gaze. "But this baby changes everything. And I know you have your own dreams to follow, so I want to figure out how we can both get what we want and be the best parents to this baby."

"Anything worth fighting for is never easy. We're athletes. We know about putting in the work and reaping the sweet benefits in the end. You want to go to med school and be a mom, then that's what will happen."

I look up at him. "You make this all sound so simple."

"I'm trying to reassure you that it can be done. I'm also trying to show you how good I look naked again."

He waggles his brows, and I can't help but laugh.

I take a deep breath in and smile. "Being around you and getting to know you—it has made all this easier to process, for sure. I also like spending time with you, and, yeah ... you're easy to look at with or without your clothes on." I smile at him.

He huffs a laugh. "You know it, darlin'."

"So, I guess what I'm saying is, I would also like to keep spending time together and see where it goes. And at the end of the day, if all we are to each other are parenting partners, we'll be the best partners out there." I turn my palm and link my fingers with his.

"Does this mean I can keep kissing you? Maybe we can even fool around a little? I mean, for the sake of getting to know each other." He has a small smile on his face, but his eyes ... they just got a little bit of heat in them.

And I can't even deny that it's turning me on. It's safe to say my hormone levels are elevated, and while I've been around him the last few weeks, it has been getting harder to keep my hands to myself. I want to touch him all the time. And the kissing just makes me want to rip his clothes off. But I'm trying to be patient. If he keeps looking at me like this though, I might just jump him.

"Yeah, we can keep kissing, and I wouldn't mind fooling around. Based on my memory of that night we were together, I'd say we have pretty good chemistry." I feel heat reaching my cheeks the more I talk.

"Good chemistry? Darlin', it was fire, and you know it. All you have to do is say the word, and I'm yours." He brings my hand to his lips and kisses it.

I pull my hand away and clear my throat. "Right. Agreed. So, that's settled. Do you want to watch a movie or something after we eat, or do you need to get home?"

"I can hang out for a while. Do your roommates mind me being here? I've only met them a few times, but I don't want them to get sick of having me around."

He's only met Mia and Peyton a few times, but Livi has been here more, and they've gotten to talk some.

"Not at all. Livi thinks you're cool, and Mia and Peyton are in and out so much with their schedules, so they aren't really here that often. I think they've been hanging out with some basketball guys lately or something."

"They all seem cool. But you haven't told them about the baby yet? Just Livi, right?"

I nod. "Yeah, I was waiting for confirmation, but now that we have it, I still don't feel quite ready to tell them. I mean, you know Livi knows, but I might hold off on telling the other two. The last thing I want is for either one of them to let it slip at practice before I'm ready to notify Coach."

"I'll take your lead, but I think we'll have to tell our families sooner rather than later. I mean, you said you used your parents' insurance card, and your dad is in insurance, so I think it's probably better to tell them before they see it, no?" He takes another bite of pizza.

"I know. I have two tournaments left for the fall season. If I can make it through this coming weekend and the next one after, I'll tell them then, so maybe we can tell our families around the same time. Speaking of, will you guys be practicing, or are you going home?"

"I'll talk to my family about the baby as soon as you tell yours." He nods. "We'll be around for practice. Our last regular season game is the Saturday after, so we can't really go anywhere."

"That's right. I wish I could have gone to the Chandler game. You guys were amazing." I take a few bites of my pasta, and then I open my Stanley and mix some Powerade and 7UP into the cup.

"It was a fun game, for sure, but it always is. Especially since we've won the last few years." He laughs.

"Definitely. So, how heavy is that Golden Hat? Is it solid or, like, a hat with a gold overlay? I've always wondered." I giggle.

He chews his food and has a closed-mouthed smile. "No, it's solid gold. Pretty heavy to most people probably, but not to us." He winks at me.

"Right. I forget you're all big manly men." I chuckle.

"I'll show you a big manly man." He laughs as he pulls my chair closer to his.

I'm laughing as he does, but also drop my fork in the process. "Guess I'm done eating?"

He hums and leans in closer, then kisses me. "Should we go watch some TV?"

I pull back. "Yes, let me just clear off the table. I'll leave your pizza here, but I'm going to save the rest of my pasta for tomorrow. I'm glad I was able to eat a little bit of it."

"Me too. Just let me know what sounds good to you, and I'm happy to bring it over. Any excuse to see you." He winks.

Archie always seems to be in a good mood. Sure, he's also a big flirt, but I think he's the kind of guy who is just happy. Being around him makes me feel good. Makes me happy. I wasn't lying about anything I said to him earlier. I do like spending time with him, and even if it didn't work out between us as a couple, I could definitely be his friend.

He helps me pack up the bag that my pasta was in, and then he closes his pizza box and sets it to the side.

I take my bag and put it in the fridge. "Do you need anything else while I'm in here?"

"If you have any more water, that would be good. Or whatever you're drinking is fine. Did I see you mix Powerade and 7UP in your cup though?"

"Ha! Yes. Don't judge. One of the days I wasn't feeling well, I was drinking some of the soda, but then got worried about getting dehydrated from throwing up, so I mixed them, and now I want it all the time. We have plenty of water though. I'll get you another one." I pull another bottle for him and grab my cup off the table.

He takes a seat on the couch and turns on the TV, changing it to—not surprisingly—ESPN. Not that I mind.

I hand him the bottle and set mine on the coffee table in front of the couch. "I'll be right back. I'm going to run to the bathroom real quick."

"You feeling okay?" he asks.

"I'm good, just need to pee." And maybe rinse out my mouth with some mouthwash.

I head into the bathroom and take care of business. Then I do a quick brush of my teeth and swish some mouthwash. My pasta had some garlic in it, and I fully intend to kiss on Archie for a bit tonight.

When I get back to the couch, he's taken off his shoes and propped his feet up on the coffee table. His water bottle is in his hand, resting on his firm stomach. He's so pretty to look at that it's not fair. I can't help but wonder what our baby will look like. I hope he or she has some of his pretty features, like his blue eyes.

I take a seat next to him on the couch, resting my body on the side with my knees pulled up. I'm angled toward him, and I reach my arm along the back of the couch. His head is resting on the back cushion, and I can't help but run my fingers through his hair. He closes his eyes and moans, which sends a shot of heat to my belly.

My attraction to him has always been at a level ten. Spending time with him and the intimacy of kissing—it has made me really horny for this man. Hell, I've been fantasizing about our night together for months. Now that he's here and moaning and looking so damn fine, my resolve is fading. As I've been feeling better, I'm definitely feeling like I might be ready to take it further than kissing.

Archie turns his head and looks over at me with a smirk. "Damn, that feels so good. You might make me fall asleep. I'm toast today."

"I'm tired, but not too tired to fool around first. Unless you aren't up for it," I tease.

"Oh, baby, I'm up for it."

He looks down at his crotch, and I follow his direction. Yep, he's starting to tent his jeans.

Leaning forward, I start to pepper kisses along his strong jaw and down to his neck. He's got a little bit of a beard going right now. It's not scratchy though.

"Archie, I'm gonna be really honest. I want you." *Kiss.* "It's been a rough couple of weeks of not feeling good, and don't get me wrong, it's coming and going, but I'm feeling good right now, and I *want* you." I bring my hand up to his face and turn it toward me, then lean in to kiss him on the lips.

He quickly takes control of the kiss, and I open willingly. Our tongues twirl, and I get lost in the taste of him. One of his hands cups my face while the other starts to drift over my shoulder and down my arm. His touch makes goose bumps break out, and I shiver.

I know that hormone levels are elevated during pregnancy, but reading about it and experiencing it are two different things. I can feel every trace of his touch, and my skin feels hot. I'm completely ready for him to rip my clothes off, but I'll let him take the lead. Not that I think he would mind if I did.

Moving my hand from his face, I slide it down his chest to the hem and slip my hand under his shirt. I trace the soft line of hair from the waist of his pants up to his belly button, and he pulls away from our kiss and takes in a deep breath.

We're looking at each other as my hand drifts across his stomach, feeling his muscles contract. I lean in to kiss him again, and my hand reaches the waistband of his jeans. I bring my other hand down from playing with his hair and tuck my fingers into the inside of his pants, right over the button. I pull slightly as we kiss, and when I do, his erection moves and is right under the tips of my fingers. The skin is smooth, soft, and hot.

He's turned his body slightly so he can touch me. One of his hands wraps around my neck, and his thumb brushes the skin right below my ear.

Just as I'm about to turn my hand that's in his pants and reach in to wrap my palm around him, he pulls back from the kiss, but he's still close enough that I can feel his breath on my lips.

"Darlin', I'm about two seconds from laying you out on this couch and having my way with you, but I need to know when we should expect your roommates back."

I reach in, take hold of his length, and lightly squeeze. "Then I guess we should go into my room. I don't know where Livi is tonight, but on the off chance she comes home, I'm not sure I want her to see you naked."

Pulling my hand from his jeans, I rest it on his stomach and lean in to kiss him again.

"Come on." I stand and hold my hand out to him.

He takes my hand and stands, and then I lead him down the hallway to my room. When we enter, he turns and closes the door, making sure he locks it. I walk over to my bed and pull back the covers.

I feel his body behind me before I feel his hands at my waist. He holds my hips firmly and tugs me back into him so I can feel his erection. I lean my head back against his shoulder, raising my arms and winding them around his neck. He brings his mouth to my neck, trailing kisses from my ear to my jaw.

I turn my head to him, and with the tip of his tongue, he traces my lips. I open with a moan, and our tongues tangle. He slides both of his hands up my shirt and cups my breasts. He kneads them softly, then tugs lightly on my nipples, which nearly makes my knees buckle.

"Archie …" I pant against his mouth.

His hands move from my chest to my stomach. "You sure you want this, Em?"

I nod. "Oh, yeah, I want this."

He kisses me again, deeper this time, and as he does, I glide my fingers up the back of his head, through his hair, holding him to me. His hands dip into my shorts, and he cups me over my panties.

"You're soaked, Emma. Is this all for me?" He slides his middle finger up and down my center, over the fabric.

"All for you." I bring my arms down, link our fingers over my panties, then guide his hand inside my underwear.

"Oh fuck. You are so fucking hot, Emma."

I move our hands, sliding them back and forth, creating a delicious friction.

My body feels like it's on fire; I'm nearly crazed with wanting him. I reach for the waistband of my shorts and lower them and my panties, pushing them down to my knees, until they drop to the floor.

Archie has one hand on my waist, the other gripping the hem of my shirt.

"Turn around, darlin'."

He tugs on my shirt, and I turn to face him. My palms smooth over the thick contours of his chest. I need to feel the warmth of his skin, so I reach for the bottom of his shirt and pull it up and over his head.

My fingers toy with the edge of his waistband. With a teasing slowness, I reach for the button of his jeans and pop it open. The teeth of the zipper make a groaning sound as I lower it, and I'm rewarded by his thick, hard erection.

"Do you ever wear boxers?"

He barks out a laugh. "Only when I have to."

I take the sides of his jeans and pull them down his legs, bending as I do. Once he's free—his cock heavy and thick, as hard as granite, standing at attention—I kneel in front of him and slide my hands up his legs. I wrap one hand around his thigh and one around his cock.

"It's just not fair," I say, before placing a kiss on the tip. "Your dick is pretty, and your face is even prettier. I'm just not sure which one I want to ride first."

The man who loves to laugh isn't smiling. Instead, he groans as I wrap my mouth around him, taking him deep to the back of my throat. It nearly makes me gag, so I pull back.

"Fuck, Emma. Just like that. You're so pretty on your knees for me."

I look up and see him looking down at me with a storm brewing in his eyes. He gives me a crooked smile and starts rocking his hips in and out of my mouth.

His hands cup my face, then slide into my hair, holding my head and moving it in time with his thrusts into my mouth.

Slick heat warms between my own legs so I reach down and circle my clit with my fingers. Archie is watching, which turns me on even more.

"That's it, baby. Make yourself come, just like that."

Releasing his cock with a pop, I say, "It won't take me much longer, Archie. I'm so hot right now."

"Put me back in your mouth. Just a few more sucks, and then I'll fuck you." He pulls my hair into one hand and tugs. "Open."

I open my mouth and lick up his shaft to the tip, then wrap my lips around the fat head and suck. Sliding my fingers through my pussy, I get them nice and wet, then reach up and work them up and down his cock, along with my mouth. My other hand slides up the back of his thigh, and I grab on to his tight ass.

"Jesus, Em. I need to get inside you. We'll have time for you to suck my cock again later." He releases my hair, then reaches under my arms and pulls me up.

I sit on the bed and scoot to the middle to give Archie room to get on the bed with me. He kneels on one knee, then climbs onto the bed and between my legs.

Archie pushes my knees apart and moves his hands up my legs. "You're soaking wet, darlin'. I need to have a taste of that honey."

It shouldn't turn me on, but it does. "Yes, please."

He leans in and swipes his tongue through my center and hums. "So good. I'm gonna make you beg for me. Then I'm going to fuck you so deep and make you choke my cock with that tight pussy." His tongue flattens, and he licks up from my hole to my clit. He flicks my clit with the tip of his tongue and slides a finger into me. With his other hand, he reaches up and holds my breast, pinching my nipple. "Come, baby. Come all over my tongue."

My body starts to warm. I feel like I can even hear my own heartbeat; I'm so in tune with how this feels right now. Between the sting of my nipple and the throbbing between my legs, my body feels like it's on sensation overload. The tingling in my lower belly spreads, and I can feel my pussy start to contract around his fingers.

When he starts to pump his fingers in and out of me and then he sucks hard on my clit, I erupt. Now, I've never been known to squirt, but if the wet feeling between my legs is what that was, I think I just soaked not only Archie's face, but my sheets.

I sit up and lean on my elbows and look down at him. Maybe I should be a little embarrassed since that's never happened to me before, but I'm not. His lips and scruff are glistening from me, and the look on his face is downright cocky.

My breathing is heavy, and even though I just came, I need him inside of me, like right now.

I crook my finger and smile. "Get up here."

He licks his lips and smiles. After dropping a kiss on my mound, he trails kisses up my body, stopping at my stomach, and pauses. He places a tender kiss there and looks at me as he does.

With one hand, I run my fingers through his hair and smile. "Crazy, isn't it?"

He nods and smiles, then continues to trail kisses up my body to my lips. "So crazy."

When he settles between my legs, I feel the tip of him at my opening.

"You good?"

"I'm so good."

I lie back and tilt my hips, and he pushes in slowly.

"Should I get a condom?" He pauses and looks down between us.

"I mean, it's not like I can get more pregnant, so unless you have something to tell me about, like an STD"—I clear my throat —"I think we're okay."

"I just got tested before training started, and I've never *not* worn a condom. And I haven't been with anyone since you." He pushes in a little further.

"Okay, same for me." I slide my hands down his arms, then back up to his shoulders, wrapping my arms around his neck.

He leans down and kisses me slowly, tasting me. His tongue rubs mine in the same rhythm as he moves in and out of me.

My hands move from his neck, down his back, and I grab his ass, pulling him in closer to me, wanting to feel every inch of him.

Archie leans on one arm while the other hand grips my thigh, bringing it up higher on his hip. The move makes me feel him deeper, and my orgasm is edging, but I want to hold off a little longer.

"You feel amazing, Archie. Don't stop."

"Not a chance. I'm gonna fill you up so good."

He circles his hips, and it hits my G-spot.

"Oh fuck, Archie. Right there. Do that again." I move my hips with his and moan. "I'm getting close."

His hips start to thrust into me again, but he pushes all the way in to the hilt. I feel his pelvis hitting me, just like the first time we had sex. When he circles his hips again, our eyes meet. Then he leans in and kisses me deep.

I can't hold off any longer, and I start to move my hips, seeking the friction from our bodies.

He pulls back from our kiss. "That's it, darlin'. Fuck my cock. Take what you need."

Heat flows through me, and my orgasm peaks, making me moan.

"You're so pretty when you come, Emma. You take my cock so well."

His praise makes my orgasm continue, and I feel like I can't catch my breath.

He pumps once, twice, then comes, yelling, "Fuuuck!"

As we catch our breath, he rests his head between my neck and shoulder and places lazy kisses on my neck.

"Em, I've never had sex without a condom, and I gotta tell you, I'm a huge fan. I mean, holy shit, I didn't know it would feel like that. I could feel you come, and I damn near blew my load right then."

I laugh, our bodies still connected. "Same. But I wasn't sure if it was because of no barrier or because my body is like a live wire right now. Every time we kiss or you touch me, my body craves more."

"You go right ahead and use me for my dick anytime, darlin'. He's ready, willing, and completely up to the task." He lifts his head and winks.

"I appreciate your generosity, Archie. I'll be sure to call you when I need the D." I push his shoulder to get him to shift off of me.

He rolls to the side, but instead of lying next to me, he gets on his knees and in between my legs. Wrapping his arms under my knees, he spreads my legs wide. His gaze is on my pussy, and he bites down on his bottom lip. He drops down and runs his tongue from my clit to my opening. Then he twirls his tongue around it and pushes it inside.

"Archie, fuck."

I hold his head and keep him in place while he licks, a whole new wave of heat rushing through me. Not only because I'm getting turned on, but also because this is a claiming move. And it's fucking hot.

I let go of his head when he places a kiss on my clit.

He hums when he rises and licks his lips. "We taste good together."

I feel heat in my cheeks at his words.

Moving back to my side, he drops a kiss to my lips before he lies down. "Just wanted to clean you up a little."

"I appreciate it."

We both smile, and then he reaches over and tucks some hair that's in my face behind my ear.

"So, I hate to ruin the mood here, and this is probably something we should have talked about sooner, but how do we think this happened?" He gently rubs my belly.

"I've thought about that. A lot. My best guess is, after round one, when you kept it in but kept pumping with a full condom, some of it leaked. Or … the condoms we took from Schuster were expired." I shrug the shoulder I'm not resting on.

"Huh. Yeah, I guess it would have to be one of those scenarios. So, I take it, you weren't on the pill or somethin' then?"

I shake my head. "No, I can't take them. They give me really bad migraines, so my doctor took me off of it to try to get control of them, and I just never went back on. I'm not a saint or anything, but I haven't hooked up much over the last year."

"Emma, let's not talk about other guys while my cum is inside you and you have my baby in your belly. I know this is all new and shit, but, damn, I don't want to be thinking about that." He squeezes his eyes shut and then opens them.

"You're right. I'm sorry. I don't want to hear about any of your conquests either."

I smile at him, and he returns it, then leans over and kisses me.

"While we're talking about this, if we're going to be hanging out and having sex, I don't want to be one of many."

"Emma, this"—he waves his hand between us—"I'm not taking this lightly. I'm aware I've been known to have some fun around campus, but I have never and would never disrespect a woman that way. Let alone the mother of my child. And just so we're on the same page"—he pauses—"I don't want you seeing anyone else either."

"I'm glad we agree."

"I should probably get going soon. I have an early class."

He starts to shift, but I hold his arm.

"You could always stay the night. I promise I won't leave like the last time." I wink to keep the mood light when, really, I want Archie to stay.

It's hard to admit, but at a time in my life where I should have anxiety and be stressing about the future, he is keeping me completely grounded. I don't know how long this bubble will last, but for now, I want to stay in it. Stay in it with him. Because with Archie, I don't have to think. We can just be.

He belts out a laugh. "Well, I hope not, considering this is your place and all."

Lying back down, he reaches for my hands and scoots closer to me again. He folds our hands together and brings them to his chest.

"Okay, darlin'. I'll stay the night, but only because you asked me so nicely. And I can't leave you lonely. You might wake up in the middle of the night, needing my dick again." He smiles.

He's right though. I might, in fact, need his dick again.

"I think I have an extra toothbrush in the bathroom that you can use. Although I don't have any boxers that would fit you."

"Oh, I sleep naked, so I'm good."

"Archie, I have roommates. You can't walk in and out of the bathroom naked." I giggle.

"Right, right. I mean, it would be a treat for them though?"

I roll my eyes and shake my head.

"Oh, come on. You can't even deny it." He brings one of my hands down to his already-hardening cock.

I nod. "It is indeed a treat. But I don't really want my friends to see my baby daddy's junk, so I'll find something you can wear when you feel the need to leave the room but can't be bothered to fully dress."

He wraps his arms around me and pulls me into his chest. I stiffen for a moment. Cuddling? Not usually my thing, but it's something I seem to be getting used to with him. And just as soon as I start to resist the embrace, I'm enveloped in the warmth of his husky scent. I relax my body into him and sigh.

"Okay, you got it, darlin'. I'm all yours." He kisses the top of my head, and I swear I feel it all the way to my toes. "So, Emma, I have a question for you. Did I see a tattoo on your back at the doctor's office?"

"Urgh. Yes."

"Are you gonna tell me what it is? Because I couldn't really see it."

I sigh. "I guess you'll see it eventually, so I might as well tell you. It's a tiny tattoo of Dora the Explorer's backpack."

He doesn't say anything, so I look up at him. His eyes are

squeezed shut, and his lips are curled in, like he's trying to hold in a laugh.

"Go ahead. Get a good laugh. I know it's ridiculous, but in my defense, I was drunk, and peer pressure is harder to fight while intoxicated. We went on spring break our freshman year, and it just kinda happened."

The rumbled laugh that comes out makes me smile through my mild embarrassment.

"Oh God. This is so good. I'm sorry, Em. I can't help it."

I laugh with him. "No, it is kinda funny. I honestly forget it's there. My memory of getting it is super fuzzy, but I guess I was going on about traveling, which morphed into me wishing I had a Dora backpack, and ... well, here we are."

"Gold, baby. Solid gold." He kisses the top of my head again.

After a few minutes of silence, Archie lets out a yawn, and I tilt my head to look at him.

"You getting tired?"

He closes his eyes and yawns again. "Yeah, a little bit. You?"

I nod against his chest. "I don't know how much longer I can keep my eyes open. Especially after that. But I do need to go to the bathroom and get ready for bed."

With his eyes still closed, he says, "You go do what you need to do, and I'll go when you're done."

I uncurl myself from his hold and scoot over to the side of the bed. I make a mental note to grab a towel so I don't need to sleep on a wet spot. Is there anything worse? When I get out of the bed, I move over to the closet and grab my white terry-cloth robe and lay it on the foot of the bed.

"You should be able to wrap this around you. I'll leave it here for you."

His eyes are still closed, but he nods and gives me a thumbs-up.

I go into the bathroom across the hall and take care of my business. When I get back into my room, Archie has one arm over his eyes, and he's not quite snoring, but breathing loudly.

Walking over to the bed, I lay the clean towel I brought from the bathroom and spread it on the wet spot. I guess I'll have to scoot really close to Archie to avoid it.

Damn.

My phone is sitting on the nightstand, and I double-check my alarm. Then I curl into Archie. Even in his sleep, he wraps an arm around me and pulls me closer. I cuddle in and find I like being in his arms. The sound of his heartbeat is the last thing I remember.

CHAPTER
EIGHT

ARCHIE

IT'S BEEN a few days since our doctor's appointment, and I haven't seen Emma since I left her house the next morning. But we've been talking every day. She is starting to feel better and is able to eat a little more.

She still hasn't told her parents or friends, aside from Livi. I plan to tell my dad this weekend when he comes up for my game tomorrow. To my friends, on the other hand, I haven't really said anything about my whereabouts and don't plan to until Emma is okay with telling everyone. And I haven't said much to Liam about it since he found out.

Hanging out with Emma, talking to her, fucking her … better than I could have imagined. But this is something bigger. We aren't just hanging out casually. We're having a baby. And I'm stoked about it, truly, even though it doesn't exactly fall into my timeline. It's happening, so I can embrace it for the gift that this baby is or freak out. And I'm not the type of guy to freak out. Plus, my dad would kick my ass.

It will still be good to talk to him about this. I think I just need to make sure I'm doing all the right things to support her. And if anyone knows how to treat his lady, it's my dad.

I'm walking back into the locker room from the practice field when Casey comes up next to me.

"Hey, brother. Are you gonna be home tonight, or are you going out?"

It's Halloween tonight, but since we have a game tomorrow, none of us are really planning to do anything. Or at least I'm not. My plan was to go home and drop my gear, then grab some food and crash. I need to check in with Emma too.

"I'm coming home, but I want to shower first. You aren't going out, are you? You're starting tomorrow." I pat his chest.

"Oh, yeah. No, I'm not doing anything. I think Charlie's cooking for us tonight and then handing out candy to trick-or-treaters. We were going to watch *Scream* after. She just texted me to ask if you would be there or not since you haven't been around a lot lately."

I push open the locker room door and head to my locker to undress. "That's my plan. But, dude, *Scream* is lame. Let's watch, like, *The Shining* or something old school."

Casey shakes his head and moves to his locker three down from mine. "Nope, no way. Charlie can't handle the really scary stuff. She'll be up all night, and Beck needs some sleep. I can't babysit her either."

"Charlie is scared, or you are?" I look over at him and laugh.

"Fuck you." He laughs. "I'm not scared, but I can't have creepy shit in my head all night either." He tosses a dirty towel at me.

"Uh-huh. That's what I thought. It's okay that you're a little bitch baby, King." I love to rib my guys.

"Who's a bitch baby?" Beckham walks in with Callaway.

"Your boy here. I didn't know he was afraid to watch scary movies." I nod to Casey.

Beck barks out a laugh. "He and Charlie are both big babies. They can't handle it, and honestly, I can't deal with either one of them tonight, so whatever we watch needs to be on the lame side of scary."

I finish pulling off my shoulder pads and then strip off the rash guard I wear. I undo the belt on my pants and push them off my legs. Then I toss my practice gear in the laundry bin and walk into the shower room.

A few guys are in there, shootin' the shit while they shower, and I hear Casey, Beck, and Bo following behind me.

After a quick wash, I grab a towel on my way back to my locker and scrub it over my head first before wrapping it around my waist. My phone chimes from the top shelf in my locker. There are a few texts from Emma, my mom, and my brother Aiden. I check Emma's first.

> Emma: Hey. Hope you had a good day today. Just wanted to see what you were doing tonight.

> Archie: Hey, darlin'. I just got out of practice and showered. I'm still at the field house. I was going to go to my place and eat with my roommates and watch a movie. What are you up to?

It's been about thirty minutes since she texted, so I'm surprised when she texts back right away, before I have a chance to set my phone back down.

> Emma: Well, my roommates are all going out tonight for Halloween, but I'm not in the mood to go, for obvious reasons.

> Archie: You feeling bad tonight?

> Emma: No, I'm fine. I was going to watch a movie and probably crash early. So …

> Archie: Emma, if you want me to come over and take care of you, that's all you have to say.

> Emma: HA! I mean, I don't need anyone to take care of me, but I wouldn't hate it if you came over.

> Archie: Want me to grab some food for us? I'm starving.

> Emma: I already ate, but you're welcome to bring something or see if we have anything here you can eat.

> Archie: I'm gonna run back to my place and grab some food, and then I'll head over. Does that work?

> Emma: Sounds good. See you in a bit.

> Archie: 🙂

After I set my phone back on the shelf, I loosen the knot on my towel and run it down my legs to finish drying off. I pull out the fresh clothes from my bag and get dressed in a T-shirt and sweats quickly, then slip my feet into my slides.

I'm zipping up my bag when Pitz walks into the locker room. "You just coming in?" I ask.

He nods, not looking too happy.

"What's up, man? You good?"

I hold out my fist to him as he walks by. He ignores it and keeps walking to his locker.

"Yo, Pitz, what's going on?"

Standing in front of his locker, he has his hands on his hips and shakes his head. "I just got out of a meeting with Coach." He looks around the locker room. "He's starting Callaway tomorrow," he whispers.

I pull a deep breath in and nod. "I can't say I'm surprised. He's been killing it this week, but I know it sucks for you. Sorry, man."

"I'll be fine. I just feel like my time is coming to an end here because, Griff, I'm not sitting on the bench next year." He shakes his head.

I walk over to him. "I get it. You'll have to do what is best for you and your career, but you have to stay focused on the rest of this season. We only have three more games before the bowl games. You will be playing in not only the games leading up to that, but we need you to be ready to go so we can get to the championship game. Do you think you can do that? You think you can be the leader we need you to be on that field, even if you aren't starting?" I place a hand on his shoulder.

He looks up and meets my eyes. "I am one of the captains on this team, and I won't let you guys down."

"That's my guy." I hold out my palm to him, and he grabs it to do our handshake. "You had me worried you were pussing out on me."

That gets me a smile.

"Fuck you, Griff. You heading back to the house or to see your girl?"

I look around the room before I answer, "I'm gonna run home first and see if dinner is ready. I guess Charlie is cooking and doing some Halloween stuff, like handing out candy, and they're all watching a movie, but I'm not sticking around after I eat."

"Gotchu. Are you coming home tonight though? We have to be here at, like, nine a.m. tomorrow," he mentions.

I nod. "I know. Right now, I plan to come home tonight, but if I don't, I'll come back early." I turn and start to walk out.

"Dude, don't let her wear your ass out tonight." He chuckles.

"Yeah, yeah. See you at home." I hold up my hand but don't turn around.

Ten minutes later, I'm parking on the street in front of my house. When I walk in, the scent of a home-cooked meal makes my stomach grumble.

Charlie is in the kitchen, pulling something out of the oven.

"Hey, Chuck. What up? Smells awesome in here."

The sound of my bag dropping to the floor makes her jump.

"Jesus, that scared me!" She looks at me and laughs. "Sorry, I'm a little jumpy. I've been watching scary movies for the last few hours while I was waiting for you guys to get home. I'm thinking that probably wasn't the best idea now. Every little noise has me looking over my shoulder."

I walk over to where she's standing and look into the pan she just pulled out. "Brownies, huh? Is that our dinner?"

She clears her throat. "No, it's just a treat for us for after dinner. I made some lasagna and a salad for us. I know you guys like to carb-load the night before. But this is a healthier lasagna. The sauce is homemade versus canned, so less preservatives. And the cheese is organic, and the noodles are whole grain with added protein."

I nod a few times. "Awesome. Thanks, sugar. Is it ready now, or do I need to wait around for a bit?"

She opens the oven, then closes it. "I'd say another ten to fifteen minutes."

"Sounds good. Thank you for doing this."

"Of course. Are you sticking around to hand out candy and watch a movie, or do you have plans?" she asks.

I bring my hand up behind me and scratch my neck. "I'm not going to be around for the movie and trick-or-treaters, no."

She nods and smirks. "Okay, got it."

"I'm going to go drop my stuff in my room and call my mom. Give me a shout when dinner is ready."

"You got it." She shoots me a thumbs-up.

I pick up my bag and take it to my room. My room setup is pretty plain. I have one of the smaller rooms in the house, but it doesn't bother me. I'm a simple guy. I just need a bed, bathroom, a dresser or a closet for my clothes, and I'm good to go. I set my bag on the floor at the end of the bed and then sit on the edge.

I pull my phone out of my back pocket and call my mom.

"Hey, Arch. Whatcha doing?" she says when she answers.

"Hey, Mama. Just got home from practice and going to eat

some dinner. What are y'all up to? Doing anything for Halloween?"

"Well, the boys have a game tonight at seven, but then some of the guys are coming back to the ranch to stay the night. Dad made the corn maze again this year, and we set up some snacks and stuff in the shack for them. But I have a feeling it's going to be a late night. Austin is already asking if he and his friends can sleep out there with the older boys, but that's a big no. I know Ace and Anders won't keep an eye on them. And apparently, some girls will be coming over, too, although I said they can't spend the night."

She keeps talking, and I lie back on my bed and smile. I miss my family. The past few summers, I haven't been able to spend a ton of time there due to training. About the time I get home and get on a schedule, I have to turn around and come back here for the school year to start.

My family plays up the holidays big time. Mom and Dad decorate the house and the shack—which is an old ranch-hand cottage that we converted into an entertainment area for us and our friends. I lost my virginity in that shack, and by the fact that my brothers are having girls up there tonight, I'm guessing they're messing around too.

I hear the front door slam and voices in the hall.

"That all sounds like fun, Mama. I'm gonna have to let you go though. The rest of the guys just got home, and I think our dinner will be ready soon. I'll give you a call after our game tomorrow. Tell Dad to text me when he gets up here, and I'll try to see him before the game."

"Okay, baby. Keep yourself safe tomorrow. I should be able to be at the next game since the boys' regular season will be over. We'll find out if we're moving on to the playoffs after tonight. Tell the boys good luck for me. Love you!" She makes a kiss sound.

"Bye, Mama. Love you. Tell the boys I said good luck if they haven't left yet."

"Will do. Bye, Arch." She hangs up.

I get off the bed and shoot a text to Emma to let her know I'll head her way in fifteen minutes. Then I pocket my phone and walk out toward the kitchen.

The guys are sitting at the set table, and Charlie is bringing food over and placing it in the center.

I pull out a chair and sit. "This looks great, Chuck. Thank you again for cooking."

"Now, see, why can't the rest of you say that? Y'all just walked in without saying hello and sat down, waiting on me to serve you."

"Hey now, Boss. I came right over to you and said hello properly." Beck winks at her.

"Yeah, we all saw that, dickhead," Casey snipes.

Charlie giggles. "Okay, I mean, except for Beck."

Since no one is making a move, I grab the spatula that's sitting next to the pan and scoop some lasagna out and onto my plate. Leaving the spatula in the dish, I move to the salad, and with the tongs, I drop some bunny food into the bowl at my place setting. Then I hand it to Pitz on my left.

I sprinkle some cheese on the top, then add some dressing to my salad. I practically shove the food in my mouth, anxious to get to Emma now.

"Bro, Arch, you in a hurry?" Beck asks.

I chew and nod.

"Where you going?" he asks.

After swallowing, I say, "You my mom or something?"

"But seriously, Arch, where have you been?" Casey lifts his chin to me.

Liam clears his throat and has a smirk on his face, seemingly in a better mood than he was in the locker room.

"Well, King, if you must know, it takes some maintenance to look this good. I need to get my balls waxed every two weeks, and then I need to check in with my barber on the regular to trim my hair and beard. Then I work out, which you would know if you came to the gym more."

"Hey! I'm there every day, same as you." Casey points at me.

"Right, right. And then I have class and practice. But since we're asking about my whereabouts, where have you been spending time, King?"

"Yeah, Case, where have you been lately?" his sister asks him with a smirk on her face. "We all know where he's been. He's with Noelle probably as much as I'm with Beck."

"You know what? I don't have to answer to any of you. Y'all suck." He throws down his napkin, laughing.

Everyone laughs and keeps talking. They chatter about the movie they're going to watch and what kind of candy Charlie bought. Casey asks her to keep some stashed for us and not give it all out, so we can have some after the game.

With my last bite shoved in, I stand and pick up my plate. After I finish chewing and swallow, I check to make sure the dishwasher is dirty, and then I rinse and load my dishes.

"All right, fellas and Chuck, I'm out. Have fun tonight." I get a water bottle out of the refrigerator.

They all say goodbye as I leave the kitchen.

I grab one of my baseball hats from the hooks by the front door and put it on. Then I pull my keys out of my front pocket and pull the door open.

I get into my truck and text Emma.

Archie: You need anything before I get there?

Emma: I'm good. See you soon.

The streets are starting to get busy with kids and college students alike all dressed in costumes. It makes me smile when I see a little boy dressed in a Walker football uniform and he's wearing my name and number, so I honk and wave.

I wonder if we'll have a boy or a girl. I'm good with either, but my family is largely male. Even on my mom's side, she's the only girl, so chances are high that we'll have a boy. I wonder if Emma has a preference.

When I pull up to her building, I see her roommates walking out. All three are dressed up in a glittery bikini top under a vest, bottoms under silver chaps, white cowboy hats with rhinestones on the band, and white cowboy boots on their feet.

I grab my water out of the cupholder and step out of my truck. "Ladies." I nod at them. "Let me guess. Space cowgirls?"

"OMG, no way did you guess that on the first try! I told you it was too easy," Mia whines.

"Babe, it's not that hard. Only so many options with us dressed like this, but I will say I'm impressed at the speed of the guess, Archie," Livi says.

I wink at her. "You ladies have a good night and be safe. If y'all need a ride, give us a call."

Peyton puts both of her hands over her heart. "Aren't you the sweetest, Archie Griffith? Emma's a lucky bitch." She giggles as Mia pulls her along.

"Bye, Archie," Livi says.

"Later," I say and head toward the building.

Before I can knock on the door, it opens. Emma is standing there in light-pink pajamas with golf clubs and golf balls on them. Her hair is wrapped up in a loose bun on the top of her head. She looks so fucking cute.

"Hey," she says, breathy.

"Hey, darlin'. Sorry it took so long. I had to get some food."

I walk in, and she shuts the door behind me.

She takes my hand in hers and leads us to the couch. "That's okay. I was just helping the girls get ready. Or really, just sitting there, talking to them, while they got ready." She laughs.

"Yeah, I saw them on my way in. They look ready to have some fun." I chuckle.

Emma laughs. "I'm sure they will. Do you want to watch a movie? I think I have some popcorn. Or I can grab some other snacks."

I shake my head. "I'm not really hungry right now, but if you are, go ahead and make something, or I can do it for you."

We sit down next to each other on the couch, and I take off my slides and push them under the coffee table with my foot. I grab her legs and pull her closer, draping her legs over mine. We smile at each other.

"Hi," I say with a smirk.

"Hey," she says, smiling.

I take ahold of her feet and start rubbing them a little. I notice her second toe is longer than her big toe. I pinch in between my fingers and wiggle it.

She reaches over and tries to swat at my hand, laughing. "I'm super ticklish. Stop."

"Okay, but I'm just fascinated by the fact that this toe is bigger than the rest."

"Don't make fun of my tootsies. I read somewhere that if your second toe is larger than the rest, especially the big toe, it means you're naturally athletic."

"Interesting." I lift my foot and see my second toe is also slightly longer, but hers … it's long like a finger.

I drop my foot and continue to rub her feet for a minute and hear a content sigh.

"That feels so good."

"I'm glad."

Not able to wait a minute longer, I reach up and turn my hat backward on my head, and then I lean in and kiss her. I trace my tongue along the seam of her lips, and when she opens for me, I slide my tongue into her mouth.

She sucks on my tongue, and my half-mast dick is now fully saluting. One of her hands moves into my hair, and she palms the back of my head. Her other hand moves to the band of my sweatpants. She moves her hand back and forth, teasing, which makes my stomach muscles constrict, and she must feel it because she smiles against my lips.

Her hand makes its way into my sweats, and when she wraps it around my erection, I groan.

She breaks the kiss but keeps her mouth against mine. "You

really do have the perfect cock, Archie." She slides her hand up and down, and when she reaches the head, pre-cum leaks out, and she smears it with her thumb, rolling it around the bulb.

"Well, you have a unicorn pussy, so I guess we're a good match." I smirk.

She hums, sliding her hand up and down my shaft, then starts to kiss me again.

I slide my hands up her thighs, which are resting on my legs. I keep one hand on her leg and move my other around her waist, pulling her in a little more. I'm about to pull her completely onto my lap when she breaks the kiss, covers her mouth, and jumps up.

"Emma, what's wrong? Are you okay?" I get up and follow her down the hall to the bathroom.

She barely makes it to the toilet before throwing up. I kneel behind her and pull her hair back with one hand.

After a few minutes, she leans back against me, and I let go of her hair.

"I'm so sorry. That's gross." She reaches over and pulls off a piece of toilet paper and wipes her mouth.

"It's okay, darlin'. You've been feeling pretty good, right?" I rub up and down her arms.

"Yeah, I haven't thrown up in a few weeks, but maybe I ate too much tonight. I was sitting, a little bent over, and I just felt a wave of nausea. How embarrassing." She leans her head against my shoulder.

"Don't apologize. I should be the one apologizing. I did this to you." I place a kiss on the side of her head. "Can I get you a water or something else that sounds good?"

She shakes her head. "Nothing sounds good, but I should probably drink something."

I move my hands down to her waist and wrap my arms around her. "You feel like you can get up, or do you want to stay still for a few more minutes?"

"It feels like it's passed now. I should be fine. I'm going to brush my teeth though." She places her hands over mine on her stomach.

I give her one more kiss on the side of her head and unwind my arms from around her and stand. I hold out my hand for her to take as she gets off the floor.

"Why don't you brush, and I'll go grab you a cold water?"

We walk over to the sink.

She looks up at me and smiles softly. "Thank you for holding my hair, Archie. That was really sweet."

"That's what I'm here for, darlin'. Here to spend time with you, yeah, but I want to take care of you and the baby." I kiss her forehead and squeeze her hand. "I'll meet you on the couch when you're ready."

She nods, and I walk out and into the kitchen. I don't see any bottles of water in the refrigerator, so I nose around through the cabinets, looking for a thermos.

I find a Stanley and pull it out of the cabinet. I put ice in first, then fill it with water from the door on the refrigerator. Then I think about the weird mixture she likes with the 7UP and blue Powerade and grab another thermos from the cabinet and mix that for her too. As I walk over to the couch, I see her coming down the hall.

"Feel a little better?" I wait for her to come closer and let her sit down first. When she sits, I hold out both to her. "This is water, and this one is the mixed drink you like. I wasn't sure which one you'd want."

"Thanks, Archie," she says as she lifts the cup with the mix slightly, then shifts her body so her knees are bent and she's angled.

"Not a problem, darlin'." I set the other one on the coffee table and take a seat and turn toward her. "Why don't we pick a movie and you get some rest?"

She nods, then rests her head on the back of the couch cushion.

I pick up the remote control off the coffee table and lean back.

The television is playing *Hocus Pocus*, but it looks like it's almost over. Yes, I've seen it before, and I know when the ending is near.

"Do you want to watch the rest of this or find something new?"

"It doesn't matter to me. I had this one on because my sister and I had watched it the Halloween before her last surgery."

I haven't wanted to ask too many questions, but since she's giving me an opening, I'm gonna take it.

"Tell me about your sister. What was she like?"

I look over at her. She has a soft smile on her face, so I don't think she's upset that I asked.

"My sister's name is—was Sunny. She was only six when she died, but in the short time she was with us, she was just special, you know?" She looks at me.

I reach over and put my hand on her knee. "So, she was a happy kid?"

"The happiest, but she was born with pulmonary atresia, which is a congenital heart defect. What happens is the pulmonary valve, which is the one that carries blood flow to the lungs, doesn't develop properly and forms a solid sheet of tissue, forcing blood flow through other parts of the heart. Surgery is necessary in order to fix it. She had her first surgery when she was just a baby. The cardiologist successfully repaired it, and she did continue to develop fairly normal, but when she was five, she started getting winded easily just from running around the house or in the yard."

She looks at her hands in her lap and twists them.

"After they ran tests, the doctors determined she needed a new valve. From what I remember and what I've been told since, she got an infection likely before the surgery. When they went in, her immune system was too weak, and the infection spread. They put her on medications, but it was too late. She died days after her second surgery." I pull in a deep breath and exhale. "My dad's younger brother had the same defect, but he didn't live past two months old. Medicine wasn't as advanced in the '70s as it was when Sunny was born."

A tear has fallen, so I reach over and wipe it with my thumb.

"We don't have to talk about it anymore, darlin'. But I'm glad you told me so I know more about you and why you would want to talk about it with the doctor. I'm sure it's a little scary, but just know that no matter what, I'll always be here for you and the baby." I wipe another tear from her cheek and then tuck a loose piece of hair behind her ear.

She looks up at me. "No, I'm glad you asked. I don't talk about her enough. None of us do really. Sometimes, I feel so guilty that I'm here and living a pretty nice life, but she's gone. My parents didn't cope well with her death for a long time. They grieved, and in turn, they essentially ignored me. It might not make sense, but being the perfect daughter was important to me, so my parents didn't have anything else to worry about. You know what I mean?"

"Did they ever consider having another baby?" Maybe I shouldn't have asked that, but I'm curious since I come from a large family.

She shakes her head. "No, I don't think so. My guess is, they were too worried that the same thing could happen with another baby. I was lucky and never had any medical issues. Not even a broken bone."

"But she was happy in the time she was here?" My hand rubs her knee.

Emma smiles and looks up at me. "Yeah, she was. Even though we were three years apart, we were really close. When she was born, I didn't want anyone else to hold her. Then as she got bigger, she was my little shadow."

She shakes the Stanley in a circular motion, making the ice clink around inside. "In the summer, we would go visit my grandparents, and they had these huge sunflowers that grew super tall. She and I would go sit in the middle of one of the rows and look up. She loved it and would say we were in a tent.

The last time we visited, I remember looking over at her, and with the shadows of the flowers, it looked like she was wearing a halo. I will never forget it. And when I think back, she always seemed older, if that makes sense. Like she was an old soul or something."

She shakes her head, making some of her hair fall over her shoulder, and she takes a piece between her fingers and twists it. "Sunny used to call me Emma Bean. And the last thing she said to me was that she would wait for me in the sunflowers."

I place my other hand over hers that's resting on her knee. "I like Emma Bean. Maybe I'll start calling you that."

"Don't even think about it, Archie. Besides, I kinda like when you call me darlin'." She smiles at me, then leans forward and kisses me.

When she pulls back, her head rests on the back of the couch again.

"Why don't you get some rest? I can sit here with you until you fall asleep."

"I was hoping you would stay with me tonight. As much as I want some naked time with you, I am really tired." She laughs.

"I can stay with you, but I have to leave early, and I should probably go to bed soon myself. Do you still want to watch a movie or just head to bed now?" I really am tired too.

"Let's go to bed. I think I have an extra toothbrush some-where. Let me find it for you. I forgot to look the other night, but you were already asleep anyway."

She gets up and holds her hand out to me. I follow her to the bathroom, where she looks in a drawer. Then she hands me a packaged toothbrush.

"Thanks, darlin'." I lean in and kiss her cheek.

We brush our teeth at the same time, taking turns to rinse.

"I'll go get my bed ready if you want to use the bathroom first?" she says.

"Thanks." I wink at her.

When I'm done, I walk across the hall to her room. She's

leaning over the bed, and I take a minute to just watch her. She's so beautiful, and the person I'm getting to know makes her even more beautiful. And I can't lie—I'm also tempted to walk up behind her and push her down onto the bed and slide into her tight heat.

But I won't. She needs rest.

After she's done organizing her pillows, she stands and turns around. "I'll be right back." She pauses to give me a kiss on her way out.

I move to the other side of the bed and pull off my shirt first, then take my phone out of my pocket and set it on the night-stand. As I'm pushing my sweats down, Emma walks back into the room.

"You're wearing boxers tonight?" She looks surprised.

"Ha! You disappointed?" I shoot her a smile.

"I mean … a little, but it's probably for the best. Self-control and whatnot." She giggles as she gets into the bed.

"Oh, hey, I don't have a charger. My phone battery is low, and I can't miss my alarm."

"There should be an extra around here somewhere."

She pulls open the drawer of the nightstand next to her side of the bed, and I spy a hot-pink vibrator sitting right on top.

"Found one. Here you go."

She reaches across the bed, and I take it from her.

"Thanks, baby."

I plug the cord into the outlet on the wall and sit on the edge of the bed. Opening my Alarm app, I set the alarm for seven a.m. I need to make sure I wake up early enough to run back to my house, eat, and get to the field by nine.

I set my phone down and move fully onto the bed. Emma is already lying down on her side and facing me.

"Hey, Archie? Thank you for asking me about my sister. It means a lot to me that you care, but it is something I needed to tell you about anyway. One of the biggest reasons this pregnancy scares me is because Sunny's condition was hereditary. So, there is a chance our baby could have the same defect." She reaches over and places her hand on my shoulder.

I turn onto my back and hold my arm out to her. "Come here."

She scoots over and rests her head on my shoulder while bringing her hand to my stomach.

"I'm really glad you told me about her. But, Emma, if he or she does have the same issue, we'll do whatever we need to do to make sure our baby has the best life. And like the doctor said, there have been advances in medicine between then and now."

She nods. "You're right, and logically, I know that. I mean, that's what I'm in school for, but I never thought about it for myself, if you know what I mean. Just surreal, honestly."

She looks up at my face, and I meet her gaze.

"Going through this with you though is making that fear lessen. I'm not sure why I feel this sense of peace or ease with you, but I do."

I kiss the top of her head. "Good. I'm glad I can help you feel better about it all. I'll do everything I can to take care of you and the baby. You won't ever have to question that."

"I'm just so used to taking care of everything on my own that it's hard to trust, but I do trust you." She strokes her hand up to my chest, and it rests right over my heart. "You ever going to tell me what this tattoo means?"

"The cards?"

"Yeah, I noticed it the first time we were together and have been curious."

"Well, it represents my brothers. Aiden, the ace of hearts. Aston is the ace of clubs. Ace is diamonds, and Austin is spades. The Joker is Jesse. He was also a surprise baby."

"I love that. Can I see a picture of them? I don't know why I didn't think to ask sooner."

I grab my phone off the nightstand and pull up my photos. "This is my mama, my dad, Aiden, Ace, Aston, Austin and Jesse. And this good-lookin' guy on the end is yours truly."

She takes the phone from my hand and really looks at the picture.

"I think you and Aiden look the most alike, but you can definitely tell you're all related. I wonder what my relationship with Sunny would have been like as we got older. Are you all pretty close?"

"Yes, we are. I don't know what I'd do without them. I love my friends, and I know they have my back, but nothing beats the bond I have with my brothers. Emma, I know you've been alone in a lot of ways since your sister died, but letting someone in and allowing others to help you don't make you less of a force. In the small amount of time we've spent together, I can see you're strong and very capable of taking care of yourself. But I'm asking you to let me take care of you. I promise to never forget how strong you are." I lean in and kiss her lips.

"Okay, Archie, I'll try."

She kisses me this time, but before we get carried away, I break the kiss.

"Let's try to get some sleep. Big Griff and Baby Griff are growing and need the rest." I reach down and pull her shirt up slightly to touch her lower belly, where my baby is.

She hitches a breath. "That tickles." She places her hand on top of mine. "But, yeah, I don't think I can keep my eyes open." She yawns. "A year ago, would you have guessed you would be spending Halloween in bed by nine p.m. with your ..."

"Baby mama?" I belt out a laugh. "Never in a million years, darlin'."

We both laugh and then settle into the quiet. After a few minutes, I feel her breathing steady, and I hear a soft little snore coming from her.

After a while, she turns away from me, but I curl around her, wanting to feel her body against mine. I kiss the back of her neck and wrap my arm around her waist and rest my hand on her lower belly under her shirt.

With a feeling of contentment, I fall into a deep sleep.

CHAPTER
NINE

ARCHIE

WE'RE PLAYING LOUISIANA TODAY, and they're a good team, but we're better. Callaway is in as the quarterback today, as expected. He's on fire too.

The clock is winding down, and we're all getting tired. In the huddle, Bo called a passing play to Beck, which means I need to execute zone protection—leaving space for him to get the ball down the field. Beck is one of the best running backs not only in our conference, but in college ball. So, I know if I give him the room he needs, he'll take it all the way.

We take our positions, and I get myself positioned on the yard line. The defensive end across from me starts talking shit.

"Griff, you pussy. How's your mom? Did she call my name when she was giving it to your dad last night?"

Does it make me mad? Hype me up? Nah. But it does make me laugh.

"Awww, you're cute, Pickens. Listen, it don't matter to me that your coaches put a JV lineup out here. I've been here all day, schooling your ass. I like this kind of party, baby."

"Fuck you and your mother, Griff."

"Ha-ha! He's scared, boys. Come on now, Pickens. I want you right here." I point in front of me.

Bo calls the play, and I jump from my position. I take ahold of Pickens's shoulder pads and throw him to the ground.

Standing over him, I yell. "Get off the field!"

Then I look up and see Beckham reach the first down marker. We're down to three minutes left on the clock. Bo calls a passing play, which will send it off to Casey. We line up, but this time, Pickens doesn't say anything.

Instead of moving straight at him when Bo calls the snap, I shift to my left and back to protect him while he throws the ball off to Casey.

A lineman comes up on me before I can brace for the hit. He gets me right in the ribs, and even though I have my pads on, it still hurts like a motherfucker. It'll definitely leave a bruise.

As I get up from the ground, our band starts playing our fight song to signal a touchdown. I look down the field and see Casey in the end zone.

We win the game by ten points.

After the game, I find my dad in the family waiting area. When I walk up to him, he folds me into his arms and slaps my back twice.

"Good game, son. How you feelin'?"

"Thanks. I'm good, just a little sore, but that's pretty much the norm." I laugh.

He chuckles. "You hungry?"

"You know it. Let's go grab a steak. I need some red meat to help the swelling in my side go down."

"Got it. Let's go to the Stockyard. We don't have one of those near home, and I like their potatahs." He lets go of me but keeps his arm around my shoulders.

Twenty minutes later, we're sitting at our table at the restaurant, both with a beer in front of us.

"So, tell me how you've been, how you're feeling. We should meet with your agent soon. I think there were a couple of endorsement deals he wanted you to look at."

"Yeah, we should definitely do that. But, hey, listen. Um, there's something I want to talk to you about. And I wish Mom were here, too, but this really can't wait."

He looks at me and crosses his arms over his chest. "Okay, what is it?"

I rub the back of my neck. "Well ... I'm going to be a father."

He blinks. "Come again? I think you just said you were going to be a father."

I drop my hand and look up at him, smiling tightly. "Nope, you heard me right. I'm gonna be a dad."

The look on his face isn't upset or disappointed, but he does look well and truly stunned, like someone knocked the wind out of him with a well-aimed horseshoe. "How did this happen, Arch?"

I chuckle and can't even help myself when I say, "Well, Dad, you see, when a man and woman—"

"Cut the shit, son. Who is she? Do we know her?" he asks.

"Dad, when have I ever introduced y'all to a girl here at college? Never. But ... this girl is different."

"How did you meet her? And do we know if it's yours? Should we get a paternity test?"

All logical questions that he's asking, but it also kinda pisses me off.

"Yes, Dad. It's mine, and, no, I'm not questioning the paternity. We went to the doctor to confirm. And before you get too carried away with your questions, she also has her own dreams to follow, so the timing isn't great for her either. But we're gonna figure it all out together. We're spending time together. And, Dad, I really like her." I take a drink of my beer.

He's staring at me, probably trying to figure out if this is all bullshit. I sit back and drink my beer, giving him time to process.

I set my beer back down on the table. "Her name is Emma. She's a premed student and a golfer for the university's team. Super smart and gorgeous. Honestly, I can't get enough of hanging out with her. When I'm not on the field or in class, I want to be around her."

He tilts his head to the side and nods. "Okay, I hear you. So, what will you do when you get drafted? Does she plan to come with you and drop out of school?"

"Well, we haven't talked much about all of that yet. I would never ask her to give up on her dream of being a doctor. It's too important to her. She lost her sister when they were kids, and I think she's made it her mission to understand and help kids with the same issue."

Dad blows out a breath. He bows his head, as if in quiet prayer. "That's a shame. No one ever wants to lose a child—that's for sure. Sounds like she's got a good head on her shoulders then. Doesn't mean I won't have some questions and concerns. You're my son, and that's my grandchild she's carrying. When will we get to meet her?"

"Not sure yet. Soon, hopefully. We might be a lot for her to handle though. Her family is pretty small. It was just her and her sister until she died. Sounds like, after her sister's death, she felt a lot of pressure to be perfect."

He smirks. "We can be a lot. Your mama is going to be over

the moon—you know that, right? Seems like we just got Austin out of diapers though."

"Ha! Dad, he's fourteen."

"Still acts like a baby sometimes though. God love him. We should have invited her to come with us tonight."

"She had to take care of some things at her parents' house this weekend. She didn't make it to the game today either."

Dad's expression sobers again. He folds his hands on the table, then leans in. "Son, I know I don't have to tell you to do right by this girl. You're a good man, but this all means you can't be messin' around with any other girls now. You need to step up and be the best dad to this baby. Whatever happens between you and Emma is between the two of you, but don't ever put the baby in the middle of your relationship. The baby will come first. And if you can make it work as a couple, that's a bonus." He pauses, eyes locked on mine. "But hear me when I tell you, I still can and will kick your ass if you mess her around."

I nod slowly, the weight of it all settling on my shoulders—but not in a bad way. Just … real. Heavy and full and somehow still right. "You don't have to worry about that, Dad. I'm all in for this girl. And I know it seems soon, but I think we'll be able to make this work."

"You sure she won't get sick of your ass? You can be a lot to handle, Arch." He laughs.

"I'm a treat, and you know it. How could she not love me?" I wink at him.

"That you are, son. I hope she's ready for you and all the stuff that's coming your way with being a pro athlete, but if she's an athlete at this level, she must have some idea. You been golfing with her yet?"

I shake my head. "No, she just finished her fall season, and I've been so busy, as you know, so no, but I wouldn't mind. She'll probably smoke me."

Our food arrives, so we take some time to eat and catch up on the goings-on around the ranch.

After we finish eating and pay the bill, we walk out to my dad's truck.

He pulls me in for a hug. "Archie, I'm so proud of the man you're becoming. Even if the timing isn't the best professionally, babies are a blessing, and we'll be so excited to meet the next little Griffith."

I squeeze him a little harder, fighting the tears that just sprang. "Thanks, Dad. I just hope I can be as good of a dad as you've been to us. And I also hope I can treat Emma with the same love and respect you show Mama."

He pulls away but keeps his hands on my shoulders. "Oh, you will, son. 'Cause if you don't, I won't have to worry about kicking your ass; your mama will."

We both laugh as he releases me.

He turns and opens his door. "We'll see you soon, but you'd better call your mama and tell her about the baby because you know I will when I get home, and she should hear it from you first."

I nod. "You got it. I'll call her on my way home. Drive safe and text me when you get there. Tell everyone I said hi and I love and miss them all."

He tips the bill of his hat. "Will do. Love you, son."

"Love you, Dad." I tap the top of his door when it closes.

I watch him drive away and think about how different my path is than his was. While I love the ranch I grew up on, I never had any interest in taking it over. Once I made that first hit in peewee football, I knew where I was meant to be.

Now, I just need to figure out a way to make my dreams and Emma's mix, so we can both be there to raise the baby. Because I can't imagine being away from any child of mine. And the more time I spend with Emma, the more I realize that I'm not interested in being away from her either.

CHAPTER
TEN

EMMA

TELLING my parents I was pregnant went about as well as I'd expected it would. They both started crying, which made me cry. They're natural worriers, so I wasn't shocked when they started asking questions. Important ones. Namely about how I'll be a mother and a student, an athlete, a young woman experiencing life in her twenties.

They're nervous about my future and the impact that Archie's career will have on all of this and how we'll be able to raise a baby together. Will he get drafted and move away? The travel that's involved and how unavailable he'll be. I'm not as concerned about that part as maybe I should be. Things with Archie have been relatively easy so far, and while we haven't had any talks about what we'll do, I do think we'll be able to make some of these decisions together.

Technically, I have one more year of premed left, so there are not only considerations to be made about medical school, but also how I'll finish my premed program and be a new mom. Where the baby and I will live and how I'll be able to support him or her are at the top of the list of worries. Who will watch the baby while I'm going to school full-time and finishing out my last year on the golf team? I know sacrifices will have to be made, but school and the team come first, especially since the latter is giving me my scholarship.

My parents have assured me that they will be supportive every step of the way. I know they will, mostly because they worry and their love is unconditional. I don't want them to feel obligated to raise my baby. I know I need their help, yet that independent woman in me fiercely wants to try to do as much of this on her own.

And of course, they want to be as involved as possible with the baby and making sure the baby's health is okay. My parents' love was never in question with me growing up; it was their emotional presence. But time has healed some of their grief, and I think this baby could bring a new connection for me and my parents too.

I know they're worried like I am about the possibility that the baby could have the same heart defect, but right now, all we can do—all I can do—is take care of myself the best that I can. Which means I need to get a little more rest and make sure I'm eating and drinking plenty of fluids.

Once we got through our talk and got some dinner, it was getting late, so I decided to stay the night with them. I called Archie to let him know I would be staying with my parents. Plus, I wanted to check on him after his game, and he told his dad about the baby, so I wanted to see how that went, but … mostly, I just wanted to hear his voice. It was an emotional day, and he just has a calming presence that makes me feel better.

When I get to my apartment the next day, I grab a small duffle bag of clothes from my car. When I was home, I found a few pairs of larger leggings, T-shirts, and sweatshirts that I'll probably need sooner rather than later. I'm not really showing yet, but the waistbands on all my pants are definitely getting a bit snugger.

When I push open the door to the apartment, I find all three of my roommates home. Mia and Livi are on the couch, watching some show about a virus taking over the world, and Peyton is in the kitchen, making quesadillas.

"Yum! Smells good in here, Pey. Did you make enough for me?" I ask her.

"Of course I did. Do you want yours with chicken or just cheese?" Peyton asks.

"Cheese is good. No, wait. Add a little chicken in there, too, if there's enough." I need to add more chicken and protein to my diet, although my appetite is finicky.

I walk in and set my duffle bag down next to the couch. I tug on Mia's ponytail, and Livi holds her hand up for me to take.

"What's up, bestie? We missed you last night. It was the first time in a while that we came home after a football game and you weren't here," Livi says.

I squeeze her hand lightly. "I needed to run up to my parents' for the day. It's been a while since I've spent time with them, and I ended up staying the night because it was getting late and I didn't want to drive back to campus in the dark."

"Fair. Well, you're just in time for dinner, so yay!" She smiles at me.

My phone chimes from inside my bag, so I bend down to take it out. I see Archie's name on the screen with a text.

Archie: You home yet?

Emma: Just got back.

Archie: Feel like hanging out, or are you tired?

"Who are you texting with, Emma?" Mia asks with a smile.

I return her smile and feel some heat hit my cheeks. Not because I'm embarrassed though. He just makes me feel some sort of way.

"It's Archie."

"Hmm. You two have been spending a bit of time together.

You guys hooking up or just hanging out?" Peyton asks from the kitchen.

"Both." I shrug, laughing. "He's a really cool guy. Super sweet and funny too."

"Okay, so he's hot, about to go to the NFL, and he's a sweetheart? You lucky-ass bitch. We practically shoved him your way. Although who would have guessed that one of the biggest players on campus would be locked down?" Mia laughs.

"Thanks?" I laugh and meet Livi's gaze. Then walk over and sit next to her on the couch, my phone still in my hand.

"Is he coming over tonight?" Livi asks.

"Oh, I'm not sure. He just asked if I was home and if I wanted to hang out tonight."

"And you'll say yes, right?" Mia leans over Livi to ask.

"I mean, probably. But y'all need to tell me if having him over all the time annoys you. We are spending a lot of time together, and that might not be fair to you guys."

Livi takes my hand. "Babe, we like him—right, girls?"

Mia and Peyton both agree.

"So, if spending time with him makes you happy, that makes us happy." She pulls me in for a hug.

"And may I just say," Peyton chimes in, "I wouldn't mind if I accidentally saw him walking around in his boxers."

"He doesn't wear any, so that probably won't happen." I let it slip out before I can really think about what I'm saying.

"Period," Mia says with a snap of her fingers. "You really are a lucky bitch."

"I'm not even gonna deny it. Although I've really only seen him naked a few times. And I do like him for other reasons too. He's a total sweetheart, super caring and attentive too."

"Well, young Emma, I feel like you're missing out on a lot of opportunity here. If he doesn't wear boxers, why are you not climbing him every second you're together?" Peyton asks.

"You know we're the same age, right, Pey?" I giggle. "But, yes, I one thousand percent agree. I should be naked with him at all times. There's a little thing called school, along with golf and football, that prevents that from happening though."

We all laugh, and my phone chimes again.

> Archie: You leavin' me hangin', Em?

"Oops. I forgot to reply to him. So, you're sure you guys don't mind if I invite him over?" I ask them and release Livi's hand.

"Totally fine," Livi says.

I look at Peyton, who gives me a thumbs-up, and then at Mia, who smiles and nods.

> Emma: Sorry, I was just catching up with my roommates. Do you want to come over?

> Archie: Yeah, I can do that. We just finished dinner here, so give me a few, and then I can head out. I just need to help with cleanup tonight.

> Emma: How nice of you. 😊 See you soon.

"Okay then. I'm going to go take a quick shower before he gets here. I didn't shower before I left my parents'." I walk around the couch, grab my bag, and start down the hallway to my room.

"Oh, hey, Em!" Mia shouts. "If you need any condoms, let me know. I have some in my room."

They all laugh.

"We got it covered, Mi, but thank you!" I shake my head when I get to my room.

When I finally tell Mia and Peyton that I'm pregnant, I wonder what they'll think about our situation then. Not that I think they will be upset with me, but I have no doubt they'll be shocked.

After a quick shower, I'm dressed in my PJs and brushing out my hair when I hear a knock at the front door. When I open the bathroom door, I see Mia opening it to let Archie in. He's standing at the door in joggers, a T-shirt, and a backward baseball hat.

Why does that have to be so hot?

"Ladies. How we doin' tonight?" He looks around at each of them with a smile.

They all start chattering at the same time, but I'm struck speechless, just looking at him. I really am a lucky bitch. He's the complete package—kind, sweet, thoughtful, has a good head on his shoulders, ambitious, and utterly sexy.

He meets my stare and smiles wider. "Hey, darlin'. You shower without me?"

"Marry him, Emma! Right now, or I will," Mia yells.

Of course, this makes Archie laugh, but then he says, "I'm sorry, Mia, but I'm spoken for."

They all look over at me at the same time.

Not sure what to say in response to that in front of everyone, I settle on, "Get over here and kiss me."

"Yes, ma'am." Archie makes his way to me.

When he's standing in front of me, I look up at him and smile. "Hey."

"Hey, baby."

Then he slides his hands into my wet hair, tilts his head, and devours my mouth. He isn't shy about kissing me in front of my friends, which I'm happy about, so I wrap my arms around his shoulders and return the kiss in kind.

He releases me from the kiss and moves his hands from my hair to my waist, then around to my ass. He lifts me up and carries me to my room. I look over his shoulder and wave to my roommates.

"What about the quesadilla I made for you?" Peyton asks.

"I'll come get it in a bit," I reply before Archie shuts the door with his foot behind us.

He walks us over to the bed, then gently lays me down.

Bending over me, he kisses me deeply again, and I reach for his waistband, but he pulls his waist away from me and stops the kiss.

"Before I get lost in you, are you hungry? We can pick this up after you eat something." He kisses my nose.

"I am a little hungry, but I can wait." I try to pull him back into me.

"Well, I don't plan to let you leave this room for a while, so if you're hungry, we'd best get that out of the way first."

He stands and holds his hands out for mine, and I let him pull me up. Then he brings me in for a hug, and I wrap my arms around his waist.

"So, how did it go with your parents before you left? Did they say anything else about the baby?"

For just a minute, I close my eyes and breathe him in. I love the way he smells, and, good Lord, when I'm in his arms, I feel so safe and protected.

"They were good. No more tears today. I told them I would keep them updated and let them know how my next appointment goes. I think they'll be nervous up until the baby is born." I move my hands up and down his back.

"Okay. Well, that's good. My mom called me again today, even though I'd told her everything after my dad and I had dinner. She's gone all Mimi mode already. She said she's clearing out my old room and making it a nursery. When I reminded her we don't know where I'll end up, that didn't stop her from filling me in on details. She asked me a lot about you today. We should probably meet each other's family as soon as possible, yeah?"

I nod against his chest, then look up at him. "I agree. I want this baby to be loved by both of our families. And I want my parents to meet you. I think they'll feel much better about the whole thing."

"Plus, I'm pretty to look at, so they can be assured the gene pool is good." He winks at me.

"That you are. I feel like it's pretty safe to say the baby will be blond?" I ask.

"Probably. My mom is blonde, and my dad is like a light brown, but he's got some gray in there now. All of my brothers are blond too. But you never know, I guess. Was your sister blonde?"

"She was, but hers was lighter than mine. Almost white blonde."

"Like an angel," he says.

"Yeah, like an angel." I smile.

We stand in silence for a minute until my stomach rumbles.

"Okay, let me go get some food so we can come back in here."

He pulls back but tilts my chin up to him with his finger. There's no mistaking the heat in his eyes. "You want my cock, Emma?"

"Yep, I sure do."

Am I drooling? I'm definitely feeling my panties getting wet, and we've only been holding each other.

"Fuck, you're perfect for me." He leans in and kisses me.

I pull back and take his hand in mine. "Come on. Let's go before I change my mind and let you feed me your cock instead."

"Whoa ho ho, darlin'. Them's teasing words. I might just tie you to that bed if you keep talking like this."

"Promise?" I wink, then walk toward the door and pull it open.

"Now, darlin', that's not very nice to tease me like that."

"Don't you worry, Arch. I'll take care of you later. Our last interruption a few days ago only left me craving you more, so I'm a sure thing tonight."

I tug on his hand, and we walk out into the hallway.

"Fuuuck," he mumbles.

The girls are all sitting at the table when we walk into the room.

"We didn't think you guys would make it back out here tonight. But I did leave your quesadilla in the oven for you, Em, so it didn't get too cold," Peyton says.

"Thanks, Pey. Archie, do you want anything?" I leave him at the table and head into the kitchen.

"I'll take a water if you have one," he says as he sits down in the empty seat at the table.

"Got it." I reach in and grab us each a bottle of water. Then take my plate with the quesadilla on it from the oven.

When I walk back over to the table, Archie reaches for me and pulls me onto his lap.

It makes my roommates laugh.

"You the caveman type, Archie Griffith?" Livi asks him.

"I mean, I'm the Emma type, so if that's caveman, sure." He winks at her.

We all laugh then and continue to eat and chat. They ask him about his game, and Mia mentions a hit he took near the end of the it.

I turn around to look at him over my shoulder. "Did you get hurt and not tell me?"

He kisses my forehead. "I'm good, baby. Just took a hit in the last play. Guy got me on my blind side."

"Did you get one of those gnarly bruises?" Peyton asks him.

"We always get a little bruised and battered in the games, but nothing I can't handle. I'll go see the trainer this week, and she'll get me feeling ready for the next game."

"I wish you had said something. I felt bad enough, missing the game on TV."

He laughs. "I'm fine, I promise. I'll let you examine it later." He kisses my lips.

"I can't decide if that's hot or kind of gross," Livi says.

"Well, she did say she wanted me to feed her—"

I cover his mouth with my hand.

"Don't you dare!" I remove my hand from his mouth and kiss him quiet instead.

"While you guys are cute and all, I am trying to eat. Can you put your tongues away for a few so we can finish?" Mia asks.

I pull away from his mouth and laugh. Then I turn around and eat a few more bites of my food.

My stomach is beginning to feel full, and I've noticed when I start to feel this way, it's best to stop eating to avoid getting sick. So, I hold it toward Archie to feed him a bite.

He takes the bite from my hand and practically swallows it whole.

As he finishes chewing, he stands with me in his arms. "Grab the waters, Em."

I lean over and grab the water bottles, and then he carries me down the hall to my room.

Over his shoulder, he yells out, "Night, ladies."

We hear them laughing as he closes the door to my room with his elbow.

He sets me on my feet, then moves over to the other side of the bed and toes off his shoes, removes his hat, then starts to take off his shirt.

"Arch, does it bother you that we're always at my place and not yours?"

He pauses for a second, then continues to toss his shirt on the nightstand. "Honestly, yeah, a little because my friends are like family. However, if I introduce you to my friends, I'm gonna want to introduce you as more than the girl I'm seeing. I want to show you off as the mother of my child, and until you're ready to go all in with the news, I'm okay with waiting."

I smile. "I know I should tell all of my roommates, but I kind of like living in our little bubble right now. This relationship is so new that it's inevitable people will have their opinions."

"And the only ones that count are ours. I'll protect our bubble and I won't let anyone fuck around with what we have here."

"Have I ever told you how attracted I am to your assertive nature?"

"I thought you liked my dirty mouth?" he says with a wink.

"Well, yeah, that too."

His eyes gleam a midnight shade of want and need.

"Sit on the bed, darlin'," he instructs, and I do as he asks.

He walks around the bed to me. "You feel okay?"

I nod. "Yeah, better than fine. Come here." I reach for him.

Archie smirks. "Take off your shirt."

I drop my arms and reach for the hem of my T-shirt, pulling it over my head. I'm not wearing a bra, so my breasts are bare to him.

"Fuck me. I think they're getting a little bigger. I love how your body is changing." When he stands in front of me, he cups my breasts in his hands. He moves his thumbs over my nipples, and the sensation makes me shiver. "That feel good, darlin'?"

"So good." I'm practically panting.

"Take my cock out."

I don't hesitate. I grab on to the waistband of his joggers and pull them down far enough to reach in and pull out his erection. My hands start moving up and down the shaft, pre-cum already leaking out of the head.

"I'm gonna feed you my cock, just like you wanted. First, I want you to lick the tip and clean up that pre-cum real good."

My tongue licks around the head of his cock, and then I take it in my mouth, twirl my tongue, and suck, making him hiss. My hands move to his tight ass.

"That's my girl. Now take it all the way to your throat. I want to see you gag on my dick. That's it, nice and slow."

Archie is too big for me to take him all the way to my throat, but I'm gonna give it my best shot. Taking orders like this doesn't usually work for me, but this … is hot. And I'm totally here for it.

I work my mouth down the shaft, using my tongue to apply pressure along the center. He twitches in my mouth.

His hands work their way into my hair, framing my head.

When I get as deep as I can, he rocks his hips, moving his cock in and out of my mouth.

"You're taking me so good, Emma. Is this what you needed? You wanted to taste me?"

I hum and look up at him, my eyes starting to water from him hitting the deepest part of my mouth, but not quite touching the back of my throat.

Saliva is pooling and starting to spill out with every move.

He's still holding my head in his hands and guides my head in tandem with his thrusts. "Fuck, Emma. I'm getting close already. Your mouth is a prize, baby. Is this making you wet? When I pull those panties off of you, will I find them soaked?"

I pull off of him to answer, "I'm so wet for you, Archie."

His head drops back as I bring him back into my mouth.

When I bring one of my hands to cup his balls and tug, he pushes as far as he can into my mouth, making me gag. He holds still, and I can feel the tears fall down my cheeks. Taking his hands from my head, he uses both of his thumbs to wipe them away.

"Gorgeous," he whispers. Then he pulls out of me. "Lie back on the bed. I want to see how wet you are."

I scoot back further on the bed and turn so that my head is resting on a pillow. Then Archie sits sideways on the edge of the mattress and takes my shorts and panties off in one fell swoop.

After tossing them on the floor, he moves his hands to my thighs and pulls them apart.

"Darlin', you are so gorgeous. Your pussy is dripping for me."

He lies down between my legs, moves one hand to my center, and pushes a finger into me while his other hand rests on my lower belly.

His tongue slides from my opening to my clit. "You taste like honey, darlin'. I can't get enough of you."

Moving his tongue faster back and forth, he has me on the cusp of an orgasm when he pulls back completely.

"What are you doing? Keep going!" I put my hands on his head and try to force him back between my legs.

He chuckles. "Baby, I want to be inside you when we both come, but I promise I'll eat your pussy again later. First, I want you to ride my cock." Archie moves to the other side of me and spreads out on the bed. "Come here, darlin'."

I roll to my side and get on my knees. I climb over him to straddle his waist. Bending down, I rest my hands on either side of his head, and I kiss him, tasting myself on his lips.

Archie takes ahold of my hips and moves me back and forth over his erection as we kiss. I'm so wet and worked up that I could come just like this.

On the next pass of my opening, the head of his cock slips inside, and we both moan.

I place my hands on his chest and start moving my hips back and forth. When his hands move to cup my breasts, I nearly explode. They are so sensitive to the touch, and it's like I can feel every inch of his skin on mine.

"You feel so good, baby. I love feeling you stretch around my cock," he pants.

"Archie, I'm gonna come soon. I can't hold it. It's too good. So. Good."

He keeps one hand on my breast, and the other hand circles my clit with his thumb. That's all it takes for me to explode.

Archie's hips thrust up, and his pace quickens. His hands move to my face, and he guides me down for a kiss. His tongue strokes mine until he starts coming, and then he's panting into my mouth. I touch the tip of my tongue to his top lip, and he groans.

His hips pump into me once, twice, and then he reaches down and holds my hips in place as he spills into me.

I kiss him along his jaw as he comes down from his orgasm.

"Emma, you are perfect." His hand slides into my hair, and he kisses me.

"I mean, I think you're kinda perfect too." I roll off of him and lie on my side, facing him.

He's smiling at me, and he looks like he wants to say something.

"What are you thinking about, Archie?"

His hand strokes my arm. "I'm just thinking about how lucky I am. My baby is going to have the best mom. And I know this might sound weird, but I can't wait to see your belly get bigger. Knowing that it's my baby inside … yeah. It's pretty amazing, right?"

I bring my hand to his chest. "Yeah, Archie, it is amazing. And I think you'll get to see that belly sooner rather than later because my pants are starting to feel a little snug. I had to bring some looser sweats, shirts, and sweatshirts back with me."

Rolling onto my back, I take his hand in mind and place it over my stomach. "I know you might not be able to feel much of anything yet, but I feel it. There's a slight swell to my stomach now where there wasn't before. I think the fact that I'm starting to see the change in my body is making it feel more real."

His hand caresses my stomach softly. "Yeah, I can feel a little bump there now." He looks from my stomach to my eyes. "Emma, thank you for telling me about the baby. I know you could have kept it from me. But getting to know you, spending time with you … I just feel really damn lucky to be a part of your life and this baby's life. I don't want to miss any of it."

Tears spring to my eyes. I'm not usually an emotional person, but these hormones are no joke. I'm either horny or see a commercial on TV and feel like crying. "I'm really glad you're here with me, Archie."

He leans in and kisses me again.

"You know, you might want to start keeping a few things here if you're going to be staying over from time to time." I smirk.

"Is that right? You want me to be your roomie, darlin'?"

"Ha, no. I'm just saying that if you're going to be spending time here with me, it might be a good idea for you to have some clothes and whatnot here, so you don't have to rush back to your place in the mornings."

He hums. "I could probably do that."

"Okay." I smile.

I untwist the sheet and pull it up to cover us both. "Should we watch a show or something before we go to bed?"

"Yeah. What do you have in mind? What's your favorite show?"

"It depends on my mood. I'm guilty of binging my share of reality TV, but my go-to show is *Grey's Anatomy*—because, you know, med student." I point to myself.

He props a pillow up against the headboard. "Okay, let's do it. I've never watched that show."

I grab the remote off the nightstand and pull it up.

"Tell me a little about it first."

"Well, I don't want to spoil too much, and there are so many interweaving storylines, so it would be hard to give you a complete rundown. But Meredith is pretty much the star of the show. She's a doctor in the same hospital that her mother worked in, and she basically feels like she's living in her mother's shadow and she constantly has to prove herself. Then McDreamy arrives and shakes everything up."

"Wait, who's McDreamy?" He holds up a hand.

"Never mind. Let's just watch, and I'll explain as we go." I press play and lie back to cuddle into Archie.

After the first episode ends, I look over at Archie and see his eyes are shutting. When I shift to get up and go to the bathroom, he startles awake.

"Sorry, baby. Did I fall asleep?"

I nod. "Yeah, your eyes were closed. I didn't mean to wake you. I just need to go to the bathroom before I go to sleep."

"Okay, I'll be here, waiting for you."

Smiling, I walk out of my room and across the hall to the bathroom.

When I come out, I look down the hallway and see all the lights are off in the apartment.

Then I walk back into my room and over to the bed. Archie is lying on his back, eyes closed, one arm behind his head. I take a minute to look at his tattoos. He's got quite a few, but I'm still fascinated by the deck of cards on his heart. I'm not really sure why it calls to me. Maybe because I know that each card is for one of his brothers. I wish Sunny and I had been able to have the kind of relationship Archie has with his brothers. I think we would have stayed close despite our age difference.

As I get into the bed, I curl up next to his body. His eyes are still closed, but he moves his arm from behind his head and wraps it around my shoulders, pulling me in closer.

"You okay?" he asks sleepily.

I nod. "I'm good. Let's get some sleep."

With my arm wrapped around Archie's waist, I drift off to sleep with thoughts of the baby, praying he or she will be okay.

CHAPTER
ELEVEN

ARCHIE

THE LAST FEW weeks have been busy between classes, spending time with Emma, and football. I haven't been home much, and when I am, it's usually just for short periods of time to grab clothes or to eat with my roommates on dinner nights.

I'm sure they're wondering where I've been. It's been months since I've been to a party with any of them, and when we're at practice, I don't really say much about anything other than football. It's not that I don't want to tell my friends. I would love to, but until Emma is ready for more people to know, I'll keep doing what she's comfortable with.

Tonight, my roommates and I are having dinner together for a Friendsgiving type of thing since we won't be together for the actual holiday. We've each made a Thanksgiving recipe from our families. My mom makes the best cornbread stuffing, so I called her yesterday, got the recipe and made it this morning. Casey made the turkey and didn't overcook it. Beck made some mashed potatoes. Liam made some green-bean thing that I'm not sure anyone will eat, but he said it's a classic Thanksgiving Day side. Charlie made homemade mac 'n' cheese and rolls, along with two pumpkin pies with fresh whipped cream to top it with. The house smells so good.

I invited Emma to come over, but she had a lab she needed to make up, so she couldn't come. But I really think she's just not ready to meet my friends yet.

We also invited Bo Callaway over because he's been getting pretty close with Casey. Or at least I see them together a lot at practice.

Casey's friend Noelle came over too. She's got some boyfriend who plays on the baseball team, but I've never actually seen them together. I guess she's bringing an apple pie.

Arbor and Lily—Charlie's friends—are here too.

We borrowed an extra-long table from Arbor's mom, Lindsay. So, the guys have been tasked with setting the table while the girls make sure everything is done cooking.

"Well, boys, our last game of the regular season is coming up this weekend. How we feelin' about it?" Pitz asks us all.

Casey chimes in, "I think it'll be a good game for sure. Close maybe."

"Their run game is strong, so our D needs to stay one step ahead and anticipate their moves before they make them." Beck is the one who likes to watch tape and analyze the other teams. He's good at it too.

"I agree with Beck. We need to be ready for them and not take this game lightly. They could surprise us and catch us off guard if we get lazy," Bo says.

"What do you think, Arch?" Pitz asks me.

"I mean, yeah, I'm not too worried about this particular game, but we can't be negligent either. We need to prepare for them. Just because we have a spot in the playoffs doesn't mean we can slack here, but I don't think we will. We're ready."

"Okay, boys. Dinner is ready. Come help us carry all the food in," Charlie instructs us, like the bossy little thing she is.

We all walk into the kitchen, and the girls are putting the

dishes on the small table in the kitchen that are ready to be brought out to the large dining table.

"Casey, come over here and help me cut the turkey," Charlie tells him.

"Wait, are we sure we want Casey to use a big knife?" Noelle asks. "Remember that time in tenth grade when he almost cut off his finger in culinary?"

"Oh my God, I completely forgot about that." Charlie laughs. "Okay, wait. Beck, maybe you should do it then."

"Char, are you serious right now? I'm not going to cut off my fucking finger. Be so for real. And, Noelle ... you're a traitor. Why wouldn't you have faith in me, bestie?" Casey looks like a wounded puppy.

"Step aside, Boss. I got this under control." Beck takes the carving knife from Charlie and drops a kiss on her lips. "Case, why don't you just grab the plate that I need to put the turkey on?"

Casey mumbles something to Beck when he walks over that I can't hear.

I grab my dish and take it into the other room and place it on the table.

Bo steps up behind me and puts a hand on my shoulder. "Hey, I saw you on campus the other day. You were with a blonde and were kissing her. Is she your girl or something?"

I turn to look to see who might be in earshot, and then I lean into Bo. "I mean, we haven't made anything official. We've been spending a lot of time together, but I haven't said anything to anyone about it while we figure it out, you know?"

"Oh, okay, so the other guys don't know—got it. I couldn't see her face clearly, but she looked sort of familiar."

"I'm not sure if you would know her—" I get cut off when everyone starts to filter into the room.

Casey brings in the platter with the turkey on it.

Bo taps me on the back. "I got you."

"Thanks, man."

I'm not gonna lie and say that not telling my friends isn't bothering me. I can't wait to tell them all about the baby. As we get further along, I not only want to tell them about it, but I really want her to meet my friends, like I have hers.

There is a pitcher of water and some bottles of wine on the table—because we think we're fancy or some shit. And once everyone is seated, we all start piling food on our plates.

"Wait!" Charlie shouts.

My fork is almost to my mouth, so I pause.

"Sorry, sorry." She laughs. "I just want us to go around and say something we're grateful for. We do it at our house every year, so we should do it here too!"

"Oh, she's right. This will be fun. I'll go first," Arbor says. "I'm grateful for being halfway through the school year. It's been a killer. I'm grateful for my roomie, Lily. And I'm grateful that Charlie finally made her way to Walker. It's been so much fun, having you here. Also, I'm grateful for getting the chance to get to know all of you. For a bunch of jocks, you're all pretty great. Cheers!" She holds up her wineglass.

"Okay, I'll go next. Really just because I'm starving and want to move this along so my sister will let me eat," Casey jabs. "I'm grateful for all of you and for an amazing season. Beck, you go."

"Uh, okay. I'm grateful for Charlie." He picks up his water glass and takes a drink.

"Dude, that can't be the only thing you're grateful for. You're having a killer season, and we're awesome roommates, so there's that," Pitz says.

"Okay, sure. We can add all that in there too." Beck shrugs.

"I love you, babe." Charlie leans over and kisses him.

Everyone else says something they're grateful for. Mostly each other, passing classes, winning the regular season.

"Archie's turn. Go, Arch," Charlie prompts.

But I can't say what I'm really grateful for. Sure, all the things they've mentioned, but I want to say Emma and the baby too.

"I guess same as everyone else. I love y'all, and I'm grateful to be healthy and killin' it on the field. Cheers." I hold my water glass up.

"Oh, wait, Bo hasn't gone yet," Pitz says.

"That's okay, man. I'm good. I'm just glad to be here and part of the meal. Thanks for the invite." He smiles and lifts his wineglass.

This really is a great group of people, and I'm honored to be a part of this group on and off the field. These guys are the kind of friends you keep forever. I really can't wait to tell them I'm going to be a dad.

A few days later, Emma and I show up at the doctor's office for her next checkup. After we get called back into the room, she undresses, but this time, she doesn't turn her back to me.

I have no idea what to expect, so I ask Emma, "So, what do you think they'll do today? Do we get to see the baby again, or is that a different appointment?"

"Well, I'm not really sure. I think we'll get to at least hear the baby's heartbeat. Other than that, your guess is as good as mine." She ties the gown around her waist.

Just as she's sitting down on the table, there's a knock on the door, and the doctor walks in.

"Emma, good to see you." Then she says to me, "And I didn't catch your name the last time."

I hold out my hand to her. "Archie Griffith, baby daddy."

That makes her laugh, and Emma joins in.

"Nice to meet you."

"Likewise. So, Doc, what do we have in store for us today?" I ask.

"Do we get to see the baby again?" Emma asks.

"I'm going to check your measurements, your vitals, and we'll get the baby's heartbeat. Emma, go ahead and lie back."

She stands to the side of Emma and pulls apart her gown, keeping the sheet draped over her legs. The nurse who followed her into the room hands her a little machine that has a wand attached to it. Then she squirts some clear fluid on Emma's belly, and then the doctor turns on the device.

She swipes it back and forth across Emma's stomach. We hear a whooshing sound and then a nice and steady rhythm.

"Okay, Emma and Archie, this is your baby's heartbeat. It's nice and strong—one hundred fifty-four beats per minute. I don't see a need for an ultrasound today."

The nurse wipes off the liquid, and then the doctor gets a measuring tape out. She runs it across Emma's belly and reads off some numbers for the nurse to record.

"Everything look good, Doctor?" Emma asks.

"Yes, it does, but you are measuring a little small, which could simply be just a miscalculation in the due date. But you're also tall and lean. I'm going to go ahead and order some blood work for you. I also want to talk to you both about the genetic testing. You have some choices. You can find out the sex of the baby through blood work. But I think it would be in your best interest to also get the additional tests based on your family history."

Emma looks over at me. "Do we want to find out the sex of the baby, or do we want it to be a surprise?"

"I'm good either way, baby." I ask the doctor, "Can you tell us more about the other tests?"

"Absolutely. You should ask questions, too, for anything you don't understand." She smiles at us both. "We'll continue to do regular ultrasounds, and I'm going to go ahead and order a fetal echocardiogram for the baby, but that won't need to be scheduled for a few more weeks—closer to your eighteen- or nineteen-week marker. It's time to get some blood work done, which could show us anything we need to monitor, but I also want to consider doing an amniocentesis, which could potentially tell us more from taking a sample of the amniotic fluid."

"How is that done?" I'm trying to work it through in my head, and I can't figure out how they would get the fluid.

"We would take a needle and insert it through the stomach and into the uterus and pull fluid through to test. There are some risks involved, so I would encourage you both to do some research before we make that decision. But at least plan on regular ultrasounds and fetal echocardiograms for the baby as your pregnancy progresses.

"Call the office once you've gone over all the information about genetic testing options. When you check out, you can make your next appointment for four weeks from today."

"Oh, I did have a question, Doctor. I'm not sure if I mentioned it, but I'm a golfer. I'm finished with my fall season, but I do need to make some decisions about the spring. I'm pretty sure I'll be too far along by mid-season, but I guess I just need to know if it's safe for me to continue to practice. I'm on a full scholarship to play," Emma says.

"I'm going to take a guess that the reason why you aren't seeing one of the university doctors is because of this, correct? You don't want the coach to know you're pregnant yet?" She looks at Emma.

"Yes, I'm just not sure what my options will be for school if I lose my scholarship because I can't play. I'm premed, so not exactly an ideal time for me to lose my scholarship," Emma tells her.

"Okay, so the good news is that you can still play golf as long as you're comfortable and assuming there are no complications with the baby. But I have to suggest that you inform your coach and the training staff that you are pregnant." She pats Emma on the shoulder. "Archie, take care of Mama."

"You know it. Thanks, Doctor." I tip my chin at her and smile.

After the doctor walks out, the nurse hands Emma a few papers with orders for blood work and a pamphlet with the testing options. We walk to the checkout counter and schedule her next appointment, which falls right around Christmas.

When we leave the office, I reach for her hand. She looks over at me and smiles.

"What?" I ask her.

"Nothing. I've just never really been in a relationship before. I mean, I had a boyfriend in high school, but it wasn't that serious. Not like hold-my-hand-in-public serious." She squeezes my hand.

"Me neither, but if you're gonna let me hold your hand, I'm gonna hold it." I bring our hands up to my mouth and kiss hers.

"Archie Griffith, you are a softy. And I dig it. I'll allow the hand-holding." She tugs my arm to bring me down far enough to kiss me.

"I think you like me, Emma Tucker." I grin against her lips.

"I think you might be right, Archie Griffith." She gives me one more kiss, and we continue our walk to my truck.

Once we get in my truck and get buckled, she turns to me. "So, I've been thinking. You can't go to your parents' for Thanksgiving, right?"

"Right. I can't get there and back before the game. And we have practice, so timing doesn't work out. My parents host Thanksgiving, so they can't get up here either. Why? What did you have in mind?" I reach over and put my hand on her leg.

"Well, I know you had a meal with your friends, but what if you came home with me for the day? It's only an hour away, so you wouldn't miss any time from practice. And I think my parents should meet the father of their grandchild." She puts her hand on top of mine.

"I can do that. My parents are anxious to meet you, too, so we'll have to make that happen at some point before the baby is born."

"The next few months will be busy for you if you guys keep winning, so I'm not sure when that can happen, but I would like to meet your parents and your brothers for sure." She looks out the window and then back at me. "I want this baby to be loved so hard."

"Darlin', this baby will be spoiled rotten and will always be loved." I smile.

She nods. "And do you think your family will like me?"

I bark out a laugh. "My mama has been praying for another female in the family for years. I think I mentioned she's the only girl in her family, and she is close to both her mom and my dad's mom, but I think they're always looking for another hen in the henhouse."

She laughs. "Well, I am definitely that." She rubs her belly.

"So, we should talk about what the doctor told us today and make some decisions, right? I'd like to take a look at some of these tests, but I want to know what you're thinking too."

"Well, the ultrasounds will happen regardless, but it does bring me some comfort in knowing that they're going to do fetal echocardiograms to monitor the baby's heart. As for the amniocentesis, I'm not sure that's something I want to do just because of the potential risks involved, but we can talk about it more once you've had time to look at it. The fact that my belly is still smaller concerns me a little, but I haven't gained much weight, just mostly changes in my shape, so I'm going to try not to stress about that unless she seems worried." She wraps her fingers around mine and squeezes.

"Okay, I'm here for you, and I just want to make sure you and the baby are okay." I lean in and kiss her forehead. "So, Thanksgiving is tomorrow. Are we going together, or should I meet you there?"

"I'll probably head up early and help my mom cook. You have practice in the morning or no?" she asks.

"No, we have tomorrow off, but I have to be back tomorrow night. We have an early Friday practice."

"Okay, I haven't decided if I'm spending the night. I might even go up tonight actually."

"You sure you want to drive up there at night? I know it's only an hour away, but I'm not crazy about you driving in the dark."

If she wasn't pregnant, I probably wouldn't think twice about it.

"I'll be fine. I think I'll text my mom real quick to see if she needs any help tonight or if she just wants me to come in the morning." She pulls her phone out of her bag and taps on the screen. "She's making some of the dishes tonight, so I think I will head up in a bit. After you drop me off, I'll pack a small bag and head out before it gets too late. The other girls left earlier today anyway, so I might as well."

"You don't want to hang out with me?" I pout.

"I'll see you tomorrow. Don't give me that pouty lip. Makes me want to bite it."

"I can arrange that. I'm happy to give you a few orgasms before you leave. Just sayin'." I move my hand up her leg and in between her thighs.

"Didn't you just say you didn't want me to be driving in the dark?"

She laughs, but she doesn't stop my hand. In fact, she spreads her legs further apart. I rub my fingers up and down the center along the seam. I can feel the heat from her through her pants.

"Baby, I could probably get the first orgasm right here in this truck. While I'm driving."

"Hmm ... I'm not so sure about that. And you should really be paying attention to the road. There's a baby on board, you know."

I stop moving my hand and glance over at her. "You want me to stop? Am I making you nervous?"

"I mean, no." Her cheeks are tinted pink, and I can tell she's getting worked up.

So, I continue to rub. Up. Down. Then she starts to lift her hips up and down, matching my movements.

My eyes are watching the road, but I can't help but glance at her to see how this is affecting her. And I'm not gonna lie— seeing her getting worked up is making my dick hard.

As soon as I pull into her complex, she unbuckles her seat belt and moves over as far as she can toward me, but she's blocked by the center console.

"Keep touching me, Archie." Her hips continue to move.

I pull into a parking spot and throw the truck in park. My hands are on her before the engine's even fully off. I turn toward her, one hand already trailing up her thigh. This time, I don't tease; I pop the button on her jeans and slide my hand inside.

The heat hits me first, and then the slick glide of her arousal coats my fingers before I'm even all the way there.

"Fuck, darlin'," I groan, my voice low and rough. "You are so wet for me, aren't you?"

Her head's tipped back against the seat, lips parted, breathing shallow. She turns to look at me, eyes heavy-lidded and glassy with need. "It feels so good, Archie. Don't stop."

"Wouldn't dream of it, baby."

My middle finger is sliding into her folds. On the next lift of her hips, I push my finger inside of her, and she moans.

"Oh fuck, Arch. Right there. Oh God. I'm gonna come!" She's gripping the door handle with one hand, and she has her other hand on my forearm, like she needs something solid to hold on to while she comes apart.

I watch her—the way her body arches, the way her breath breaks, the flush blooming across her chest—and it nearly undoes me. My dick aches behind my zipper, so hard that it's painful.

As the first pulse of her orgasm starts, she looks over at me, mouth slightly open. I think I could come in my pants, just watching her come like this. She's so fucking sexy, coming undone.

"Come for me, Emma. Let me feel you coat my fingers. That's it, baby. Ride it out."

I move my fingers faster as she comes. She bites down on her bottom lip.

"You're so pretty when you come for me, Emma."

"Ahhh ..." She moans as the last of her orgasm flows through her with a cry of, "Holy shit. I think I saw stars."

I can't help but chuckle and shoot her a wink. "You're welcome."

Then I pull my hand out of her pants, bring my fingers up to my mouth, and suck her wetness from them. She's watching me, and I'm watching her.

I twirl my tongue around my fingers and hum, "Delicious."

"Fuck, that's hot, Archie," she whispers.

I lean in and kiss her, my tongue seeking hers. Our tongues twirl, and she moans into my mouth.

When she pulls back, she looks at my mouth. "I'd better get inside."

"Okay, darlin'. I'll walk you in."

She nods and then reaches for the door handle.

I pull the handle on my door and push it open. Then I walk around the front of the car and take her hand as she reaches me.

"Do you want to come in while I get ready?" she asks, a wicked smile on her lips.

"Ha! We both know that if I come in and watch you get ready to leave, you won't be leaving any time soon. So, if you really want to go to your parents' tonight, I'd better just kiss you goodbye at the door."

"Okay, fine. You're no fun." She giggles.

"Baby, there is nothing I want more than to slip inside that tight pussy, but there's no way I'll be letting you leave if I do."

When we reach her door, she lets go of my hand and pulls her keys out of her bag. "Thanks for coming with me today." She looks up at me and smiles.

"Of course. Always be here for you if I can be."

"I know, but I still appreciate it." She reaches for my hands and takes them in hers. "Give me one more kiss before you go."

"You don't have to ask me twice." I lean in and kiss her, but instead of letting this kiss grow hot, I kiss her sweetly.

She has a smile on her lips when I pull back.

"Good night, darlin'." I step away, so I don't follow her in.

"Night, Arch. I'll text you the details and my parents' address for tomorrow." She walks into her apartment and turns, shooting me a smile before she closes the door.

As I walk down to my truck, I can't help but laugh to myself. I have never had to meet the parents before. The girls I took to prom or other school dances, I grew up with all of them, so no introductions were necessary. But the stakes are higher on this one. I mean, I get along with everyone, so I don't think anything will go wrong, but still. Just another situation I couldn't have imagined being in this year.

CHAPTER
TWELVE

EMMA

I GOT TO MY PARENTS' house just before nine p.m. last night. I stayed up with my mom for a while, and we made a pumpkin pie and a sweet potato pie. I don't like the sweet potato pie, but I could seriously eat the entire pumpkin pie. I'm kind of wishing we had made an extra.

We talked about the baby and started to make a list of all the things we needed to buy. There are so many things these little babies need. And even though it's slightly overwhelming, I can't deny that I'm getting excited to buy some of the basics. The big stuff will probably need to wait until we figure out our living situation, but I think starting to get some onesies and picking out bedding and some of the cute gender-neutral items will be fun.

Archie is due to get here any minute now. I don't really feel nervous, but I'd be lying if I said I wasn't anxious. Our relationship has only come up a few times in conversation, but I think it will be easier to answer some of the questions they have when he's here with me.

My dad is excited to have another man in the house. It's a bonus that Archie also plays football, and now he has someone to watch the Dallas Cowboys play the Detroit Lions. It's a game that has been played for years between the two teams. My dad is a huge Cowboys fan.

I've told them who he is, so I'm sure they've looked him up. My tip that they have looked him up is that they aren't asking a ton of questions about him, which is surprising. Even with the friends I've made at school, they've always been very curiously cautious about who I spend my time with.

Just as I'm taking the stuffing out of the oven, I hear the doorbell ring.

"I'll get it," I holler from the kitchen so my dad doesn't jump up and answer.

I want to have a minute with Archie before I have to share him with my parents.

After setting down the dish, I take the potholders off my hands and place them on the counter. I look over at my mom and see her watching me with a soft smile on her face.

"What?" I ask her.

She shakes her head. "Oh, nothing. You just seem excited."

"I am excited. He's nice to look at." I giggle.

"Ah! Emma Grace!" she scolds with a laugh.

I rush over to the door and pull it open.

Archie is wearing a freaking cowboy hat and cowboy boots. Scoop me off the floor. To make it even better, he's wearing a distressed pair of Wranglers and a plaid shirt with pearled buttons. He looks like he just stepped out of *Yellowstone*. Or the ranch he grew up on, but whatever. I like the *Yellowstone* thought better.

He's watching me with a smile on his face. "Hey, darlin'."

If we didn't have to go inside and talk to my parents right now, I'd probably pull him in and rip those clothes off. Except for the hat. He could leave the hat on. While I ride him again. Save a horse and all that.

"Hi," I finally say. "Come on in. We're just pulling the food out, so your timing is perfect."

When he steps in, he tilts his hat back on his head and bends down, lifting me in his arms. We're face-to-face now, and he leans in and kisses me.

"There. That's better," he whispers against my lips.

With my arms wrapped around him, I bury my face in his neck, breathing him in. "I'm glad you're here."

"Me too. Should we go in so I can meet your parents?" He sets me down. "Can I put my hat somewhere?" He looks around, eyes landing on the bench near the door.

"Oh, yeah. I'll just drop it here on the bench, if that's okay." I take it from him and place it on the bench. Then I grab his hand. "Come on. Let's go meet the parents." I smile.

We walk into the kitchen first, and my mom has her back turned to us. She is bent over, looking in the oven.

"Mom, Archie is here."

She stands with a casserole in her hands. Dad strolls in, tight smile on his face.

"Hey, Dad. So, this is Archie."

Archie reaches out his hand to my dad first. "A pleasure to meet you, sir. Thank you for inviting me here to spend the day with you and your family."

Dad takes his hand and shakes it. "We're glad to have you. You can call me Van."

Mom puts the dish on the counter and walks around it. "Hi, Archie. Welcome to our home."

"Mrs. Tucker, thank you for having me."

He holds his hand out to her, but she leans in and hugs him instead. I'm slightly shocked by the gesture, and I look over at my dad, who looks equally surprised.

"Archie, it's so nice to meet you. But please call me Stacy." She pulls back and gives him a warm smile.

"It's nice to meet you both as well. Is there anything I can help with?" he asks.

She shakes her head. "No, I don't think so. Emma and I got most of it done last night and this morning, so you made it just in time. The food is coming out of the oven, and it's time for Van to carve the turkey."

"Okay. Well, it smells delicious in here. I can't wait to try it all."

I step into him and wrap my arm around his waist, tugging him into me. His arm wraps around my shoulders, and he leans down and kisses the top of my head.

My mom is watching us, eyes getting glassy.

"Let's eat, so we can be done when the game starts. Archie, you a Cowboys fan?" Dad asks him.

"That I am. Grew up a few hours south of Dallas."

"Glad to hear it; otherwise, we'd have to ask you to leave." He smiles over at Archie, who just laughs.

"I get it. I think I'd be disowned in my own home if I wasn't a Cowboys fan."

My mom walks between us. "Okay, everyone, grab a dish, and let's head to the dining room."

I let go of Archie and grab a dish off the counter, and Archie follows. Dad carves some turkey off and places it on a platter.

We sit in our seats, my parents at each end of the table, and I'm next to Archie on one side of the table.

"Do you want some water, darlin'?" Archie asks me.

"Yes, thank you." I put my hand on his knee under the table.

"Okay, let's pass this food around and get to it," Dad says.

We all take servings, and Archie has a little more than anyone else, which makes me smile. Dad says grace, and then we all start eating.

While we eat, my parents ask him questions about his family and general questions about football and where he sees the season going. I wasn't worried about Archie being able to handle it or feeling awkward. He's just so confident in who he is, and he has the ability to make people feel comfortable.

But I have a feeling some of the tougher questions are coming.

Once we've finished eating, my mom suggests we go sit in

the family room. She gets a coffee for herself and my dad. I go into the kitchen and get a bottle of water for me and Archie.

He and my dad are talking about football, commenting along with the commentators.

I take a seat next to Archie on the couch, then lean over and kiss his cheek. He puts his arm behind me and rests it on the back of the couch. I scoot into him a little more and place my hand on his leg.

My parents have never seen me behave this way, so I'm sure they're surprised by how affectionate I'm being in front of them. But the fact that Archie came today and has gotten along so easily with my family has driven me further into my feelings for him. Because I can't deny I'm falling for him hard. And it's not just for the baby. It's about us.

"So, Archie, I'm glad you and my daughter seem to get along nicely, but as her father, I need to know how you plan to take care of her and the baby." Dad sets his cup of coffee on the end table next to him.

When I look from my dad to Archie, he's nodding.

"Yes, of course. I completely understand why you're asking. Emma might have mentioned it, but I am declaring for the draft after this season is over. So, I intend to play professional football for as long as I can. Ideally, I would love to play for a team that isn't too far from my family. And now that Emma and I are creating our own family, I don't want to be away from her or the baby for long periods of time either. A lot of discussions need to be had between teams and my agent, but I'll do what I can to make that happen."

"Archie, I appreciate you telling us all of this, and really, we're excited for you and your future, but like you said, this involves our daughter, too, so I guess we're just trying to understand how Emma fits into the plan and how she can still follow her dreams too. And what happens if you get injured? What would you do to provide for the baby?" Mom says.

"Well, I can't speak for Emma, and I'd be afraid to do so."

We all laugh.

"Smart man." I lean over and give him a pat on the cheek.

"At the end of the day, I want Emma to be happy and also pursue her dreams. But the fact of the matter is that we are having a baby, so we need to figure out a way we can accomplish our dreams together, but also make sure we are giving our baby the best of us. As far as a backup plan if I get injured, I'd like to stay in the sports world in broadcasting or even coaching maybe. My family also owns a ranch, so there's that option too."

I clear my throat because this man is about to make me cry. "Mom and Dad, I know you're worried about all of this, and Archie and I have a lot to figure out for sure, which we'll likely have more answers for soon. But we've been spending a lot of time together, and I truly believe we will figure it all out as we get more information. There's still too much up in the air."

Archie takes my hand in his and squeezes gently.

"I will look at schools near where he'll be playing, and we'll make a plan together."

"You'd do that?" Archie looks at me with a surprised expression.

Dad shifts on the couch. "Well, wait a minute. I don't know how I feel about you uprooting your life, Emma, to follow Archie around. What if your romantic relationship with each other doesn't last? You'd be stuck all alone in a state you had no support in. You can't just uproot a child. There are laws, and ... well, this could get very messy."

There's that word I dread. Messy.

I want to create this family with Archie, no matter what our status is. That said, if this relationship continues on its path and he decides one day that he doesn't want me anymore, I'll be devastated. Being alone will be even more difficult.

However, my child needs to be near his or her father, and that notion currently trumps all other feelings I have.

Archie must feel the unease in my body at my father's questioning because he squeezes my hand and sits up to level with my father.

"Look, I care about your daughter, and I can't wait to be able to spend more time with her and get to know her as we go through this together. I'll do whatever it takes to be there for them both. She will never have to doubt me."

And ... my damn eyes are leaking again. Freaking hormones.

There's not much left to say after his declaration, so my parents seem satisfied by the answers he's given them for now. So, we watch the Cowboys game when it comes on after the half-time show, and then a few hours later, Archie needs to head back.

I'm debating on whether or not I want to go with him or stay here one more night.

After he says his goodbyes to my parents, I walk him out to his truck. "Thank you for coming today. And thanks for being a good sport with all the questions."

He opens the door of the truck and tosses his cowboy hat onto the passenger seat. When he turns around, he sits sideways on his seat, and then he reaches for me and pulls me closer so I'm standing between his legs. "You don't have to thank me; I should be thanking you. It was nice to meet your parents and get to know my baby's grandparents."

I wrap my arms around his shoulders. "I think they like you, so that's good." Leaning in, I kiss him. "I like you too, by the way."

"Is that right? Emma Tucker likes me? Hmm ... must be the orgasms." He grabs my ass and brings me into him so we're as close as we can be in this position. "I like you too." Then he kisses me and sucks on my bottom lip.

My mouth drops open slightly, and I'm about two seconds away from pushing him down on that seat and straddling him.

With a pop, he releases my lip and pulls back, smiling. "Are you coming back tomorrow?"

"Yes, I think so, but I'll let you know for sure."

"Okay, darlin'. I'll text you when I get home, but if you're asleep, I'll talk to you after practice." He smacks my ass lightly.

I step back from the truck, and he shifts to face the wheel.

"Bye, Archie."

"Bye, darlin'." He shuts the door and starts the engine.

I watch him drive away, missing him already. Maybe learning to depend on someone else isn't all that bad.

CHAPTER
THIRTEEN

ARCHIE

DECEMBER IS FLYING BY. Between wrapping up the semester—and really, my college career—practice, and games, I'm pretty much running on empty.

The brightest spot in my day is the time I get to spend with Emma. We've gotten into a pretty good routine together, and there's barely a night we don't spend together. I know her roommates like me, but I'm not sure they planned on having another roommate this year. And not one who eats as much as I do. But I do bring groceries, and I've even cooked for the girls a few times.

Although they haven't been around much lately either. Mia and Peyton are still hanging out with the basketball players; they've been around a few times and seem like decent guys. And Livi has been spending time with a guy from one of her classes. He's been over a bunch of times, but we don't really hang out with them.

Emma is nearing the halfway marker on the pregnancy and is slowly starting to show even though the doctor said she's still a little on the smaller side. She's hid it well with baggy clothes, but when we're alone, she doesn't hide it, and I get to see her gorgeous belly carrying my baby.

Tonight, my roommates and I exchanged gifts for Christmas. Casey got me a box of condoms. For a minute there, I thought Liam was gonna break and tell everyone about the baby, but he didn't.

It's getting harder for me not to tell my friends. I spend every day with them on and off the field. And I gotta admit, I'm getting even more excited the more Emma shows. It's becoming more real every day.

I just left my house after our gift exchange, and I'm on my way over to Emma's, but I made a quick stop at the store. She was craving some ice cream, and what my girl wants, she gets.

> Archie: I'm at the store now. Is there anything else you need before I go in?

She doesn't reply after a few minutes so I try her again.

> Archie: Darlin', I'm missing my girl, and I want to get this done so I can get to you. Do we need anything else?

Emma: Archie, don't tell me you miss me. Tell me you're outside my door with my ice cream and wearing gray sweatpants. It's about actions, babe.

This girl. Our appetite for each other hasn't lessened. If anything, we crave each other even more. And thankfully, Emma seems to be one of those pregnant women who wants sex all the time. Not complaining. Not at all.

> Archie: Be there in ten.

Emma: 🍆💦👀

Emma: Oh, wait! Grab some gummy worms.
And some Sour Patch Kids too.

I shake my head and laugh. She's been getting more cravings lately, and some I can get, but others are just weird. Like putting peanut butter on a pickle. I walked in on that in the kitchen one night and gagged, but she wolfed it down like it was the best thing she'd ever eaten.

Exactly ten minutes later, I'm knocking on her door. She opens it, wearing nothing but my Texas Forever T-shirt and, from what I can tell, no panties.

"Okay, so ice cream first or later?"

"Archie, I'm about to lick you like an ice cream cone, so dick first, sweet treats later." She grabs my shirt and pulls me in.

I wrap my free arm around her and lean in to kiss her. "Hi, baby."

"Hi," she says, smiling.

She takes the bag from my hand, and I follow her into the kitchen. With her back to me, I walk up behind her and run my hands up her sides and under her shirt. And I was right. No panties. Her back arches against me, and I take the opportunity to take ahold of her breasts, plucking her nipples.

I run my tongue up the side of her neck, and she tilts it to the other side to give me better access. I release one of her breasts and run it down over the swell of her belly to her bare pussy.

My hand grazes her, and I push my middle finger through her folds, finding her wet.

"Is my girl ready for my cock?"

She moans when I circle her clit with my thumb and nip at her neck. "Yes. Ahh! I need you, Archie." Her hips start moving with my hand.

"Come on. Let's go into the bedroom." I remove my hand from her pussy and take her hand in mine.

When we get to her bedroom, I pull her in, then close the

door. We walk together to the bed, and I drop her hand and reach for the hem of her shirt. I slide it up and over her head.

Her full tits bounce when she brings her arms back down. Bending slightly, I take both breasts in my hands and push them together. I run my tongue over one of her nipples, then suck it into my mouth.

"That feels so good, Arch. Suck a little harder."

She pushes her chest into me. Not that I need any encouragement. I could spend hours with these beauties.

I move to her other breast and nip, suck, nip while my other hand pinches her other nipple between my thumb and forefinger. When I release her nipple from my teeth, I turn her body and guide her to lie down on the bed.

She reaches her arms around my neck, pulling me into her and kissing me, tongue plunging deep into my mouth. I groan and move to settle my body between her legs.

I break the kiss and trail kisses down her neck, over her breasts. When I reach her stomach, I place my hands on either side and lean in to place a kiss there. I feel Emma's hands run through my hair. I look up at her and smile.

"Archie, you're going to be the best dad. I'm so lucky."

"I'm the lucky one." I place another kiss on her belly and continue kissing down to her pussy. I push her thighs apart. I lean in, flatten my tongue, and run it from her opening to her clit. Then I suck her nub, and it makes her hips lift.

"Holy hell, that feels good."

I hum against her opening, making her moan.

"Archie, lie down next to me. I want to do something." She tugs at my hair, which makes my hard-as-rock dick twitch against the bed.

I kneel and then scoot to the side of the bed I sleep on as Emma rolls to her side, then sits up. She reaches into her nightstand drawer and pulls out the hot-pink vibrator I've seen before but we've never used.

"What are you doing, darlin'? You want me to tease your pussy?"

"No, this is for you, not me."

"Uh … I'm not really curious about that, baby, but I'd be happy to try it out on you."

She leans in to kiss me. "Do you trust me?"

"Emma, darlin', of course I do, but, uh, what do you plan to do with it?"

Without a reply, she moves up and over me. Her pussy right over my face. I don't waste a minute and swipe my tongue through her slit. I reach up and grab her ass cheeks and pull them apart, then run my tongue from her clit to her opening.

She moans, then sets the dildo down on the bed next to her and takes ahold of my dick with one hand, sliding it up and down my shaft. I hear her spit, and then her wet hand moves along my erection, pumping slowly.

Her mouth wraps around the head, and she sucks, making me moan. When I pull her hips back down toward my mouth and I circle her clit with my tongue, she takes me deep into her mouth.

I'm so lost in the taste of her and the feel of her mouth on my dick that I barely register the sound of the vibrator clicking on. Just when I'm about to pull my mouth away from her to ask what she plans to do with it, she runs the vibrator along my balls and the underside of my cock.

"Fuck!" I move my mouth from her pussy and bite down on the inside of her thigh. "Emma, keep doing what you're doing."

Her mouth comes off my dick with a pop. "I will. Let me make you feel good."

Instead of replying, I thrust my hips toward her mouth and feel the vibrator run along my shaft again. Holy hell. I've never felt anything like this. It's like my mind doesn't know where to focus —her pussy or the tingle that's working at the base of my spine.

I run my tongue up and down her center, then thrust it in and out of her pussy. I can feel her muscles start to contract against my tongue. Knowing she's about to come and feeling her mouth move up and down my cock, along with the vibration on my balls, I'm ready to blow.

Her movements are less controlled so I know she's close. I brace my hands on her hips and move her up and down onto my face, thrusting my tongue inside of her.

She's moaning around the head, and she's dropped the vibrator next to my leg. I thrust inside her mouth and feel the pressure from my balls up my shaft.

I pull my mouth away from her as I start to come. My forefinger and middle finger replace my tongue, and I feel her orgasm squeeze me.

"Suck, Emma. Take my cock to the back of your throat. I want you to swallow every drop of my cum." I thrust one more time and spill into her mouth.

She sucks hard as she pulls off my cock. Taking every last drop.

Emma shifts and moves to lie down beside me. She reaches down and grabs the vibrator and turns it off. "Well, did it feel good?"

"Fuck yeah, it did. Never would have thought a pink dildo would work me up like that, but damn."

She breaks out in a deep laugh, and I roll over to pull her into me.

"I'm glad you find that funny, darlin'. I'd love to try it on you. Maybe a little ass play?"

She stops laughing and looks at me. "I mean, I never really had any interest in that, but I'm not opposed to trying it with you. But maybe that should wait until after the baby is born?"

I pucker my lips and nod. "Yeah, we can wait." Then I lean in and kiss her.

"Oh!" she gasps and puts her hands on her belly.

I sit up quickly. "What's wrong, darlin? Are you okay?"

She smiles and looks over at me with tears in her eyes. "I think I just felt the baby move!"

"Are you serious? Where? Show me where." I put my hand on top of one of hers.

Lying back and resting her back against the headboard, she takes my hands and moves them along her stomach, stopping right under her belly button. I feel a movement under my hand, and my eyes snap to hers.

"Did you feel it?" she asks me.

I nod and move my head closer to her stomach. "I already love you so much, little one. I promise I'll always take care of you." I kiss her stomach, and when I do, I feel another movement.

I hear a sniffle and look up at Emma.

"You okay? It doesn't hurt, does it?"

She shakes her head. "No, not at all. It feels a little like when you ride a roller coaster and there's a wave or flutter in your belly." A tear escapes the corner of her eye, but she wipes it away.

"Why are you crying, baby?" Keeping one hand on her stomach, I sit up and lean in to kiss her.

"Feeling the baby kick ... it's just surreal. Like, I've felt my body changing, and logically, I know it's all happening, but feeling the baby move is, like, whoa. You know what I mean? Like, there is a life inside of me."

"It's wild, for sure. I bet it's a weird feeling for you, but it's also really awesome." I kiss her again. "You're going to be an amazing mom, Em. Like, really amazing."

"You think so?"

For the first time since I met her, she looks uncertain.

"Fuck yes. You're going to be the best." I lie back on my pillow and pull her to rest her head on my chest.

"Hey, Arch. In case I haven't told you lately, I really like you." She's tracing the tattoos on my chest.

"Hey, Em. I really like you too." I kiss her on the top of her head.

"Oh shit! The ice cream! It's probably melting." She sits up.

"I got it. Do you still want some or wait until later?"

Her lips purse. "Hmm ... let's wait until later. I had a craving to put the gummies in the ice cream, but it's passed now."

I shake my head. "The regular or sour ones?"

"Uh, probably both, with the chocolate ice cream."

"Baby, that's not right."

"Archie, I literally cannot help it that the baby wants these things."

I rub my hand up and down her arm. "But can I remind you of all of them once the baby is born?"

"Absolutely not."

"Okay, fine." A rumbled laugh escapes me, and then I kiss the top of her head.

I run to put the ice cream in the freezer then climb back into bed with Emma. After a few minutes, I feel her breathing change and realize she's fallen asleep. Since she's lying on her side, I don't have a good angle to touch her stomach again, but I drift my fingers back and forth along her side, feeling the curve of her belly.

When I close my eyes, I think about what our future is going to look like, and I realize that not only do I see Emma in every scenario, but I see lots of babies. And damn if that doesn't make me smile.

CHAPTER
FOURTEEN

EMMA

ONE OF THE things I've been experiencing lately is vivid dreams. I read that it happens to some women during pregnancy. It's definitely happening to me, and not only are they vivid, but they're all sex dreams.

When I told Archie about it, he assured me that I could wake him up anytime.

I think his exact words were, "Darlin', if you feel the need to take a ride on my cock in the middle of the night, you go right ahead and hop on."

I can feel the rise and fall of his chest under my head, knowing he's in a deep sleep. And even though I know he doesn't mind, I start to move my hand across his chest to try to stir him awake.

Still naked from earlier, I move my other hand between my legs, and I'm definitely wet. Then I move my hand from between my legs and slide it along his semi-erect shaft. This man is hardly ever flaccid. Not that I'm complaining.

He shifts only slightly, and when I look at him, his eyes are still closed. I'm moving up and down his shaft lightly, just enough to get him hard. And I'm so turned on from my dream that I could probably get myself off by just working him over.

Once he's standing at full attention, I move to straddle his waist. Lifting up, I position his head at my opening and slide down his cock. I can't help the moan that escapes, and my head falls back as I get lost in this feeling.

I start to move my hips up and down, my head still tipped back, when I feel Archie's hands grab ahold of my hips. He starts to move me fast and deeper.

When I look down at him, I don't see the typical smirk, but I see an intensity in his stare, and I feel heat rush from my core right up to my cheeks. There are no words between us, but our eyes stay locked.

He brings one of his hands up to my breast and kneads it as I move up and down. My hands are resting on his chest, and I move them across his pecs, feeling the muscles contract under my touch.

His hand releases my breast, and he takes both of his hands and reaches around me to take hold of my ass. The position pushes me up a little further, so I lean down and kiss his slightly opened mouth. His breaths are getting faster, but I can tell he's trying to hold himself back.

I lean in again, running the tip of my tongue along his, mouths open. He takes my bottom lip between his teeth, pulls it in, and sucks. When he releases it, I slant my mouth over his and circle my tongue around his.

My orgasm is close, so I sit back up to feel him as deep as I can. He must sense that I'm close because he moves one hand between our bodies and circles my clit with two fingers.

I can feel my pussy starting to contract around him, and he thrusts up deeper into me as I squeeze his cock. When I look down at him, he's watching our bodies where we're joined, but he must sense my eyes on him because he looks up.

He pushes up into me and holds me still, and I can feel his dick jerk inside me as he comes. I don't know if it's partially hormonal from the pregnancy or what, but I'm totally here for these intense orgasms.

Once my orgasm subsides, I lie down on top of him, chest to chest. I tip my head up to kiss his jaw. I don't stay like this for long because while my belly is still not big, it is a little uncomfortable.

After a few minutes, I sit up and lift off of him, and his cock slides out. I lean over and give Archie a kiss, then turn on my side, back facing him. He curls up behind me and wraps his arm around my waist, holding my stomach.

I feel light kisses on the back of my neck and hear a whispered, "Perfect," before I drift back to sleep.

CHAPTER
FIFTEEN

ARCHIE

EMMA IS GOING TO HER PARENTS' to spend the holiday with them. Since her hometown is so close to campus, she plans to come back for the rest of break and stay in her apartment. She invited me to come with her, but I can't leave because of training. So, today, I'm giving her a gift before she leaves.

I'm kind of surprised she hasn't found it. I put it in her closet a few weeks ago, waiting to give it to her for Christmas.

The other girls have already left for break, so it's just the two of us. I got up early and made her some breakfast. I joke around with my roommates that I'm like Betty Crocker, but no lie ... I'm a decent cook. So, I've made Emma some protein pancakes, sliced up some fruit, and made some orange juice. I tried eggs the other day, and even though she hasn't gotten sick in a while, the smell turned her stomach, so protein pancakes it is.

After setting the table, I walk down the hall to wake her up. Now, under normal circumstances, I would let her sleep, but we're both on a schedule today. I need to get to the field, and she needs to get to her parents'.

I sit on the edge of the bed and watch her sleep for a few

minutes. She has one leg out of the sheets, which exposes her ass. I can't help but run my hand over it, and it makes her stir.

"Hey, Em. Breakfast is ready." I lean down and kiss her cheek.

She rolls onto her back and brings her arms over her head and stretches. The sheet, which was only partially covering her to begin with, shifts, exposing her breasts with her stretch.

Again, I can't help myself, and I reach out and cup them. I lean down and kiss one. "Good morning." Then I kiss the other. "Good morning."

Emma gasps. "Did you just say good morning to my boobs?"

"Sure did, baby. They deserve to be acknowledged too."

"Archie, you're too much, but I love it."

She sits up, then reaches over and grabs my dick. "Good morning."

I belt out a laugh. "We will not make it out of this room if you don't let go of my cock, Em."

"Oh, fine. I am hungry anyway. I should eat and then get ready to head out. What time do you have to be at the field?"

"I don't need to go until eleven, but I want to have a little time with you before we leave." I stand up, bend over, and lift her out of the bed.

"You know I'm capable of getting out of bed by myself, right?" She rests her head on my shoulder.

"I do know that, but since I can't fuck you right now, I'm gonna hold you." I carry her into the bathroom and set her down. "I put your robe on the hook behind the door, not that I want you to wear it, but I know you don't like to sit bare-assed on the furniture."

She lifts up to kiss me. "Thanks. I do not enjoy that, no. Although I'm surprised you have joggers on. If the girls aren't here, you usually stay in your boxers if you have them on or shorts."

"I can't let you tempt me this morning. I had to cover my

goods. You're a temptress." I smack her ass. "Now pee and come out so we can eat."

"Okay, I'll be out in a few."

I walk back into her room and into the closet and grab the bag off of the top shelf. She's still in the bathroom, so I make my way to the table and set the gift bag on top.

She walks down the hallway toward me. "What is this?"

I stand and pull out her chair. "Well, it's pancakes, fruit, juice."

"You know that's not what I meant, smart-ass. What's in the bag?" She reaches over and takes it from the center of the table.

I touch her forearm to pause her movement. "It's just a little something for Christmas."

"Oh, okay, let me go grab yours." She starts to stand.

"You can give me mine after." I lean forward and kiss her. "Go ahead and open it, unless you want to wait until after we eat."

She pulls out the tissue paper lying on the top and sets it on the table. When she puts her hand into the bag, she pauses and looks over at me with a smile, and I give her a wink.

She moves the bag slightly off the table to pull out my jersey in her hand. Turning the shirt around to the back, she sees my name and number sixty-nine. "Archie, I love it."

"Good. I'm glad. I just thought even if you can't be at the game, you can still wear my jersey if y'all are watching here or whatever." I shrug.

All of what I'm saying is true, but I also want her to wear it because she's mine. She's been mine since that very first night we met.

She stands and takes off her robe, then pulls on the jersey. It hangs long, covering her ass. She walks over to me and stands between my legs. My hands immediately slide up her bare legs.

"This is seriously sweet. And the least I can do is represent my guy, right?" She leans down and kisses me, slipping her tongue inside.

My hands move, truly, of their own accord, up the back of her thighs, and I take hold of her juicy ass.

Her legs spread over mine, and she straddles me. The tip of my dick is already peeking out of my joggers, so it doesn't take much for her to reach down and pull them down enough to free me. Then she puts one hand on my shoulder to brace herself, and with the other, she positions my cock at her entrance. When she sinks down, we both groan.

"Fuck yes, darlin'."

"Archie, did you really give me your jersey just because you want me to wear it for the game? Or did you give it to me because you want to claim me?" Arms wrapped over my shoulders, she starts moving her hips back and forth.

My hands move up her back, and I pull her into me closer. I lick a path from her throat, over her chin, and then slip my tongue into her mouth. I slide one hand up to the back of her neck and grip it. Then I pull my mouth away from our kiss and look her in the eyes while she rides me.

"Yeah, darlin'. I want you to wear my name on your back." I lift my hips and thrust up into her heat. "Because you're mine."

"Fuck yes, I am. Just like you're mine." Her pace quickens as she starts to bounce up and down my cock.

"That's it, baby. Ride me. Take me as deep as you can." I continue to thrust up as she comes down.

Then she slows her pace and starts rolling her hips, grinding. "You make me feel like I can't get enough. I want you inside me all the time. Your dick was made for me, Arch."

"All for you, Em. It's all yours. Now come for me. I want to feel you soak my cock." I move one hand between us and circle her clit with my thumb, and she gasps. " That's it, baby."

My hand still on the back of her neck, I pull her in, and I kiss, lick, suck on her neck as she starts to come. I can't hold back anymore. I push up into her as deep as I can, and I feel my cum shoot into her hot, tight pussy.

Once we've both stopped coming, she pulls back and smiles at me. "Thank you for my jersey."

"You're welcome, darlin'. It looks good on you. Especially when you're riding me."

She smiles and lifts off my dick, and when I look down, I see my cum dripping out. I hold her still and take two fingers and push it back inside of her.

"Arch, I'm already pregnant." She smiles.

"I know, but I want to stay inside you as long as I can." I wink at her, then bring my fingers to her lips. "Open." Her mouth opens, but she takes my hand in hers and licks my fingers clean. "That's fucking hot, darlin'. You need to do that again sometime." I grab her hand and pull her in for one more kiss.

She smiles when we stop kissing and moves back to her chair. Pulling the hem down past her ass, she sits.

"Worried about leaving little Archies on the chair?"

"The little Archies are all mine." She winks at me.

"Damn straight. Now eat. My baby needs food."

"Okay, okay. This all looks really good. Thank you for making me breakfast."

"Anytime, baby."

"Oh, so tell me about how the present exchange went last night? What did you get?" she asks.

I chuckle. "Well, funny enough, Casey got my name and bought me a box of condoms."

"You're kidding! It's kind of funny though." She takes a bite of her fruit.

"I mean, yeah, it is. But I can't lie. It's getting harder not to tell them about you and the baby. I'm with them all the time, and they're my best friends. I mean, Liam knows, but it's not like I can talk to him about it. We're either at practice with everyone or someone is always home."

"Sorry, Archie. I know I'm asking a lot to keep it quiet, and we really won't be able to for much longer. I guess I've just been putting off how to manage my scholarship and figuring out what my choices are going to be once my coach finds out I'm pregnant."

"I know, and I get it. But I'm crazy about you, and every day that I look at you and I see your belly growing, I want everyone to know you and that baby are mine. You're gonna need to figure out how to tell your coach soon, Em. Your season starts up right after break."

She nods and pulls in a deep breath, then blows it out. "I know. Let's just get through the holidays and your game, and then we can figure out what to do from there, I guess."

"Okay. We can do that."

"Wait, before I forget to give it to you, let me go get your gift."

She pushes away from the table and walks down the hall to her room. Seconds later, she comes out, holding a small box.

"Thank you, darlin. You didn't have to get me anything though." I take the box from her hands.

"Well, actually, it's kind of perfect, so just open it." She sits back down in her seat and takes a sip of her juice.

"Okay, here we go." I rip off the red-and-white striped wrapping paper and let it fall to the floor. I lift the lid and see a white bundle with a small number sixty-nine and my last name above it. I pull it out of the box, and it unrolls. "Holy shit, this is cute. Is this one of those baby T-shirts?"

Emma snorts out a laugh. "It's called a onesie. I saw something on Instagram the other day, and it was a couple doing a gender reveal with a similar concept. I just thought it was cute, and then the idea of making it a little jersey hit me, and I thought you might like it."

"Baby, I don't like it; I love it. After he or she is born, you can both wear your jerseys together." I set it down on the table. "Thank you. It's perfect."

"You're welcome. I'm glad you like it. How funny that we both got jerseys though?" She picks up her fork and takes a spear of melon.

"Pretty funny, but I'm also thinking about how spoiled this baby is going to be. So, this means I can get some things for the baby?" I lift up the onesie again and trace my name with my finger.

"I think we should probably start getting some things here and there. My mom and I started a small list at Thanksgiving, but you and I will have to make a bigger list later for sure."

I lay the onesie over my shoulder and move the box off the table. We've been having fun together, but this moment right here just brought reality crashing in. A baby is coming in months, and our world is about to change in more ways than one.

"Em, I think we need to talk about what we're going to do. I meant what I said to you and your parents. I fully intend to stand by you so you can also accomplish your goals and dreams, but I also want to make sure we are on the same page. I know it's uncertain right now about where I'll be, but what are you thinking about all of this?"

She sets her fork down. "Well, I have been thinking about it, and I think it makes the most sense for me to transfer to a school near where you will be playing. I mean, it would be great if that ends up being Dallas since the University of Texas Southwestern is there and has an amazing program in my field of study. But it would be helpful to know what the other possibilities might be just so I can start thinking about what to do with school. I have to apply and get accepted into a program."

"And I wish I knew. I think once we get through the playoffs, I'll know who has serious interest in me, then, of course, after the combine. But my agent knows I want to stay close to home if at all possible. I just hope the Cowboys are watching and have some interest in me."

"Okay, so I think the only thing we can do right now is just know that my path will kind of depend on where you go. If you think Dallas is a strong contender, then I'll go ahead and get all the information for my possibilities there. Once you have a better idea about the other options, I'll look around. But I've also been thinking that it might be a smart idea for me to take a break for a year when the baby is born." She looks down. "It's not that I'm putting anything on hold for myself, but with you starting with a new team and us having a new baby, it might be smart to settle into that before I dive into a transfer." She looks up at me and tilts her head. "What do you think?"

"Darlin', I don't want you to do anything you don't want to do. So, if you think that's the best thing for you and the baby, then I'll support you completely. I want to make things as easy as possible for all of us. But hear me when I say, I want you with me, no matter where it is. So, anything I can do to help with school, tuition, you name it, I'm going to take care of it and you."

"I can't ask you to do that." She shakes her head.

"You aren't asking me. I'm telling you that it's what I want."

"Okay." She gives me a crooked smile. "So, I suppose we're at least on our way to having a plan now?"

I nod slowly. "I think so, as much as we can anyway."

"All right then."

CHAPTER
SIXTEEN

ARCHIE

WALKER MADE it through the semifinals, then on to the quarterfinals. While this isn't my first playoff season, it feels different because it will be my last. Since we made it to the championship game, I'm still technically enrolled at the university, but I don't need to attend classes. None of us do really. The school takes these types of games seriously because they bring in a lot of money.

We arrived in Miami early today. We got settled in at the hotel and watched some film before going to the stadium.

After dropping our gear in the locker room, we move out to the field. We'll be running some drills, but we also have to do commercial shots. Like the ones you see on TV when they talk about the players and the guys are twirling balls around in front of a bunch of strobe lights in a hallway. Or at least that's what I think it looks like, and it kind of does in real life too. Then our media coordinator told me one of the reporters from ESPN wants to interview me. It's not uncommon for us to be interviewed before big games like this, and this season, I've had to do more.

There's a lot riding on this game for me in terms of what NFL teams will be watching me. But I'm trying to soak it all in and have a good time too. This is my last collegiate game. My parents and brothers are here for the game, but I probably won't see them until after the game tomorrow since they're staying at a different hotel. Having them here for this means everything. I wish Emma could be here, too, but I know it's hard for her to travel with her school schedule, and training has started for golf as well.

I see Beck and Casey in front of me. I walk to them and put them both in a headlock. "Hey, dickheads. Can you believe this? This is the tits. We're gonna blow those Southeast fuckers away —ya feel me? Oh shit, hold up. Where's Pitz?"

I look around and spot him on the other side of the field with Callaway and the QB coach. I put two fingers in my mouth and whistle, causing half of the team to look my way. "Pitz, get your ass over here for a minute."

Liam runs over and behind me, jumping on my back. "You dick. I was going over a few new plays with the coach."

I take hold of his shoulders and easily flip him off my back. I don't let him hit the ground though. "Can't have you getting injured before your last game as a Stallion."

"Ow, asshole. That hurt. I don't have pads on yet, you dick," he says, shoving me.

I laugh at his effort to move me. "Okay, fellas. Let's be real for a few minutes. This is my last college game. Linson, I didn't know when I met you—what, two years ago now?—that you would become one of my best friends. You're a hell of a player, but an even better friend. And, King, you level out Linson's moodiness, which is why we've kept you around."

They laugh.

"I'm just playin'. You would do anything for any of us, and that's appreciated more than you know, King. We know you have our backs, no matter what, on and off the field.

"Now, Pitzy, we've been playing together for three seasons.

You've been my QB, my wingman, and one of my best friends. I'm really going to miss seeing your ugly mug every day.

"Okay, enough sappy shit. Let's bring it in." I hold out my arms and wave them into a circle. "Come on, fuckers. Let's do this."

We stand together, shoulder to shoulder, arms around each other.

"Here's to the games we've won together and the one we're about to win. And here's to our brotherhood. We might not be related by blood, but I wouldn't want to do this without you guys. Now let's go get that fucking trophy!"

They yell, "Hell yeah!"

"Hold up. Let me get a pic of the four of us on the field." Beck pulls out his phone, then hands it to Pitz.

We all scrunch together to fit in the frame.

After a few snaps, I squeeze Pitz's shoulder and start to walk back toward the tunnel leading to the press area. "I'll see you all later." I lift my arm and wave to them.

Before I walk into the room though, I take out my phone from my back pocket and text Emma.

> Archie: You should see this. It's the big show, darlin'.

> Emma: I wish I could see it! I'm so excited for you. What are you doing now?

> Archie: I'm about to go into an interview, but I just wanted to text you first.

> Emma: Well, that was sweet. Go do your interview and then call me when you're back at the hotel later.

> Archie: Okay, will do. You feeling good?

> Emma: Yep, the baby has been kicking a lot today.

The baby has been more active lately, and we've been feeling him or her move and kick. It seems to be reactive to our voices, but also after Emma eats. It's the coolest thing ever.

> Archie: Give your belly a rub for me. I miss you.

Emma: Okay, Daddy. I will rub my belly for you.
And I miss you too.

> Archie: You called me Daddy.

Emma: Go to your interview, Arch.

> Archie: But now I'm getting a boner because you called me Daddy.

Emma: Not in the way you're taking it! LOL.
Bye, Archie. 😘

I pocket my phone and smile. I'm not really getting a boner. Sometimes, I just like to mess with her to see what she says. Luckily for me, we both have a pretty dirty sense of humor, so she's never really shocked by the things I say.

Twenty minutes later, I stand and thank the reporter, then head out to find out where I'm supposed to be next. I'm starting to get pumped about this game, and I just want today to end so we can win tomorrow.

The adrenaline pumping through me right now is electric. I'm ready to get out on the field and kick some ass. This is our time. This is my last college game, and I want a win.

The music from the band is loud, the fans are cheering, and we're ready to play. From where we're standing at the entry of the tunnel, we can only see the pyrotechnics, our cheerleaders, and the mascots. Not being able to see much builds the anticipation.

Bo, Liam, and Coach are standing just in front of me, ready to lead the way out on the field. I'm standing next to Beckham, Casey on his other side. The buzz in my veins is getting stronger, and I can't stand still. I want to get my team as pumped up as I am.

I turn in a circle and yell, "Let's fucking go! Who are we?"

"STALLIONS!" the team yells.

"What are we gonna do today?"

"WIN!"

That's better. I want to feel the energy of the team. I want them to be hungry for this win like I am.

"Let's go, baby! Linson, I got you, man. I won't let anyone get by me today." I smack Beck's helmet, then look at Casey. "King, you get the ball, and you run like your life depends on it!"

"You know it, baby. Let's GO!"

Casey and I clasp hands, and I pull him in for a chest bump.

Our fight song starts playing, which signals that it's about time to charge the field.

"Please welcome the Walker University Stallions!"

As I run out, I look around at the fans and can't help but bounce my way to the bench, raising my arms up and down, trying to get the fans to cheer louder.

Once I reach the bench, I lift my helmet up enough to get a better look around the stadium. These are moments you never forget. Playing football at this level is a privilege, and there isn't a day that goes by that I'm not grateful that I get to play and that I've stayed healthy in the three years I've played at Walker.

After the national anthem and the rest of the ceremonies, it's showtime. I go out to center field with Liam for the coin toss. We call heads and select to defer, which means we'll get first pick in the second half.

We jog back over to the sideline together and watch as the defense takes the field. After the first snap of the ball, we can tell this game is going to be a battle. They're good, but we're better. Now it's time to prove it.

After a fourth down by Southeast, it's time for me and my squad to get on the field. We are one of the best, if not the best, offense in college football. We utilize a spread offense, which relies on a tight end, three receivers, and a running back. This type of offense helps to give us the ability to make variations and a quick strike approach.

In the huddle, Bo calls an inside zone play. Which means he'll pass it to Beck, and then he'll run it around the right side of the line and try to get the first down. I need to make sure he gets through the hole and down the field.

Once we're on the line of scrimmage, I eye up the defensive player across from me.

"Hey, fifty-six! We gonna be here all day, baby. I like this kind of party. You ready for me, baby?"

Taunting the other team is one of my favorite things to do. It gets in their head, and they make mistakes, or it pisses them off, and we can really put on a show.

"Fuck you, Griff. You can't hurt this! I'm a machine, yo! I'll put you in the dirt," he answers.

"Okay, son. Okay. Let me see you try." I raise both of my hands and wave them toward me.

Bo snaps the ball, and the play is in motion. I leap across the line and grab fifty-six—who I know is David Wilson from watching film and seeing him on TV this season. It doesn't take much for me to knock the shit out of him and lay him on his ass.

"Welcome home, son!" I jump off him and look back over my shoulder at him as he gets up. I smirk, then blow him a kiss.

"That's cute, you trying to hit. You hit me here"—I pat my chest—"and I didn't go nowhere."

Chris Schuster, one of my linemen, bumps me with his shoulder, and he's laughing. "You razzing him already, or did he start in first?"

"Who, me?" I point at myself and smile.

Bo calls another play—for him to make a long pass to Casey and get him in for the touchdown. But once the ball is snapped, their defense reads the play, and Casey is covered so there's no way he can get the ball. With no other options, Bo runs through an opening in the line and takes off down the field, giving us our first touchdown of the game.

We go on and off the field with little progress in the game the rest of the first quarter.

But in the second quarter, Casey catches a rocket from Bo and runs it in for another touchdown, giving us the lead by one touchdown.

During that play, Wilson tried and failed to lay me out.

"Fifty-six, you gonna take me out? You've been giving me more hugs than my girlfriend gives me. Hey, I know it's hard, but you signed up for this."

He shakes his head at me and turns to walk off the field. But I point at him and look at his teammates.

"Hey, you guys might want to try somebody else at left tackle. Son, you gotta do better than this." And then I jog off the field, laughing. I fucking love this game.

After halftime, the game moves fast. We're now in the final seconds of the game and losing—twenty-eight to twenty-four. We need one more touchdown to win.

We're bloody, tired, and ready to take this game. We won't give up. We came to win.

Bo calls a swing pass that will give Beck the ball, which means it's my job to seal the outside of the D end in order for it to work.

"Okay, boys, this is ours! Let's finish this now! We won't need a fourth down! All right, trips right, two swings, X left, shotgun, on one!" Bo claps once.

I see the Bulls shift into a blitz, which is what we want in order for our play to work.

Bo calls, "SET," and I start to move with my line into pass blocking before shifting to the right to zone block.

The ball is tossed to Beck, and he runs down the field and right into the end zone. I push off the defensive player and jump back.

"Help is on the way, boys! Don't you worry; help is on the way!"

Then I run my ass down to the end zone to celebrate with my team, tossing my helmet off along the way.

When I reach Beck, I lift him up, and we're all cheering, screaming, jumping up and down. Helmets flying, guys crying, and then fans start rushing the field.

After that, everything feels like it happens so fast. We're gathered to go to the stage where the trophy presentation will be. Because I'm one of the captains, I jump up onto the stage. We've been given hats and shirts to wear.

I haven't been able to find my parents and brothers yet, but I'm sure they're making their way onto the field.

Coach comes over to me and hugs me. "We fucking did it, Griff!"

"Hell yeah, we did, Coach! Let's go, baby!" I lift him in a bear hug, and he just laughs until I put him down.

The presentation starts, and I finally spot my family to the left of the stage, all smiles and yelling my name. Mama has tears in her eyes, and she's holding on to my dad. I wish Emma were here to see this too. I want to share all of these moments with her.

I'm awarded the Offensive MVP of the game. After I get my trophy, I find my teammates and point to them, then tap my chest. I love these guys. They've been like family to me.

When the presentation ends, I'm directed to a few reporters

for interviews. Once I'm done, I make my way over to my family, waiting by the exit.

I run up to my mom and lift her up into a hug. "We did it, Mama!"

She's laughing and crying. Then I set her down, and she cups my face with her hands.

"We are so proud of you, Archie! You were amazing out there today."

Dad works his way in and wraps me in a hug. "So proud of you, son!"

Then each of my brothers hugs and congratulates me.

"I need to go get cleaned up, and then I think the team is having a banquet or something at our hotel. The families are invited, so y'all head that way, and I'll meet you there."

"Okay, we'll meet you there then. Love you so much, Archie!" Mama gives me another hug.

Then I turn and wave at them one last time before I head into the tunnel that takes me to the locker room.

When I get in there, there's beer, champagne, music blasting. It's like a party in here, and I fucking love it!

Tempting my fate by pulling my phone out of my locker to take pictures with my team and record some video, I see a text message from Emma, saying congratulations, but I can't see the whole message because Pitz dumps a beer over my head.

After about thirty minutes or so, Coach tells us to get cleaned up so we can head back to the hotel for the banquet. We all shower, pack up, and head to the bus.

Once I settle in my seat, I pull my phone back out and open Emma's text.

> Emma: Congratulations, Arch! I'm so fucking proud of you!
>
> *picture of her in her jersey*
>
> Emma: Call me as soon as you can!

> Archie: Hey, darlin'. You still up? We just got on the bus.

My phone rings, and I see Emma's name on the screen. I'm sitting alone right now, and the team is still loud, so no one is paying attention to me.

"Hey, baby. I didn't wake you, did I?"

"Hey, no, not at all. I've been waiting for you to call. I did something crazy."

"Crazier than that time I caught you talkin' to the toaster and chanting, 'Come on, toaster. I know you can do it'?"

"How embarrassing. I was late to class and needed to get some food in my belly. I thought you were still asleep."

"I was hovering in the corner, waiting to see which inanimate object you'd talk to next."

Her laugh echoes through the phone, and I find I'm smiling like a fool, just listening to her.

"God, I miss you."

"Well, that's good to hear because ... I'm actually here!" she squeals.

"You're *here*? As in *here in Miami* here?"

"I couldn't get a room at the hotel you're in, but I'm, like, one block away. I know you have some stuff to do with the team, but if you can sneak over after, I would love to celebrate with you!"

"Are you serious? Why didn't you tell me? I would have gotten you seats with the families of the team."

"It was a last-minute decision, and I didn't want to ruin any game-day rituals you have. You get all caveman when I'm around, and I knew you'd be focused on where I was sitting and if I was okay—"

"I can't believe you came to Miami."

"It was weird. I was sitting in my parents' house and telling them about your big game when it dawned on me that I should be with you. I've never done anything spontaneous like this. Ever."

"Ever?" I ask her, knowing full well there was a time a few short months ago when she was very spontaneous.

"Okay, well, not hop-on-a-flight-to-Miami spontaneous."

"Darlin', you just made my day ten times better than it already was!" I laugh.

She giggles. "Well, I'm glad. I wanted to be here for you. This is a big deal, and I couldn't miss it or the chance to wear your jersey at an actual game."

"Fuck me. I can't wait to see you in it."

"I sent you a picture. Did you get it?"

"Not the same. Not the same at all."

"Okay, well, lucky for you, you'll get to see it in person! Do you know what time you can come over, or do you want me to meet you somewhere? Livi and Mia are here with me, but they have their own room. They're planning on heading out to the bars soon."

"Fuck. There's an event when we get back to the hotel. I wish you could come with me; it's for the team and our families. I had to give them a list beforehand, but I'm sure I could add you on if you want to come. I would love it if you did. My entire family is here, and my parents got a suite. We plan to head back to their room after the dinner event thing. I would really like for you to meet them."

"I definitely want to meet your parents. Why don't you go to the banquet and I can meet you all after? Does that work?"

"Really? You'll come meet them? My mom is going to lose it. I apologize in advance for any smothering or my crazy brothers."

"Why don't you celebrate with your team for a bit? While the girls get ready to go, I'm gonna rest first because the travel and the excitement of the game was a lot. But I can't wait to meet your family. And, Archie, I'm so excited for you! I'm glad I could get here to see it."

"Me too, darlin'. I'll just text you when we're wrapping up."

"Sounds good to me. I'll be waiting." She makes a kiss sound and disconnects.

The next few hours are going to be brutal. I want to see my family and spend time with the team, but I really want to go see my girl too.

She's become the person I want to share all of these big moments with, as well as the little ones. And I can't wait to see her in my jersey, my baby in her belly … yeah, this night needs to end fast.

CHAPTER
SEVENTEEN

EMMA

BEING at the game meant more to me than I'd realized when I booked the ticket. It wasn't just about showing up; it was about showing *him* I'm here. For him. For this baby. For us. He's shown up for me in ways no one else ever has. He deserved to see someone in the stands just for him. I wish I'd realized it days ago, but I'm here now, and that's what matters.

I've seen Archie play before, but this time was different. Now that he's mine—now that we're *real*—it's like I felt every hit in my own bones. Every time he pulled himself up off the ground, I had to remember how to breathe. And when they won? God, the happiness on his face was everything.

But it's been almost two hours since I saw him after the game. I've been scrolling the team's feed, screenshotting every glimpse of him. And even in the photos, grinning with his helmet under one arm, there's still something else there. A shadow behind his eyes. A weight I'm just starting to notice.

I'm getting anxious to see him, so I put my phone down and head into the bathroom. Wouldn't hurt to brush my teeth, hair, and maybe do a quick wash of my face.

My phone buzzes. FaceTime.

"Hi, baby," he says, and my chest immediately loosens.

"Hey. Did you have fun?"

"Emma!" someone calls from behind him—blond, tall, and full of charm.

"Hi, um … Ace?"

"Aston," he corrects with a wink. "The better-looking twin."

"Oh no." I laugh. "Definitely Archie's brother."

Archie pushes him aside. "Go away," he mutters, half amused, half feral. He steps into the hotel bathroom and closes the door for privacy. "I'm coming to get you."

"I can just meet you there," I offer. "I'll call while I walk—"

"Emma." His voice drops into something low and resolute. "You are not walking anywhere alone. Not in a strange city. Not at night. I'm coming to get you. Be ready."

I swallow hard. That tone. It should annoy me, but it doesn't. It lands somewhere deep. Safe.

"Okay," I say, quieter now. "I'll be downstairs."

"Damn right you will." His eyes soften. "Can't wait to see you, darlin'."

When we hang up, I stare at my reflection. Heart fluttering, lips curved into a smile I didn't know I was wearing. He's stubborn, yeah. But he's mine. And this caveman thing? It's kind of hot.

Looking in the mirror, I run my fingers through my hair. I'm not sure why I'm starting to feel worried about how I look. Overall, I'm a confident gal. But meeting his parents? This is a big deal.

I swipe on some lip gloss, grab my coat, and head for the lobby.

Ten minutes later, I step outside just as Archie rounds the corner with another guy—I think it's his brother Aiden—striding toward me like he's afraid I'll vanish if he blinks.

"Hey—" I start to say, but he cuts me off by pulling me into his arms, lifting me off my feet.

"You shouldn't be out here alone." His voice is rough against my ear. "Couldn't relax, knowing you were walking."

"I was fine—"

He pulls back just enough to look at me. "Don't care. You're mine. And you're carrying my baby. That means you don't get to be *fine* out in the dark. Not on my watch."

I should bristle. But I don't. Because the truth is, it's been a long time since someone cared enough to be this ... intense about me. My parents have always erred on the side of caution, but this is different. It's Archie. He doesn't smother. He shields.

"I'm glad you came," I whisper.

He brushes his lips over my forehead. "I'm glad you came."

"I should have made this plan days ago—"

"All that matters is you're here now." He holds his mouth to my skin a beat longer than usual and then presses his forehead to mine. "I'm the luckiest motherfucker alive."

"Hate to break this up, but Mama is going to lose it if we make her wait any longer to meet Emma."

Archie releases me and sets me down. "Aiden, this is Emma. Emma, this is Aiden."

"It's so nice to meet you, Aiden. Archie talks about y'all all the time."

"Nice to meet you too, Emma. The family is pretty anxious to meet you, so we'd better get back."

"Ha! Anxious is an understatement. I think they're more excited to meet you than they are about my win." Archie looks down at me with an expression I can't read.

"You okay?" I ask softly.

"I am now." He glances at me. "You showing up tonight? That meant everything, Emma. You don't even know."

As we walk, Archie tells me bits about the game—how the second quarter nearly gave him a heart attack—and I laugh. But I don't miss the way he rolls his shoulder. He took a few good hits earlier, one that had me gasping from the stands.

The walk is short, but he stops a few strides before his hotel's entrance.

"Okay. Fair warning. My family. I know they're a lot," he says. "Loud. Physical. All up in your business."

"Sounds like you."

He smirks. "Exactly. They'll love you. Just … be warned. My mom might cry. My brothers will flirt. And my dad'll probably try to feed you."

"Bring it on."

Archie holds the door open for me. We walk into the building and take the elevator up to the seventh floor. As we exit the elevator, we see Liam Pitz coming out of a room.

"Griff! What up, man? Aiden, as always, excellent to see you." He walks up to us and gives Aiden one of those bro hugs and pounds his back.

"Pitzy, good to see you too, man. Congrats on the win."

"Thanks. It was a good game." He turns toward me and Archie.

"Emma, this is Liam Pitz, my roommate and teammate." As Archie says the words, I hear a falter in his voice but ignore it, just as Archie does as he slaps that big, beautiful smile on his face.

I hold out my free hand. "Hey, Liam. I'm Emma. It's nice to meet you."

"My guy!" Liam says, giving Archie a backslap before turning to me. "So, this is *the* Emma. Hi, I'm Liam."

Liam's grin is genuine as he looks at me and then to Archie. "Man, look at you. Championship ring and a beautiful girl. I'm happy for you."

When Liam goes to hug Archie, I try to step away, but Archie squeezes my hand. Won't let go. My heart tugs a little, and I'm not sure why.

"You heading out to party?" Archie asks him.

"Yeah, I just wanted to say goodbye to my parents before

they leave in the morning. I assume you're taking Emma to meet the family?"

"Yep, and we'd better get in there before they all pile into the hallway," Aiden chimes in.

"Okay, y'all have fun. Emma, nice to meet you. Take care of my guy here."

"I'll do my best." I feel a little heat spring to my cheeks when I smile at him.

I do want to take care of Archie, like he takes care of me. And these last few days apart have made me realize just how deep my feelings have gotten for him.

Liam walks over to the elevator as we walk down the hall. Aiden pulls out a card from his pocket and unlocks the door. I can hear people on the other side talking. Loudly.

Once we're inside, the volume hits me like a wave. Laughter, voices, movement—it's a lot.

"We're back!" Aiden calls out.

A shorter-than-me blonde woman comes barreling toward me. "Emma! Oh my word, aren't you pretty? Archie, those pictures you sent me did not do her justice. I'm Alicia, and I couldn't be more excited to meet you."

She wraps me in her arms, so I let go of Archie's hand to return her embrace.

"Hi, Mrs. Griffith. I'm happy to meet y'all too." I turn back and look at Archie, who has the biggest smile on his face.

"No, no. Call me Alicia. Mrs. Griffith is my mother-in-law, but even she won't let you call her that. Come meet the rest of my boys since you've already met Aiden."

A tall, middle-aged man with brownish hair stands from the couch. "Emma, it's so nice to meet you. I'm Archie's dad, Shane." He leans in to hug me.

I'm not used to all the hugging. My family isn't all that touchy-feely.

"Nice to meet you, Shane."

"These are the twins, Ace and Aston."

They both stand and take turns hugging me.

"And this is Austin, and Jesse is the baby of the bunch."

"Mama, I'm not a baby." Jesse shakes his head as he leans in to hug me. "Nice to meet you, Emma."

"Nice to meet all of you." I feel and see Archie's tattooed arms come around my waist, and he kisses the back of my head.

"All right, now you can all settle down. Let's give her a minute to breathe." He places a kiss just under my ear.

I catch his mom's eye, and she has her hands together, covering her mouth, but drops them when I smile at her.

"Emma, would you mind if I felt your stomach?"

The question stuns me a little. It's really just been me and Archie, and the realization that there are other people excited about the baby hits me full force.

"Oh, of course!"

Archie's arms drop, but he steps to my side when his mom comes up to me.

She places her hands on either side of my stomach. It surprises me how tender it feels. How real. Her hands are gentle.

Her voice cracks. "This is just a miracle. Hi, baby. I'm your Mimi, and I'm going to love you so hard. I already have your room ready at the ranch. We're gonna have so much fun together."

I look up at Archie, and he has a soft smile on his face when he looks at me. I feel tears starting to form so I bite down on my bottom lip to try to keep from full-out crying in front of his family.

"Okay, sweetheart, let's let the girl go." Shane comes up behind her and places his hands on her shoulders. "She gets emotional about the grandbaby thing," Shane says with a wink.

She stands and wraps an arm around his waist. "Shane, that's our grandbaby in there. Can you believe it?" She swipes at a tear running down her face.

I'm overstimulated, but oddly ... comforted.

Archie steps closer. His eyes hold mine. It's almost too much

—this wave of love that feels so different from what I grew up with.

When she pulls away, I have to blink fast to keep tears from spilling. Archie's arms come around me again like a shield.

He moves me to the sofa, where we take a seat. Archie places his arm around me, and I notice him shift uncomfortably again.

"You okay?"

He shakes his head. "Nah. I'm good. I'll ice it later. Nothing worse than usual."

It's just us for a moment, until his brothers come crowding around us, ready to pounce.

"So, Emma," Aston says, plopping down on the arm of the sofa and grinning like he's known me forever, "has Archie told you about the cow stampede?"

Archie groans.

"No," I say, eyes lighting up. "But I'm suddenly dying to know."

Ace jumps in, practically bouncing. "Picture this: fourteen-year-old Archie, already convinced he's invincible, dares Aiden to jump the fence into the back pasture."

"I didn't *dare* anyone," Archie mutters.

"Right, right. He *strongly encouraged* it," Aston corrects. "Anyway, Aiden hops the fence, not realizing the cows are behind the barn, and they come charging like something out of a Western."

"Archie panics," Austin adds, already cracking up. "Runs *toward* the cows, full sprint, waving his arms like a lunatic, trying to scare them off."

"He got knocked clean off his feet," Ace finishes, dramatically miming the fall. "Came home covered in cow poop and completely pissed off."

"I was being a hero," Archie says, deadpan. "They were stampeding my idiot brother."

"And he still asked his ninth-grade girlfriend to the dance, smelling like a barn," Aston says.

"Oh no." I laugh. "Did she say yes?"

"Shockingly, yes," Archie mutters. "Then she dumped me a week later for a kid with a four wheeler."

"So, this idiot got a dirt bike to show him up," Austin says with a wink.

"And I got asked out by three girls that day." Archie beams as his arm's still around me, and his thumb strokes lazy circles into my side like he doesn't even notice he's doing it.

"Thus began the era of Archie," Austin laments.

"How you landed Emma is beyond me," Aiden adds.

"You're just lucky she's already knocked up," Ace says cheerfully, tossing a grape into his mouth. "Otherwise, she'd have better sense than to date *you*."

"Bold of you to assume she's dating me," Archie replies coolly. "Maybe she's just using me for my genetics."

That gets a bark of laughter from the whole room.

I smile, already feeling strangely at ease with them. There's a rhythm to the banter, a love underneath all the jabs. I'm still adjusting to it, almost like an outsider looking in, but with a front row seat to it all.

After a while, the conversation splits into side conversations—football talk with Shane, Alicia googling a list of baby names and suggesting them out loud to the room, only to be met with a bunch of vetoes. Apparently, the Griffith boys have dated a girl with every name on the top one hundred baby names and have a reason why we shouldn't name our baby that.

I'm looking out the hotel window. Miami is beautiful and bright, even in the dark of night. I turn to look at Archie. He's so handsome and strong. I can't believe I wasn't going to be here tonight. I'm surprised I missed so many moments with him. I guess I'm still waiting for the shoe to drop.

For the messy to begin.

For the bad news to come walking into the waiting room of life and tell me it's all over.

I want to fully relax into this reality. I'm almost there, and with every day that passes, I feel like it could be true, and it scares me.

I'm so lost in thought that I don't realize Aston has walked over until he speaks.

"You probably noticed he's a little ... off tonight," he says under his breath.

My gaze flicks to Archie, who's standing with Aiden now. He's laughing at something his brother said, and yet there's something in his mannerisms. His posture is a little too stiff, and his eyes look a little tired.

"Yeah," I admit softly. "I figured he's exhausted from his game. He looks like he took a good hit too. And I'm sure I also threw him for a loop with this surprise visit. You know Archie, always trying to make everyone happy."

"Exactly," Aston says.

I tilt my head in question, wondering what he means.

Aston nods. "He found out earlier today that Liam Pitz is transferring out."

My stomach drops. "His best friend?"

"Yeah. They've played together for three years—roomed together, trained together. Even though he won't be at Walker anymore either, Archie's taking it hard. He won't talk about it, of course. Just keeps saying he's happy for Liam and understands why. But we can tell. And I think the reality of his college career being over is a little bittersweet for him too."

"That's ..." I trail off, glancing back at Archie. "That's a lot."

"He's not great at losing people," Aston says gently. "He's loyal to a fault. When someone leaves, even for a good reason, he takes it to heart. And he also doesn't like to leave people behind."

That makes something in my chest ache.

"Thanks for telling me," I murmur.

Aston just pats my shoulder. "You're good for him. Don't let the caveman act scare you off."

I glance over at Archie again—and this time, his eyes find

mine across the room, like he felt me looking. He gives me a small, weary smile. The kind of smile someone only gives when they're tired, but glad you're there.

It hits me, all at once: He's always the strong one. For his team. For his family. For me.

But tonight, maybe he needs someone to be strong *for him*.

I squeeze Aston's hand in thanks and stand up.

Time to remind him he's not alone anymore.

I walk over to him and take his hand.

When he looks down at me, he smiles. As I start to smile in return, I yawn instead.

"I think it's time for me to get my girl to bed." He releases my hand and wraps his arm around my waist.

"Boo. Okay. Emma, promise you'll come see us soon. And I hope you don't mind all my excitement about the baby, but I can't wait to show you the nursery. And don't you hesitate to let me know if you need anything. Oh! We could do some baby shopping if you come down too!" Alicia pulls me in for a hug.

"I would like that. Thank you. And I'm glad you're excited. Shopping would be fun. I definitely need to start getting some of the things off my list."

"You just tell me what you need, and it's yours." She nods and smiles.

"Okay, Mama. Dad. Boys. We'll see you soon. Aiden, call me when you get back to New England."

A collective goodbye is said, and we wave as we leave.

Once we get into the elevator, I release a breath I didn't realize I was holding.

"You okay, baby?" Archie turns to face me.

I nod. "I'm so good."

"Thank you for meeting them. It means a lot to me."

"I'm really happy I got to meet them too. I love the way your family is so in tune with each other. You can literally feel the love in the room. I want that."

"You'll have that, darlin'. I promise you." He leans down and kisses me.

As we walk back to my hotel, he tells me some more about the game, and a peace settles in me. This beautiful, kind, caring, talented man, who loves his family, is mine. And even though this pregnancy wasn't planned, I couldn't have picked a better daddy for my baby.

When we get to the room, I drop my bag on the dresser, and he sets his wallet and phone next to it.

I take his hand and turn him to face me. "Hey, babe. I'm really glad I got to meet your family." I tilt my head up to look at him.

He leans down, frames my face with his hands, and takes my lips. When he breaks the kiss, he smooths my hair back off my face and just looks at me.

"Emma, you're so fucking beautiful. How did I get so lucky to knock you up? Turn around and let me see my name on your back."

Okay, maybe he is feeling the buzz a little. When he releases my face, I turn but look over my shoulder at him.

"Aww, you're the sweetest."

I laugh.

"Do you need to get something to eat? Want some water or anything?" he asks.

"I'm good. I have a bottle of water on the bedside table, and I ate earlier."

He moves the hair from my back and sets it over my shoulder. Then he brushes one hand across his name and hums. "I sure do like this." He buries his face in my neck and kisses me softly.

"You know, if you wanted to stay with your family or go party with your friends, I wouldn't have minded. I just wanted to be here with you to celebrate a little bit." I sit down on the edge of the bed.

He moves in front of me, and I open my legs for him to stand between them. They kind of spread anyway with my growing belly. He places his hands on my shoulders and looks down at me as I look up at him.

"Darlin', there is nowhere else I'd rather be than here with you and my baby. And I gotta say, I think you like me a lot if you flew all this way to see me play. Oh, and you're wearing my jersey, so this feels like a big moment." He winks at me, then kneels between my legs.

"I mean ... I might like you a lot. You're pretty fun to hang around with, and you're a beast on the football field, but the orgasms ... that's the clincher."

He knows I'm mostly joking with him, but he also knows he blows my mind in bed too.

"You know it, darlin'. Now let me see my baby." He brings his hands to the hem of my jersey and slides it up over my belly. "Hi, baby. Daddy had a really good day today. Someday, I'll be able to tell you all about it and maybe even show you the game. Although things will probably be weird by then, and I won't understand technology, but I'll tell you all about it. And then Mommy came to surprise Daddy, and she all but claimed me as hers by wearing my jersey. Then she met your grandparents and uncles and didn't get scared away."

"Okay, babe, I think you're going a little overboard here." I huff, even though it's pretty much the truth. "There were a lot of people wearing your jersey today, and you know it. And your family is amazing."

He places a kiss on my belly but looks up at me. "Mommy is trying to pretend it doesn't mean more than it does, but I know she can't resist me."

I try to hide my smile by puckering my lips and shaking my head back and forth. We both start laughing at my attempt to deny that I can't resist him. It's the complete truth.

He starts to push the jersey over my breasts and then up and over my head. I'm wearing a sports bra since none of my bras are fitting me anymore. And I can't say that it's a bad look for me. Archie must agree because he buries his face in my boobs every chance he gets. Like right now.

"You are so perfect. I feel like you were made for me and only me. Did I ever tell you that the first time I saw you at that party, it felt like everything faded around me, and all I could see was you?" His face is in front of mine now, and he's looking into my eyes.

"Archie ..." I breathe.

"I'm not lyin'. I looked up, and there you were. And the best part was that you were looking at me too. I think we both felt something that night, am I right?" He tilts his head slightly.

I nod. "Yeah, you're right. There was definitely something happening."

"So, I kinda feel like the baby happened because we really are supposed to be together or tied together in some way. I'm so excited to be a daddy, but I'm even more excited that I get to do this with you. Wins like today, and hopefully more and even bigger wins in the future ... won't mean as much if you aren't with me."

My eyes must be leaking because Archie swipes away a tear from my face with his thumb.

"Emma Tucker, I am madly in love with you. And I'm not just saying it because you're having my baby. I mean, I'm all in. I will forever be there when you need me, and I want to have you by my side through all of this." He holds his arms out wide.

"Me too, Arch. I love you too. I know this is all happening in a timeline we didn't plan, but I sure do love coming home at the end of the day, knowing I'm going to see you. And I find I sleep a whole lot better when you're with me too, so I'd better keep you so I can sleep because doctors need sleep." I smile, lean forward, and kiss him.

"Goddamn, how did I get so lucky? Thank you for coming, baby. It means more to me than you know."

"I want to be there for you, like you've been for me."

"I am really glad you got to spend time with my family too. They probably wouldn't have let us leave when we did if they didn't have an early flight tomorrow. And Aiden has to get on a red-eye back up north. He had to get permission to leave for the weekend to come down, but his team only gave him, like, twenty-four hours so he could be here for the game. But he made it and got to see it all, so he didn't mind the late-night flight."

"I would like to be able to spend some more time with them before the baby is born too. Might be a little tough with my golf schedule." I sigh.

"I say this with all the love, okay?"

I nod.

"Darlin', this baby ain't gonna get smaller. You won't be able to hide this bump, I would say, even in another month. You've gotten away with wearing baggy clothes, but you'll have to wear your uniform."

"I know. I know I can't avoid telling my coach much longer. I guess it's just hard for me to imagine not playing golf if I lose my scholarship. Like even though I never planned to play past college, other than for fun, it's just always been a part of my life, you know?"

He nods, then leans forward and kisses me. "I do know. But whatever happens and whatever you find out about your scholarship, it will work out. And maybe—and hear me out—maybe it's time to stop golfing for now. Once I get drafted, I want you with me."

"I know. I've thought about it a lot too. I think I just want to be able to let it go on my terms. Does that make sense?"

"It does. Let's see how things go in the next few weeks. That will give you some time to make some decisions, and I'll have a better idea on the direction I'll be going as far as where I'll end up after the combine. I mean, I won't know until draft day, but I'll start to get some feelers."

"Come here. Right now, I want to feel my guy."

I put my arms over his shoulders and pull him into me. He buries his face into my neck, and we just sit there for a second. Archie truly does give me peace. And in just this short time we've been together, I can't imagine my life without him, and now, I don't want to.

"You feeling good, or are you tired?"

I feel him start to kiss my neck.

My hands drift from his shoulders into his hair. "A little tired, but not on the verge of falling asleep yet."

"Okay, good. Because I need to taste you. I feel like it's been days since I've been inside you and had a taste of what's mine."

He starts kissing his way down my chest and pulls my sports bra down. His tongue trails a path across my nipple and back until he sucks it into his mouth, making me moan.

He makes his way further down, stopping again to kiss my belly. When he reaches the waistband of my shorts, I lift my hips, and he takes the sides and pulls them off, along with my panties.

"Oh, baby. You're so ready for me, aren't you? Your pussy is already soaked, and I've barely touched you." He runs a finger from my clit to my opening, sliding it inside just a tease.

Leaning in, he flattens his tongue and runs it up and down my pussy. "I need more," he says as he lifts my legs and puts them over his shoulders.

I lie back on the bed and relax into his touch, his tongue. He's devouring me like he's never done before. I brace myself on my elbows so I can watch him. I mean … this giant man is between my legs, having himself a feast. And I'm here for every second of it. Watching him watching me is pushing me over too. It's so fucking hot.

My hips rock against his face, and I try to reach down to hold his head in place, but grip the sheets of the bed instead, feeling my body tingle and a flush runs up my body.

Just as soon as I start to come, Archie pulls away. "Turn around, Em."

He holds his hand out to me and helps me to sit. Then he lets go of my hand, and I turn on the bed, my back to him.

I look over my shoulder to see him undressing. "Do you want me on all fours?"

He shakes his head and climbs back on the bed behind me, his chest to my back. "I'm gonna fuck you just like this, but spread your legs wider."

One of his hands is resting on my shoulder while the other runs up my inner thigh. Then he cups my pussy and rubs me, and I feel his hand getting wetter as I start to move with him. His dick is resting on my ass between my cheeks, and I can feel it sliding up and down, which just turns me on even more.

Just as I'm about to hit the edge of my orgasm again, he pulls his hand away, and I turn my head to look at him.

"Archie, I swear to fucking God, if you don't make me come, I will do it myself."

"Patience, baby."

He trails kisses up my neck, licking, biting, and his hands move to cup my breasts. I relax into his touch and rest my head on his shoulder.

He takes my nipples between his fingers and pinches, which

sends a rush of heat down to my pussy. I swear I could come just from him playing with my nipples and kissing on my neck.

When he moves to the other side of my head and starts licking and sucking, he pulls on my nipples, then releases and pinches again. The sensation is bringing me closer to the edge, and my hips start rolling, seeking friction. He pulls his hips back slightly and repositions his body so his cock is now sliding between my folds, the head hitting my clit in just the right way.

Then, just when I'm about to come again … he releases my neck and my breasts.

"Archie, please."

"Emma, baby, I'm not gonna deny you for one more second. I need inside your tight pussy. I wanna bury myself so deep inside that you feel me in your throat."

"Yes! Yes, I accept. I beg you. Put. Your. Dick. In. Me. NOW!"

It sounds kinda like he growls, but I'm so lost in my lusty haze that I'm not really sure. But then I feel him wrap his arm above my belly, and he lifts me slightly, bracing me against him, my back to his chest.

He pushes into me, and we both groan, but then he stops.

"Why are you stopping? Move, Archie."

He rests his head on my shoulder, breathing heavy. "Darlin', I'm about to blow my load just from getting inside. Give me a minute to calm down."

I shake my head. "No."

And then I reach up and behind me to wrap my arms around his neck. I start to circle my hips and—oh, the sweet, delicious friction. I could come just like this, even without him moving.

"Fuck! Yeah, I'm not gonna last."

His one arm still keeps me held to him while his other hand takes hold of one of my breasts. The entire position feels so erotic to me, and my hips start to roll faster as he thrusts up into me deeply, hitting my G-spot.

His one hand moves from my breast and reaches down to circle my clit. That's all it takes for me to erupt.

"Oh fuck, babe. I'm coming!" I'm all but bouncing on his cock now as I come.

"Come on, Em. Come for me." He thrusts up a few more times and groans. "Fuck yes. You feel so fucking good."

I unwrap my arms from his neck and rest my head on his shoulder. My hands hold on to his arm that's still around me.

"So good, Arch. So good. I've missed you these past few days. My vibrator just doesn't feel the same."

He chuckles with a rumble in his chest. "I think the next time I'm gone, we're gonna have to FaceTime so I can see that. I don't like the idea of you coming without me."

"You don't jerk off when we aren't together?" I lift my head and turn back to look at him, as much as I can.

"Of course I do. But it's not all that often that I'm not with you."

"True, true. Okay, I need to move now, and I'm thirsty. Do you want something to drink?"

He pulls out but puts his hand between my legs and pushes his finger inside me.

I look down and smirk. "You done?"

"Yep." He turns my face and kisses me.

After cleaning up in the bathroom, I come back out to find Archie lying on the bed with his phone in his hand. He's got a smile on his face.

"Whatcha looking at?"

I climb on the bed and curl up next to him. He lifts his arm so I can tuck myself closer and rest my head on his chest.

"Just looking at some of the guys' stories on Instagram. Casey and Liam are fucking hammered. Looks like they went out to some bar, and there are girls hanging all over them. Maybe Casey will actually get laid tonight."

"I thought you mentioned a girl at the Christmas party with him."

"Oh, they claim they're just friends, but he's completely obsessed with her." He shakes his head. "She's got some boyfriend—or she did. Not really sure. Anyway, they spend a lot of time together, but they aren't a couple."

"Well then, I hope he does get laid tonight. He's got a lot to celebrate. That touchdown he scored was awesome. I'm sure he could have his pick of girls too. He's a good-looking guy."

"Hey now. That's my friend. I don't want to have to kick his ass because you think he's hot."

"I didn't say hot; I said good-looking. Besides, I have my hands full with you." I slide my hand up his chest and move it back and forth.

"That you do, baby. I am a lot to take in. And by that, I mean—"

I cover his mouth. "I know what you mean." I giggle. "I heard about Liam transferring. How do you feel about it?"

"It's kind of a weird feeling. I knew it was a possibility, and I'm not even gonna be there, but knowing he won't be at Walker just makes me feel sad, I guess. I understand why, and I do think it will be good for him from a future career perspective, but I don't know. I guess I'm always the one to leave, and any kind of change is usually by my choice. But knowing we'll be far apart and our schedules won't sync—I don't want our friendship to end."

"I get that. But like you said, you'll be gone, starting your own adventure. In more ways than one." I rub my belly. "And just because he won't be playing at Walker doesn't mean he won't still be your best friend. You guys just have to make the effort to be there for each other when you can."

A soft smile lights his face. "You're right. I'll just miss him, and I think that's harder for me to admit than I thought it would be. And today, we played our last game together. It all came crashing into me, you know?"

I tilt my head and place a kiss on his jaw. "Makes sense. The last goodbye is never easy."

We lie there in silence for a few minutes, and then he yawns and stretches his arm that I'm not lying on to the side.

Then he looks at me and smiles. "I can't believe you're here. You really have no idea how much this means to me. And I meant it when I said I love you. I really, really do."

"I couldn't have missed it. And I really, really love you too."

We lean into each other and kiss.

And I do mean it. I couldn't *not* have been here for this beautiful man who shows me every day that he's there for me and the baby. He's a special man, and I need to make sure I continue to show *him* how much he means to me.

CHAPTER
EIGHTEEN

ARCHIE

AFTER THE CHAMPIONSHIP game before the banquet, Liam told me privately that he was going to leave Walker once the transfer portal opened. Now that the celebrations around campus for our win have come to a close, Liam informed the coaches that he has decided to transfer to Michigan. We're at the field house, cleaning out our lockers today. Watching him pack up his personal belongings is a little tough, even though I won't be here next year either. It just feels like so much is changing all at once.

I pack up the rest of my things and toss what I don't need into a bin. Most of it will get thrown out, but they will sometimes take things out and wash them for memorabilia. Almost all of my stuff needs to be burned or shredded.

I turn around and see Liam sitting on the bench in front of his locker, looking into it. As I walk over to him, I sniffle.

I set a hand on his shoulder and squeeze. "You okay, brother?"

He shakes his head. "I don't know. I just never pictured leaving here until I was done, but I just can't sit on the bench for a year, and I know that's what would happen. Callaway won the season for us. And I know I had some good games, but there's no way I'd see time on the field next year if I stayed here."

As much as I hate to agree with him and don't want to see him go for the sake of our team and friends, I do think it's a smart decision.

"I know, man. But you have to do what's best for you and your career. You need to give yourself the best chance to get drafted. And you know we'll all stay in touch. A bond like ours doesn't just end when we go our separate ways." I ruffle his hair.

He chuckles. "Oh, I know. I won't let any of you forget me."

"Wanna go grab a bite or something before we head back to the house?"

"You not going straight to Emma's?"

"Not yet. She has an afternoon class this semester that she's not too happy about and doesn't get a break between class and practice. So, I was just going to head back home and chill, but now I'm hungry."

He stands and picks up his bag from the floor and sets it on the bench. "Yeah, I could eat."

We say our goodbyes to the coaches, training staff, and equipment managers before we stop to sign some footballs and jerseys. As we walk out, it hits me that this is the last time I'll leave this field house as a player. My time—along with Liam's time—at Walker is done. Chokes me up a little, and I wrap my arm around Liam's shoulder.

Neither of us says anything in my truck on the way to the restaurant. I pull into The Font, which is a place we've spent a lot of time together. When we walk in, some of the longtime staff that works there all shout a hello to us.

They let us pick our own table, so we move to our usual spot in the corner, away from most of the regular crowd, although it's still pretty quiet in here right now.

"I just realized how long it's been since we've been here together, man. This season flew by, and with all the Emma stuff, we haven't hung out together much outside of practice." He leans forward, resting his arms on the table.

"Yeah, I know. It's just been so wild. I almost feel like it's been a fever dream. And now I need to gear myself back up and get training. The combine will be here before I know it."

The waitress interrupts us and takes our order.

"So, how is Emma handling all of this? Does she understand what's coming? What your schedule will look like?"

"She knows my schedule for the combine, and I think we have some plans for what happens next, but you know I won't know for sure until I ... know. But she says she's looking into schools near where I could possibly go, and once we know for sure, she'll send in her applications and whatnot. She might decide to take a break after the baby is born too. We'll just have to see how she feels." I shrug.

"Arch, I still can't believe you're gonna be a dad. When do you think you'll tell the others? I mean, they'll have to know soon. You can't exactly hide it unless you cut everyone off, but you know they won't let that happen."

Our drinks are set on the table. We each got a bottle of beer, and we clink them together before we take a drink.

"No, I know, and I want to tell them. Hell, I've wanted to tell everyone for months, but I was following Emma's lead. She needs to figure out what will happen with her scholarship, but honestly, I'm not sure it really matters anyway if she's coming with me. But I suppose on the off chance she doesn't or can't get into another program, she doesn't want to jeopardize it. I can't wait to tell everyone. I want to introduce her as my girlfriend and the mother of my child all at once though. Hopefully soon." I take another drink and set the bottle on the table.

"You love her?" he asks.

"Yep. Head over ass in love with that girl. Pitz, she is everything. She's wicked smart, funny, confident, caring, and has some weird little quirks that should be annoying or gross, but they just make me love her more. I mean, dude, her pregnancy cravings are weird as shit, but I sit there with a smile and watch her destroy perfectly good food." I bark out a laugh.

"I don't even want to know. You know I'm a picky eater as it is, so I don't know if I'll be able to deal with that someday." He shakes his head.

"Ahh … you will, and you'll do it with a smile because you love the girl and she's growing your baby. Speaking of the little nugget, you want to see some pics?"

I pull out my phone. I take pictures of all the ultrasound photos so I can send them to my family. This is the first time I've shown anyone else though. The sense of pride I feel makes me feel ten feet tall.

He takes the phone and zooms in on the baby's face. "This is pretty fucking amazing, man. That's a little you, bro! So wild. I can't wait to meet the baby. And Emma sounds awesome, man. I'm so happy for you. Grabbin' life by the balls and shit."

After the food arrives, we talk about what comes next for us both. I talk to him about some of the training I'll be doing for the combine, and he tells me a little about his new coach at Michigan.

Liam Pitz is one of a kind and someone who I know will be a lifelong friend.

A week later, we all say goodbye but not without tears.

Before he gets into his dad's SUV, Pitz hugs each of us, but I hold on a little longer than the others.

When he pulls back, he grabs my shoulders and squeezes. "This isn't a goodbye; it's a see you later, right?"

I nod. "See you later, brother."

We do our handshake, and then we all watch as Liam and his dad drive away.

CHAPTER
NINETEEN

EMMA

IT'S BEEN three weeks since the championship game, and to say things have been hectic would be an understatement. Between all the excitement around campus and my golf season starting, Archie and I have barely had time together. I mean, we still stay together pretty much every night. The only time we don't is if I have a big test or heavy studying to do. I can't focus when he's around. He's hot and an incredibly sexy distraction.

He left three days ago for the combine in Indiana. The amount of training he had to do to prepare was insane.

I talk to him every night, and we text during the day when he can, but he's tired.

He's had some meetings with his agent, who he can officially meet with now that he's no longer a collegiate athlete. His agent is telling him that there are several teams that want to meet with him and are anxious to get his scores from the combine.

The golf team is in Arizona for a tournament, which is helping me stay distracted from not feeling all that great today. I've been pretty lucky that I've been able to keep playing, but I'm going to have to come clean with my coach about the pregnancy. For my uniform, I've had to get larger sizes two times now, and I'm surprised they haven't questioned my weight change. My height and body shape have definitely benefited me in making my belly easier to conceal, but I think that time is over.

I'm in the third rotation on the course, paired with Peyton and a girl name Sarah from Arizona State. The sun is pretty hot today, which isn't helping with me not feeling good.

Peyton takes her shot, and then the girl from Arizona takes hers. I pull out my driver and tee and walk over to the tee box. After I set my ball, I look out at the course and determine where I need to aim in order for me to get close to the green near the hole.

I take a few practice swings, then step up to the tee. Then I spread my legs slightly and tilt my hips back. Pulling my club back, I take my swing and feel a twinge in my lower belly when I rotate my hips. I nearly drop my club, not because of the pain, but it startles me so much, and I feel a wave of panic rush through me.

As I walk back to the cart, I hold my lower belly, no doubt showcasing my bump to Peyton and Sarah.

"Em! OMG! You're bleeding."

Just as she says it, I feel a trickle of blood run down my inner thigh. I'm trying not to panic, but it's kinda hard not to.

"Pey, I need you to get Miranda for me."

I sit down on the cart bench as Peyton and Sarah stand near me. I watch as Peyton gets on the walkie-talkie to call for Miranda. In all the reading I've done about pregnancy, I'm trying to scroll through my memory to see if I can think about what to do until I can get to a doctor. Putting my feet up makes sense, so I pull my legs up onto the short bench. At the very least, if my blood pressure is elevated, it should help with that.

But now I feel like I'm moving toward panic mode. I need to get ahold of Archie.

"Okay, Em. Miranda is on her way. I should let Coach know

too, right? Or does Miranda do that?" She's biting on her thumbnail and staring at me with big eyes.

Sarah is just standing there, eyeing me. "So, this isn't your period?"

I shake my head. A pain shoots through my lower belly, and I clutch it and bend forward.

"Emma, you're pregnant, aren't you?" Peyton asks.

I sigh and look at her. "Yeah, I am. About twenty-six weeks."

"Twenty-six weeks! Why didn't you tell us? I live with you, for fuck's sake, and I just thought you were in that new relationship glow, not a pregnancy glow! You have been in baggy clothes all the time though lately, so I guess this is all making sense now. But, Em! OMG, you're pregnant!"

"Look, Pey. I'm sorry I didn't tell you guys, but I still haven't told Coach yet. Archie and I needed to get some things figured out before we made it public. But right now, I'm kinda freaked out, so can we talk about this later?"

"Totally! Yes, totally! Oh God, I'm sorry. What can I do?"

"Can you find my phone? I need to text Archie."

"He's in Indiana, right? Oh shit, Em. Can he get here?"

"I'm not going to ask him to come, but he needs to know what's going on. He might not be able to answer right now, but I need to tell him."

Miranda pulls up in a cart and rushes over to me with her medical bag in hand. "Emma, what's going on?"

"I'm bleeding, and I have some lower abdominal pain."

She nods. "Okay. Ladies, can you give us some privacy?" She turns to look at Peyton and Sarah. "Actually, you should just take my cart and go to the next hole."

"Yes, of course." Peyton hands me my phone, and she and Sarah walk to the other cart and get in. "Em, text us later, okay?"

"Thank you. I will."

"Emma, you need to tell me some more information so I know what's going on."

"I'm twenty-six weeks pregnant. I haven't had any issues

with my pregnancy, but I haven't been feeling all that great today. After my last shot, I felt a twinge in my lower belly. When I was walking back to the cart, Peyton called out to me and pointed out that I was bleeding. I felt the trickle of blood as I was walking."

"Okay, let me take your blood pressure. I want you to drink some water too. It could be a few different things, but this is not my area of expertise, so we should get you to a hospital to get you checked out."

She puts the cuff around my arm, and I feel the pressure as it inflates, then slowly deflates.

"Your blood pressure is normal, so that's good. Let's get you back to the clubhouse and make arrangements for you to get to the hospital."

"I'm not going to have to get in an ambulance, am I? I don't love the idea of everyone seeing me leave that way."

"Maybe. I need to let Coach know too. Have you told her about the pregnancy yet?"

I shake my head. "I haven't. It gets a little tricky with my scholarship, and I was hoping to play as long as I could and thought I maybe had a few more weeks to figure it out."

"I see. Okay, let's head out. Drink the water slowly."

We make our way to the clubhouse, and as we get there, Coach is already there, waiting for me.

"What's going on, Emma?" Her hands are on her hips, and I can't say she looks pleased.

"I've been feeling a little off all day today and had some cramping and now some bleeding." I'm not sure why I can't just say that I'm pregnant, but the words feel stuck.

She nods and then she waves her hand toward my body. "Go on. Tell me everything."

My eyes start to tear up, and I just look at her. I truly hate disappointing people, and I'm not a deceitful person, but this whole situation has put me majorly out of my comfort zone.

Even though it's turned out to be a happy thing, I've spent the last few years playing on this team.

"I'm pregnant."

She puts her hands on her hips and looks down and sighs. "Oh, Emma. Those are not the words I wanted to hear. But we need to get you to the hospital, so we can have this conversation later. I'll come check in after the tournament. I'm going to have Miranda get you over there, and she can go with you." Walking over to me, she puts a hand on my shoulder. "I hope everything is okay. We'll talk later." Then she turns and walks away.

Twenty minutes later, I'm loaded into an ambulance and on my way to the local hospital with Miranda. Once we arrive, they keep me on the gurney and take me to one of the rooms in the emergency room area.

I've texted and called Archie, but he hasn't answered. I can't remember what skills he will be tested on today, so it's better if I just have all the information first anyway.

After all my vitals are taken and they've hooked me up to an IV, I sit and wait for what seems like an hour. Good news is, the cramping has stopped, and I'm no longer bleeding.

A doctor walks in, looking down at a tablet. "Emma Tucker?"

"Yes." I shift on the bed to sit up a little bit.

"I'm Dr. Jones. I'll be taking care of you today. So, I see that you're twenty-six weeks pregnant. You haven't had any complications during the pregnancy, which is good. You don't drink or smoke, right?" He looks at me and rests the tablet against his stomach.

"No. Even when I wasn't pregnant, I didn't drink much, and I was never a smoker. I'm a golfer on my university team, so I'm in pretty good shape."

"Okay, good. I'm just waiting for the blood work to come back to rule out anything serious, but in the meantime, I'm going to have you get an ultrasound, so we can see what's happening with that little one in there." He taps on the tablet and then holds his stethoscope in his hand for a second. "Go ahead and sit up for me if you can."

He holds out his hand, and I take it and pull myself up. Not something I would usually need help with, but I feel like I need to be cautious.

"Okay, deep breath in." He holds the stethoscope to my back. I breathe in.

"Good." He moves it around to the front, above my heart. "Everything looks and sounds good, but like I said, I want to rule out anything serious with the blood work and the ultrasound. My guess is that you were probably a little dehydrated. Traveling, being out in the sun, physical activity—you can dehydrate faster than normal. Which can cause some cramping. As for the blood, likely related to the cramping. I'll be back in when we get some results. Just try to rest." He taps the bedrail, then turns and walks out.

Not even five minutes later, a younger girl—probably close to my age—comes in, attaches my IV bag to a hook on the bed, and tells me she's taking me to get an ultrasound. Once we reach the sonography room, she locks the bed in place. "I'll be back to get you when she's done."

Then she walks out, and another woman in scrubs walks in. "Hi, Emma. Can you tell me your full name and date of birth?"

"Emma Tucker. June 29, 2003."

"Okay, thank you. I'm Shari. I'll be doing your ultrasound today. Anything you want me to know before we get started?" She sets up the screen and then puts a pair of gloves on.

"No, I don't think so. I'm guessing you know I had some bleeding and cramping today, so nothing else to report."

I'm lying down with a gown on and a blanket over my lap. She pulls down the blanket to my hips and moves the gown to rest right under my breasts.

"Perfect. Okay, so just relax, and let's get a look at this baby."

She squirts some liquid on my belly and starts to smear it

around with the Doppler. The baby's heartbeat fills the room, and I release a breath I didn't realize I was holding in.

The baby is wiggling around and looks like maybe sucking a thumb. I can see the features more clearly than the last ultrasound we had.

"Would you mind getting a few pictures for me to take home? My boyfriend isn't here, and we usually do all of my appointments together." I think this is the first time I've referred to Archie as my boyfriend.

"Of course. Do you live here in town?" she asks.

"No, I'm from Oklahoma. I go to Walker University. I'm in town for a golf tournament with my team."

"Oh, wow. That's fun. Although this isn't so much fun, huh? You had some bleeding and cramping, right?"

"That's right." I watch the screen and then see the baby. "Hi, nugget."

My eyes water. I wish Archie were here to see this. But also, I just wish he were here.

"Baby looks good. Although I'm not a doctor so he'll go over the results with you. Do you know the sex of the baby?"

"No, not yet, but I don't want to know without my boyfriend."

"You got it." She wipes off the Doppler and sets it on the cart, then grabs some tissues and hands them to me. "You're all set. Someone will come get you and take you back to your room. Good luck, Emma." She smiles.

"Thank you," I reply.

She walks out, and minutes later, the girl who brought me here enters. "You ready to go?"

"Ready as ever." I laugh.

My anxiety has decreased significantly after I saw the baby and heard the heartbeat. When I get back to the room, I should at least call my parents and let them know what's going on. After I talk to the doctor, I'll call Archie again.

We reach the room, and the girl hooks the IV back on the pole. "Do you need anything before I go?"

"Um, I don't think so."

"Do you want me to get you some fresh ice water?"

"Oh, yes, that sounds good."

"You got it. Be right back."

She leaves the room, and I reach for my phone on the rolling table next to the gurney.

Archie still hasn't responded, so I pull up my parents' number and press the green button to call.

My mom answers after a few rings. "Hey, Em. Aren't you supposed to be on the course right now?"

"Hey, Mom. Yes, but I had a little incident today. I had some cramping and some bleeding, so they sent me to the hospital."

My mom gasps. "Oh my God, Em. Are you okay? Is the baby okay?" I can hear the panic in her voice, which is why I should have waited to call her until I had more information.

"I'm good. The baby is good. They think it was likely dehydration, but we're still waiting to get the blood work, and I just had an ultrasound. I'm guessing the doctor will be in here soon —or I'm hoping anyway. I really don't want to have to stay overnight. I want to get home."

She releases a breath, and then I hear Dad in the background say, "Oh, thank God. Emma, please call us as soon as you see the doctor."

"I will let you know when I have more information."

"Have you called Archie yet? He's at the combine, isn't he?" Dad asks.

"Yes, he is. I tried getting ahold of him, but he hasn't replied yet, and I'm not really sure what he has going on today. I don't want him to be distracted or worried about me though until I have more to tell him."

"Honey, you need to keep trying to reach him," Mom says.

"I will, I promise."

"Do you want us to try to call him?" Dad asks.

"No, I've texted and called. If he can have his phone on him, he'll see me calling."

A new doctor in white a lab coat walks into the room.

"I have to go. The doctor just came in. I'll call you later."

"Okay, we love you. Call us back as soon as you can. You know I'll be here worrying until you do. And if they want to keep you overnight, we'll come down."

"Mom, gotta go. Love you." I disconnect the call before she can reply.

I look up at the doctor. "Sorry about that."

"No problem at all. My name is Dr. Romano, I'm the chief obstetrician here at the hospital. I heard you had quite the afternoon. Will you go over the details of your day?"

I restate the events that led me to be in this hospital bed and answer a few more questions about my pregnancy and family history while Dr. Romano listens.

"Is everything okay with the baby?" I ask, watching as Dr. Romano looks at the tablet in her hand.

She looks down at me and smiles. "Your blood work looks normal, and the ultrasound looks good, and the baby's heart rate is good, but we did want to mention that there might be a small hole in the baby's heart. Has your doctor mentioned that to you?"

My entire body freezes.

Hole. Heart.

Sunny.

The one thing I worried about with this pregnancy has just washed over this room like a black cloud. My chest tightens, and I feel like I might be sick.

All of a sudden, I'm nine years old again, sitting in a sterile waiting room with a stranger and feeling so very alone.

My baby's heart. I can picture it already. The surgeries, the worry. The dread of always thinking the worst is about to happen.

I can't reply, so I just shake my head.

"Okay, I'm going to send the report to your doctor back in Oklahoma. They can schedule some additional tests to monitor you further. You should be okay to be discharged tonight and go back with your team."

"Thank you." I can't bring myself to tell her about my sister right now.

She places a hand on my arm. "There's no need to panic. When you get back to Oklahoma, you can have a fetal cardiogram and get a better idea of what you're dealing with. It is something that happens and often resolves on its own. Right now, the baby looks good. Strong heartbeat, good growth. But like I said, get an appointment scheduled with your doctor when you get home."

I nod and clear my throat. "Okay, thank you. I need someone to let my team trainer know I'm ready, and I need to get in touch with my coach and let her know I'm being discharged. Do you know when that will be happening?"

"We'll go ahead and get the paperwork started and get you out of here as soon as we can. I know you have a flight to catch tomorrow, and I'd prefer you get a good night's rest tonight."

"Okay, thanks."

"Take care of yourself, Emma. If you have any problems tonight, don't hesitate to come back in." She walks out before I can reply.

My hands are shaking a little as I text my coach, telling her I'm ready to go. She replies right away, saying she's walking into the hospital.

I feel like I'm in a daze. Sitting here, thinking about everything she just told me. Thinking about my sister. Panic is rising, and I'm starting to feel like I can't breathe. When my sister died, I remember that feeling inside of me. It hurt so bad, and I never wanted to feel like that again.

In the months I've been pregnant, I've accepted, bonded, and allowed myself to get so excited about our little nugget. I truly don't think I will survive it if something is wrong.

Coach walks in, and my gaze snaps to hers. "Hey, Emma. How are you feeling?"

I sit up in the bed. "I'm okay. I haven't had any issues since I've been here, so that's good."

"Good. I'm glad to hear it. They're working on discharge papers now? And they say you can travel tomorrow?"

"Yeah, they're working on everything now, and said I'll be good for tomorrow. She told me to get some rest tonight, so when I get back to the hotel, I'll probably just go right to bed."

"Yes, that's a good idea. We can get you something to eat if you're up to it."

"I'll probably go to bed."

"Emma, we need to talk about this. I need to understand how you are pregnant and I didn't know. As your coach, any changes, especially physically, I need to be made aware of. We could have made changes or had certain provisions available for you. It was negligent on your part for not telling me. I understand why you didn't, but this could have been worse than it was, and I wouldn't have known what was going on."

"I know, and I'm sorry. It was such a shock at first that I wasn't really sure what to do. I was just trying to get through as much of the year as I could before the baby was born. I knew I wouldn't be able to finish out the season, even though I was cleared to play by my doctor, but I also wasn't sure how this was all going to affect my scholarship."

"Understood. We can talk about that when we get back to campus. I'll need to review protocol on this because I've never been in a situation like this before. Can I ask if your roommates knew?"

I shake my head. "Mia and Peyton had no idea. Livi was with me when I took the test, so she knows."

"I see. And who is the father?"

"His name is Archie Griffith."

"Archie Griffith, the football player?"

"Yes, that's him." I nod.

"Interesting. Did his coach know about the baby?"

"Not that I'm aware of. I think he would have told me if he had said something to his coach, but I asked him to keep it quiet until I could figure out what to do with my scholarship and whatnot."

She inhales deeply. "I can see how this would all be somewhat complicated. Isn't he going into the draft?"

"He is. He's at the combine right now actually."

"Well, Emma, you have a lot to deal with, it seems. The last thing you need is a lecture from me. So, let me find out what we need to do for you, and we'll meet sometime this week. I think it's safe to say that you shouldn't be at practice until you're feeling better and you've seen your doctor."

"Yes, ma'am. I understand. For what it's worth, I am sorry I didn't tell you sooner."

"You know, Emma, I've been coaching for a long time, and I know my players have had a lot of secrets over the years." She sighs. "But I do think you're my first pregnancy."

She walks over to the bed and takes my hand in hers. "I'll miss you this season, but I still expect to see you."

"I will be around for sure. Once we know what's happening and what my doctors say, we can figure it out, right?"

"Absolutely. And, Emma, congratulations on the baby." She squeezes my hand, then leans in for a hug.

My freaking eyes tear up again. "Thanks, Coach. It's certainly been wild."

"I hope Archie has been supportive. He's had a lot going on with his season."

"He's the best, seriously. I lucked out in the baby daddy department." I snort.

"Glad to hear it. Okay, let's get you out of here so you can get some sleep. These hospital beds are the worst."

A few minutes later, the discharge nurse comes in, and I sign everything I need to sign to be released. They tell me they've already sent my records to my doctor in Oklahoma.

Focusing on everything they're telling me is keeping me distracted from my panic, but it still there, lingering. I need to call Archie.

CHAPTER
TWENTY

ARCHIE

WE'RE JUST FINISHING up for the day, and I hear my ringtone coming from my duffel bag. I pull it out and see Emma's name, along with several missed calls and texts. I miss her so much it hurts. Even though I've been going nonstop since I've been here and pretty much fall into bed every night, I still miss my girl.

"Hey, darlin'. How did you do today?"

"Hey. Um, well, not great." She huffs.

"What's wrong? What happened?" I can tell something isn't right by the tone of her voice.

"I, uh … I had some cramping and bleeding, so I had to stop playing, and they sent me to the hospital."

"What the fuck?! Why didn't you call me right away?" I start pacing. My heart is racing, and I just feel … helpless right now.

"Babe, I did. You were in drills all day, right? There wasn't anything you could do anyway. You're in Indiana, and I'm in Arizona. No way would you have been able to be here, and besides, I'm okay. I had all the blood work done and got an ultrasound. I got to see and hear the baby. I'm good. We're good."

"Emma, I'm so sorry I didn't see my phone sooner. You're my girl, and that's my baby." I whisper the last part, not wanting anyone around me to hear my conversation. Not now.

"I know, but, babe, it's okay. I do need to see the doctor when I get home. They saw something in the ultrasound about the baby's heart. They didn't seem to be too worried, but definitely want me to follow up." Her voice cracks.

"Darlin', are you on your way home or still in Arizona?" I'm trying to calculate if I can make it there to be with her or if I can rearrange my plans to meet her when she gets back to Oklahoma.

"We leave early in the morning. I'm at the hotel now, already in bed. I'm going to get some sleep. I'm physically exhausted, but it's been a bit stressful today, and it's worn me out."

"Yeah, okay. You should get some rest. I'm going to see what I can do to get home tomorrow."

"Archie, no. Don't you still have some things to do?"

I shake my head even though she can't see me. "No, I'm done for the most part. Let me talk to my agent and see what I can do. But, Em, I'm going to have to tell him why I need to come home early. It's only a day early. And I need to be there with you."

"Okay, well, I guess I'll see you tomorrow then. I'm going to get some sleep. I hope everything went well today. I can't wait to hear about the whole thing when you get home."

I put one hand on my head and pull on my hair, frustrated. "I'm not gonna lie, Em. I'm really not happy that I can't be with you to hold you tonight."

She sniffles and then clears her throat. "I know, babe. I'll see you tomorrow. Night."

"Night. Get some rest. I should be there around the time you get home, too, so I'll meet you at your place. Love you, baby."

"Yeah, that sounds good. I'll see you then."

She ends the call, and I stand there, staring at my phone.

Something doesn't feel right. Maybe it's because I'm not with her, or she didn't tell me she loved me, too, but I'm worried.

I shoot off a text to my agent and ask him to call me when he gets a chance. My phone rings seconds later.

"Archie, my man. What's going on?"

"Hey, Scott. I need to get home early tomorrow. Do you think that will be an issue?"

"Home to Texas or home to Oklahoma?"

"Oklahoma. I need to see my girlfriend."

"Is there a problem, Archie?"

"Yeah, um … so my girlfriend is pregnant, and she had an issue today. I really need to get home to be with her."

He huffs. "You mean to tell me that you haven't mentioned that you're going to be a dad, knowing I'm trying to negotiate deals on your behalf, for your future. You didn't think I should know that?"

"Look, it's a little complicated, but she's nearing the end of her pregnancy now, and we can't really hide it anymore anyway. I'm not asking for your opinion on my personal life or my reasons for not discussing it with you before now. Just figure out a way that I can get home without causing an issue. Can you do that?"

He mumbles something I can't decipher. "Right. Well, we'll deal with it. I think we need to sit down and have a meeting, and she should be included in the conversation going forward— because whatever move you make will involve her."

"Yes, it absolutely will. You and I both know where I want to be, so now more than ever, we need to get there with negotiations."

"I hear you. I'll start digging deeper and let you know if anything interesting happens." He moves his phone away and speaks with someone. "I gotta run, Arch. Talk later."

Tomorrow can't come fast enough.

CHAPTER
TWENTY-ONE

ARCHIE

IT'S BEEN a few days since we've been back, and I've been at Emma's every day. She's going to classes, but comes back home right after. It's almost like she's moving on autopilot, and I can't figure out why. And I feel like she's pushing me away.

I'm waiting for her at the doctor's office now. We decided to meet here because she had class before this and drove to campus; she didn't want to leave her car there, and we wouldn't have had time to run it home before coming here. Before the scare in Arizona happened, we would have come together, no matter what.

The door opens, and she walks in, looking a little flustered.

"Hey. Sorry I'm late. There was some traffic when I was trying to leave campus."

I stand when she walks over to me and wrap her in my arms. "All good. I got you checked in."

"Thanks," she says, pulling away.

Just as we're about to sit, the nurse opens the door to the back and calls Emma's name.

When we get to the room, Emma is instructed to undress and

wait for the technician to come get her. I look over at her in question.

"We're doing the ultrasound first?"

She nods. "Yeah, I guess so."

"Okay, good. I can't wait to see the baby." I reach for her hand and squeeze gently.

She won't look at me. She just stares at the wall in front of her.

Something has changed with Emma. When we got off the phone yesterday, she seemed fine, but then stopped taking my calls.

"Darlin', can you look at me for a minute?"

Her head turns, and she looks at me.

"What's going on, Em?"

"I'm fine. Just want to hear what the doctor says so we know what we're dealing with." She releases my hand and stands, then turns her back to me to undress.

I nod. "Okay, yeah. But the doctor in Arizona said everything looked okay, right?"

"I mean, other than the possible hole in the heart, yes."

"Are you worried that it's the same thing as your sister?"

She looks over her shoulder at me and scoffs. "Yes, Archie. My sister literally died from a heart issue, so, yeah, I have feelings about this."

"I'm sorry. I'm just trying to get you to talk to me. I want to understand how to help you."

"You can't really help me, Archie." She turns back to face me once she's tied the gown.

"Well, I want you to tell me how you're feeling."

The technician comes in before Emma can reply, and she preps her computer and probe thing that she uses on Emma's stomach.

She lifts Emma's shirt and squirts some liquid on her belly, then takes the probe and runs it across her stomach.

We hear the baby's heartbeat right away, and I reach over to hold Emma's hand again.

"Okay, Mom and Dad, let's take some pictures of baby." She moves it around, stopping to take some measurements, and taps a few things into the computer. "Heart rate looks good. Measurements are good. I'm not sure if they went over this with you yet, but we're measuring the possible hole in the heart that they believe they saw in Arizona."

"Yes, I'm aware," Emma says, not in a mean way, but more mechanical-sounding. Robotic almost.

"I have all the numbers the doctor needs. Do you guys want to know the sex of the baby?" She looks at Emma first, then me.

"I think we decided to wait, right, Em?" I answer for both of us.

She just nods and lets go of my hand to take the tissue from the technician.

"No problem. I love surprises, but sometimes, parents want to know for nursery design and clothes. Moms start to want to nest near the end of their pregnancies."

"Nest?" I ask.

She hums. "It's when the mom feels the need to get everything prepped and ready for baby. Bedroom, clothes, all the baby needs."

"I see. Well, baby, if you want to do that, we can."

Emma finishes cleaning off her belly. "I'm good. Let's just wait."

"Okay then, I'm all set. Here are a few pictures for y'all to take home. Have a good rest of your day, you two."

No reply from Emma again, so I answer, "Thank you. Same to you."

Emma shifts around on the table and sits up.

"You need anything, darlin'?"

"Archie, I'm good. I appreciate you asking, but I'm fine. If I need something, I'll tell you."

Now, I only grew up in a house with one woman, but I know that tone well enough to know to keep my mouth shut.

A few minutes later, the doctor comes in with her nurse.

"Hi, Emma, Archie. Good to see you both here. I'm going to get right to it because I have to head out for a delivery. Emma, you look great. Baby looks great. All of your blood work from previous tests and the one from Arizona all look normal. We do see a small secundum—which is a hole in the heart—located in the upper part of the baby's heart, in an area called the atria septum. This type of defect does typically close on its own without medical intervention. Because of the size, I don't see any reason to believe that in this case, it won't close on its own after birth. But due to your family history and this development, we will have you monitored by one of our high-risk OBs in our practice and continue the fetal echoes. Do either of you have any questions for me?"

Emma shakes her head. "No, I think I understand everything."

"Archie, how about you? You have any questions or concerns?"

"Well, I mean, I'm sure I'll have more after I do a little more research on this, but my primary concern is if Emma is okay. Is the baby okay and not in any type of pain?"

"Of course. Good questions. Emma is doing great. I have no further concerns about Emma. What happened in Arizona was most likely caused by dehydration, but also, as your baby grows, you may experience spotting from time to time. We want to know if that happens, but it is pretty normal in most cases. As for the baby, the baby is growing nicely; measurements are all good. Even though you're on the smaller side, it's still within range. The heart rate is strong, and I don't see any murmurs or problems with heart function. But because of Emma's family history, we need to monitor the heart closely."

"Thank you. That's helpful. I just want to make sure I can

give them both anything they might need, and the more I know, the better."

The doctor smiles at me, points at me, and then looks at Emma. "He is one of the good ones, Emma. Hold on to him." She looks back at me. "Try to enjoy the last few months of the pregnancy. Once the baby arrives, your lives will change completely."

I smile my signature smile. "Why, thanks, Doc. I appreciate that and also agree with you. One more question: is it safe for us to have sex? I don't want to do anything to hurt Emma or the baby."

"Archie, Jesus." Emma looks at me, then at the doctor. "Sorry."

"Don't apologize. I'm glad you asked. You can absolutely have intercourse over the next few months. Emma, you can really do anything you want as long as you feel good. So, take good care of her, Archie."

"Yes, ma'am. I fully intend to." I stand from my chair. "Thank you, Doctor."

"I'll see you in two weeks. We'll start seeing you every two weeks, and then once we're in the last month, we'll want to see you weekly. Now the high-risk OB will set a schedule with you, but we'll try to schedule your appointments on the same day to make it easier on you." She touches Emma's arm on her way out.

"Thank you, Doctor," Emma says.

After the door closes, I reach out to Emma and help her move off the table to get dressed. She accepts my hand, but releases it right away once she stands.

"You can go out and see if you can schedule the appointments with the high-risk doctor. Might be easier for you to do it because I don't know your schedule yet for when you'll be here and when you'll be in Texas for training."

I watch her as she takes her gown off and starts to dress. She won't look at me.

"Sure, I can do that. We should probably talk about my schedule soon. I would like you to be with me as much as possible. Do you know when you have your meeting with your coach yet?"

She shakes her head. "Not yet. I should hear something by tomorrow."

"If you want me to go with you, I can do that. Just say the word."

"I'll let you know, but I'm sure I'll be fine. I'm gonna run to the bathroom real quick, so I'll meet you at scheduling."

She opens the door and walks out. And I just stand there for a minute, hands on my hips. I don't do well with guessing games. I know she's going through something right now, and I'll be as patient as I can be, but I won't be able to deal with this for long. I need her to talk to me so I know what she needs.

After we get the next appointments scheduled, we walk out to the parking lot. I walk her to her car, and before she opens the door, she turns to face me.

"Arch ... I ..." She grabs on to my shirt with her hands.

I pull her into me and wrap my arms around her. "Tell me what you need, Em, and it's yours."

She shakes her head into my chest. "I'm not really sure. I feel like everything is happening at rapid speed now, and I just need to process it all, I guess. I mean, we've been living in this nice little bubble where everything is perfect. You went from being one of the most notorious players on campus to basically living with me. But, Archie, you're leaving, and then after that, you'll be gone a lot. I can do this alone. Hell, I've been alone for so long that I don't think anyone realized it. I'm just thinking that maybe we need to—"

"Don't you start pulling away from me."

"It's just a lot of pressure. You need to get through the draft, and I need to figure out what I'm doing. It's just a lot."

"I see." And I do. "It is a lot. But I know we can work it out because I think we're worth trying for, but also, I will be there for my baby. Yeah, it's not always going to be easy or go according to plan, but we'll figure it out."

"How do you know though? Like, how can you be so sure that we'll still like each other once the baby is born? I don't want either of us to feel resentful of each other, you know. Like what if we're just caught up in this baby bubble?"

"Are you only with me because of the baby bubble?"

"Me? Archie, I've never been so intertwined with someone before. It scares the hell out of me. It scares me so much that I'm going to move to another city to be with you and you're going to be gone half the time. I'm scared that, one day, you'll realize the party is over, and you'll walk out the door, and the baby and I will be alone. I'm afraid that our baby will be sick and need a strong parent, and I want to be that person, but I don't know if I can do this on my own. Not again. I can't risk losing anyone. Not this baby and definitely not you."

"You're scared. I get it. Before we got to know each other, you only knew me as a player and not the kind of man who wouldn't leave. But trust me—this is real, Emma."

"How do you know? How do you know we're not just playing house?"

"Darlin', I don't know how to explain it other than … I just know. When I saw you at that party that night, there was just something there for me. I know I've told you this already, and I know you never planned on seeing me again, but for me, it was different. I couldn't get you out of my head. And it wasn't just because of the sex. It was you. I love you, Emma."

"But what if you really don't know me? And then we have this baby, and you get to know me without all the hormones, and you don't like who I am?"

"Well, I can tell you what I know, what I'm crazy about. Your weird toe, the one that's longer than your big toe? I dig it. And maybe our baby will have your weird toe, and I love it because it will obviously mean he or she will be a natural athlete, but also because it will be something from you."

She pulls back to look up at me.

"And I don't mind that you take all the red Sour Patch Kids out of the bag and leave the rest for me. Works out really because the orange is my favorite anyway."

"Orange is gross," she mumbles.

"That's your opinion, darlin'. You got your favorites; I got mine." I kiss her forehead.

"I also love the adorable little tattoo you have of Dora's backpack on your lower back because I love the story that goes with it. Now, I will say, I hope you get over the craving you have to put peanut butter on pickles. Now, that … is gross. The 7UP and Powerade—I can get on board with that. It's not bad at all."

I rub my hand up and down her back.

"I'm still on the fence about your choice in who Meredith belongs with, but I love that you know the outcome and would still want to pick McSteamy over McDreamy."

"You know all that about me?"

"I pay attention, Emma. But at the end of the day, I know it'll work out and that everything will be okay because you and I will make it okay. We'll work hard at making sure our schedules sync or whatever we need to do."

"I don't know, Archie. It just all feels stressful, and I'm used to having solutions and plans."

"Maybe you should spend some time with the girls tonight. Do you think that would help or at least take your mind off of some of this?"

She looks up at me. "I don't really want to sleep without you, but, yeah, maybe that's a good idea. I kind of feel like I owe them all a catch-up too—you know, since I've been hiding big things from them the last several months."

I bend my head and kiss her—it's sweet and entirely too short. "If you need me, just call, and I'll be there. Go have a night with the girls."

She nods and steps back, then opens her door and gets into the car. I watch as she pulls out of her spot and wave as she leaves. I'll give her tonight, but we will talk about this.

We have a lot to figure out, but I think I need to make a call to my parents and my agent.

I'm at my house with my roommates. It's been a while, and I'll be packing up the last of my things soon. Not having Liam in the house feels so strange. I've been so busy lately that I haven't checked in with him much, and I should make a point to do that soon.

Tonight, I'll make dinner for my roommates, who now officially includes Charlie. She's moved in completely. After the championship game, Beck wasn't gonna let her go anywhere again.

Bo Callaway is planning to move in sometime right before training, but first, he'll head back to California for a few weeks in the summer. It seems like he's been hanging out around here a lot from what I can tell in the times I stop by.

I'm making burgers on the grill. I cut up some potatoes and put them in the air fryer that someone must have gotten for the house.

"What up, man? Good to see you." Casey walks over and pats me on the back. "Do you need any help?"

"I'm good. Just need to get the ketchup and mustard out of

the fridge." I walk over and open the fridge door, pulling out what I need.

"How are you feeling about the draft?" He leans up against the counter, arms crossed.

"I feel really good. I have a meeting with my agent this week, so hoping to have some feelers. I talked with the general managers of the Dallas Cowboys, Kansas City Chiefs and the Denver Broncos, but I'd like to stay closer to home." I grab the spatula on the counter and a clean plate for the burgers. "Walk with me."

"So, you want to get a conversation with Kansas City or Dallas then?" He opens the sliding door for me.

"Ideally, Dallas, but we'll see. They don't have a high selection this year, unless they trade up, so I'm not sure. I would like to go in the first round, but all the magic needs to happen to get me where I want to be." I hold the plate in one hand and open the grill cover, then pull out the cooked patties.

"The dream, Archie. You'll be living the dream. I'm so excited for you. It'll be awesome, watching you out on that field."

"Thanks, man. I can't believe it's finally here. It feels like I've spent half of my life preparing for this, you know?" I close the lid, and we walk back into the house.

"No doubt. I've wanted to play ball since I was little. Getting my chance to start this year was a dream come true. I can't imagine what it would feel like to be in your shoes."

"I think I'm more excited than nervous. I feel like the time is right, and I'm in a good position. If the logistics work out the way I want, I'll be one happy man." I grab some cheese I set out on the counter earlier and lay a few slices on a some of the patties. Then I look over at Casey and laugh. "Just gotta believe, ya know?"

"It'll be something to see, for sure. We about ready to eat? I'll call for the others. I'm not going to get Beck and Charlie though. I've learned my lesson." He shivers. "Can't see that again."

"Buddy, you gotta knock." I laugh and punch him in the chest lightly.

"Oh, I did. And we'll leave it at that." He shakes his head and shouts out to them. "Hey, Char, Beck. Dinner is ready."

Charlie walks in first. She's wearing shorts and a T-shirt that's ... inside out. Beck follows shirtless and in gym shorts, hair disheveled.

"Archie! I didn't know you were here." Charlie walks up and hugs me.

"How's it going, Chuck? Settling in officially around here? Love the organization in the pantry." I put my fist out, and she bumps it.

"You should see our bathroom." Beck shakes his head as he walks over to the table.

Charlie follows, and he pulls a chair out for her, pushes her in, and then kisses her on the head.

I bring the burgers over to the table, then go back to the counter and pull out the potatoes from the air fryer. I dump them in a bowl, then take them to the table.

Casey grabs a beer for me, Beck, and himself and a water for Charlie.

Once we're all sitting, I look around and soak it in. This is probably the last meal I'll eat with them in this kitchen. Their friendships, even though Casey and Beck have only been here for two years, have meant a lot to me. On and off the field. We've had a lot of fun together, but they've also become brothers to me. I can't wait to tell them about Emma and the baby.

"Let's raise our glasses." I lift my beer. "Here's to it and from it, then back again. And if you don't do it when you get to do it, you may never get to do it again. Grab life by the balls, boys. Take your chance while you have it. And you too, Chuck." I wink at her. "I love y'all. Cheers!"

"Cheers!" they all say in unison.

Three years ago, I came to Walker University, ready to take on college ball. I feel like I have accomplished everything I set out to do and then some. Winning the championship this season … what a wild ride.

I'm so ready to move on though. Playing in the NFL will be an amazing accomplishment, but becoming a dad and hopefully having more with Emma … life-changing. And I can't wait to start living this next chapter.

CHAPTER
TWENTY-TWO

EMMA

GETTING in my car and driving away from Archie today was hard. I meant it when I said I didn't want to sleep without him tonight. But the reality of all of this is pushing me way out of my comfort zone. Bringing up things I don't really want to think about. My parents keep calling me to check in, and it just makes me feel more anxious.

When I walk into my apartment, my roommates are sitting on the couches, watching some reality show that I couldn't get into.

"Hey," I call out.

"Emma! You're home. Where's Archie?" Livi asks.

I drop my bag on the chair by the kitchen table. "He went to his place tonight."

"Everything okay?" Mia asks.

"Mmhmm. It's fine." I walk into the kitchen and grab a bottle of water from the refrigerator.

"Come hang out with us then. It's been a while since we've had a girls' night." Peyton pats the spot next to her.

When I walk past my bag, I grab my phone from inside, then go sit on the couch.

"So, I guess I'll be the one to just say it." Mia pauses. "Emma, how the fuck did you hide being pregnant all this time? I am completely shooketh, but also, I feel super stupid for not noticing. So, for that, I'm sorry I've been an oblivious and selfish friend."

"I mean, honestly, Emma. I am sure this has been bananas for you. I can't believe you didn't tell us. Although it all kinda makes sense now that you and Archie started hanging out suddenly. I knew you hooked up, but you said you didn't want anything more than that?"

"I didn't. And I probably wouldn't have contacted him again, but I guess there was another plan." I rest my hand on my belly, grateful I don't have to hide anymore and I can just relax in front of them.

"Because of school or something else?" Peyton nudges my leg with hers.

I look at her and shrug. "I mean, yeah. I've had a singular focus since I've been here. When I was with him that first night, I just had a feeling he could be a dangerous distraction."

"I totally get that, but it doesn't seem like it's been a bad thing, having him around," Livi pipes in. "Archie is completely obsessed with you, girl. We see the way he treats you around here. Guy is hooked."

I feel a blush in my cheeks, and I nod because what's she's saying is true. He treats me so well, and if anything, he's been more than supportive of my studying and schedule.

"So, what's the plan then for after the baby? Will you live happily ever after and have all the football babies?" Mia gasps. "OMG, I love this for you. Your babies are going to be so fricking cute."

"Let's settle down for a minute. I am having one baby right now. We have no idea where we're going yet. That's actually why he's not here. I've been a little ... I don't know ... not doing great since Arizona. Handling that alone brought up some things for me. This has all happened so fast, you know."

Livi reaches over and places her hand on top of mine on my belly. "This is okay, right? Sorry, I probably should have asked, but now that it's out in the open, I really want to feel her."

"Well, we don't know that it's a she yet."

"Stop being a downer, Em. Of course it will be a girl." She moves her hand from the top of mine and to the side of my stomach. "Baby, this is your bestie, Liv. I'm going to be your favorite, obviously, because I will spoil you rotten. OH! Can we do a baby shower? Please, please!"

"YES! OMG. Do you even have anything for the baby yet?" Mia puts a hand on her chest.

"I mean, I feel like we would have noticed baby gear in the house, no?" Peyton sits back and puts her arm around the back of the couch and behind me.

"Well, first of all, who else would we invite to the baby shower? You guys are pretty much my only friends. My mom has gotten a few things that she's been keeping for me at their house. And Archie's mom renovated a whole room for the baby. We have a few basics in my closet, but not a ton yet. We don't know if the nugget is a boy or girl yet or where we'll even be living, so it's been hard to make a lot of plans."

"OH! Holy shit. I think the baby just moved. Em, did the baby move?" Livi asks, eyebrows raised.

I move my hand to the side of hers. "Yeah, here. The baby is twisting around or something right now. I drank a little water on my way home, and I usually get a lot of activity after."

"I want to feel!" Mia jumps up.

Peyton puts her hand on my stomach. "So cool." Peyton looks at me and smiles. "What does it feel like?"

"Flutters. I don't know how else to describe it. Like butterflies in your belly. Although now that this little nugget is getting bigger, the kicks are a little stronger."

"Emma, in all seriousness, how are you doing with all of this though? Like, what are you going to do about golf and school when he gets drafted?" Livi asks.

"I have a meeting with Coach on Friday, and Archie leaves for Texas soon, because he wants to be home for the draft. So, I need to figure it out."

"But have you guys talked at all about what to do? You have pretty clear goals for your future, so I'm just curious about how you'll make it all work with his career." Livi takes my hand in hers.

"Well, right now, it looks like it's between Dallas, Kansas City, and, I guess, Colorado. I've been looking at schools in those areas, and I have the applications filled out. So, once we know for sure, I'll send them off. My first choice would be Dallas because it's closer to my parents, and Southwestern has an amazing medical school."

"Do you feel like you're letting go of your dreams so he can follow his?" Mia asks.

I shake my head. "No. I mean, if Archie were telling me instead of being supportive, we'd be in a different boat. But at the end of the day, I love him, and he's going to be an amazing dad. I would never keep him away from his child, and I don't want to do any of this without him."

"So, did you have a fight or something? Is that why he's not here?" Peyton asks.

I shake my head. "Not a fight exactly. We had our doctor's appointment today and went over everything that had happened in Arizona. I don't really talk about it, but my sister died when we were young. She was only a few years younger than me. She had a genetic heart disorder and died from complications from her last surgery."

"Oh, Emma. I'm so sorry," Mia says.

"Our baby looks fine, and things have gone fairly smoothly until now. They saw a small hole in the baby's heart. I think because I was alone when I got the news and then couldn't get ahold of Archie, it just made me shut down a little. You all know

I like structure and routine, and this is something I can't put into a box and control. So, my response is to keep myself protected from feeling too much. The loss of my sister was really hard on my family, and I don't ever want to go through something like that again. Then I spiraled and started to think about what I would do if Archie wasn't in the picture and if he was only with me because of the baby. It wasn't pretty, looking at it now." I swipe the tears that have started to fall.

"Em, I'm not an expert by any means, but I am your friend, so I feel like I can say this freely. You cannot push this man away because you're scared. You've already laid out tentative plans, so it will all work out. I think the uncertainty and not knowing where you'll be is scary enough, then add in a complication with your baby … I get it. But let him help you through the scary parts. It sounds like he's supportive and he wants to be there for you too." Livi leans forward and hugs me.

"She's right, Em. You need to talk to him." Mia wraps her arms around Livi and me.

"Well, I want in on this too." Peyton joins the hug.

These girls have been really great friends and teammates to me.

"You're right. This relationship is really the only one I've ever been in, and we're going at it at full speed. Skipping a lot of the steps, you know? But I do love him, and even with my fears, I know I'd follow him anywhere. There's just some scary in between, but I need to have faith in the doctors and in Archie."

"Yes, girl! Now, go get your man." Mia jumps up out of our hug circle.

We break apart.

"I think he needs some time with his friends, so I'll text him in a bit. I think this has been a lot for him too. And y'all, there's only a few weeks left of school, and then the baby comes in May. I can't imagine the pressure he must be feeling to take care of me, train for the combine, and prepare for the draft. We have big life things coming at us hard."

"Okay, let's order a pizza then. I'm starving." Peyton grabs her phone from her pocket.

"Can we circle back to the baby shower?" Mia pipes in.

Livi claps her hands. "Oh, yes. So, what do you think, Em? Let's do it the weekend after the draft or something."

"Okay, maybe. Let me talk to Archie first." I stand from the couch, grab my bag, and head to my room. "Call me when the pizza gets here. I'm going to lie down for a bit."

"'Kay, we will," Livi chimes.

When I get to my room, I lie down on my bed. I'm almost asleep when I feel the baby moving. Lying on my back like this makes nugget move around a bit more, I've noticed. I rub my belly with one hand and place my other on the spot I felt the kick.

My emotions have definitely been heightened lately, but I can't help the tears that fall. I'm overwhelmed by the miracle of this life. How amazing this whole process of growing a baby is. I know we have to stay cautious until the baby is born, but I have to believe that this baby is strong and healthy and will have an amazing life because they have parents who will pour every ounce of love into them. I wish Archie were here right now to share this moment with me, but at the same time, maybe this moment was meant for me alone.

I'm still lost in thought when I hear my phone buzz from my bag. I roll off the bed and grab my bag from the floor. I see it's a text from my mom, but I call her instead of replying.

"Hey, Mom."

"Hey, sweetie. How are you feeling?"

"Good. I was just taking a rest."

"Did you see the doctor today?"

"We did. She is sending me to the high-risk OB in the office to monitor me for the rest of the pregnancy, but she says everything looks good. So, I think that's all we can do for right now."

Mom lets out a sigh. "Okay, well, that's good news. I feel better that they're keeping a close eye on the baby."

"Me too. It helps ease my mind every time I hear the baby's heartbeat. It sounds so strong. I wish you could hear it."

"I'd be happy to come to an appointment with you sometime. Do you think they would let me in with you?"

My parents have been much more available since they found out about the pregnancy. And I actually like it. I've been so independent for so long, so between Archie and them, having support is kind of nice.

"I don't see why not. You should come for the next one in two weeks."

"I would love that. Thank you." She sniffles.

I hear the door to the apartment open, so our food must be here, and I'm getting hungry.

"I need to go eat with the girls, but I'll send you the details for the appointment."

"Okay, sounds good. I love you. Tell Archie we said hello."

"Will do, Mom. Love you too. Bye." I set my phone on my nightstand.

When I get to the kitchen, there are two pizzas sitting on the counter. I grab a few slices of plain cheese and sit down at the table with the girls. I won't have these moments with them much longer, so as much as I miss Archie, I do think I should spend time with the girls tonight.

"So, should we watch something tonight, or do you all have plans?" I ask.

"Oh, let's watch the new season of *Love Island!*" Mia suggests.

"Yes, I'm in," Peyton answers.

Livi looks at me with a raised brow. "Em?"

"Sounds good to me. Let's do it."

We eat and laugh and talk about the baby some more. And talk about their love lives. Then, when we finish eating, we all crash on the couches and watch TV together.

I must have fallen asleep because I feel Livi gently trying to wake me. "Emma, you should probably go into your room so you're more comfortable."

Lifting my head, I look around the room and see Mia is also passed out. "What time is it?"

"It's ten. Why don't you go get some sleep?" She stands and holds out her hands to help me up.

When I get to my feet, I pull her in for a hug. "Thanks, Liv. I love you."

"Love you too, babe. Go to bed, but call that man of yours first. He's probably worried about you by now."

I nod and start down the hall, stopping at the bathroom to get ready for bed before heading to my room. As I walk in, I strip off my clothes and change into one of the shirts Archie left here. I can even faintly smell him on it.

Pulling back the covers, I look over on what's become Archie's side, and it makes me miss him. I climb into bed and grab my phone off my nightstand.

Archie has called a few times, and I see a few texts too. Instead of texting back, I call him, and he answers right away.

"Hey, darlin'. You okay? I was just about to come over there to check on you."

I can hear the worry in his voice.

"Hey, yeah. I'm good. I took a nap earlier, and then we had dinner and watched TV. I must have crashed at some point, and Livi just woke me up. Sorry to worry you."

He lets out a breath. "It's all good. I hope you had a nice time with them. Are you feeling better?"

"Yeah, I am. I just think everything is coming all at once, and I have very little control of it all, but I feel better. I miss you though."

"I miss you too. So much."

"Did you have fun tonight with your friends?" I ask.

"Mmhmm, yeah. It was a good time. It's weird doing family dinners without Pitz, but it was good to spend time with them. I can't wait for you to get to know everyone."

"We should do that soon, for sure. Maybe this weekend?"

He clears his throat. "Well, I got a call after dinner, and the trainer I had planned to work with here canceled on me, which really sucks because I wanted to be here with you while you finished classes before the draft. But, baby … I think I'm going to have to go to Texas. I'm not having any luck finding someone who can work with me here."

"Oh, okay. So, when would you have to go?"

"I'm not sure, but soon. I can do some things on my own, for sure, but I really need to work with someone. I don't want to put more stress on you, so let me try to work on it some more and see what I can do."

I can't help but tear up. It's just been a few rough weeks, and I thought we would have some time to work out some of these details, but it doesn't look like that will happen.

"Okay, we'll figure it out. Just see what you can do, and we'll go from there."

"Darlin', I'm sorry. I really didn't want to tell you this tonight, but we will need to figure out what to do. I don't want to be away from you. Especially with everything going on and you going into your last trimester."

"I know, but we can't stop the draft." I laugh half-heartedly. "Want to meet for breakfast in the morning?"

"Yeah, that sounds perfect. But are you sure you don't want me to come over tonight?"

"I mean, I do, but I'm also so tired that I'd probably be asleep by the time you got here. Do you want to pick me up or meet?"

"I'll come get my girl. I'll be there at eight a.m. Is that good? Or too early?" It sounds like he's moving around and closing a door or drawer.

"No, that's fine. What are you doing right now?" I'm nosy and kind of curious about what his room looks like. How he organizes everything. What his bed looks like.

He chuckles. "Sorry, is it too loud? I'm just going through my clothes and stuff and sorting it to pack up. I'm going to have to take my stuff back to Texas soon either way."

"Right," I whisper, then hold out my phone and press the FaceTime button.

He answers right away with a smile on his face. "Hey, baby."

"Hi. I just miss you and wanted to see your face. I also want a little tour of your room. You know … since you're moving out."

"Right, right. Well, this is it. Not much to it really." He turns his phone around and slowly shows me his room.

There really isn't much in there. Nothing on the walls. I see his bed with a plain blue comforter and a high dresser, and that's about it. There are a few pictures of his family on his dresser. My heart pinches a little that I'm not on there or the baby isn't, but then I can't be sad about it because it's my fault I'm not on there.

"Archie, I'm sorry I asked you to keep me from your friends. Or the pregnancy at least."

"Baby, I get it. Do I wish you could have gotten to know them better? Sure. But I'm also glad that we got so much time together to get to know each other too." He smiles at me softly.

"I love you—you know that?" I touch the screen, wishing I could touch his face.

"I love you too, darlin'. Get some rest, and I'll see you in the morning."

"Okay, bye, babe."

I blow him a kiss, and he puckers his lips in return.

If he has to leave early, that could change some things for me. But tonight, I'm not going to think about it anymore. Tonight, I'm going to sleep and be grateful that, today, everything is okay.

CHAPTER
TWENTY-THREE

ARCHIE

I'VE BEEN awake since five a.m. I got my workout in for the day, talked to my mom about getting the shack ready for me since she converted my room into a nursery, and made a few calls to some trainers in the area. I'm not having a lot of luck, so it looks like I'll have to go to Texas before the draft. But I can manage here for a few more weeks until we can figure out what Emma's options are. I need to talk to her about it today though.

Pulling into her complex, I can see her already waiting for me outside. She looks beautiful, standing in the early morning sun. Her long blonde hair is down, and she's wearing some long, baggy pants, but her shirt is formfitting, showing off her belly. Before I can put the truck in park, she's walking toward me and over to the passenger side. She opens the door and hops in.

"Hi," she says with a shy smile.

I lean in and kiss her quickly. Then I open my door and walk around the front of the truck. She's watching me through the front window, shaking her head.

I open her door and scoop her into my arms, bride-style, and kick the door closed with my boot. Then I set her down and wrap her in a hug. When I pull back, I frame her face and kiss her.

"Hi." Then I bend down a little so my face is near her stomach and set my hand on it. "Hi, nugget."

"What are you doing?" She smacks my chest when I stand.

Instead of answering, I reach around her and pull open the door. I take her hand and hold her as she gets back into the truck. I give her another kiss—because I can—then shut the door.

When I get back into the driver's seat, I have no doubt there's a shit-eating grin on my face, but I don't fucking care. This is my girl, and she needs to be treated like a queen.

She has a huge smile on her face, and she's shaking her head. "You're too much, Archie Griffith."

"Nah, darlin'. I'm just yours. Now give me those lips again. I missed you last night." I lean in closer, then wrap my hand around the back of her neck, pulling her toward me.

Her mouth opens to me, and I slide my tongue into her mouth, tangling her tongue with mine. She moves her hands into my hair and holds my head in place, deepening the kiss.

She pulls away after a few minutes, breathing heavy, but there's a soft smile on her lips. "I missed you too. Should we just skip breakfast and go back inside?"

My hand moves from her neck, and I tuck some of her hair that's fallen into her face behind her ear. "There's nothing I want more, but I'm starving, and I need to get you and the baby fed too. And I think we need to talk about some things, don't you?"

She takes my hand in hers and nods. "No, you're right. I want to talk some more about what we need to do before the draft. I was thinking about it a little this morning before you got here."

Releasing her hand, I pull out of the parking spot, and we start for the restaurant. I set my hand back on her leg as I drive.

"Okay, I want to hear about what you think, and I need to have some idea on what you have left to take care of here and honestly if you're ready for all of this right now. I know it's a lot, and I want you to feel good about the choices you're making."

The place I'm taking her to isn't far, so within ten minutes, we're pulling into the parking lot.

Once we're seated and we've ordered our food, I take her hands in mine. "Talk to me, baby. Tell me how you're feeling today."

She squeezes my hands. "I feel pretty good. Much better than yesterday. What happened in Arizona really rocked me more than I thought it did, but I didn't realize just how bad until I got back, you know. And then I felt like everything was happening all at once, and then add in fears about the baby … so I'm thinking I might have had a slight panic attack or something. Thank you for being patient with me. I understand that you're going through all the same things, and I don't think I've been taking that into consideration, and I'm sorry for that."

"Darlin', I hope I'm proving to you that you aren't alone in all this. I'm so sorry I couldn't be there when you were in the hospital. It truly kills me to think about you being there by your-self. And I'm not gonna lie—you know I'll be gone a lot during the season, so we'll need to make arrangements for those times so you aren't alone with the baby. I just ask that you talk to me and not shut me out. Go through what you need to go through, but let me stand by you while you do. Can you do that for me?" I pull her hands up and kiss her knuckles.

"I can do that. So, I think this is a good place to start talking about what I think I should do to support you. I have a meeting with my coach tomorrow, so I'll discuss my options with her, but I think it's best with everything going on that I take a medical hardship so I can finish the school year. Although I'm sure with, like, six weeks left in the school year, it's already covered. But this way, it will be on record."

"Are you sure you're good with this decision? I want you to feel good about it. You asked me about resentment yesterday, but it's really me who should be worried about you resenting me."

"Archie, no. I've thought about it a lot after our appointment and our talk yesterday and getting a good night's sleep. Then when you mentioned your trainer not being available ... well, it just felt like it was my turn to be there for you the way you've been for me."

"No. Your school and golf scholarships are too important to you."

"Yes, but now you and the baby are what's important. And I will become a doctor. That won't change. But let's be honest— I'm not going pro. Golf has given me amazing opportunities, and that's good for now. Besides, it's not like it's gone forever. You know, people play golf into their seventies."

I shake my head and smile. "I suppose you don't see a lot of forty-year-olds on the football field."

"And you don't see a lot of men who have the chance to play in the NFL. And you only get a few chances to love on your newborns before they're grown. I mean it, Archie, this is what I want."

"Emma, this means more to me than you know. I've been working on this all morning. Trying to figure out a way to stay here so you can finish, but also get the training in that I'll need. The only solution was that I was going to just go back and forth between here and my parents' house. The other thing we need to factor in here is the doctor, but I suppose we take one thing at a time for now?"

She nods. "Let's get through the meeting with my coach and see what your options are, and then we'll make arrangements for what works for us."

"I love you, baby. I know this is chaos right now, but it will all settle down."

"Ha! No, babe, it won't. You'll get drafted, and then we'll have to find a place to live while you're training with your new team. And, oh, we'll be having a baby during all of that too. It's not gonna settle for a while. But I love you, so we'll make the chaos our bitch."

"Damn right, baby. That's my girl." I laugh a little too loud.

"So, what else do you need to do today?" she asks, pulling her hands from mine to take a drink of the water the server just set on the table.

"My mission is to serve you, baby, so whatever you want to do is what we'll do."

"Well, I have class at one and three, but then I'll be done. Coach told me to take this week off for practice, so I'll just head home after class. But I was thinking … maybe we could go look at some baby furniture. I know we don't have an actual house to put the baby in, but I feel like it might be fun to look. What do you think?" Her eyes are bright, and she looks genuinely excited.

"We can absolutely do that, baby. Do you want to go before class or after?"

"Let's go after we eat. Then we can just relax later. Assuming you want to come over?"

Our food arrives before I can reply. She ordered pancakes and a side of eggs. She butters her pancakes, then pours syrup all over the pancakes and then the eggs. I just watch in fascination.

"Got enough syrup, darlin', or do you need some more?" I tease.

"Hush, Archie. I can't help it. The baby needs some sugar." She giggles.

We eat and talk about things we need for the baby and a little about the different schools she'll be applying to depending on where we land. It sounds like Dallas would be the best option, so I'm really hoping I can make that happen. For both of us.

CHAPTER
TWENTY-FOUR

ARCHIE

THE LAST FEW weeks have been pretty busy. Emma and I made it down to my parents' ranch and have settled in the best we can under the temporary circumstances. My mama hasn't scared her off yet with the way she's excited about the baby. And I have to admit, the nursery looks awesome. I think Emma likes it too.

Emma had to stay back for about a week to wrap up some things and pack up some of her stuff from her parents' house. While we were apart, we tried the FaceTime sex, and I got her to use that pink vibrator while I watched and jerked off. It's definitely something we'll be doing again when I'm on the road. Ten out of motherfucking ten.

She was able to get approval to take two of her finals online, and she had already turned in three of the papers that counted as her final, so for all intents and purposes, she's been done with her school year.

We did have to get a referral from our doctor for an OB down here and a high-risk doctor, but really, we're in good hands, especially considering one of Emma's top choices in schools is where our doctor's office is. It's a little bit of a trek into the city from the ranch, but I don't mind because I get to have Emma all to myself.

It's the morning of the draft, and I opted to be at home. My entire family and Emma's parents are waiting for us at the main house. But I want a little more time with my girl before I have to share her with our families. I mean, my entire family is here, and the news crews are already parked outside the house. We're a good mile from the main house, but there's nothing between us but wide-open space. I can see everything happening there from the window.

I'm too anxious to sleep, but not ready to go, so I do the only thing that can settle me. I strip off my shorts and crawl back into bed with my girl.

Emma's lying on her side, naked, her hand cradling her face. She looks so peaceful and calm. I snuggle in behind her and wrap my arm around her waist. I kiss the back of her neck, which makes her stir. When I lick a path from her neck to her earlobe and then bite down softly, she moans.

I drift my hand from her waist, over her belly, and in between her legs. She opens her legs just enough for me to get my hand between them. Her pussy is slick, and my fingers slide from her tight hole to her clit easily.

Her hips start to rock, and she moans my name. "Archie, what time is it? Do we need to get up to the main house?"

"We have time, darlin'. Just relax. Let me make you feel good."

My fingers move faster, and her hips buck against my hard-on.

"Babe, I don't know if we have time this morning. Maybe we should put this on pause until later."

"How about we just cuddle and if it slips in, it slips in?" I can't help the laugh that comes out of my mouth.

I absolutely intend to slip it in, and she knows it, which is why she laughs too.

Bringing her arm up, she wraps it around my head, and she grabs on to my hair. It's not painful, but just enough pressure to spur me on. "Just give me enough time to shower."

"You got it, baby." I trail kisses on her neck again, then suck as I flick her clit faster. I can tell by her breathing that she's getting close, and it's not going to take much for us both to come.

I take my hand from her pussy and pull her hips back a notch, then move her thigh so her pussy is exposed to me. With her hips tilted, I can push right in from this angle, so I do just that.

My dick is rock hard and takes no guidance sliding into her tight heat. With her legs closed like this, it makes her pussy practically choke my cock. Yeah, I'm not gonna last long.

"Archie, that feels so good. I'm so close."

"Me too, darlin'." I move my hand back between her legs and slide my middle finger back and forth over her clit. "Get there, baby. I can't hold it much longer."

"So. Close." Her hips stop moving as I feel her pussy begin to contract around my cock.

"That's it, baby. Come for me." My own orgasm erupts, and I pump into her harder.

"Fuck, Arch. That was the best cuddle we've ever had." Then she bursts out laughing, which makes me laugh.

After our breathing calms from our orgasms and laughing, I pull out. "I guess we should get cleaned up. Mama should have some food put out for everyone soon, if not already. I saw my dad go into the house from the barn around six a.m., so she's probably on breakfast, round two. And I have no doubt she's offered those news crews food too."

"Okay, babe. Let's get moving. My parents are probably waiting for me too. They aren't used to all this noise. Which I say with love." She laughs. "What time is Scott going to be here?"

She shifts and moves her legs to the edge of the bed and

stands. Her arms lift in a stretch above her head, and I stare in awe at this beauty that's mine.

When I don't reply, she turns to face me. "Arch. Focus. Scott?"

"I can't help it, darlin'. You're just too pretty."

I move off the bed and wrap my arms around her waist. Her belly is getting bigger and rests between us. I lean in to kiss her and feel a swift kick from her belly.

"Nugget is excited for today too, I think." She brushes her hand over her stomach.

"Nugget is about to be a very spoiled baby with all the money Daddy is about to get, so I would be excited too," I grumble into her neck.

"All right, hotshot, let's get ready, but don't distract me with your big peen. We have to get going."

I reach down and tap her between the legs with the head. "This big peen?"

"Archie, seriously." She pushes me away.

"Okay, okay. Let's get going."

While we get ready, I think about what part this draft plays in our future. Then I think about us, the baby. All of it. This life we're going to be living together as a family, and I feel a sense of urgency to make it official.

After I put my best jeans, shirt, and boots on, I grab my phone and my girl's hand. "Let's roll, baby."

A few thoughts on how to propose run through my mind. Maybe I should take her back to Walker since that's where we met. Or maybe I should wait until the baby is born and propose with our little nugget in the room. I can't decide. Yet, now, with her hand in mine as we walk on my parents' ranch, a strong wave of serenity weaves through my bones, and I know this moment is the right one.

"Emma, stop."

"What's wrong? Did you forget something?"

I grab her hands in mine and pull her in closer. "No, I didn't forget something. Or, well, shit. I guess I did." Fuck. A ring.

"Okay, we can go back and get it."

She tries to let go of my hand to start walking, but I hold on tighter.

"No, darlin'. I didn't forget something at the house. I just want to tell you that you being here with me today is more special than me actually getting drafted because I feel like I've already gotten the best of this life. You are everything to me, Em. Every. Thing. Over football, all of it. And I don't want to do anything in this life without you by my side." I drop to one knee.

"Archie, oh my God. What are you doing?" she cries, but has a watery smile on her face.

"Emma Grace Tucker, love of my life, mother of my baby, I would be honored if you would agree to be my wife. I love you, baby. I love you so much. Will you marry me?"

"Yes! Yes, I'll marry you! I love you so much!" She pulls me up and wraps her arms around my neck and kisses me.

This kiss is a promise. This kiss is a symbol of our commitment to each other and the love we feel. It's tender and sweet, and I don't want it to end.

She breaks the kiss first. "We'd better get inside. I can see the family watching out the window. They'll come out here if we don't get in there."

I look over at the house and see the family, my mom literally bouncing up and down. "Okay, so I don't have a ring yet, but I'll get you one first chance I get." I give her one more kiss before we start walking.

"Ha! Okay, babe. Now, let's go!" She leans up and kisses my cheek.

When we reach the house, my family erupts in cheers. My mama is sobbing and laughing. My brothers all come up to us and congratulate us.

For the next few hours, Scott and I have a lot of conversations about what's going to happen. It looks like I'll get my wish and go to Dallas. Stranger things have happened at the last minute though, so I'll be holding my breath until that call actually comes through.

Just as it's about to start, I talk to my friends, but honestly, I don't even know what's being said. It's so loud in here, and my mind is racing.

Aiden comes up to me and puts his arm around my shoulders. "You okay?"

"Yeah, I mean, this is pretty crazy in here. I can't even focus right now."

"Well, I mean, you proposed to your girl today—I'm guessing on the fly—and you're going to be getting the biggest chance of your career, so I can't imagine why you can't focus."

"Okay, funny guy." I wrap my arm around his neck and pull him in. "And, yeah, the proposal was on the fly, but I meant it. That girl is it for me."

We both laugh, and it sounds the same.

"Oh, I had no doubt about the sincerity of the proposal, but the fact that you did it just before you walked into this madhouse was so typical Archie. You should have seen Mama. We were all standing around the kitchen, eating, and out of nowhere, she starts screaming. I thought Pops was gonna have another heart attack, and Dad belted out a, 'Jesus Christ, Alicia.' But when she started jumping up and down, we all ran to the window to see what she was looking at, and we all saw your ugly mug kneeling on the ground." He hits me lightly in the chest.

"Hey, if I'm ugly, you are, too, since we look alike, dickhead."

"No, but seriously, I'm happy for you, man. Love you." He pulls me in for a hug.

"Love you too, Aiden. You'll be doing this in a few months. You think you're ready for it?"

"Fuck yes. I can't wait to get in the league. I'm not even nervous. I'm just ready. The lottery was interesting though.

Dallas didn't get the bid, so we'll see what happens. Scott thinks I'll go early, so now we wait."

"Bro, it would be so sweet if we both ended up in Dallas. You haven't really lived here in years, so Mama would be in heaven, having all her boys here. Then add in my baby, she'd be nuts."

"Yeah, we'll see. I'm stoked though. But it's Archie day today. Let's fucking go, man!"

"Hey, Archie, it's time. We want you to sit here in the center. Mom and Dad, you can sit on one side. Emma, you can sit on the other side."

We all take our seats and watch the opening of the show. Minutes later, the commissioner stands at the podium. Scott is pacing the room, eyes glued to his phone, fingers moving a mile a minute.

"Archie," he says, waving me over, nodding.

"Be right back." I kiss Emma on the cheek, stand, and walk over to Scott.

"Okay, thanks, Jerry." He nods at me. "Okay, it's happening. Third pick. They'll be calling in a few. They agreed to all of our terms, so it looks like you're gonna be a Cowboy, like you wanted. Congratulations, Arch. Big day for you."

He puts his hand out, and I take it in mine.

"Thank you, Scott. This is great news. I know my girl will be happy, and my mama will be over the moon. Thanks for making it happen."

"My pleasure, buddy. Let's go wait for that call."

I sit back down next to Emma and my parents, and my phone starts ringing immediately. I pull it out of my front pocket, and I feel Emma's hand land on my knee.

"Hello?"

"Archie! Coach Heimer here. How you doin' today?"

"Yes, Coach. Doing good. Thank you."

"Are you ready to be a Cowboy?"

"Yes, sir, I am. Thank you so much."

"Congratulations, Archie, to you and your family. We'll see you in Arlington tomorrow."

"Yes, Coach, thank you. See you tomorrow." I press End and look at Emma and smile and whisper, "Dallas."

My dad wraps his arm around my shoulders and squeezes a few times before letting go.

Minutes later, the commissioner comes back on just as the Cowboys' clock runs down to zero. Not gonna lie—I have a slight moment of panic, thinking they might change their mind, but as soon as the commissioner starts to speak, I know it's done.

"With the third pick of the 2025 NFL Draft, the Dallas Cowboys select Archie Griffith, tackle from Walker University."

Relief washes over me, followed by pure, unadulterated excitement. My entire life, I've worked toward this moment. From peewee league to tackle and getting a spot on the varsity team as a freshman, running extra sessions with my trainer while the other kids were at the swimming pool or goofing around. It hits me that it all paid off. My dad taught me to lift weights, and my mama cooked all day long because I was only twelve, yet training like a D1 athlete. The money they invested, the time and miles on the trucks. We all gave something for this moment, and the celebration isn't just for me; it's for my whole damn family.

I stand when someone from the news crew hands me a Cowboys hat, and I put it on my head. I turn toward my mom first and hug her, then kiss her on the cheek as she tells me she loves me. Then I hug my dad, and my brothers pile on too.

"Love y'all," I say as they all cheer in my ear.

When I walk over to Emma, she's watching me with tears in her eyes. I take her by the hand and pull her up. I wrap her in my arms and kiss her quickly.

"Love you, baby."

"Love you, Arch. Congrats, babe." She pulls back and wipes a tear from her cheek.

We sit back down, and the guy with the headphones near the

camera spins his hand, then points at the camera. I can see myself on the TV behind the commentator onstage.

"Congratulations, Archie. Do you have anything to say to all these Cowboys fans out here today?"

"Yes, sir. How 'bout them Cowboys?"

Everyone in my house cheers so loud that I can hardly hear myself speak. The camera cuts to the crowd at the draft, also cheering.

"Are you ready to win? I can't wait to get out on that field and work. Let's go!" I clap my hands a few times, and then the camera cuts back to the show.

As soon as the light turns off, everyone jumps up and cheers. I stand and pull Emma up by the hand again and pull her into me. We both tuck our heads into each other's neck. I'm trying not to cry like a baby, so I take deep breaths in until I feel like I can speak.

"I love you, Arch. I'm so happy for you. This is incredible and exactly what you wanted." I can hear the tears in her voice too.

I squeeze her a little tighter, then pull back and look her in the eyes. "You are my world, Emma. Sharing this with you is a dream come true. Thank you for standing beside me, carrying my baby, loving me, and for just being you. I hope I can give you as much as you give me. I love you so much, baby."

"I love you, Archie. So much." She takes ahold of my face and kisses me. She slips her tongue inside, which takes me by surprise a little since her parents are here, but I ain't gonna stop her.

"Yo, get a room!" one of my brothers—I think it's Ace—yells.

I give him the finger over my shoulder, but I feel Emma laugh against my lips, then pull back.

Emma's parents walk over to us then, and it's only slightly awkward because I honestly don't give a fuck who sees me kissing my girl. I'm marrying *the* girl, my family is surrounding me, and I just got drafted to my hometown team. The only thing that would make it better was if my boys were here. Charlie too.

"Archie, congratulations. We're just so excited for you!" Stacy hugs me, and then Van gives me an angled hug around his wife.

"Thank you both. This is a great thing for all of us. I'm glad y'all could be here today."

Emma's arms wrap around my waist, and I put mine around her and pull her in.

"We wouldn't want to be anywhere else." Stacy looks at Emma and smiles. "We're so happy for you both."

The rest of the day flies by, and when I check my phone, I see texts from my friends and several missed calls. I'll call them all back tomorrow, but for now, a text will have to do because I'm ready to get back to the shack and spend some time with my girl.

CHAPTER
TWENTY-FIVE

EMMA

YESTERDAY WAS A WHIRLWIND. By the time we got back to the shack, I could barely keep my eyes open. But Archie was worn out too. I think between the emotional roller coaster and keeping up with conversation, we were both exhausted. We pretty much stripped and fell into bed with barely a kiss.

The sun is coming up, and I'm sitting at the little kitchen table, looking out the window. It's so pretty here. Peaceful. I'm so glad my baby will get to spend time on the ranch. And by the looks of the nursery, Alicia plans on having Nugget here a lot. But I love it. She planned a baby shower for me this weekend, too, since a lot of family will be around anyway, so my friends are coming down tomorrow for the weekend.

I can see horses grazing in the distance and cows in a pen outside of the barn. A thought hits me when I see Archie's dad riding up from the south of the property. He's got a cowboy hat on, and he's riding alone. I get a flash-forward of what Archie might look like when he gets older. And in that thought, I decide I don't want to wait to marry Archie.

He has to leave in a few hours to go to Arlington, but I think we need to have this conversation now. I pad back to the bedroom and crawl in next to him. He's naked, like usual, so I run my hand up from his stomach up to his chest and rest it on his heart.

I'm propped up on my elbow and watch him stir. "Arch."

"Hmm? What's wrong?" He opens an eye and looks at me. "You okay?"

"Yeah, I'm good. I was just thinking, what if we just get married this weekend while everyone is here and my friends are coming for the baby shower? I mean, I don't really see a reason to wait, and I would like to have your name when the baby is born."

He sits up and props his back on the headboard. A slow smile forms, and it's incredibly unfair for a person to look this good first thing in the morning. "You wanna marry me, darlin'? This weekend?"

"Well, I mean, I feel like it just makes sense. Everyone is already here, and the baby is coming sooner rather than later. And after the baby is born, will we even have time to plan a wedding? Effective time management is key here, babe." I feel like I'm rambling a little, but now that the idea is rolling around, the more it feels like the right thing to do.

"I don't want to deprive you of your dream wedding. Don't you want to walk down the aisle in your dream dress that you picked out months before and have everyone you know dance with you at a party that has everything you ever wanted because you'd been thinking about the flowers and music and all the other stuff that girls think about with weddings?"

"That's the thing. I have everything I've ever wanted right here. I've never dreamed of my wedding, so I have nothing to compare it to. And as for dresses, I'd marry you in the T-shirt I stole from you the night we first met."

"I wouldn't argue with that."

I grin.

"But seriously, I don't want you to wake up in five years and wish you had done this differently."

"Archie, I think we're a little late on wanting to do things on a traditional timeline. What do you say? Make an honest woman out of me and make me your wife this weekend."

"Darlin', I'm gonna marry the shit out of you."

We both laugh, remembering when he said the same about dating me.

"Tell me what you need, and I'll make it happen. We have the big bucks now, so let me know how you want to do this."

I shake my head. "No, I don't want to spend a lot of money or anything. I just want to get married here. On the ranch. Simple, easy. I just need you." I lean in to kiss him.

"Okay, baby. Let's do it. But I want my friends to be here too. I can't wait for them to meet you and, of course, to tell them about the baby. Your friends are coming tomorrow?"

"Yes, you're right. I do want them here if they can be. Let's call them all today and see if we can make it work. Should I ask your mom to help with the wedding too? I mean, we should probably ask if we can get married here first, right? Or do you think a wedding is a lot to put on her on top of the baby shower stuff?"

He barks out a laugh. "Oh, baby. You are gonna be the favorite in the family. She's going to push me and my brothers aside, maybe even Dad, just so she can have you all to herself. You're gonna make all her dreams come true."

I can't help but laugh because it's funny, but also, I can actually see this and don't hate the idea. I really like her, and I think we'll have a good relationship.

"Okay, then let's do this! Yay!" I lean in to kiss him again, but his alarm goes off.

"Shit, I need to get up and get ready to go. Did you eat yet? We should probably eat before we shower and get in the car."

"I had a piece of toast because my tummy was rumbly. But I

can definitely eat more. Do we have an agenda for the day, or do we just wait until we get there?"

His parents and I will be going up with him to tour the facilities and meet the coaches and staff.

"I don't have anything yet, but maybe something will pop up when we're on the way. Either way, let's just plan on not eating for a while and maybe have my mama bring some snacks." He jumps out of bed, and his tight ass is on full display.

"You wearing your boots and hat today, babe?"

He turns to look at me and smirks. "You want me to wear my boots and hat?"

"I mean, I don't hate it when you do." I can't help but smile.

"Okay, baby, I'll wear them for you."

He winks, and I can't deny that he can still make my stomach flutter. And the sex, even though I'm getting bigger every day, I still want it all the time.

But right now, we need to go meet the Cowboys.

On the way up to Arlington, Alicia, my mom—on the phone —and I pretty much mapped out the whole baby shower, then wedding, including a small reception for after the ceremony on the ranch. I gave my mom some ideas on what I wanted for the cake so she could place the order for that, and we talked about what I would wear, so we'll probably shop while we're in the city before we go back this evening.

The cake is ordered, and the food ... I left to Alicia. The local pastor is a family friend, so she called him, and he can marry us. So, everything is pretty much set. The only thing left for us to do is call our friends and get them down here. Although I think Archie already texted Liam—since he's the farthest and would need more time to make arrangements. The rest of his friends and mine can make the three-hour trip easily.

As for the tour, it's been incredible. We saw the facility, and Archie got to see his locker. His nameplate was already on it, and his jersey, with his number sixty-nine, was hanging in it. We took a lot of pictures, and Archie took some video of what he was permitted to share.

Now his parents and I are waiting for him to finish up with a few meetings. They have us sitting in a lounge that overlooks the practice field. The whole operation of this place is impressive. My dad would love to see it.

"Emma?" A woman, perfectly manicured, walks into the room.

"Yes, ma'am?" I stand and rest my hand on the top of my belly.

Shane and Alicia stand, too, almost in a protective way. I nearly laugh, but hold it in.

"On behalf of the Dallas Cowboys, we want to welcome you to the Cowboys family. Congratulations to y'all!" She hands me a small box wrapped in silver paper, a big blue bow, and a star with the words *Baby Griffith* on it.

"Oh, okay. Thank you so much."

Alicia comes to stand next to me when the woman walks out.

"Emma, sweetie, open it." Her hands are folded and tucked under her chin.

I'm pretty sure she's more excited than I am, but I tear into the paper anyway. When I lift the top of the box, I see a Cowboys blue onesie with the number sixty-nine and *Griffith* on the back. It's just like the Walker one I bought for Archie for Christmas, but this one probably cost a bit more. He's gonna love it!

"Oh! That is just precious. My word. Shane, come look at this. Emma, pull it out so we can see it."

I set the box on the chair I was sitting in and pull it out of the box and hold it up. It's adorable, I have to admit.

"It looks like there might be something else in the box." Shane lifts it and pulls out white pants with a blue stripe running down the sides. The whole ensemble looks like a tiny uniform.

"Well, if it's a girl, we'll add a big bow for her hair." Alicia giggles. "I just remembered the cutest thing I saw on the Pin network."

"Pinterest?" I question.

"Whatever, yes. The place you can find recipes and whatnot? That one. Anyway, I saw the cutest idea, and since the cat's out of the bag about the baby, with you being on national TV and all, we should do it!"

"Okay, what is it?" I ask, but we're interrupted by Archie coming into the room.

"I think we're done for the day, but I'll need to be back up here by Monday. Which means, Em, we will need to start looking for a temporary place to stay until we can come up and look for a house."

"Wow, this moves fast. Okay, well, let's make a stop at one of the stores I found for a dress. Arch, you and Dad can just wait in the car or something. I don't think it will take long. I just want to show Emma a dress, which looks exactly how she described the one she wants for the wedding."

"All right, let's get a move on it then. We have a lot to do, and I'm beat. I want to get Emma off her feet and rested too. The next few days will be a little hectic."

Once we leave the complex and make our stop at the store

Alicia found, which did indeed have the perfect dress, we make our way back to the ranch.

We eat with the family before heading back to the shack, where we once again practically fall into bed.

The next morning, I hear Archie talking in the other room.

"So, your flight leaves in an hour, which will put you in Dallas around two p.m. Central. We'll be here. I'll order a car for you so you don't have to get a rental." He pauses. "No, dumb-ass, I'm calling an Uber for you." I hear a loud cackle from the other end of the call. "Later, man. Thanks for coming."

"Hey, who was that?" I walk into the room and hug him.

"Mornin', darlin'." He kisses the top of my head. "That was Pitz. He just got to the airport in Detroit, and he'll leave soon. I spoke with Beck this morning, and he, Charlie, Casey, and Call-away are heading down in a few hours. Beck said if he wakes Charlie up now, she might cut him. And I'm not sure if it was a joke or not."

"I should probably text the girls then to get an ETA, huh?" I walk back to the bedroom and send out a text to Livi, Mia, and Peyton.

They all respond immediately, which is surprising since it's so early. They'll make their way down after eleven a.m.

Archie comes back into the room, looking down at his phone. "My mama wants us to come up to the house. She gave me instructions to not dillydally or fool around." He gives me an annoyed look.

"We'd better get moving then," I say, laughing.

Once we get to the main house, Alicia takes us up to the nursery. She must have grabbed the box with the onesie in it from the car because it's sitting on the changing table. I kind of forgot about it just because I was so tired when we got back. Sitting next to it are two white T-shirts and two baseball hats. One says *Mommy*, and the other says *Daddy*.

Does she just have this stuff lying around?

"Okay, I need you two to change into these T-shirts and holler when you're ready." Then she bustles out of the room.

Archie grabs both shirts from the table and hands me mine. "Do you know what this is about?"

"It might be the Pinterest idea she had, but I'm not sure."

Once we're dressed, Archie yells out to his mom.

After about twenty pictures, she lets us see the photos. I have to admit, it's so freaking cute. I love it. It's a picture of Archie and me, our backs facing the camera. Our hats are on backward, also facing the camera, and we're each holding a shoulder of the onesie we got from the Cowboys, with his name and number.

Archie, well, he's eating it up, and he quickly posts it on his social media. The caption is simple though. It says, *My life, my love.*

Gah, this man. I just love him.

CHAPTER
TWENTY-SIX

ARCHIE

I'M RUNNING on adrenaline at this point. I don't know what day it is or what time it is. I'm just going where I'm told to go.

We went to the courthouse this morning to get the marriage license, and luckily, the judge found out I was there and signed it for us on the spot. His son was a year younger, and we had played football together in high school. Then he wanted my autograph and a few pics before we left.

Our friends arrived a few hours ago, and my mama had a whole spread set out for a little barbeque. Her friends brought baby gifts, as did Charlie, so it's turned into a little baby shower/pre-wedding bash today.

My friends, as I knew they would, seem to love Emma. I can tell she feels comfortable with them and is enjoying having them here. It was a good call, inviting everyone up. And my brothers are here too. Although Austin had to leave early for a baseball game.

Ace and Aston have been flirting with Mia and Peyton shamelessly. I think they think they really have a chance with those two. Cocky little fuckers. I love 'em.

Aiden has been hanging out with Bo and Casey mostly. He's met Casey a few times, but this is the first time he's getting to meet Bo. They're sort of alike, now that I think about it.

Emma's friends pulled me aside earlier with a plan. I'm not sure if Emma will like it or hate it, but they really want to pull this off, so like the good sport that I am, I agreed. I ordered a car to pick up the girls and booked a block of rooms in downtown Dallas since it will be late by the time we're done. The girls will all head out first, and me and the guys will show up a bit later—minus my brothers because where we're going, they need to be twenty-one to enter.

The car arrives, and Emma has no idea what they're doing, but she seems to be having fun. Charlie is going with them even though Beck wants her to stay with us. Because where we're going, Beck is likely to go apeshit if some guy starts rubbing up on his girl. And I don't blame him. The difference between us though, I'm putting a ring on it. Tonight. And she's having my baby, so I'm not too worried about it.

When my truck pulls up to the club where the girls are thirty minutes later, Casey looks out the window and shakes his head.

"Uh-uh. I'm not going in there. Is that where the girls are? Beck, you're okay with Charlie being in there?" His voice squeaks, and his eyebrows shoot to his hairline.

"Fuck no, but I'm here now, so it doesn't really matter."

"Be a good sport, King. This is about my girl. Don't ruin it for her."

He shakes his head as we all get out of the car.

Liam wraps an arm around my shoulders. "She digs the hat, I guess?"

I have on my favorite Stetson. Not the one I'll wear for the wedding, but my everyday hat. It's black with a thin black leather band around it. I'm wearing my boots that she likes too.

"She loves the hat." I wink at him.

We hear the girls before we see them. Peyton, Mia, and Livi are sitting near the front of the stage, whistling at the guy dancing in front of them. Emma and Charlie are sitting around the back of their table, not watching the show but talking to each other.

"I'm gonna go find the guy I need to talk to in order to get backstage. You guys hang back here so Emma doesn't see you."

They all nod, and I make my way to the back.

"You Archie?" a guy in a black shirt asks me.

"That I am."

"You're dancing for your girl, right?"

"Yeah. I'm the only one who can dance for her. I don't want any other guy onstage but me while she's up there."

"Not a problem. Hey, I gotta ask though. You just got drafted to the Cowboys, right?"

"Depends on how you plan to use this information."

The guy tilts his head back and laughs. "Buddy, you don't have to worry about anonymity here. We have to sign pretty strict agreements. You'd be surprised if you knew who came in here. So, no offense, man, but you ain't newsworthy enough to lose my job over."

Okay then. I hold my fist out for him to bump, and he does and laughs.

"Good luck this season, man. We need some guys like you on offense."

"Thanks. I can't wait to get out there and get it done."

He nods, then looks around the curtain. "Looks like you're up. Your girl is sitting in the chair onstage."

"Thanks, man."

I walk up the few stairs to the stage, and the lights are off. As soon as "Pony" by Ginuwine starts playing, I walk out onstage. Now, I'm not a dancer, but I do know how to move my body. And I've been known to eat up attention, so the loud cheers that erupt when I slide around the stage feed my ego just a little.

When I get to the chair, Emma is blindfolded, and she's wearing a sash that says *Mother* and *Bride-to-Be*, written in marker. I try to hold in my laugh, thinking about how much Emma probably hated the whole idea of this.

Because I have zero patience, as soon as the lyrics start, I take hold of her blindfold and slowly lower it down. When she opens her eyes, she looks up at me and smirks.

"I knew it."

Instead of answering, I place my hat on her head and start dancing up on her. I straddle her lap while standing and take hold of the back of the chair with one hand while brushing my fingers down her face with my other hand.

My friends and Emma's are whistling and catcalling from the table in front of the stage. But my eyes, they're on Emma.

I roll my hips because I'm here to put on a show after all. Her eyes move down my body, and I see the heat in them. This is turning her on. I know that look well.

When I push off the chair to stand, I grab the hem of my shirt.

"Oh, babe. You're pulling it all out, huh?"

Instead of answering her, I give her the smile I know makes her melt, then take off my shirt and toss it to her. She catches it and sets it on her lap.

Emma motions me toward her with her index finger, so I slide my way back over to her. When I'm straddling her, she works her hands from my stomach up to my chest.

"You want this, baby?"

"Oh, yeah, and you're all mine. Fuck, Arch. I'm almost embarrassed to say it, but this is turning me on. We might have to make this a regular thing. But, like, in our home. Privately."

"Only for you, darlin'."' I take hold of the back the chair again, but with two hands this time, and I tilt it back far enough for me to lean down and kiss her.

My hat slides back on her head a little, so I slide one hand toward the middle and let go of the chair with the other hand to catch the hat before it falls. I catch it by the brim, and while I'm still hovering over her, I flip my hat and set it on my head and wink at her.

The hollers and whistles from the crowd are near deafening as the song ends.

I pull Emma up by her hands, then lift her, cradle-style, and carry her off the stage. When I set her down, her hands wind around my neck, and she lifts up to kiss me. It's deep. It's dirty. And my cock feels like it's gonna bust through my zipper.

"Baby, I can't fuck you here. Let's go back to the hotel."

"Yes, the hotel. Wait, what hotel?"

"I got us all rooms here in Dallas for the night."

"Okay, yes, let's do that. I'm sure they can figure out their way back, right? Like, we don't need to wait for them?"

I let out a deep laugh and tilt my head back. "Yeah, darlin', we can leave. I sent the hotel info to everyone with their room numbers and digital keys on the way up here. We're good. Let's get out of here."

I set my hat on her head while I slip on my shirt, then reach into my pocket and take out my phone. I text Beck to tell him we're leaving.

We reach my truck in the parking lot, and I pick her up and set her in the seat. Then walk around to the driver's side and hop in.

"So, were you surprised or no?" I lean over and kiss her nose.

"Well, I mean, I had an idea something was gonna happen when they pulled up to that club. There was no way you would be okay with me going there without you, so I just followed along with the plan. Curious more than anything. But, babe …" She leans in and whispers against my lips, "You got me so worked up that I hope you're ready for me to ride. You. All. Night."

She licks my mouth from my bottom lip to my top. And I don't know why that's so sexy, but it is.

"Oh, yeah?" I ask, sliding my hand up her thigh. "How wet are you?"

"Soaked."

My fingers reach her center, and she's right. She's soaked.

"Let's see how long you can last."

I brush my fingers across the top of her panties, and she rolls her hips.

"I can't wait. I need you now. Like, seriously. Let's get in the back seat."

"Baby, I'm not sure how comfortable that will be for you. There's not a ton of room back there."

Instead of answering me, she jumps out of the truck. I see her look around the parking lot, and then she gets in the back seat.

I can't help the laugh that slips out. This night has been pretty crazy as it is, so why not fuck my very pregnant fiancée in the back of my truck? In a parking lot at a strip club. *Sorry, male revue.* So, I jump out and get in the back with her.

"Archie," she moans as I push my hand between her legs.

"Be good, Emma. Don't come yet." I lean in and kiss her, capturing the next moan that tries to escape.

With the limited space we have, it'll be tricky to get her completely naked like I want, but I need to feel as much of her as possible. Her skirt and panties come off first. Then I take my hat off her head and put it back on mine. Then I pull off her shirt.

"Lift your arms."

She's fumbling with the button on my jeans, but it pops open when I lift my hips. She pulls down the zipper, then drags my jeans down my legs. Then she slides her hands back up my legs and takes my cock in her hand and smears the cum around my crown.

"Darlin', if you keep playing with my cock, I might come before you get yours. How do you want to do this?"

She climbs over my lap and straddles me. "I think I'm gonna go ahead and take that ride. But, Archie, leave the hat on."

"Yes, ma'am." I take hold of the rim and tip it toward her.

"Fuck, that's hot." She lifts up and reaches between her legs and grabs my cock. As I sink into her tight heat, we both moan. "Holy hell, you feel so good, Arch."

"That's it, baby. Bounce on my cock."

My hands slide around to cup her ass, and I help her lift her hips up and down. When she starts to roll her hips, I slide my hands from her ass to take hold of her breasts.

"Squeeze a little. Your hands feel so good on me, babe. Your cock is so deep. I just want to stay like this. I feel like I can't take you deep enough."

I start to roll my hips in sync with hers. It's slow, controlled, and I feel like our bodies are truly and deeply connected. Needing to taste her lips, I move one hand to her neck and pull her toward me, then meet my mouth to hers. Our tongues tangle, and I feel her hips start to move faster.

She breaks the kiss, breathless. "I'm so close. Keep moving your hips just like that, Archie. You're hitting that one spot that drives me crazy, and I feel like I'm on fire."

Just as she says it, I start to feel her pussy contract around my cock.

"Take it, baby. Ride it out," I pant out.

I've been holding back my orgasm, waiting for her to reach hers first. With a few more deep pumps, I can't hold back anymore, and I erupt.

She leans back and rests her head on the back of the front seat. "Oh fuck, Arch. That was so, so good. We're definitely gonna do this again. And preferably when I'm not pregnant."

I place my hands on either side of her belly. "Baby, you are so beautiful to me. Watching you come is my very favorite thing. I'm the luckiest son of a bitch that I get to call you mine. And tomorrow, I'll get to call you my wife."

"Yeah, you are. I can't wait. But right now, I'm not sure I can move. You're gonna have to help me get off your dick." She snorts out a laugh.

"You can stay on board. Hell, we can even go another round

if you want. You keep moving those hips, and I'll be ready to go in just a few pumps."

She shakes her head and starts to lift her hips, making my dick slide out. "Let's go to the hotel. I know the wedding isn't until the evening tomorrow, but I don't want your mom to be left taking care of everything tomorrow."

"Baby, she won't let you lift a finger, and you know it. You just need to show up at the end of that aisle and say yes."

She puts on her top, then pulls her panties and skirt on. "I'll definitely show up, and I will one hundred percent say yes."

I pull up my jeans, zip, and button. "Let me get you out, just sit tight."

Then I open the door and walk around to her side. When I pull the door open, she's got a strange look on her face.

"Baby, what's wrong?"

"I think I just had a contraction." She's holding her stomach.

I put my hand over hers. "Is it one of those early ones? What are they called? Braxton something?"

"Braxton-Hicks, but I'm not sure that's what this is." One of her hands grabs on to my forearm. "Okay, that was a little stronger."

"Do we need to go to the hospital?" I'm trying to stay calm for her.

She scoots forward a little closer toward me, and I take her arm and hold it while she starts to climb out.

"Maybe I just need to stand for a second."

As soon as her feet hit the ground, a gush of fluid splashes on the pavement.

"Baby, either you just peed or it's time to go."

"It's time to go." She looks up with panic in her eyes.

"Hey, I got you. We got this. Let's get you in the front seat and get moving." I lean in to kiss her and wrap my arms around her.

Her hands grip my shirt, and she nods into my chest. "Okay, I guess we're going to have a baby."

CHAPTER
TWENTY-SEVEN

EMMA

ARCHIE IS SITTING in the chair next to my bed, holding the most beautiful little girl I've ever seen. Ten perfect little fingers. Ten perfect little toes.

When we arrived at the hospital, I was already dilated to four centimeters. However ... they wouldn't give me the epidural until I was seven centimeters. Then my labor lasted for thirteen hours, and I pushed for one hour. But I had an incredibly supportive cowboy by my side. He was so calm and attentive.

"Well, Mama, I think we should decide on a name for our perfect angel here before our families offer their input. We probably should have thought about it a little more before she was born."

Archie called his family and Liam on the way to the hospital to let everyone know, and his mom called my parents. They're all waiting to meet her. Archie and I wanted to have some time with her before everyone descends on the room. Plus, she's been having some tests done on her heart to get a better idea about how large the hole is and if there are any other mechanical issues. So far, they don't see any sign of pulmonary atresia, but they want to keep her here for a few extra days just to make sure she isn't having any trouble breathing.

"Yeah, we should have, but there's been so much going on, and we didn't know the gender."

"I think the next time, I'd like to know."

"Next time?"

He gives me that sexy smirk of his. "I mean, whenever you're ready, of course."

"Let's let it rest a bit before we start making plans for another baby. It's only been three hours."

"You got it." He leans down and kisses the baby's head. "Darlin', I just want to say thank you for giving me this gift. I knew I wanted to be a dad someday, but this is more than I could have imagined. This is a true gift right here, and I will forever be grateful to you." He reaches over and takes my hand. "I love you so much."

A few tears run free, and I wipe them away with the back of my hand. "I love you too, Archie. She's a gift of life for both of us. Unexpected, but the best gift I've ever gotten."

"What would you think about honoring your sister? We could use her name as a middle name or something."

"I think … that would be perfect."

Archie stands and brings her over to me. When he places her in my arms, a peace comes over me, and I know without a doubt that this little girl was meant to be mine.

"Doesn't it feel like she's really looking at us? I mean, I read somewhere that they can't really see or something, but I think she's looking at us."

"Yeah, I think so too. She's just so perfect." I trace her little nose and lips, which makes her mouth open, and she starts rooting. So, I bring my gown down and nurse her. I can't say it's a pleasant experience, but I think we'll get the hang of it.

"Baby, you're both perfect." He kisses the top of my head.

"What do you think about Lainey for her first name and

Sunny for her middle name? I love the idea of using my sister's name, but I want the baby to have her own identity too."

"Lainey Sunny Griffith. I like it." He leans down and kisses her head. "What do you think, Little Sunshine? You like that name?"

"I like it too. Okay, so we'll go with that. Should we introduce everyone to her now that we have a name?"

He nods. "I just want to sit here with my girls for one more minute."

"Hey, come here." I tilt my head up and pucker my lips, and he leans down to kiss me. "You're already the best daddy. I love you so much."

"I love you, too, darlin'. I'll be right back. Do you need anything before I bring everyone in?"

I shake my head. "Nope, I think we're ready."

Archie kisses me, then the baby again and walks out the door.

The baby is no longer sucking, so I place her over my shoulder and rub her back. "I hope you're ready for this, Lainey. You're part of a rowdy family, but they sure will love you."

The football season is upon us already. Archie is doing amazing and has had the opportunity to start in most of the games. This week, they'll be playing the Monday Night game, which worked perfectly for us because it's a big game at Walker this weekend and Archie wanted to be here.

His friends love Lainey, as do mine. Anytime we get to see any of them, they all want to spoil her rotten. The only one we don't get to see that much is Liam, but he and Archie talk all the time. I know he misses him and the rest of the guys.

We're staying at my parents' house this weekend. They're getting ready to move to Dallas to be closer to us and will be helping me with Lainey when I go back to school. And to help me with any final details for our spring wedding.

One of the hardest things for them about leaving Oklahoma is that my sister is buried here. But my mom says she feels Sunny around her every day and that the gravesite is just a place. Sunny *is* around us, and I have to say, I agree. Because since Lainey has been born, I feel like my sister is watching over us.

Lainey has had to continue to be monitored, but so far, we haven't had major concerns. Definitely a few bumps in the road in terms of irregular heart rates, and the hole is closing a little slower than they hoped, but no matter what happens, I just have faith it will be okay. And Archie has been a huge support and a big part of why I've been able to stay calm about all the testing.

We have to leave soon for the game, and we'll be taking Lainey with us. Archie likes to show her off to all his friends. But we're going to make a stop at Sunny's grave before we go. Like my mom says, I know it's just a place, but I want to take Archie and Lainey anyway.

"You ready to go?" Archie comes into the guest room we're staying in with Lainey in his arms. She has a fistful of his hair that's peeking out of his Walker football hat and trying to eat his jaw.

Her own hair is growing in, with some ringlets starting, and as predicted, it's blonde. Her eyes are blue, like Archie's. I know I'm biased, but she's the most beautiful baby I've ever seen. She's the perfect combination of us, but I will admit, she does favor the Griffith side of the family.

I'm not sure there is anything sexier than seeing him with our daughter. Even when he changes her diaper. Sexy.

"Yes, I think I have everything she'll need. I'll feed her in the car before we go into the game."

"You don't have to feed her in the car. We'll be going in the players' entrance and be able to use the family waiting area. You'll be fine there, unless you don't feel comfortable."

"Oh, no, that's fine. I have my little sheet to drape over my shoulder. We just need to stop at the florist to grab Sunny's flowers on our way to the cemetery."

"Okay, baby. I'll go put Little Sunshine in the car seat. Did you grab the baby carrier, or do I need to grab it on my way out?"

"I got it. I'm ready, so I'll come out with you."

My mom is in the kitchen, drinking a cup of coffee and scrolling on her phone. "Emma, did you see this idea for a photo shoot? We could dress her like a bumblebee! How cute is that?"

Archie's mom is rubbing off on my mom, and collectively, we've done several photo shoots of the baby in various settings. But they love it, and it makes them happy, so I play along. Archie thinks it's funny, and he's not at all surprised by their Pinterest obsession with finding new trends to try with our daughter. They did a football set at the start of his season, which I think was his favorite so far.

"That's super cute, Mom. We can do that one once you get settled. Let's not take that on in the middle of the move."

"Oh, I'm sending it to Alicia. I thought we could do it on the ranch. Can you imagine the backdrop? Perfection."

"Whatever makes you happy." I laugh. "We're gonna head out and stop to see Sunny before the game."

She gives me a soft smile. "Okay, sweetie. I love you. Let me kiss the baby before y'all leave." Mom walks over to Lainey, still in Archie's arms. "I just know your auntie would have loved you. You're our Little Sunshine, aren't you?" She kisses Lainey on the cheek.

"We'll see you later, Mom. Tell Dad we said goodbye. I haven't seen him since breakfast."

"Oh, he ran out to the store to get more packing tape."

"Stacy, I told y'all I would be happy to pay for movers. You don't have to do this alone." Archie has tried repeatedly to get them to let him pay for the move, but they won't let him. He's already bought them a house not far from ours, so they don't want to feel like they're taking advantage, even though he insisted.

"Not another word about it. Besides, Van is very particular about his things. He would annoy them by giving them instructions." She laughs and shakes her head.

"That's so true. Okay, we need to go if we want to make it to the game on time." I start walking to the door, trying to move this goodbye along.

"Say goodbye to Grammy, Sunshine." Archie lifts her arm and waves it at my mom.

"Bye, my sweet girl. I'll see you later!" Mom blows her a kiss as Archie starts to walk out.

After leaving my parents', we stop at the florist and get some sunflowers for Sunny's gravesite.

Archie is carrying Lainey as we walk to her headstone. Lainey fell asleep in the car and has barely stirred since he took her out of her seat.

When we reach her stone, I kneel on the grass, set the sunflowers against her headstone, and run my fingers across her name. "I brought someone to meet you today. Well, two someones." I turn and look at Archie, who is now sitting on the grass behind me.

He smiles and places a hand on my shoulder.

"This is my baby girl, Lainey, and the love of my life, Archie.

I'm sorry we haven't been by sooner, but I think about you and feel you every day. I wish you could have been here to meet them. You would love them. They both have the same happy nature you had." I wipe a tear from my cheek. "I wanted you to know that I'm not scared anymore because I know you're watching over her and I have faith that everything will be okay." My tears are coming faster now, and I need a minute to breathe.

Archie gives my shoulder a squeeze and clears his throat. "Hey, Sunny. I wish I could have met you, but your sister talks about you a lot, so I feel like I know you." He pauses. "I promise you, I'll do everything in my power to take care of your sister and our baby girl. They are my entire world. But I know you'll have our backs too." He squeezes my shoulder again, then lets go. "I'm gonna give you a minute alone with her."

I nod and wipe the tears from my face. "Okay, I'll be right there." I set my hand on top of the stone. "We have to get going, but the next time we're here, I'll come back. I miss you and love you so much." I sniffle. "I'll see you in the sunflowers."

EPILOGUE

ARCHIE

MY FIRST SEASON in the NFL is in the books. It was an incredible experience, and I can't wait to go back to training camp in the summer. But right now, it's all about my girl. It's finally our wedding day.

Emma wanted to get married on my parents' ranch, which, of course, thrilled my mama. It took some time for Emma to decide on exactly the right spot for the ceremony to fit her rustic ranch wedding theme, but she did, and I gotta say, it's perfect.

The location is a little far from the main house, so we have tractors with trailers to bring guests to the wedding site. Then the reception is closer to the house, under a tent. My brothers, friends, my dad, daughter, and I jumped on the trailer and are all heading over now. Some of the guests are starting to arrive, so we figured it was time to make our way out there too.

I have Lainey in my arms, but she's reaching for my brother Aiden. She's obsessed with him. And my dad too.

"You want to see Uncle Aiden, Sunshine?"

"Gimme my girl." He reaches for her and takes her from me.

She's dressed in a pale yellow dress, and a headband is

holding her wild, curly locks from her face. She's almost a year old now and getting so big.

Lainey puts both of her hands on his face and squeezes his cheeks together for a very drooly kiss.

"Lucky you." I laugh because he now has drool on his face, but he just smiles and wipes it away.

"A little drool never hurt anyone—right, princess?" He kisses her cheek, then turns her so she's facing everyone. "So, brother, you ready for this?"

"You know it. It feels like forever since I asked her to marry me. It seems like we've been married though, so it's just a formality at this point. But I wanted her to have the wedding she wanted, and it was impossible to try to make it work with me in season."

"No doubt. I'm just glad it worked out for me to be here, too, with my bye week." He hands Lainey off to my dad because she's getting squirmy again.

"Me too. I wouldn't have wanted to get married without you here."

The tractor starts to slow as we climb up a small hill and approach the wedding site. I haven't been out here since the wedding planners and florists were out here earlier, so I'm a little surprised when I see it. My mama is already there to welcome guests and direct any last-minute details.

There's an aisle between bales of hay in rows for seating with blankets lying on top of the bales, and at the end of each row is a bouquet of sunflowers in what looks like glass mason jars. The altar is formed by an arbor, woven with sunflowers and other white and yellow flowers. A small acoustic band is sitting along the side of one of the rows, playing music as guests take their seats. It's exactly what Emma wanted, and I can't wait for her to see it.

Casey, Beck, and Liam step off the trailer first, followed by my brothers. My dad stands and steps toward me, and Lainey reaches out for me to take her. God, I love this little girl. She's everything good. I kiss her on the cheek before she wraps her little arms around my neck.

"You ready for this, son?"

"Hell yeah. I can't wait to see her coming down that aisle. For me, this is just a formality, but I wanted her to have everything she wanted. I would have married her the day I asked her—actually before then—but my baby girl here had a different plan for us, and I couldn't be happier." I pull Lainey back a little to look at her face. "I have everything a man could want."

"That you do. Take care of them, protect them, put their needs before yours. Always." He reaches out to run his hand over Lainey's head. "You're a good son and an amazing father, and we're so proud of the man you are. Love you." He leans in and wraps an arm around my shoulders and the other around Lainey and me.

"Thanks, Dad. I learned from the best. Love you too."

I step away and grab Lainey's tiny cowboy boots off the bench. I bought my girls matching white cowboy boots for the wedding. Emma squealed, but I think she was more excited about the baby's than her own.

"All right, old man. Let's do this."

"Lead the way, son."

We step off the trailer and move toward the arbor at the end of the aisle. My brothers and my boys are huddled around each other when we get there, so I hand Lainey to my dad and go stand with them.

"What're y'all doing over here?"

I see Liam pouring whiskey into red shot cups and passing them around. When he gets to Austin, I swipe it out of his hand.

"Mama would kill you, and I can't have you ruin Emma's day."

"That's not fair. Ace and Aston get to have one, but I don't?"

"Settle down, Austin. You're only fifteen. You don't have enough hair on your chest to appreciate the taste of this fine bottle of whiskey."

"Says the brother only four years older than me. You shouldn't be drinking either, Aid. This is some bullshit right here."

"All right, Griffs, hush up. This isn't about you. It's about Archie." Liam hands me a shot. "Okay, boys, let's gather round."

"Hey, that's my line." I smirk.

"Yeah, but I'm taking the reins today." He lifts his cup, and everyone in the circle follows suit. "I'm not as good at these as you are, but I'll take a stab at it." He clears his throat. "May you always walk in sunshine and never want for more. May good fortune and peace always be at your door. May the love and friendship you have guide you whenever you're in doubt. And may the good luck that's with you never run out. Here's to you, my friend and brother. We couldn't be happier that you locked this girl down with a baby."

Everyone laughs.

"Cheers to Archie and Emma!"

"Cheers!" rings around the circle, and we all take our shots.

"I love y'all, and I couldn't ask for better friends and brothers to be standing up here with me today. Come on now. Bring it in."

I open my arms wide, and we all wrap our arms around each other. We pull apart when we hear the other tractor coming up the hill.

"Showtime, Arch." Aiden pats me on the back, and we all move to stand by the arbor.

In my gray suit and my best white cowboy hat and my best boots, I wait for my girl. The pastor steps up and stands behind me and puts a hand on my shoulder. I look over at my mama, Dad, and Lainey and wink. My mom is bouncing Lainey on her lap, which means she's probably getting a little restless or hungry. My baby girl doesn't like to sit too long. She's always moving. I can't imagine what she'll be like when she actually takes off. Trouble.

I see more of my family, some of my old teammates,

including Bo Callaway, and some of my new teammates. I give a few waves and smiles.

But then the music starts to play, and I see Emma's bridesmaids—Livi, Peyton, Mia, and Charlie—step off the tractor, but they're blocking my view of her. Then I see her mom, and then her dad. Finally, there she is. Emma holds her dad's hand as she steps down. When she looks up, our eyes meet, and her smile is so wide. I nearly run down the aisle to grab her.

She decided to have both of her parents walk her down the aisle. Their relationship has gotten much closer since Lainey was born. And then when they moved down to be closer to us and help with the baby, my family just kind of scooped them up into our crazy brood.

When she reaches the end of the aisle, I walk up to her and her parents, and I reach for her hands. "Hey, darlin'."

"Hey, Arch." Her smile is wide, and her eyes are shining.

She looks as happy as I feel. Then she looks over at my parents with our baby girl and squeezes my hands.

The pastor starts speaking, but I can't hear anything he says. I'm completely locked in on my beautiful bride. She's wearing a cream-colored lace dress that just seems to flow down her body. It dips a little low between her breasts, and it's sleeveless, and there's a strap that hangs loosely along her shoulder. She's absolutely gorgeous in it, and I can't wait to take it off her later.

"You look good enough to eat, babe." Emma squeezes my hands.

"Darlin', I can't wait to get you in the shack tonight. While that dress is gorgeous on you, I'm dying to get you out of it."

I can't help but lean in and kiss her. She tastes like cinnamon.

We pull back when Lainey lets out a giggle and claps her hands. The guests all laugh, and Emma and I both look over to see our happy baby girl. Emma gives her a little wave, which makes Lainey bounce up and down on my mama's legs.

"Okay, friends. Let's get this started. We're gathered here today to celebrate the love between Archie and Emma. As I've spent time with these two, I can honestly say the love I feel from them is pure and the kind that never ends." He opens the book in his hands. "They've asked that we not take too long to get to 'the good part.' Archie, Emma, I see you're already holding hands, so you're moving things along for me."

Everyone laughs again.

"Archie, did you have a few words to say to Emma?"

"That I do, sir." I clear my throat because I feel like I'm getting a little choked up. "Emma, today, I make this vow to you, but in truth, you've had me wrapped in your world since I saw you across that dance floor. I think I knew even then that we were meant to be together. You're my greatest love, my best friend, my biggest cheerleader, and the best mom to our baby girl. I promise to nurture all your dreams and help you reach them, as you have with mine. I promise to share my whole heart with you and remember to show you how deeply I love you every day. And I promise to love you loyally and fiercely for as long as I live." I reach out and brush a tear off her cheek.

"Okay, well, wow. I have to follow up after that, huh?" She looks at the pastor, then back at me. "Archie, how lucky am I to call you mine? Your love and trust in me make me a better person. You love me and complete me in ways I never thought possible. You are always there to stand by me through my greatest challenges and fears. You encourage me to grow, and you help me believe in myself. With you by my side, I know I can accomplish anything. And I promise to be there by your side to celebrate your successes and mourn your losses as if they were my own. I promise to be the best partner I can be because you deserve the best of me. Watching you love our daughter just makes me fall for you even more. Archie, my love, my husband, father of my child, I am madly and deeply in love with you, and I can't wait to walk through this life with you." She places a hand on my chest.

"Now we'll exchange rings."

I let go of Emma's hand and turn to my brother Aiden. "You didn't lose it, did you?" I smirk at him.

"No, I didn't lose it. Jeez." He takes the ring out of the pocket on the inside of his jacket and hands it to me.

When I face Emma, she's sliding my ring onto her pinkie.

"Archie, do you take Emma to have and to hold from this day forward till death do you part?"

"I absolutely do." I slide the platinum wedding band on her ring finger to join the engagement ring I gave her the night Lainey was born.

"Emma, do you take Archie to have and to hold from this day forward till death do you part?"

"Yes, I do." She slides my ring on my ring finger. It's also platinum and matches hers.

"By the power vested in me by the great state of Texas, I now pronounce you husband and wife. You may kiss your bride."

He doesn't have to tell me twice. Before he even finishes his sentence, I tip my hat back and lean on in.

My arms wrap around her waist, and hers come over my shoulders. I tilt my hat-covered head to the guests to give us a minute of privacy while I devour my wife's lips. She opens to me, and I slide my tongue in and tangle it with hers. It's deep and probably a little dirty for a wedding kiss, but I don't give a fuck. I'm gonna kiss my wife however I want.

Our guests are cheering, and I hear a few whistles too.

Emma pulls away, a little breathless. "Well, husband, should we get to our party so we can wrap this night up?"

"Baby, we can go to the shack right now and fucking ditch the party. I'm ready to be wrapped up in you all night." I lean in to take her lips again.

The pastor clears his throat in an attempt to interrupt us, but it doesn't work. "Seems like they're gonna keep going, so I'd like to introduce you to Mr. and Mrs. Archie Griffith!"

I keep kissing my wife because I can.

More whistles and cheers go around until Emma pulls back and laughs. "All right, let's do this."

We turn toward our family and friends, then make our way down the aisle and to the same tractor she came in on. Our wedding party joins us a minute later, and we make our way to the tent.

If someone had told me nearly two years ago that I would be a father, husband, and drafted by my dream team, I wouldn't have believed them. But here I am, the luckiest son of a bitch in the whole world.

EMMA

This day couldn't have been more perfect. The sky was a gorgeous shade of blue, and everything turned out exactly as I had envisioned. We had an amazing meal, and our friends and family seem to be as happy as we are.

Lainey was ready to call it a night about an hour ago, so I nursed her one more time before my parents took her back to the main house for bed a few minutes ago. She was the belle of the ball in her little dress and boots.

We've been really lucky with how easy she is. She is starting to get quite busy, and I think she's ready to take off any day now, but she's a very good baby. We've never been away from her overnight, but she'll be close by if they need us to come get her. She'll be going with us on our honeymoon, which is what we wanted. She's too little for us to leave her for too long. But honestly, I'm looking forward to having my husband to myself tonight.

When I saw him standing at the end of the aisle today, I nearly melted on the spot. His hair is a little shorter now and doesn't curl out as much under his hat, but he sure did fill out that gray suit nicely. I seriously don't know how I got so lucky. He's everything to me. The best dad, the best partner, the best man.

Walking back into the center of the tent, I see him talking with his friends and brother Aiden. They're all laughing about something I didn't catch when I walk up to them.

I wrap my arms around his waist and rest my head on his back. Just feeling him against me brings me peace.

He turns to bring me around to his side. "Hey, darlin'." He tilts my chin up to kiss me.

"Hey, husband. Do you want to have one more dance before we call it a night?"

My friends come over and join us. Livi seems to be having a good time with Liam, which means I'll have to ask her about that later. Mia has a bottle of Fireball in her hand, and Charlie has some red shot cups in hers.

"Okay, before these two take off, let's do a celebratory shot together!" Peyton claps.

Everyone takes a cup from Charlie, and Mia fills hers and passes the bottle around the group. Once everyone has a full cup, Archie raises his.

"Emma and I …" He looks down at me. "I can speak for us both, right?"

I can't help but laugh. "Yeah, babe, you can."

"Emma and I would like to thank you all for being here with us today. We love y'all like family, and it means the world to us that you could be here."

"Um, Arch, I am your family." Aiden speaks up. He has possibly been dipping into some other drinks tonight.

"Dude, don't ruin my flow." Archie smiles and shakes his head. "Anyway, thanks for being there for us today and every day. Cheers to the best group of friends we could ask for!"

"Cheers!" everyone chimes.

"All right, darlin', let's go have that dance." He takes my hand and leads me out to the dance floor.

Our wedding song was "I'm Gonna Love You" by Cody Johnson and Carrie Underwood, and it was perfect for us. But the song that starts playing is "Speechless" by Dan + Shay.

I wrap my arms around his shoulders. "Archie, thank you for making this day everything that I wanted. It was everything I dreamed, truly. And how lucky did we get that Lainey was also good? I was worried she was gonna start up when she saw us at the altar. I thought we might be saying our vows with our baby between us."

He huffs a laugh. "Yeah, she sure is a perfect baby. I think she knew we needed our moment together. Baby, you nearly took my breath away when I saw you coming toward me. I'm happy you got to have your day. And to think, we were gonna rush it." He winks at me.

"Ha! Yeah, Lainey definitely had different plans for us. But I'm actually glad everything turned out this way. I got to take the time with my mom and yours to make it special. Not that it wouldn't have been great to get married sooner, but we were able to focus on her, and we needed to." I run my hands up to his neck and into his hair. "Now, I feel like we were able to really enjoy the day and remember it, you know?"

"I know what you mean. I think it turned out exactly how it was supposed to though." His hands start to move lower down my back, and then he leans in and kisses me.

I can taste the cinnamon from the shot on his tongue, and I suck on it, making him groan. With him pressed into me like this, I can feel his erection against my stomach. All the kissing and touching and anticipation of having him to myself tonight makes me feel like I'm waiting to erupt.

I pull back, but my lips are still touching his. "I'm so ready to get out of here. What do you say, Cowboy? You up"—I run my hands down his back and over his nice, tight ass, then pull him into me even more—"for a ride?"

A slow, sexy smile spreads across his face, and he kisses my lips again. "Giddyup, darlin'."

Want to see what Archie and Emma are up to now? You can get the bonus chapter on my website: avasuttonbooks.com

Walker University Stallions
Counter Play
Zone Protection
Strong Side
Silent Count

STRONG SIDE SNEAK PEEK

Noelle - End of Second Year at Walker University

One more month. I can make it one more month. This has been my mantra all day. It's the end of not only my second semester of my second year at Walker, but almost the end of the school year at the elementary school where I not only student teach, but also volunteer for their various school programs.

Today was field day, and the chaos from the day with kids ranging from five to eleven just about pushed me over the edge. Of course, it didn't help that it was hotter than hell out there. And on my way home, I realized that I hadn't eaten at all today, and the headache that's coming on needs some immediate attention or it'll turn into a migraine.

My cell phone rings and I quickly glance at the display screen in my car and see it's my best friend, Casey King, calling me. He's been my best friend since middle school and is one of the reasons I chose to attend Walker University instead of Chandler State University. Outside of school and my boyfriend, Trey, I spend the most time with him.

I tap on the screen to answer his call. "Hello, Casey King."

"Hello, Noelle James." He chuckles. "How was your day today?"

"Well, I'm hot, tired, and ready for a two hour shower to try to get rid of this headache that's coming on. It was field day today, so it was a long day. I went straight to the elementary school from my last morning class, and I'm just now on my way home." I huff.

"That sucks. What can I get for you? Do you want me to bring anything over?"

This is one of the things I love about Casey. He is always there for me. No matter what.

"No, I'm good. Trey is supposed to come over later, so if I can't get this headache to drift away, I'll have him bring me something."

"Uh huh, yeah right. Well, let me know how that works out and when he bails on you, just text me what you need," he grumbles.

Trey is my first boyfriend, and well, first everything. He was my first real kiss, I lost my virginity to him, and the first guy to make my heart equally burst and hurt. And Casey, has seen it all. He's not a big fan of my boyfriend, and nothing I say will change his mind.

When I met Trey in our freshman year, I was smitten. He was in my history class and asked me for my notes after the first week, then sat next to me every class afterward. Within a month, we had gone on our first date.

"Case, he's been pretty good about not ditching me lately since they lost in the playoffs. He's just goofing around until he leaves for the summer league in Minnesota. He came over last night, too, and it was all good." My voice hitches slightly. It wasn't all good really. He was on his phone the entire night and barely talked to me at all. So I went to bed, and when he came in later, he woke me up for sex that lasted all of maybe ten minutes, then immediately rolled over and went to sleep.

"Right. Well, why don't I just come over with some of that soup you like from The Font? It always helps you feel better. And I'm guessing you didn't eat much today."

"Casey, I'm good. In fact, I'm pulling up to the apartment now, and surprisingly, Trey is already here. So if I need anything, he can get it for me. But you know I appreciate you, right?" I spot Trey's Jeep in the guest parking spot next to mine.

"That I do, James, that I do. Alright, call me or text me later so I know you're feeling better." There's a slight edge to his voice, but then softens. "Please."

I pull into my assigned parking spot in front of my apartment building and turn off my car. I tilt my head back onto the head-rest and close my eyes to try to ease my headache. "Okay, I will. You should go out and have some fun with the guys tonight."

He laughs. "Yeah, okay, I might. Later."

"Bye." I open my eyes and press end on my phone.

Taking in a deep breath, I try to summon the strength to get out of my car and climb the one flight of stairs to my unit. My headache isn't lessening, and if I don't get some meds in me stat, I'm going to be in trouble. I grab my backpack from the passenger seat and get out.

On my way up the stairs, I hear loud music playing, but I can't tell where it's coming from until I reach the landing on my floor. It's definitely coming from my apartment, which doesn't make sense. I don't think that Trey would be blasting music while hanging out in my apartment. Maybe it's my roommate, Cassie.

As I'm putting my key in the lock, I hear Trey shout, but I can't make out what he's saying. When I push open the door, I see him pounding into my roommate, who is bent over the arm of the couch. They haven't noticed me yet, and I'm too stunned to say anything.

"That's right, Cass. Take my dick like a good little slut. I'm gonna wreck your fuckin' pussy." He grabs her hair and pulls it as he pistons into her, forcing her head back.

When I move my gaze to her and look at her face, her eyes are closed, mouth open, clearly enjoying the wrecking of her pussy. Strange thing is...we have never, I mean ever, in the two years we've been together, had sex like this. But I'm literally struck speechless.

"You feel so good, Trey. Fuck me harder," she moans.

My bag slides off my shoulder and hits the ground. The sound makes them both look over at me. And he. Keeps. Pumping.

"Oh, shit, fuck. Noelle!" Cassie screeches and at least has the decency to try to pull away from Trey and cover herself up with *my* blanket that's draped over the back of the couch.

He backs up, cock still hard and without a condom, and not bothering to cover it and lifts his arms. "What the fuck, Noelle. Why are you home early?"

I can't seem to make my mouth move, both from the pain in my head and the scene before me. But when Cassie starts to walk over to me, I raise my arms out in front of me to stop her from getting anywhere near me. "Do not come near me."

"I'm so sorry, Noelle. We didn't think you would be home so early." Not a *I'm sorry I'm fucking your boyfriend on our couch*, but sorry I came home early.

I glance over to see Trey pulling up his boxers. The ones I bought him for Christmas this year that have little baseballs printed all over them. Un-fucking-believable.

"Right, well, I'm so sorry to interrupt. You two go ahead and enjoy yourselves." I pick up my backpack and turn to reach for the handle on the door. "Oh and Trey, we're so fucking over. You need to be gone when I come back, and I never. I mean, *never* want to see or hear from you again." I point a finger at Cassie. "And since my parents are paying for this apartment, you need to leave too."

"What! Where am I going to go? We still have a few weeks left of school." She whines.

"Cassie, I really don't care. Go stay with Trey!" I start to laugh humorlessly.

"Come on, Noelle. You're over—"

"NO." Shaking my head and closing my eyes, I can't muster

the strength to engage with him further, my head is full on pounding now, and I need to get out of here. Fast.

When I open my eyes, I look at them both one last time. "Get the fuck out of my apartment by five pm or I'm calling the cops." I walk out the door, letting it slam behind me.

I rush down the stairs and get back into my car, throwing my backpack into the back seat. I know what I just saw, but also... what the fuck just happened? I never had any reason to suspect that they were messing around in my apartment right under my nose.

My hands are shaking, and my breathing is unsteady. I try pulling in some deep breaths to calm down, or at least clear my head enough so I can leave the parking lot, and don't have to watch them leave.

I search for my phone and realize I put it in the side pocket of my backpack when I got out of the car earlier. So I turn and reach for it, feeling it buzzing when I get a hold of it. When I look at the screen, I see it's Trey calling, and I immediately hit decline.

I can't hear his voice right now. And literally nothing he could say to me would erase what I just walked in on. I'm so fucking stupid staying with him for as long as I did. I heard rumors that he had been fooling around with girls when we would break up, and it hurt, but I convinced myself it was okay because we weren't together. But this, I can't ignore.

There's only one person I want and *need* to see right now. The only person who could make this hurt less. I open my recent calls and tap on his name, dialing immediately.

"Well, that was—" he starts to say, but I interrupt.

"Casey, I need you." And then I start to cry.

ACKNOWLEDGMENTS

To my family, thank you for riding through book two with me. I know it's not easy, especially when I haven't showered for days. You are my reason for everything. I love you all, eternally.

Compass Press, thank you for walking me through the author journey. Let's get cookin' on book three!

Jovanna Shirley, once again, thank you for your patience and expertise. I can't wait to work with you on the rest of the series and many more!

Jeannine Colette, no words can express the gratitude I have for you and your creative mind. Thank you for helping to identify the holes and improving the overall story. Now, let's get to work on Casey. ;)

Sarah Sentz, you do more than I could ask or probably even realize. Thank you for your support, feedback, and for helping make Autumn's life easier.

Tina Otero, thank you so much for working with us to polish and shine this book baby. Looking forward to working on the rest of the series with you!

Sam B, thank you so much for taking the time to read Archie and

Emma. I can't tell you how much it meant to me to receive your feedback. Thank you for loving them like I do.

Sam R, your excitement and enthusiasm for this series makes me absolutely giddy! Every piece of feedback I get makes me smile. Thank you so much for everything!

To all the readers, thank you for giving me a chance! Your reviews, edits, and simply the fact that you are reading my book is surreal. Thank you!

Wordsmith Publicity, Autumn and Roxie, thank you for helping me reach readers and your guidance and support!

ABOUT THE AUTHOR

Ava Sutton is a sports enthusiast and author of spicy college and professional sports romance.
When she's not writing, you can find her nose in a book, scrolling social media or planning dream vacations she someday hopes to take. She lives in Dallas, Texas with her two dogs.
Connect with her on Facebook, Instagram, and TikTok.
@avasuttonbooks

www.avasuttonbooks.com

www.ingramcontent.com/pod-product-compliance
Lightning Source LLC
Chambersburg PA
CBHW021406110726
47901CB00008B/2071